Seduced by a Scoundrel

Barbara Dawson Smith

St. Martin's

To my parents
Your fifty years of marriage are truly golden!

Titles by Barbara Dawson Smith

A Glimpse of Heaven

Never a Lady

Once Upon a Scandal

Her Secret Affair

Too Wicked to Love

Seduced by a Scoundrel

Acknowledgments

A special thanks to Mike Hermann for providing this math-challenged author with the right numbers.

My gratitude also goes to my fellow critiquers Joyce Bell, Christina Dodd, Betty Traylor Gyenes, and Susan Wiggs for their extraordinary perception.

And last but not least, thanks to Debbie Thomas for introducing me to the real Drake and Alicia, who very graciously lent me their names.

SEDUCED BY A SCOUNDREL

Chapter One

Lady Alicia Pemberton braced herself to commit an act of desperation.

Holding tightly to the wrought-iron balustrade, she subdued her inner agitation and followed the butler up the grand staircase in Wilder's Club, St. James's Street. Their footsteps echoed through the soaring entrance hall with its tall white columns and dark green walls, decorated with paintings and statuary. The place might have been a mansion in Mayfair.

But she knew it to be a glorified gaming hell.

To her left loomed a spacious salon, the groupings of leather chairs empty save for a portly man engrossed in the *Times* of London. In the vast room to the right, a pair of gentlemen played billiards. A crack resounded as a yellow ball shot across the green baize and disappeared with a muffled thump into a hole in the corner of the table. The players were so intent on their game, they never even noticed a lady had invaded their exclusive club.

It must be too early yet for drunken revelry.

The elegant decor made Alicia aware of her own drab appearance, the outmoded spencer with its sadly frayed cuffs, the blue muslin gown gone pale from many washings, the bonnet with its girlish cluster of white ribbons more suited to the frivolous debutante she had once been.

She entombed her regrets. Those carefree days were gone. Dreams were for starry-eyed girls, not a mature woman with a family to protect. A family in dire trouble.

The butler stopped before a gilt-trimmed door. "Ye don't look the usual sort," he said in a gravelly Scottish burr.

His voice jolted Alicia out of her dark thoughts. "I beg your pardon?"

"Wilder's sort." A giant of a man with a leather patch over one eye, he stuck his grizzled face down to her level and subjected her to an unservile scrutiny. "If ye want a bit of advice, miss, ye should run along home and back to yer needlework."

Alicia thought he was the one who needed advice—in manners. "I have business with Mr. Wilder."

"Business, ye call it? He doesna pay for his pleasure, if that's what ye're thinking. Never has, not with the females swarming 'round him like ants to honey."

Her stomach clenched despite her resolve to numb her emotions. Was her purpose so obvious?

She schooled her features into an expression of aristocratic dignity. "Mr. Wilder is expecting me. You may show me in now."

The butler shrugged. "Have it yer way, then." He swung open the door with his ham-fisted paw and motioned her inside.

Determined to get this loathsome interview over with and done, Alicia marched past him. The impertinent servant went out. The door clicked shut.

She was on her own.

The dim antechamber smelled faintly of expensive leather and musky cologne. Above a half-moon table hung a painting of some wild, rocky landscape. A patterned carpet in crimson and blue muffled her footsteps. She kept her gloved hands at her sides, her posture erect. It seemed perversely important that she maintain a ladylike demeanor.

Going through an arched doorway, she entered a large room lit by a silver branch of beeswax candles. The draperies were closed to the late afternoon sunlight, and a mahogany desk dominated the chamber. On the polished surface, a ledger lay open, and beside it a gray-feathered quill stood in a silver inkpot.

She scanned the marine-blue walls and wine-dark leather chairs, the bookcases filled with volumes. It might have been a wealthy banker's office—except for the pair of ivory dice scattered on the desk. Shuddering, she turned quickly from the sight.

The coal fire hissed into the silent air, a counterpoint to the tension inside her. She had sent up her calling card with the nosy butler. So where was Drake Wilder?

She had taken a chance on finding him here. Leading a heathen life, he'd probably been gambling until dawn. He would sleep during daylight hours while decent, hardworking folk went about their duties. And if he deliberately meant to make her wait, let him. She was well acquainted with games of power. She had, after all, once been the toast of society.

Too restless to sit, she perused the titles on the shelves. The books must be for decoration only. A man who owned the premier gaming club in London could have no interest in the philosophy of Plato, the plays of Shakespeare, the intricacies of Euclidian geometry. Drake Wilder exploited the hopes of gullible gentlemen, nurturing their dreams of glory, then fleecing them of their wealth. He spared not a qualm for the disaster he caused to their families. Or the lives he shattered.

Anger stabbed Alicia, but she blunted it with the armor of reason. She must keep a calm, clear head. She must strike a hard bargain.

And if she failed? No. She would not allow herself to consider the possibility. The consequences were too dreadful.

As she paced the office, an alabaster statue on the marble mantelpiece caught her gaze. Slightly larger than her hand, the carving depicted a man and a woman locked in carnal embrace.

They were naked.

Alicia averted her eyes. But only for a moment. Curiosity proving stronger than prudery, she took the heavy piece into her hands. In the light of the fire, the sculpture seemed to glow with life. The man sat on a rock with the woman straddling him. The juncture of her opened legs pressed against his lower region. Her head was arched back as he nuzzled her breasts, and happiness lit her fine features.

The celebration of lust appalled Alicia. She told herself to put the statue back in its niche. Instead, she clung to it in morbid fascination, her wayward mind projecting her into the arms of a lover. Drake Wilder's arms.

How could she do *this* with a stranger?

Sometimes, late at night and alone in bed, she would picture herself lying with an imaginary husband, his hands moving gently over her nightdress. She could almost feel the warmth of his body pressed to hers. . . .

How innocent was fantasy compared to stark reality. Never had she dreamed the act was accomplished without a stitch of clothing. That she would be expected to do more than lie on her back and allow him liberties. That she would have to behave like *this* with the scoundrel who had pushed her family to the brink of ruin—

"Shocking, isn't it?"

The deep male voice sliced through her trance. She spun around, her gaze scouring the shadows. A door in the far corner stood ajar, and a man loomed there, his hand braced on the gilded panel. He had entered silently, stealthily. His black hair and swarthy coloring caused him to blend into the gloom. He wore the dark tailored coat and white cravat of a gentleman, yet there was something uncivilized about his tall, muscular form. Something that raised the fine hairs on her skin.

How long had he been watching her?

"That piece is rather old and priceless," he went on. "It's attributed to an apprentice of Michelangelo's. But feel free to fondle it."

Alicia realized she still clutched the indecent statue to her bosom. With unhurried hauteur, she set it back on the mantelpiece. "Do you always spy on your guests?"

"Only the female variety."

"How very reassuring."

His low chuckle disturbed the air. He watched her from beneath level black brows, taking his time studying her, his appraisal blatantly masculine. "You must be Lady Alicia Pemberton."

"And you must be Mr. Drake Wilder."

He inclined his head with the arrogance of a king, and she clenched her teeth to keep from raging at him. It wasn't like her to speak sharply to a stranger. Especially one whose good favor she so desperately required.

Drake Wilder was bastard born, a cardsharp who had risen from the seething darkness of London's underworld to become the richest, most notorious rogue in all of England. He had an aura of aggressive confidence, a face that showed hard lines of experience. He made her nervous, and she had never before been nervous around any man.

Strolling closer, he settled himself on the edge of the desk. He scooped up the dice and idly shook them, the ivory cubes rattling in his palm. All the while he kept his gaze on her. His eyes were a deep midnight-blue, riveting in their intensity. His scrutiny made Alicia uncomfortably aware of how vulnerable she was, alone with him in his dominion.

"Please sit down," he said, waving his hand with lazy grace. "I'm surprised a lady would venture here without a chaperone."

Unwilling to concede any advantage, Alicia remained standing. "You shouldn't be surprised. I've come to discuss my brother's debt."

"So. The Earl of Brockway would send a woman to plead on his behalf."

"Gerald doesn't know I'm here." In truth, her hotheaded brother would be livid. But she was acting for his benefit. And first, she must pursue the faint hope of finding an honorable solution.

Please, God, help me to convince this man.

She laced her gloved fingers together. "Mr. Wilder, perhaps you don't realize my brother is only eighteen. As he has not yet reached his majority, he should never have been permitted to gamble at this establishment."

"He is no longer a boy. Whether you admit so or not."

"He is prone to youthful impulse," she countered. "I should know. As his elder sister, I have been responsible for him all his life."

Drake Wilder's amused gaze flowed up and down her slender form. "Just how elderly are you?"

His heavy-lidded survey made her skin prickle again, and in a flash she saw herself unclothed, straddling him, his mouth on her breasts. . . .

"My age has nothing to do with this matter," she said primly.

"It is indeed relevant. So answer me."

Was it false pride that kept her from admitting she had been long on the shelf? Better to grant him this one concession. "If you must know, I am three and twenty."

"Teetering on the brink of antiquity."

His smile broadened, crinkling the corners of his eyes and creating attractive dimples on either side of that masculine mouth. A light-headed sensation nearly made Alicia sway on her feet. Humor relaxed the harshness of his expression so that he looked almost approachable.

As handsome as sin.

Realizing she was holding her breath, she released it slowly. "The point is, my brother cannot be held liable for a gaming debt. It isn't legal."

Wilder's humor vanished into a calculating look. "Quite so. Yet he is bound by his honor as a gentleman. And he will have nothing left to pay his other creditors. Those debts will land him in prison."

The weight of that fear threatened to crush Alicia. Only yesterday, the arrival of the bill collectors had alerted her. Bootmakers, tailors, jewelers, and wine merchants had congregated like wolves in the front hall, demanding payment before his lordship settled the gaming notes he had incurred the previous night.

In horror, she had rousted Gerald out of bed and badgered the truth from him. Hanging his head, he admitted to a night of drunken revel. He had wagered their meager savings and gambled funds they did not have. They were destitute.

"Twenty thousand guineas," she had whispered. "Dear God in heaven, what foolishness possessed you?"

He had regarded her in hollow-eyed despair. "I'll win back the money, Ali. Just grant me a little time."

"No! Stay out of the gaming hells. Lest you end up like Papa."

Gerald had flinched at her harsh words and, taking swift advantage, she had wrested a promise from him to remain at home. Then she had swallowed her pride and gone begging to their acquaintances, but to no avail. The banks, too, had refused to authorize a loan to a woman. She had even visited a moneylender on Threadneedle Street, a wily man with beady eyes who threw her out when she could offer no collateral.

Giving her no choice but to bargain with Drake Wilder.

He lounged against the desk, his long legs stretched out and crossed at the ankles. The idle clacking of the dice drew her gaze to his large hands. She wondered how many women had known the touch of those blunt-tipped, masculine fingers. The thought made her quiver with aversion and . . . something else. Something she didn't care to examine.

"Have you other family?" he asked.

"My father is dead. My mother is . . ."—Alicia paused, her throat aching—"unwell."

"Uncles? Grandparents? A guardian?"

"No one."

"Then at the ripe old age of twenty-three, *you* are liable for your brother's debts."

She had walked straight into his trap. With her eyes open and her resolve set. "Yes, I am. I trust we can work out a plan for repayment."

"I trust so."

He didn't look as though he trusted her; his eyes were impenetrable. For the hundredth time, she did a mental inventory of the town house, already shorn of all but the most shabby of contents. She could sell the furniture in the spare bedchamber and in the drawing room. She could pawn the silver tea service that she'd hidden for just such an emergency. She could take in laundry and sewing.

"I can manage twenty guineas per month," she said.

Wilder laughed. "At that rate, the debt would take slightly over eighty-three years to repay. Adding in three percent annual interest, you'd be paying forever. You see, twenty guineas per month wouldn't even touch the principal. You'd go deeper into debt each year. At the end of eighty-three years, you'd still owe the original twenty thousand plus over one hundred thirty four thousand in interest."

The magnitude of the liability staggered Alicia. She sank onto a leather chair and clenched her fists in her lap. "You must be wrong. You can't have calculated those figures without pen and paper."

"When it comes to numbers, I am never wrong."

Through the flickering firelight, his eyes glinted at her. Predator eyes.

Dear God, help me.

She rose from the chair and took a step toward Wilder. They faced each other like combatants in a boxing ring. A faint smile tilted one corner of his mouth. He seemed to relish her dilemma, but that only fired her resolve.

She could bend him to her will. He was only a man, after all. And men could be manipulated.

Deliberately she relaxed her tense muscles and curved her lips into a cool smile. Then she untied the ribbons beneath her chin and removed her bonnet, letting it drop to the chair behind her. "Perhaps I could interest you in another form of repayment."

Wilder cocked an eyebrow. "Do tell."

"I am offering to be . . . your mistress."

A scowl darkened his face. His fingers closed around the dice until his knuckles showed white. She could have sworn he looked angry, but that made no sense. Bitterly she wondered how else he'd thought she would repay him.

"Do you know the odds of rolling a seven?" he said unexpectedly.

"Sir, I am not a gamester. I truly don't care—"

"The odds are one in six." With a lightning-quick motion of his wrist, he tossed the dice into a shallow box on the desk. "Come, see how I fared."

Wondering at his purpose, she slowly approached him. A lock of black hair dipped onto his brow, enhancing his rakish look. His subtle male scent wrapped around her like a silken noose. Up close, he had an arresting face, a clean-shaven jaw and strong cheekbones, a mouth with a slight sensual curl that made her think of stolen kisses in the darkness.

Alicia blinked down at the black velvet-lined box, where the ivory cubes displayed a two and a five. "A lucky throw," she murmured, fighting to keep the venom from her voice. If rumor were truth, Drake Wilder had the luck of Lucifer.

He shook his head. "This pair of dice is weighted," he said, turning one in his long fingers. "A tiny quantity of lead is secreted beneath certain numbers, which causes the die to overbalance and fall to the opposite side. If the dice are thrown just so, the odds of winning greatly increase. Quite handy for the unscrupulous gambler."

Gripped by angry suspicion, Alicia frowned. "Are you saying . . . you *cheated* my brother?"

Something hot and frightening flashed in his eyes. It vanished in an instant, leaving a flinty chill. "Hardly. Lord Brockway played the faro table."

"You could have rigged the game in favor of the house," she said, unwilling to let go of the notion.

"There is no cheating permitted in my club. These"—he dropped the ivory cubes back into the box—"were taken from a gentleman who disobeyed that rule."

"Then what is your point?"

"That things are not always as they appear to be." His eyes sharp and piercing, he lowered his voice to a silken growl. "And *I* am no fool."

Again, she had the discomfiting urge to step backward, to put a safe distance between them. But that would be tantamount to admitting he held the upper hand. "I never said you were."

"Yet you expect me to forgive a marker of twenty thousand guineas in exchange for a romp in bed. Either you think me a fool—or you vastly overrate yourself."

His scorn struck a blow at her confidence. Did he not find her attractive?

He *must*.

Drawing on the charm that had once made her a sought-after beauty, Alicia managed a throaty laugh. "Why, you mistake me, Mr. Wilder. I certainly don't expect to discharge the debt in one night. I'd hoped we could agree upon a mutually satisfactory length of time."

"Indeed."

Encouraged that he hadn't refused outright, she fluttered her lashes like a coquette. "I should think you'd appreciate a woman who would never beg you for trinkets or favors. A lady who knows how to behave discreetly."

"I might get you with child."

Alicia controlled a shudder. There was shame in bearing a bastard, yet long ago she had set aside the dream of marriage and family, the tender yearning for children of her own. She had resigned herself to spinsterhood for a reason he couldn't know. . . .

Having no other choice, she pushed away that dread. "Then I would care for the child. You need fear no obligation."

"How considerate of you."

His face was inscrutable. Her palms damp, she slowly unbuttoned her spencer, slid the short jacket off her shoulders, and let it drop to the chair. "You'll find me pleasant company," she murmured. "I'm able to visit you each evening at nine—or later, if you prefer. You have only to agree to the arrangement."

He glanced coolly at her low-cut bodice. "I can have any woman I want," he stated. "And there might be value in making a lesson of Lord Brockway. To show others what can happen when their markers are not repaid."

Alicia bit back a horrified gasp. "No, *please*. It would be a mistake to condemn my brother to prison. He's prone to lung complaints, and you'll never get your money if he dies. Besides, I can offer what few women of your acquaintance possess. You see, I—" Aware of a burning in her cheeks, she swallowed past the dryness in her throat. "I am untouched."

He scanned her shoulders and breasts in a way that made the color rise in her cheeks. "The virgin sacrifice," he said sardonically. "You would ruin yourself for the sake of your wastrel brother."

And Mama. Dear sweet Mama. "Yes," she whispered.

He sat silent on the edge of the desk, unmoving, and she sensed a moody darkness in him, likely because he felt cheated of his ill-gotten gains. Then his arms lashed out and pulled her closer, trapping her within the prison of his legs. He tunneled his fingers into her blond hair and dislodged a few tortoiseshell pins.

His touch was an invasion that sent chills down her spine. Only by force of will did she manage to stand quietly, aware of the fear and revulsion inside herself, along with an undeniable, shameful attraction.

Though her heart thumped madly, she lifted her chin and met his gaze. "Have we a bargain, then?"

"That depends."

"On what?"

"On how well you please me." His fingers commenced a slow assault on her senses, rubbing her scalp ever so lightly. "Show me you're worth twenty thousand."

Dear God, he expected *her* to seduce *him.*

Aware of a little catch in her throat, Alicia took a steadying breath. The challenge in his eyes mocked her limited experience. How many women had known his caresses? How many had straddled him, naked, in the throes of wantonness?

No. She didn't want to think about *that.* Instead, she would entice him with a kiss. At one time, men had fought for the chance to claim that rare token of her affections.

She placed her trembling hands on his shoulders, aware of the solid muscles beneath his coat. Ever so slowly, she leaned toward him. Never before had she seen eyes that distinctive shade of dark blue. He was so close she could discern each spiky black lash. In the moment before her lips touched his, she felt the tickling warmth of his breath. Then the taste and scent of him enveloped her, and the firmness of his mouth sent a melting quiver through her limbs.

But he made no move to return the kiss. His hands rested heavily on her shoulders, his thighs exerting a subtle pressure against her legs. She was aware of the impression of strength in him . . . and jaded indifference.

Determined to make him want her, she slid her hands over his starched cravat and into his hair. The strands sifted through her gloved fingers like thickly spun silken threads. She touched him in light strokes as he had done to her, all the while brushing her closed lips over his. Men liked teasing caresses and quick stolen kisses that made them wild with longing. In her youth, she had lured more than one gentleman into a darkened corner for a few moments of flirtatious kissing. She would torment him until he groveled before her in adoration.

That sense of power flooded her now, though the excitement of it was somehow different, hotter, more intense than with her former suitors. Of course, *they* had been gentlemen. Drake Wilder was a rogue.

His lips moved slightly and her pulse leapt. He was not so impassive; he must be fighting his need to respond. Now was the time to charm him. To make him commit to a brief affair in exchange for canceling the debt.

Lifting her head, Alicia opened her eyes. And blinked.

A grin deepened the dimples on either side of his mouth. Sardonic humor danced in his eyes. "If that's your best effort," he said, "my money would be ill spent."

He was laughing at her! She stiffened. But fear overshadowed all else. "Teach me, then," she forced out. "I'm willing to learn."

"No. I prefer an experienced woman in my bed."

So that was that. He would let her brother be sent to prison. He would condemn her mother to an even more hideous fate. Alicia felt ill from the terror of failure. She could plead with him, but his contemptuous expression told her it would be useless. She could appeal to his humanity, but he was a cold, cruel man who knew nothing of kindness. She could rage at him, but all she had left was her dignity.

A bitter taste in her mouth, she took a step backward. "You have proven one fact, Mr. Wilder. That wealth will never make you a gentleman."

She turned to leave, but his fingers closed as tightly as manacles around her wrist. His expression was rigid, his cheekbones prominent in his despicably handsome face. "Now, there you're wrong," he said with soft-spoken menace. "Wealth *will* enable me to take a place in your exalted circle."

"If this is another attempt to mock me—"

"I've decided to forgive your brother's debt, after all." He silenced her with an intense, calculating stare. "On one condition."

She hated him for resurrecting her hopes. "What? What is it?"

"The condition, my lady, is that you marry me."

Chapter Two

He watched her as he had done for weeks.

Standing at the window of his office, Drake held back the heavy velvet drapery and peered down at the sunny street below. He paid no heed to the fine carriages that rattled over the cobblestones, the elegant buildings made of Portland stone, the columned facade of White's Club at the top of St. James's Street. His attention was fixed on one pedestrian.

Her head held high, Lady Alicia Pemberton left through the front gate and walked at a stately pace past the wrought-iron fence in front of his club. The spring breeze fluttered the white feathers on her bonnet and molded her gown to her curves. He knew the softness of those curves pressed against him, the warm silken skin of her neck and shoulders, her subtle scent of roses. Even now, the memory of her untutored kiss aroused him.

His response to her had surprised him. He'd thought her too frigid and aristocratic for his tastes. He preferred a warm, earthy woman without inhibitions. A woman who knew how to give as much as she took. Not a nose-in-the-air blueblood who believed herself superior to him.

He was a man who controlled his physical urges. Though he savored sensuality in many forms, he must not allow lust to distract him. Not until he had achieved his purpose in marrying Lady Alicia.

She had refused him, of course, though not without a momentary pause. He had waited, anticipating her rejection, until a trace of alarm had clouded those clear blue eyes. She did not want a husband, and he knew why. His informants had done a thorough job of investigation.

And he, too, had observed her from afar. Several times, he'd waited in a closed carriage while she headed out on her early morning errands to the fish market or the green-grocer. He took care to use a different vehicle each time so that she wouldn't grow suspicious. Watching her wasn't vital to his plan, yet he'd felt the burning need to learn all he could about the woman who was being courted by his sworn enemy—the Marquess of Hailstock.

Drake's fingers clenched around the drapery. With narrowed eyes, he stared down at his quarry. Lady Alicia had reached the corner and paused as a coalman's dray approached. One of the wheels struck a puddle and splashed her with filthy water. She didn't leap back or shake her fist; she merely waited on the curbstone until the vehicle passed by and she could cross the busy street. Her unruffled, ladylike demeanor intrigued him.

More than he could have imagined, he had enjoyed baiting her, testing that genteel composure. He could admit to a grudging admiration at the way she'd stood up to him. And he'd been stunned by her willingness to do almost anything to protect her family, even relinquish her chastity to a scoundrel.

How he would relish telling Hailstock of her offer.

With cool satisfaction, Drake knew he had read the nobleman's character well. Lady Alicia must have gone to Hailstock first, and despite his wealth, the marquess had refused to lend her the twenty thousand unless she married him. She had refused him, too. Because Hailstock wouldn't tolerate her mother.

But Drake could. It was a vulnerability he intended to exploit to ruthless advantage.

"I ken what ye're up to," said a gravelly voice behind him. "Dinna think ye can pull the wool over these auld eyes."

Drake released the drapery, letting it fall across the window as he turned to face Fergus MacAllister. The hulking man stood with his hands planted at his lanky waist and a grimace lowering his white brows.

Though Drake had reached his thirtieth year, that stern gaze could still stir a flicker of guilt in him. "I've nothing to hide," he stated. "The girl won't be hurt."

"Not hurt?" Fergus shook his head in disgust. "When ye sent me to spy on the lady, ye dinna say ye intended to milk her puir brother of all his money. Nor to use her as yer whore."

"I'm not intending to make her my mistress."

Fergus snorted. "Ye canna expect me to believe *that.*"

Annoyed, Drake walked to the desk and seated himself in the leather chair. He looked down at the ledger, ran his finger down a column, and just as swiftly totaled the figures in his head. Affecting a detached tone, he said, "Then believe this—I mean to marry her."

The older man's jaw dropped. "Of all the dastardly schemes . . ." he sputtered. "Ye're set on revenge. Ye intend to steal her away from Lord Hailstock."

"That's none of your concern."

"Hah. Is the lass to have a say in the matter?"

"No."

Fergus stomped to the desk and shook his gnarled finger in Drake's face. "Yer mither raised ye to treat folks fairly, to be a braw man. And this is how ye repay her. By maneuvering that sweet angel to yer own wicked purpose."

"As my wife, that *sweet angel* will want for naught."

"Naught but love. Naught but respect and honor." The branch of candles cast shadows on Fergus's familiar, craggy face with the black eyepatch. "Ye'll have yer vengeance at last. But how will ye live with yerself, I wonder?"

Drake refused to lower his gaze. He remembered the flash of horror in her eyes when he'd taunted her with the prospect of sending her brother to prison. But he wouldn't let himself feel sorry for her. After years of poverty, she would adjust quickly to being mistress of a rich household. In time, she would probably thank him.

"I'll live as I've always done," he said. "However I choose." In a dismissive move, he picked up the quill pen and dipped it into the silver inkpot. "Go now. You've duties to attend to. Check the invoice from the wine merchant and see that he didn't cheat us."

Fergus straightened himself. "Gettin' toplofty on me, are ye? Actin' like the laird of the castle."

"I havena forgotten my roots," Drake said, deliberately resorting to the rough burr of his youth. "Now go awa' wi' ye', Fergus MacAllister. I'll hear no more of yer bletherin'."

Fergus glared for another long moment, his meaty fists clenching and unclenching. Then, muttering Gaelic curses beneath his breath, he stalked out into the antechamber. The door slammed shut, and a current of air set the candle flames dancing and sputtering.

Drake jabbed the quill back into its holder. Thrusting his head into his hands, he rubbed his brow. He despised himself for speaking so sharply to Fergus, for treating him with the disdain the nobility reserved for lesser beings. But Drake would brook no interference to his plan, not now, when he was so close to success.

He would give Lady Alicia Pemberton a day to reflect on his offer. Then he would return her call. And if she still refused his offer, he had in his possession the means to persuade her.

Wealth will never make you a gentleman.

Her aristocratic coldness still infuriated him. On the

brink of ruin, she had stood there like a queen addressing a gutter rat. Until today, he had viewed her only as a pawn, his means of revenge. But now he looked forward to their nuptials for another reason. He wanted to shatter that cool reserve.

He wanted to show the proud Lady Alicia that she was no better than he.

"Gerald! Why are you up so early?"

Alicia paused in the doorway of the basement kitchen. Her brother sat at the long wooden trestle table, his scrawny shoulders hunched as he wolfed down a meat pasty. At the hearth, Mrs. Molesworth sliced onions into the stewpot. The stout battleax of a woman wore a mobcap over her iron-gray hair, and she gave a crisp nod to Alicia.

Seeing his sister, Gerald launched into a fit of coughing. Alicia hastened to his side and pressed a mug of tea into his hands. That deep hacking always made her tense and worried, though she strove not to reveal it to him.

He took a long gulp. "Thanks," he said in a raspy voice.

" 'Ere's a dose of 'is tonic." Mrs. Molesworth appeared with a spoonful of something that smelled of licorice.

Alicia took the spoon and passed it to Gerald, who grimaced at the thick, dark liquid. "I hate the taste."

"Drink it down quickly, then." How many times had she spoken those words to him? Since boyhood, the chest ailment had plagued him through the damp months of autumn, winter, and early spring. The physician could do no more than recommend the tonic, and a poultice for more severe episodes.

A ray of sunlight through the high casement window cast a halo on his honey-brown hair. With trembling fingers, she touched those gold-kissed strands, remembering him as a mischievous lad who would dispose of his medicine in the nearest vase if she didn't keep a close watch on him.

And now Gerald could be locked in a dank prison cell with no one to care for him. . . .

Sliding a glance upward, he thrust the empty spoon at her. "You needn't fuss, Ali. I'm perfectly fine."

There was something wary about that glance. Suspicion drilled past her worry, past the weariness of another sleepless night. Alicia set the spoon in the scullery, then went to the hearth and poured herself a cup of tea from the kettle on the hob. Her faded brown skirt swishing, she walked toward him. "Why are you dressed to go out?"

"Business," Gerald muttered around a bite of his pasty.

"What sort of business?"

He brushed a crumb from his smart blue riding coat. " 'Tis nothing to concern you."

"Tell me," she said in the stern governess voice she'd once used while teaching him his lessons. "If you're gambling again—"

"No, I am not." Elevating his jaw, he stared down his nose at her. At times, he could look as imperious as the earl he was. "Do you think me a complete ninny-hammer?"

She thought him too naïve, too achingly young. Sliding into a ladder-back chair opposite him, she cradled the hot cup in her chilly hands. "I should hope you've more sense than that. And if you wish me to cease badgering you, then tell me where you're off to at this early hour."

The lordly arrogance vanished as quickly as it had appeared. He sat silent and sullen, a stubborn boy with his lower lip jutted out.

From across the kitchen, Mrs. Molesworth banged a tin pot into the dry sink. "Go on, m'lord. Your sister'll find out soon enough, any'ow."

Pouting, he reached for another pasty and took a big bite. For all that he ate, he remained poker-thin, his ribs almost concave. He chewed a moment, then mumbled defiantly, "I'm taking Pet to Tattersall's."

Alicia gasped. "You're selling the mare?"

He gave a jerky nod. "There's an auction today. She's in prime condition and should fetch a high price."

Alicia's heart swelled and her eyes filled with tears. Gerald had raised the fine gray mare from a filly at their estate in Northumberland, before their father had gambled away their unentailed lands. Her brother's love for the horse was reflected in its name and in his devotion. For the past five years, since they'd sold the other horses, the barouche, and the traveling coach, and dismissed their stable help, Gerald had groomed and curried the animal himself. With great enjoyment, he rode Pet through the streets of London and along the bridle paths in Hyde Park. The mare was a source of pride to him, a final vestige of their former wealth.

"Oh, Ger," she said, leaning across the table to place her hand over his bony fingers. "How dreadful for you."

A telltale brilliance in his green eyes, he swallowed convulsively and looked away. Then he thrust back his chair, the wooden legs scraping the flagstones. "I'd best get on with it," he said with wobbly cheer. "Can't send off the old girl without a proper brushing." Trudging across the kitchen, he headed up the short flight of stairs to the tiny garden and the mews beyond.

Alicia sipped the scalding hot tea to ease the lump in her throat. At the edge of her awareness, she heard the tap-tap of Mrs. Molesworth chopping vegetables for the soup at luncheon. The fire whispered on the stone hearth and the clock ticked on the mantelpiece. But the familiar cozy sounds of the kitchen held no comfort today.

Blast Drake Wilder! He had lured a gullible youth to the gaming tables, milked him of money he didn't possess, and forced Gerald to relinquish his most prized possession. She couldn't excuse her brother's part in the matter, yet she blamed Wilder for trapping an unwary young man.

And after all that, he had expected her to marry him. The shock of it sent chills over her skin. She was ashamed to admit that for a fleeting instant, she'd been tempted by his offer. It would mean an end to their debts. To the effort of putting food on the table. She might even enjoy the luxury of having new, pretty garments to wear. . . .

Then she had remembered Mama. She could never, ever let Drake Wilder practice his cruelties on her mother.

To her chagrin, Drake Wilder had witnessed her brief indecision. She pictured him as he'd made his proposal: smug, overconfident, superior. With cool conceit, he had explained that he wished to be the equal of the noblemen who frequented his club. Her blue blood and impeccable lineage would grant him entrée to society.

Alicia no longer considered herself superior to any other human being, though at one time she had been concerned unduly with appearances. She had been vain and self-centered, reveling in her position as one of the leading debutantes of the Season. All that had changed in a flick of the cards when her father had lost everything but this town house and a modest annuity. His death still haunted her. And now, after five humbling years of toil and grind, she had formed an appreciation and respect for the hardworking lower classes.

But Drake Wilder was a breed apart. She felt a deep resentment that he aspired to be a gentleman. An ill-gained fortune did not entitle him to mingle in aristocratic circles.

How gratifying it had been to refuse the scoundrel. He belonged in the rookeries with the coiners and thieves.

Someone touched her back and she started. She looked up to see the familiar, care-worn face of the cook. "Mrs. Molesworth. I'm sorry, I was woolgathering."

"There, now, dearie. Don't be frettin' about 'is lordship. The lad wishes to make amends for 'is foolishness." Shaking her head, Mrs. Molesworth pursed her lips. "Though 'e won't get near twenty thousand for the mare."

"I know." Alicia despaired of obtaining the remainder of the money. God help them if they were forced to sell the house. In its dilapidated state, it wouldn't fetch much, and they needed a place to live anyway, where no one would heckle her mother. For the cook's sake, she put on a brighter face. "At least we have a roof over our heads. Mama's happy here, so we should count our blessings."

"Humph," Mrs. Molesworth snorted, and lifted her thick arm to brandish a butcher knife. "I'd sooner take this blade and carve out the innards of that Drake Wilder."

So would I.

Disturbed by her own savagery, Alicia said, "We mustn't talk like that. I shan't lower myself to his level."

"May'ap a lady like you wouldn't, but by jings, I will. Let the bastard so much as sneeze in my 'earing, and I'll spit 'im and roast 'im for dinner."

Alicia wondered what Mrs. Molesworth would do if she found out about Alicia's visit to Wilder's Club. That Alicia had offered to be his mistress. That he had laughed in her face and proposed his devil's scheme instead.

Hiding her trepidation, she left the table and collected the teapot from a shelf. The chipped china with its pink roses was the only item left of their once magnificent dinner service. Measuring out a spoonful of tea leaves from a drawer in the cupboard, she said over her shoulder, "I'll take a breakfast tray up to Mama. She'll be awakening soon."

Mrs. Molesworth bustled to the iron pot and dumped in the sliced carrots. "Soup's on, and you've other matters to tend to, m'lady. I'll take the first turn with 'er."

Alicia was painfully conscious of the fact that she'd been forced to let go the other servants, leaving a burden on the older woman. "But you do too much already."

"Bosh. I'll get a'ead on the mendin' whilst I sit with 'er ladyship. " Mrs. Molesworth thrust a plate into Alicia's hands. "You sit back down and eat. 'Eaven knows when we'll see beef for pasties again."

*   *   *

Alicia was crouched on her hands and knees in the drawing room, fiercely polishing the baseboard, when someone rapped on the front door. Lost in thought, she kept working until the knocking sounded again and she remembered there was no longer a footman to answer the summons.

Bedraggled and dirty, Alicia sat back on her heels, stuck out her lower lip, and blew a tendril of hair off her forehead. She was tempted to ignore the visitor. It was likely another creditor. But she would sooner know now than have a nasty surprise later.

Stiff from kneeling on the bare wood floor, she dropped her cleaning rag into the bucket of soapy water, wiped her hands on her apron, and clambered to her feet. Stonily, she averted her gaze from the altered drawing room as she trudged out into the hall to open the front door.

She blinked in dismay. At the curbstone loomed a fine black carriage, the horses held by a coachman. And on her doorstep stood a tall, debonair gentleman dressed in an impeccable gray coat and matching trousers. He removed his top hat and bowed, displaying a thatch of thickly silvering dark hair. Richard, the Marquess of Hailstock.

"My lord," she said, dipping a curtsy while brushing ineffectually at her soiled skirt. "This is most unexpected."

"My dear Alicia, forgive me for intruding." His gray eyes flickered over her dishevelment, though he was too well-bred to comment. "I was hoping to speak with you, but if another time is more convenient . . ."

Alicia had put him out of her mind after their angry parting two days ago. Yet his familiar distinguished features brought the spark of impossible hope. Perhaps, just perhaps, he had reconsidered.

She stepped back. "Please come in, my lord."

Pretending she wore a glittering ball gown instead of a sadly rumpled work dress, she led him into the drawing room. Their footsteps echoed in the nearly empty chamber.

The marquess stopped abruptly. "Good God," he exclaimed. "What's happened here?"

She saw the oblong room through his eyes, the bare wood floor, the forlorn expanse of space, the blank walls with pale squares where paintings had once hung. Tears prickled the backs of her eyelids. She would not weep. She would *not*. Casually, she said, "I sold everything this morning."

Not more than an hour ago, the secondhand seller's dray had hauled off the rosewood furniture and the rolled-up old carpet. Gone was the pianoforte where she had played as a girl, treasuring her father's smile of pleasure. Gone were the pretty figurines her mother had once delighted in collecting. Gone was the dainty writing desk where Alicia had sat for the past two days, working and reworking the accounts, hoping to find a way to pay off their creditors. The twenty-three gold guineas she had been paid wouldn't stretch far.

Rather than give vent to despair, she had spent the past hour scrubbing the floors and moldings with a fury.

"Please, sit down." Penury didn't mean she couldn't be gracious. She led Lord Hailstock toward the only remaining pieces: a chaise and two frayed chairs by the hearth so that she and Mama and Gerald could sit here of an evening. She might even persuade Mrs. Molesworth to bring her knitting here.

"How is James?" she asked.

Sorrow flashed in Hailstock's eyes at the mention of his only son, an invalid. "He's fine, but I haven't come here today to talk about him. I need to talk about you."

He touched Alicia's elbow and seated her beside him on the chaise. Against her will, she found herself melting at his gallantry, the genuine concern on his aristocratic features. He was a widower who had lost his second wife only the previous year. All her life, Alicia had known him as a friend of her parents, for Mama had grown up with his first wife, Claire. It had seemed awkward at first for Alicia to realize he was courting her. She had enjoyed the small luxuries he'd brought her, the sweets and the flowers and books. She had looked forward to their animated talks on everything from fashion to gardening. But though she was fond of him, she didn't love him with the wild romantic ardor she had once dreamed of feeling for a man. Yet she was certain she could be happy with him, were it not for their one momentous difference of opinion.

He took her chapped hand, gently pressing it between his sleek, kid-gloved fingers. She was distressingly aware of how reddened her skin was, no longer smooth and soft, the fingernails unbroken. "My dear Alicia," he said, "it pains me so to see you reduced to living like a pauper. You come from one of the finest and oldest families in England."

The tiny flame of hope in her flared a little brighter. Had he come here to say he'd been wrong? That he would put no stipulation on their marriage? "I have no other recourse," she said. "You know about Gerald's debt. Mr. Wilder will be demanding repayment."

Something stormy flashed into Hailstock's eyes, and his grip tightened on her. "That rabble! Your brother cannot be blamed for the weakness he inherited from his father. But I condemn Wilder for exploiting such a flaw."

"I pray Gerald has learned his lesson." She thought of him, selling his prized mare in order to help repay the note, and a bittersweet pain clenched her breast. "I know he wouldn't deliberately do anything to harm Mama and me."

"Nevertheless, the damage is done. And a fine lady like you cannot live like this." Hailstock gestured at the empty chamber.

"What else am I to do?" she murmured.

"We can do what we discussed two days ago, when you came to me, asking for my help." He touched her cheek and gazed deeply into her eyes. "Marry me, darling. Much as I dislike giving tuppence to that Wilder wretch, I would do it for you, if you were my wife. I came here today hoping you had reconsidered my offer."

How wonderful it would be to transfer her worries to him, to let him take care of her, to once again live the uncomplicated life of a lady. Alicia forced herself to ask, "Have you changed your mind in regard to Mama, then? Will you allow her to live with us?"

His mouth thinned. "You must see how impossible that is. Please, don't turn away." His cool fingertips drew her face back toward him. "You must see that Lady Brockway belongs where she can be properly cared for by people experienced in these matters."

"*I* care for her properly," Alicia flared. "I don't know how you can forsake her. She and Papa were your friends once. I remember watching from the top of the stairs, seeing all of you laughing together at dinner parties and fancy balls. It made *me* happy to see Mama smile so gaily. She was the loveliest lady there." She stopped, her throat taut.

"All that is gone now," the marquess said urgently. " 'Tis regrettable, but time marches on and people do change. Wishing will not bring back the mother you once admired."

"I *still* admire her," Alicia said fiercely. "*That* is where you and I differ. To me, she is no bit of rubbish to be tossed aside simply because you consider her an embarrassment."

His expression rigid, Hailstock sat back on the chaise. "Think, my dear. If you spurn my offer, there will be no one else willing to pay so much for your hand. Your brother will go to prison while you and your mother end up in the workhouse. Is that a better fate than what I propose?"

Alicia shivered, for beneath the heat of her anger lay a cold kernel of fear. "If I must starve first, I will never, ever give Mama over to strangers. And to such a horrible place as you propose—"

"M'lady!" Running footsteps thudded in the corridor,

and Mrs. Molesworth burst into the drawing room, her round face flushed, her mobcap askew. "M'lady, you must come, and quickly!"

Alicia sprang up from the chaise. Her insides knotting, she seized the cook's broad shoulders. "Is it Mama?"

"Aye. She was gatherin' flowers in the garden, singin' to 'erself while I pulled weeds. I nipped inside for a minute, just to stir the soup, and when I come back . . ." She paused, quivering, her plump hand pressed to her mouth.

"Tell me."

"She's gone, m'lady. She's nowhere to be found!"

Chapter Three

The flower-seller perched on the park bench, yellow daffodils and purple crocuses spilling from the basket in her lap. Her sweetly earnest face looked as delicate as a cameo beneath a wide-brimmed straw hat with its cloud of pink tulle. A tattered moleskin cape with a blue satin lining hung from her thin shoulders down to a much-mended black skirt. Near her small bare feet, a fat pigeon pecked at the dirt between the stone flags of the path.

"Flowers fer sale," the woman trilled, holding up a posy. "Please, buy me lovely flowers."

The pedestrians strolling the park made a wide berth around the bench. A nursemaid pushing a perambulator slowed and stared. A haughty gentleman curled his upper lip in distaste. A pair of fashionably dressed merchants' wives scuttled past, their mouths flapping in horrified whispers, their gait swift as if they feared venturing too near.

"Quite mad," muttered the tall, pinch-mouthed matron.

"An outrage," squealed her plump friend. "Not fit to be seen by decent folk—"

"Then it is a blessing there are no decent folk here," Alicia broke in.

The two women pivoted, gasping in unison.

Her heart beating swiftly from the frantic search, Alicia

took grim satisfaction in their discomfiture as she marched toward them. She wouldn't hesitate to use her family's sterling status to silence these insensitive boors.

The sour-faced woman dipped into a stiff curtsy. "My lady! This is a surprise."

Her apple-cheeked companion almost tripped in her haste to follow suit.

In her haughtiest voice, Alicia said, "You would do better to make your obeisance to Lady Brockway."

"We would, but . . . but . . ." the stout woman sputtered, her lips quivering in alarm, "but it is nearly luncheon time. Come along, Louise." The two women hastened toward one of the town houses along the square.

Alicia wanted to fling another insult at their departing backs. Gossipy old hens! She held her tongue; further estranging the neighbors would only worsen their narrow-minded opinions.

And it would reflect all the more poorly on Mama.

Aware of a catch in her throat, she continued down the path to the bench. The pigeon launched itself into the air in a flutter of gray wings. The flower-seller spied Alicia, and a smile bloomed on her pixie face.

Her blue eyes sparkled as she waved a limp bouquet tied with a ragged length of pink ribbon. "Tuppence, miss. Tuppence fer the finest flowers in all of London town."

Alicia smiled at her mother. To hide a stab of bittersweet affection, she gathered the wilting crocuses and inhaled their delicate fragrance. It saddened her, these times when no recognition shone in Mama's eyes. Today, Eleanor, Lady Brockway, wore the mask of a stranger.

As always, Alicia played along with her mother's latest fantasy. "Thank you. But I'm afraid I haven't brought my money purse. Would you mind walking home with me?"

"Ye may take the blooms fer free," Lady Eleanor said grandly, her soft aristocratic voice marred by a counterfeit Cockney lilt. "I'll be busy makin' other sales."

Alicia doubted that. Her mother was attracting scandalized attention not only from the people strolling the walkways, but also from the nearby houses. In more than one window, a drapery twitched and a pale oval face peered at them. A part of her wanted to stick out her tongue like a child; the more practical side saw the need to escort her mother back inside, where no one would sneer at her.

"I insist on paying you," Alicia said. "Do come with me. It's only a short walk." She straightened her mother's cape, took her by the elbow, and gently helped her to her feet.

"Oh, bother." Lady Eleanor's lower lip trembled. "Truth be told, no one will buy from me. No one at all."

The hurt in her voice arrowed into Alicia. "Never mind them. Vulgar people don't appreciate pretty flowers, that's all."

Her mother brightened. "Aye. Ye must be right."

As they walked through the park, Alicia glanced past the plane trees to the row of houses. Like the others, theirs was a tall stone dwelling with pillars and three floors of windows, the roof crowned by several chimney pots. Her gaze riveted to the vehicle slowing to a halt at the curbstone.

Guided by a liveried coachman, a pair of matched bays drew the sleek black coach. The carriage parked in the place where, only minutes ago, Lord Hailstock's barouche had stood. The marquess had quickly taken his leave after Mrs. Molesworth's agitated announcement, and Alicia hadn't had time to feel disappointed or angry at his desertion. Her attention had been focused on finding Mama.

Alicia sighed inwardly. The visitor must be one of Gerald's high-flying friends, though the young coxcombs seldom came to call anymore, in part because of her mother and in part because of Alicia's disapproval.

She might have taken Mama in the back way, except they lived in the middle of the block, and it would mean walking the gauntlet of busybodies down the street, around the corner, and through the mews. She would rather spirit

Mama inside quickly without subjecting her to another hurtful snub.

Crossing the busy street, she kept an arm around her mother's girlishly slender waist. Lady Eleanor hummed a tuneless ditty and half skipped over the hard cobbles. The basket of flowers swung from her hand, and her bare toes kicked up her hem. Lost in her own world, she didn't notice the neighbors gawking from windows and door stoops.

And just as well, Alicia thought, her chin held high. She couldn't bear it if Mama comprehended the fear and loathing her madness inspired. Better she stay indoors, protected within the warm circle of family.

Unfortunately, she had a habit of wandering off if she wasn't watched every minute.

They skirted around behind the coach, its windows transformed to mirrors by the sunlight. No insignia marked the black lacquered door. A trace of expensive leather underlay the more common smell of horses. The stone-faced coachman did not so much as glance at her.

She had just placed her foot on the first step leading to the porch when she heard the carriage door open behind her. *Blast.* Moving in front of her mother, Alicia fabricated a polite smile and swung around to ward off the visitor. She would inform him that her brother had not yet returned from Tattersall's. The dandy would scuttle off posthaste—

Her diplomatic plan died a quick death as a tall man emerged from the coach. A comma of black hair lay on his broad brow, and his keen blue eyes glittered at her in the sunlight. The fine black suit and silver waistcoat might have marked him a gentleman, but Alicia wasn't fooled by costly trappings.

She saw the devil in Drake Wilder.

Like Lucifer's gift to womankind, he sauntered toward them. The promise of sin lay in that lean, muscled physique and the sensual slant of his mouth. The sight made her heart beat faster—only because he reminded her of that mortifying kiss. And the horrid fact that she owed him twenty thousand guineas.

Had he come to pressure her for payment? To push his unthinkable proposal on her?

Even that possibility fell secondary to the chance that he might poke fun at Mama. She could hear her mother humming softly behind her, could feel the brush of her skirts as she swayed in time to the imaginary music in her head.

Thankfully, Wilder kept his gaze on Alicia as he took her work-roughened hand in his. Unlike Hailstock, he wore no gloves, and his firm grip encircled her cold fingers with a hellish heat. "My lady. How good to see you again."

"Mr. Wilder. You are not welcome here."

"Still fretting over that kiss, I see."

His eyes laughed at her. Before she could retort, he brought her hand to his lips. The caress of his breath sent a wicked warmth cascading through her insides. It was anger, she told herself. He had toyed with her, letting her make a dolt of herself, and that was not an experience she'd often faced.

She snatched back her hand. "I never *fret*," she said in a frosty voice. "And I'm not receiving visitors at the moment. If you will excuse me."

Intent on getting her mother into the house, she turned her back on him. Lady Eleanor chose that moment to peek past Alicia and chirp, " 'Ello, sir. Would ye care to buy a posy fer yer sweet'eart?"

He shifted his attention to her, one of his dark brows lifting as she held forth her basket of bent, bedraggled blooms. *Dear God.* Alicia prayed he didn't realize he was gazing at the dowager countess.

Her hopes were dashed in the very next moment. "Lady Brockway, I presume," he murmured. "I can see where Alicia gets her beauty."

"Alicia?" She blinked, her fair brows drawing together

in a wistful frown. "I once knew a girl named Alicia. A right pretty little girl she was."

Before he could recoil or make a cutting remark, Alicia slid a sheltering hand around her mother's back. She urged her up the short flight of steps toward the haven of the house. "Never mind him. He really isn't interested. Now come, I've tuppence for you, remember?"

"Not interested, bosh." Stopping on the porch, Lady Eleanor smiled innocently at Wilder from beneath her wide-brimmed hat. "Surely such a 'andsome gent 'as a girl to woo. An' no better way than with flowers."

"I'm sorry, Mama, he was just leaving. And so are we—"

"Wait. I do indeed wish to make a purchase." In two quick strides, Drake Wilder cleared the four steps to the porch and blocked their path to the front door. He dipped a courtly bow to Lady Eleanor. "Would you be so good as to show me your wares?"

"Certainly, kind sir." Giggling, she lifted the basket of flowers for his inspection. "Take all the time ye likes."

Alicia watched, tense and wary, ready to stop him if he dared to mock her mother. She would feel no qualm about slapping that too-handsome face. Or poking her elbow into that flat stomach. Or shoving those wide, muscled shoulders aside so that she could whisk her mother inside and lock the door. She would not feel safe until then. . . .

"Ye must pick the prettiest nosegay. What of this one?" Lady Eleanor fished out a rather limp bunch of crocuses. "Ye'll want only the best fer the lady of yer choice."

"Quite so." He lifted his sardonic gaze to Alicia.

Her skin prickled from the force of that masculine stare. She could feel her breasts tightening, her belly clenching, her legs weakening. Looking into his eyes gave her an elemental awareness of him as a man . . . and herself as a woman. This scoundrel wished to marry her. To use her as a stepping stone to the inner circle of society. And to take her to his bed. Her gaze focused on his beautiful mouth with its appealing half-smile, the dimples deep and tempting. . . .

Resenting his effect on her, she curled her fingers around her own posy. "Make your choice and be gone."

Slipping forefinger and thumb into an inner pocket of his coat, Wilder drew out a gold guinea, which he presented to Lady Eleanor. "I'll buy the whole lot," he drawled. "This should more than cover the price."

As Alicia gaped in amazement, he scooped up every last one of the blooms. Yellow, white, pink, purple, the flowers drooped in his big hands, the daffodils brushing golden pollen on the sleeve of his dark coat. Heedless, he presented the bouquet to her. "For you, the lady of my heart."

Flabbergasted, Alicia caught the flowers against her bosom, drenching herself in rich scent. Her voice deserted her. What nefarious purpose had prompted his flamboyant gesture? There had to be a catch; there always was with a man like Drake Wilder. In a moment he would make his cruelly scathing remarks. He would ridicule her mother until she wept.

Lady Eleanor clapped her hands. The empty basket swung from the crook of her arm, the gold coin glinting among a few bruised petals. "Ah, she's a pretty one. And sweet-tempered, too."

"Mmm." Mockery glinting in his eyes, he made a noncommittal sound in his throat. "We are a fine couple. A perfect match."

"Aye," she said, regarding them fondly, her small hands folded beneath her chin. " 'Tis like a romantic tale of yore."

"I'm glad we have your approval." In a swift move, he caught Alicia to his side, his hand firm and warm at her waist, trapping her to his hard body. Her arms were so full of flowers that she couldn't push him away. "From the moment we met, I knew we were destined to wed."

He had the audacity to wink at Alicia. As if she were a willing party to duping her mother.

She should spit in his diabolically handsome face. She despised the way he held her, as if she were his possession, won at a roll of the dice. Yet he had made Mama smile, and a curious tenderness tugged at Alicia's heart, an involuntary softening that stole the edge off her anger. Had he not clasped her so closely, she might have wilted like the blossoms crushed to her bosom.

The rogue. This charm was all an act, his way of trifling with women. He didn't care about Mama; he would want to cast her into Bedlam Hospital when he was done teasing her. That horrifying thought shook Alicia into action.

She shouldered herself free of him. "Come," she told her mother. "You must help me arrange these flowers in water."

Lady Eleanor giggled like a girl when Wilder opened the door and politely assisted her into the foyer. Alicia kept a sharp eye on him, alert for any sign of derision, the contempt she herself had witnessed in him. But he showed her mother only a courteous regard, advising her to watch her step and complimenting her on her extravagant hat.

Mrs. Molesworth came trotting down the dim corridor. "M'lady! You gave us all a start!" She aimed a puzzled glower at Drake Wilder.

She clearly didn't realize his identity, and Alicia wasn't about to enlighten her. Not wanting her house made into a battleground, she discreetly shook her head. He would be gone from here as soon as he realized that no matter how steep her debt to him, he could not use her family as playthings for his amusement.

Alicia went to her mother and deposited the cuttings back in the basket. "You'll need a vase," she said, slapping the pollen off her hands. "Will you take her to the kitchen, please?"

The cook gave a brisk nod and guided Lady Eleanor

down the passageway. Mama's excited voice drifted back to them. "Look!" she said, rummaging in the bottom of the basket. "I've a guinea! From that well-mannered gent. I do believe 'e's in love with 'er."

Alicia's face flushed hotly. Conscious of Wilder standing behind her, she held herself with ladylike dignity. To her relief, Mrs. Molesworth only smiled at Mama's ramblings, and the pair disappeared through the doorway that led to the basement stairs.

Anxious to evict Wilder, she whirled back toward him. The tart dismissal withered on her tongue. He wasn't there. Sunlight through the long window poured a thick golden bar on the empty marble floor.

She hadn't even heard him move.

Then she spied him in the library, examining the few remaining books on the mostly bare shelves. Heels clicking, she marched into the bleak chamber where, in her father's day, comfortable leather chairs and bound volumes had scented the air. Now the furniture was gone and not even a fire crackled on the hearth to lend a little cheer. In spite of the dangerous circumstances, she felt a little clutch of nostalgia in her breast.

"Mr. Wilder, I must ask you to leave. Immediately."

She might have been talking to the empty bookcases. He was scanning an old text, his face intent as he turned the pages. "A rare copy of Plutarch's *Moralia*. By God, I looked all over Rome for this."

He read ancient Latin? She tamped down her surprise. So what if he'd been educated? That had no bearing on his unwelcome presence here. "Put the book back," she said sharply. "And next time you wish to speak to me, kindly send a note. I would prefer that our discussions take place anywhere but here."

"I'd like to add this to my collection," he said absently, not lifting his gaze from the book. "Name your price."

"It's yours—for twenty thousand guineas."

That caught his attention, and he bared his white teeth in a grin. "Clever lady. But I believe I'll pass."

He shut the volume and replaced it on the shelf. Thrusting back his dark coat, he stood studying her. The shadows from the closed wooden blinds fell across his face and lent him a sinister cast. With the tip of her tongue, she moistened her dry lips. It was uncanny how he could focus his attention, his eyes burning into her, as if he could strip her bare, body and soul.

"I've twenty-three guineas for you," she stated. "Though of course you'll wish to deduct the one you gave to my mother."

"Nonsense. It was my gift to her."

"The dowager Countess of Brockway is not a beggar. She doesn't require your charity."

He cocked a lazy eyebrow, as if he were amused by her tart-tongued pride. Then he strolled toward Alicia, his every movement a study in masculine grace. His polished black shoes made only the slightest sound on the uncarpeted floor.

She would not flee, though her pulse sped and her palms dampened. Conscious of the silent, empty house, she held her place just inside the doorway of the library. Not even a clock ticked; the ormolu one from the drawing room had been sold along with the other furnishings.

He stopped mere inches away. She gritted her teeth to keep from flinching. She would show no fear to this knave.

His fingertips brushed lightly over her bare throat and down to her bodice. The caress sparked a path over her skin, and in utter disregard of her resolve, she pressed backward, her spine meeting the hard shelves. "Churl! Don't touch me."

His mouth formed that breath-stealing pirate's smile. "Crosspatch," he countered, holding up a lavender strip between his fingers. "There was merely a petal clinging to"— his gaze flitted to her bosom—"you."

His eyes an unfathomable blue, he lifted the petal to his nose and inhaled deeply. A river of heat coursed through her breasts, settling low in her belly. She had the disturbing impression that he wanted to smell the fragrance of her flesh rather than the ruined blossom.

"You needn't look so alarmed," he said in a voice as smooth as honey. "I haven't come here to seduce you."

Did he think her a fool, to trust him? "State your business and be gone. I'll not have my mother upset when she finds out who you really are."

"Empty words. I'll wager she hasn't the least notion of your brother's folly. *You* certainly wouldn't tell her."

Despising his astuteness, Alicia gripped the sturdy wooden shelf behind her. "Nor will you. I'll not have you anywhere near this house."

A hint of impatience tightened his mouth. "I see no sport in badgering your mother."

"Given half a chance, you'll sneer at her. I know your sort. You pretend to humor her, and all the while you're laughing up your sleeve."

"I'm not like those who taunt what they don't understand."

"And *you* understand her? Tell me, why would you show true kindness to her? Give me one good reason."

He shrugged, his face moody. "My mother was an actress," he said, turning away to prowl the room. "While she was learning her parts, she often played the roles with me. She might be anyone from *Hamlet*'s Ophelia to Mary, Queen of Scots." Taking a stance at the ivory marble mantelpiece, he added, "So you see, this pretending that other people find odd seems quite ordinary to me. Now, do you want to mock me and *my* mother?"

Alicia shook her head, intrigued by the insight into his past. Against her will, she pictured him as a little dark-haired boy, trading lines with his costumed mother. How strange to see the similarity to Mama, who dressed as a flower-seller or Cleopatra or whomever else struck her mad fancy.

Alicia deliberately broke the thread of connection to him. *His* mother had been sane. *She* knew she was portraying a character.

"Does she still act in the theater?" Alicia found herself asking.

"She's dead." His tone was hard, shutting the door on the past. "But enough about me. I've come to talk about us."

Us. She shuddered inwardly at the way he coupled them together. In a tumble of words, she said, "I'll have more funds for you soon. My brother is selling Pet."

"Pet?"

"His mare." Her voice threatened to choke, but she relentlessly cleared her throat. "So you see, we are making every attempt to repay you."

Wilder laughed. "Even the finest horse will fetch only a fraction of the money."

"It will have to do for now." She swallowed, then took a sustaining breath. "Unless you will reconsider my proposal . . . to be your mistress."

Even across the width of the library, his stare was fierce. "You know what I want, my lady. Your hand in marriage."

Oh, dear God, not that. Anything but that. "You ask the impossible."

"If it's Lady Brockway who concerns you, I'm willing to allow her to live with us." His face took on that calculating intensity. "Don't forget—we have her blessing."

She hated him in that moment. She hated him for the flash of hope in her, and for the way he had led her mother down a garden path of lies. She couldn't trust him; she daren't trust him. It made her ill to think of giving such a man the rights of a husband. He was a smooth-talking gambler who lured the unwary into a false belief in their own infallibility. Papa had fallen prey to such men, and now

Gerald . . . gullible, gawky Gerald, who might die if he were condemned to a damp prison cell.

But she would fight Wilder on that. He couldn't take everything. At least they had a home, bought and paid for long ago, a sanctuary for Mama.

"I'll take out a mortgage on the house," she said recklessly. "There will be enough to settle the debt."

"I'm afraid that is out of the question," Wilder said.

Reaching inside his coat, he withdrew a folded piece of parchment and held it out to her. He clearly expected her to come to him and take it. She considered standing her ground, winning this play of power. But if that paper concerned the debt, she had to know. . . .

Shoulders squared, Alicia walked slowly toward him. Those watchful eyes took in her every step. He frightened her; she could admit that to herself. But she refused to let him see.

Their fingers brushed as she took the paper. Despite her frisson of awareness, she forced herself to move deliberately, to open the vellum as she headed to a nearby window, where a sliver of light illuminated the scrawling black penmanship. Gerald's handwriting, affixed to a legal document. As she absorbed the words, horror crept in a stranglehold around her heart.

It was the deed to their house. And it had been signed over to one Drake Wilder.

Chapter Four

"I own this house now."

That supremely satisfied voice echoed as if through a long tunnel. Alicia was aware of the window frame biting into her upper arm. The dust motes dancing in a knife blade of sunshine. The deed quaking in her cold fingertips.

Mama's refuge was gone. *Gone.*

Someone touched her shoulder. "Answer me. Have you nothing to say?"

Drake Wilder loomed beside her. A moment ago, he'd stood halfway across the library, but she was too numb to feel startled. She glimpsed only his charcoal sleeve with its glinting silver buttons. She couldn't wrench her gaze from the legal document. Quite possibly, her mother's death warrant.

"You aren't about to swoon, are you?"

"Swoon?"

"You're deathly pale. Don't you have any chairs in this godforsaken place?"

"Sold." She didn't bother to mention the few furnishings in the drawing room.

What would happen to Mama?

"You'll sit on the damned stairs, then. Come."

He caught her slender wrist, his long fingers entrapping

her chilly flesh with a band of heated steel. He gave a tug and her legs moved obediently, her skirt whispering like the frantic pulse beat in her ears.

Somehow Drake Wilder had coerced her brother into signing over the house. Why hadn't Gerald told her?

She couldn't think why; she knew only that Drake Wilder had breached the last of her defenses, conquered the final outpost of her independence. They would be turned out into the street.

Unless she bound herself in marriage to this gambler.

Black dots swarmed before her eyes. In a stupor, she stumbled on the threshold of the doorway. The deed slipped from her fingers and fluttered to the checkered marble floor of the foyer. With a choked cry, she stooped down to retrieve it.

Wilder reacted more swiftly. He snatched up the document and handed it back to her. Their fingers brushed with a bolt of lightning.

Half crouched, Alicia stiffened. So did he. Their gazes locked. A frown quirked his black brows, and those uncommon blue eyes raked her features. If she didn't know better, she might believe him concerned for her well-being.

But he cared nothing for her. If it suited his ruthless purpose—and she knew it did—Drake Wilder would toss her and her family into the gutter. Who was he to destroy their lives?

Unexpectedly, he cupped her cheek in his big, warm palm. "Your skin is like ice. I'll help you up."

His sham compassion shattered the glass wall around her emotions. A storm whipped to life inside her, washing hot color into her cheeks, filling her emptiness with blinding rage.

Springing up, she shoved him away. "Villain!"

He staggered backward and caught his balance with the flat of one palm on the floor. With quick canine grace, he vaulted to his feet. His eyes glittered in the sunlight from the long window. "Virago," he said in a level tone. "Don't think you can get the best of me."

"And don't *you* ever touch me again." She crumpled the deed and hurled it at him.

He caught the wad of paper with an easy flick of his wrist. "A husband has the right to touch his wife."

"You aren't my husband."

"But I will be. As soon as arrangements can be made."

Goaded by his confidence, she yanked the tatters of composure around her. He would not cause her to lose control again. He would *not.* She lifted her chin. "We still have the entailed estate. You can never take it from us."

"That house lies in ruins. It's uninhabitable."

His knowledge rattled her. Two years earlier, a fire had destroyed their manor house in Northumberland. They could never survive the icy moorland winter by camping in the burned-out shell. "I'll find another man to wed, then. A *gentleman.*"

"With madness in your family? I think not." A strange watchfulness on his flinty features, he smoothed out the deed and tucked it into an inner pocket of his coat. "The nobility place great value on pure bloodlines. Not even the Marquess of Hailstock can tolerate such a taint."

His perception struck Alicia like a blow. How did Wilder know so much? How did he guess that Richard had refused to marry her unless she committed Mama to that hideous asylum?

Then Alicia understood the ugly answer. "You've been spying on me."

"It pays to know one's opponent."

Outrage soured her tongue. Defeat tasted even more bitter. Wilder had maneuvered her into a corner, stolen her home, outflanked her at every step. "Why me?" she asked. "There are plenty of impoverished noblewomen who would marry you for your money. Ladies from families more accepted in society than mine."

He shrugged. "Perhaps so. However, it seems that fate, in the form of your brother, has intervened. You will do well enough for my purposes."

His purposes. If she must give in to him, at least she could make some demands of her own. "I'll consider your proposal, then," she said frigidly, "on two conditions. First, you shall sign a legal document granting me sole guardianship of my mother. Wherever I live, so will she. I'll never let you lock her away in a rathole where she would suffer abuse."

A muscle jerked in his jaw. "I've already told you, I bear no ill will toward Lady Brockway."

"And why should I believe the brute who would coerce a woman into marriage?" A knot aching in her breast, Alicia shook her head. "You'll sign the agreement, else I'll never stand with you before a clergyman."

He gave a terse nod. "As you wish. And your second stipulation?"

"That we will have a chaste marriage."

His guffaw echoed through the foyer. "Don't be ridiculous. Yesterday, you were eager to be my mistress."

She battled an angry blush. "The game has changed now. The stakes have been raised."

"My prim little virgin," he said, shaking his head, his expression one of droll charm. "You can't imagine what you'd be denying yourself."

His cocky grin only fueled her fury. Lest she fly at him again like a fishwife, Alicia held herself rigid. "I assure you, Mr. Wilder, I have never been more serious. I will not allow you in my chambers. Not ever."

"People often regret vows made in anger."

"Then you know only riffraff who lack moral fiber."

"I know that moral fiber is a cold bedfellow."

Alicia compressed her lips, then said calmly, "We will make a fair exchange. *I* require cancellation of my brother's debts. And *you* require an introduction to society. I owe you nothing else."

He regarded her with a faintly calculating stare. Sunlight limned his powerful form; he had the brawny physique of a street fighter garbed in the trappings of a gentleman. A gentleman's thoughts she could read, but not this man's. Drake Wilder had risen from the criminal underworld where honor was a weakness to exploit.

"I'll accept both of your conditions with a provision of my own," he said. "You will permit me the right to coax you into my bed."

Into her mind flashed the image of herself, stark naked, sprawled wantonly astride him. She staved off a shudder as a shameful warmth slithered past her defenses and curled low in her belly like a snake. "No. I can't trust you not to force yourself on me."

Those impenetrable eyes watched her with shrewd amusement. "Quite the contrary. You can't trust yourself to resist me."

"Don't flatter yourself. I'd sooner kiss a hedgehog."

His smile broadened with a flash of white teeth. "You could use a few lessons in kissing."

"You could use a few lessons in manners."

"I propose we educate each other, then."

He strolled toward her, and Alicia refused to give ground, though a brittle panic enveloped her. Would he kiss her *now*? Would he show her how a scoundrel seduced a woman? If he dared to ridicule her again . . .

But he didn't touch her. He slid back his coat and planted his hands on his hips in a gesture of masterful male assurance. "So, Lady Alicia. Give me your answer before you take me on a tour of my new town house."

It rankled her, to obey this arrogant upstart. "Planning to move in?" she said icily.

"As a matter of fact, we'll live at my house near the club."

"Not without Mama. And you'll allow Gerald to stay here without charge."

"Agreed." He looked more amused than angered by her demands. "And now I will have your promise to be my wife."

His superior height required her to tilt up her chin to hold his gaze. With studied poise, she clasped her tense fingers together. "Only if you promise to cease your attentions when I tell you so."

That sly grin came again. "*If* you tell me so." His heavy-lidded gaze caressed her, roving up and down, lingering at her breasts and hips until her skin prickled. "Beneath all that refinement, my lady, you're flesh and blood. And before the Season is out, you'll come begging to share my bed."

Gloom shrouded the sparse furnishings in the bedchamber. Standing by the night table, Alicia measured several drops of laudanum into a cup of weak tea. She added a crumbling of coarse brown sugar, stirred the liquid until the lumps dissolved, and then turned to the woman in the four-poster. "Your posset is ready."

Sitting against a bank of goose-feather pillows, Lady Eleanor looked lost in the huge bed with its swags of aging rose velvet. A white lace nightcap perched on her silvering fair hair. She kept her tattered moleskin cape tucked close like a young child might hold a beloved blanket. The sputtering tallow candle added luminescence to her blue eyes.

"Ah, ye're a dear," she said, accepting the chipped china with the reverence worthy of a communion cup. "Bless ye for takin' me in. 'Tis ever so cold and lonely to sleep in the alleys."

Alicia concealed a grimace at the irony of her mother's current delusion. The Countess of Brockway had never spent a single night out on the streets, and never would if Alicia had her way. They shared this bedchamber, partly because it was cheaper to heat one room than two, and partly so that Alicia could keep a close watch on her mother. Before the doctor had prescribed the laudanum, she'd had a habit of wandering around the house during the night, sometimes venturing up to the darkened attic to search through the trunks of antique clothing left from decades of Pemberton ancestors. Alicia feared Mama might knock over a candle and set the house afire, not to mention cast herself into danger in other ways.

Once, after garbing herself in heavy brocaded robes as the Queen of Sheba, Mama had taken a nasty tumble down the steep wooden stairs. A sprained ankle had incapacitated her for a fortnight. Another time, fancying herself to be Joan of Arc, she had found a battered breastplate and an old dueling sword, and Alicia had caught her in the foyer, ready to charge out the front door and into the night.

Heaven knew, she needed a guardian angel. Not a devil of a son-in-law who would dislodge her from these familiar surroundings.

Torn between anger and affection, Alicia reached down and smoothed a stray curl from her mother's brow. "Drink now," she murmured. "Every last drop."

Obediently, the countess drained the cup and handed it back. Then she patted her lips with a lace handkerchief, which she tucked into her voluminous sleeve. Like a child, she snuggled down and let Alicia settle her beneath the embroidered coverlet.

A contented sigh eddied from Lady Eleanor. "I been thinkin', dearie. There's somethin' so familiar about 'im."

"About who?"

"That polite young man of yers. I wonder if 'e's bought posies from me before."

Alicia stiffened, though she was careful not to show her rancor. "I'm sure you're confusing him with someone else."

"One don't forget such a 'andsome gent. He was smitten with ye, buyin' every last flower. Ah, 'twas so romantic."

Alicia avoided looking at the vase of bedraggled blooms, which she'd placed on the mantelpiece for her mother's sake. She resented the oily charm he'd used to win over a vulnerable woman. But like it or not, she would have to endure his presence in her life. She knew her duty. She had taken him on the requested tour of the house—his house now. He had behaved with perfect courtesy, though she trusted him about as far as she could throw the contents of a chamber pot.

"His name is Drake Wilder." She bit her lower lip and tasted the metallic zest of blood. Earlier, she had forced herself to pen a note to Lord Hailstock, informing him of the news. Now she must tell her mother. "You'll be seeing more of Mr. Wilder from now on. Today . . . we became betrothed."

Those papery eyelids blinked. Like clouds parting to blue sky, Lady Eleanor's drowsy eyes grew slowly lucid, focusing on her daughter. "Alicia?" she said wonderingly. "Did I hear you right? You are to be wed?"

The elegant, aristocratic voice startled Alicia. Overjoyed by the transformation, she sank to her knees beside the bed. "Yes," she whispered. "Oh, Mama. *Mama.*"

Her eyes brimming, she smiled at her mother. She never knew when to expect these rare episodes of sanity; they might last mere moments or long, treasured hours. But why now? Why when she didn't dare pour out her fears and uncertainties?

The countess groped for Alicia's hand. "My darling girl, that is wonderful news. Who is this Mr. Wilder? Why haven't I made his acquaintance?"

"It all happened rather quickly," Alicia said evasively. "I suppose you could say we had a whirlwind courtship."

Her mother's brow pleated. Horror flirted with her fragile features, and she raised herself on one elbow. "Oh, dear. I've been drifting again, haven't I?"

"You've been . . . ill. But I'm sure you'll feel better now."

"What day is it? What month?"

"April the eleventh."

"Dear heaven. Last I recall, 'twas Candlemas Day and Gerald brought me the most beautiful bouquet of snowdrops. . . ." Sinking back onto the pillow, the countess shook her head in despair. "God have mercy. Whatever is happening to me?"

Willing her hand not to tremble, Alicia stroked her mother's slender forearm. "You'll be fine," she soothed. "You're weary, that's all, and it's difficult to focus your mind. Close your eyes now and rest. I'll answer all your questions later."

The countess's eyelids drooped. "Such a sweet daughter you've always been. I don't mean to be a burden."

"You're not! You're my pride and joy," Alicia said fiercely, leaning down to kiss her mother's pale cheek. The faint comforting fragrance of lily of the valley clung to her skin. "How ridiculous to think otherwise."

"I *am* silly, aren't I? Your papa always teased me about my fancies." A dreamy smile smoothed the lines of tension from Lady Eleanor's face. She shifted onto her side and rested her cheek on her folded hands. "In the morning, we must plan your nuptials. And you must promise to invite your betrothed here to meet me. If you love him, then so shall I."

"Of course," Alicia said woodenly.

"It shall be the event of the Season. Gerald will escort you down the aisle at St. George's. You'll carry lilies trimmed with white satin ribbons . . ." Her voice drifted off, and her breathing became quiet and regular with slumber.

A familiar twist of melancholy encircled Alicia's heart. She couldn't be certain her mother would even remember the news come morning. The countess's recollection of the distant past could be sharp and clear, while present events often slipped through her muddled awareness like water through a sieve. Though perhaps in this case, her tendency to forget was a blessing. Heaven forbid Mama should learn the true circumstances behind the marriage. Or the brutal nature of the man Alicia intended to marry.

Before the Season is out, you'll come begging to share my bed.

Too restless to sleep, she snatched up the candlestick and hastened to the door. The laudanum would ensure that her mother slept deeply for hours, and it was the only time Alicia felt safe leaving her alone. She would make her way down to the kitchen and brew a pot of tea. Then perhaps a tome from the library would provide sufficient distraction from her emotional turmoil. An hour or two of deciphering Latin never failed to exhaust her. Especially a difficult work of essays like Plutarch's *Moralia.*

Drake Wilder had traveled to Rome searching for that particular work. Was book collecting such a lucrative investment? Surely the hard-bitten owner of a gaming club could have no liking for intellectual pursuits. When would the ruffian find time to bilk his customers and seduce his whores?

When would he find time to prey upon mad widows and naive earls? To coerce a desperate woman?

In a fit of ire, Alicia surged out into the darkened corridor. And collided with a solid shape.

A yelp pierced the gloom.

Startled, she lifted the candle and saw her brother. Gerald hopped on one stockinged foot, a small box tucked beneath his arm. His hair was mussed and his cravat untied, baring his prominent Adam's apple. "Ye-ouch! You trod on my toes."

"Hush." She quietly shut the bedroom door. "You'll waken Mama. She's just now taken her draught."

"You almost burned me, too," he grumbled. "You should watch where you're going."

"It's time you came home. I've been wanting to speak to you." Prodded by anger, Alicia grabbed her brother by the arm and marched him down the passageway and to the grand staircase. "Drake Wilder came here today. On a small matter regarding ownership of this house."

"Oh . . . that." Clutching the box, her brother hunched his shoulders. "I meant to tell you, Ali, truly I did."

"When? After he had served us an eviction notice?"

His green eyes rounded. "He swore he wouldn't. By God, I'll call him out for going back on his word."

When Gerald would have leapt down the stairs, Alicia stepped in front of him. The candle flame wavered as she pressed her other hand to his scrawny chest. "Mr. Wilder has done no such thing. Instead, he has agreed to absolve the debt." The disclosure nearly stuck in her throat. "You see, he and I . . . shall be married."

"Married—?" Gerald's jaw dropped. He stared at her as if she'd sprouted whiskers. "You'll marry *him?*"

"Yes."

"But . . . you're not his sort. He likes wenches who—" Gerald cleared his throat, his cheeks turning ruddy. "That is, he likes common women."

Bitterness choked Alicia. "Nevertheless, we've come to an agreement. We shall be wed as soon as arrangements can be made."

"No! I'll find the money somehow." Her brother plunked the box down onto the floor, and the muffled chink of coins rang out in the shadowed upper landing. Dropping to one knee, he untied the twine and opened the top. The meager candlelight glinted off a small mound of gold inside the box. "This isn't much, but perhaps he'll accept a down payment."

A rush of understanding tempered her anger. "You sold Pet."

"Quite so," Gerald said with glum bravado. "Chester-field paid two hundred guineas for her. The rotter drove a hard bargain, but he'll be decent to her at least."

"Oh, Ger." Her throat taut, Alicia bent down and slid her arms around him. His baby-fine hair glided across her cheek. For a moment, his bony shoulders sagged against her in a hug reminiscent of his youth, after Mama had descended into dementia and Alicia had assumed the role of parent.

Shooting to his feet, Gerald brought his fist down on the rickety wooden railing, and the blow echoed into the vast murky expanse of the hall below. "By damn! If only I had Wilder's skill, I could turn this two hundred into twenty thousand. The lucky devil could do it in one night's play."

"I won't have you gambling." That sickening worry overshadowed all else. Her marriage would place him in close proximity to a seasoned gamester. If Gerald were to end up like Papa . . . "Promise you won't go near Wilder's Club ever again."

"But everyone gathers there. 'Tis the very crack. No harm can come of joining my friends for dinner sometimes."

She caught his sleeve. "Promise me, Gerald."

"I know my duty to you and Mama," he mumbled. "I won't gamble again."

"I pray not." Yet she couldn't feel at ease, not with the future looming like an executioner's ax. "And you should know that Mr. Wilder won't accept any down payments. He won't take anything less than my hand in marriage."

Gerald opened his mouth as if he would argue. Then he sank down onto the top step and looked up at her, his young features stricken. "It isn't fair. This is my fault, not yours."

It was Wilder's fault. "What's done is done," she said, forcing a smile. "Everything will be for the best. You and Mama and I shall have a good home and ample food on the table. That is all that matters."

Her brother didn't look comforted. "You're sacrificing yourself. I can't let you do that."

"You must." Determined to convince him, she managed an airy laugh. "Please, Ger, don't look so unhappy. Women often marry for monetary advantage. If truth be told, I'll enjoy going to parties and having a fine wardrobe again."

"But what about his . . ."—he cleared his throat—"marital rights?"

Before the Season is out, you'll come begging to share my bed.

Steeling herself against a shudder, she took a deep breath. "He's promised me a chaste marriage. So you see, it is to be strictly a business arrangement."

A cautious hope dawned on his face. "You won't mind, then? I wouldn't permit it if I thought him a bad sort. But he *is* a gentleman, regardless of his low birth."

He was a hard-hearted wretch. But Gerald needn't know the depths of Wilder's depravity.

Hoping God would forgive her the falsehood, Alicia said firmly, "Of course I won't mind. I should be quite content to be rich again. And to know that all of our troubles are finally over."

Chapter Five

Through a small iron grate in the wall, the muted strains of the violin and pianoforte drifted into the candlelit office. The music came from the salon downstairs, where gentlemen wagered their fortunes on a roll of the dice. The specially designed system of pipes carried the melody to every chamber in the building. It was Drake's design, one of the innovations that set his club apart from all the others on St. James's Street. Noblemen, he knew, could be lulled into taking greater risks in an atmosphere of refined serenity.

On an ordinary evening, Drake would be down there in the thick of the action, strolling from table to table, keeping a discreet eye on the play, offering praise to the winners and consolation to the losers.

But this was the night of his betrothal. The beginning of his revenge. If he'd guessed right, at any time he could receive a certain visitor. And it wasn't the redhead in his arms.

Ensconced in the leather chair by the hearth, Drake idly smoothed his hand over the clingy green gauze of her gown. Lydia had slipped up the back staircase, as was her habit whenever she had an evening free. The lead actress in a popular play at Covent Garden Theatre, Lydia could have any man she wished, yet she came here to him. Always before, he had taken great pleasure in her earthy sensuality.

But tonight her artifices annoyed him—the coy beauty mark she'd penciled on her generous bosom, the heavy musk of her perfume, her soft mews of pleasure as she strung kisses along his jaw. Letting her stay had been a mistake. Not even her lush figure could distract him from his restless reflections. He could think only of an aristocratic blond beauty too cold and proud for his tastes.

We will have a chaste marriage. . . . I can't trust you not to force yourself on me. . . .

"I'm afraid you'll have to leave now," he said abruptly.

Surprise flashed into her velvety brown eyes. She took his hand and guided it beneath her skirts. "You can't mean that. We've only just begun."

His fingers curled against her warm, silken thigh. *She* would marry him willingly. He had known many women like her, women who had hinted at a desire for a permanent match. Yet he felt no inclination to do more than take the pleasure they offered him.

Lady Alicia Pemberton was another matter. Toward her, he felt a burning resolve that went beyond revenge, a possessiveness that was fast becoming an obsession. In a mere two encounters, she had managed to startle him and insult him, amuse him and anger him, arouse him and intrigue him. Despite her chilly blue blood, she showed a fierce loyalty to her infirm mother. He felt a grudging respect for that.

At the same time, he resented being distracted from his true purpose. Alicia was forbidden fruit, that was all. As soon as he bedded her, the challenge would lose its appeal. He would feel no further desire for his genteel wife.

He slapped Lydia on her cushiony bottom. "I'm expecting a visitor," he said. "This isn't a convenient time."

"A quick ride, then," she said, rocking suggestively

against him. "Shall we go into the other room or do it right here?"

There was a bed in the adjoining chamber for such liaisons. But Drake felt only a mild stirring, easily mastered. He lifted her to her feet. "Neither," he said. "I'm sorry, but you cannot stay."

Her lower lip thrust out. Recognizing an incipient tantrum, he swiftly guided her through the antechamber, where he gave her a conciliatory kiss. "Go without a fuss, and tomorrow you shall have a surprise from the jeweler."

He did not feel inclined to inform her about his impending marriage. He would continue their affair, and if she became troublesome, he would find another mistress. The world was full of willing women.

As he ushered her out, he spied Fergus MacAllister stomping down the lamplit corridor, a thunderous glare on his craggy features. But it was not that one-eyed glower that struck a vigilant expectation into Drake. It was the man marching after Fergus.

Richard, the Marquess of Hailstock.

Right on cue.

Drake gave his mistress a gentle shove in the opposite direction. "Go now."

Glancing curiously over her shoulder, the actress sauntered to the back staircase that led down to the butler's pantry and the kitchen. At the doorway, she blew him a kiss. Then she vanished into the stairwell.

"Well, well," Fergus growled. " 'Tis a braw night for callers. And not a sweet angel among them." He gave Drake another piercing look, then jerked his thumb at the marquess. "I told this one to wait downstairs, but he'd have naught to do with takin' orders."

"Cheeky minion," Hailstock snapped. "You forget your place—"

"No, *you* forget," Drake cut in. "You're in my domain now."

Before the marquess could do more than scowl, Drake sent Fergus away with a silent motion and then ushered Hailstock through the antechamber and into the office.

Drake's anger transformed into dark elation as he strolled to a side table and picked up a cut-glass tumbler. Into it he splashed a golden brown liquid from a decanter. Then he pivoted toward Hailstock, who stood stiffly in the center of the Aubusson rug.

"Brandy?" Drake said, holding up his glass. "It's the finest French stock—the same as in Bonaparte's private cellar."

"Devil take your smuggled contraband. This isn't a social call, and well you know it."

"Suit yourself." Taking a long swallow, Drake sauntered to the desk and settled himself on the edge. For all his nonchalance, he could barely taste the mellow liquor. He savored only the secret pleasure of revenge.

Twenty years had passed since he had last seen Lord Hailstock at close quarters. Those years had strung silver threads through Hailstock's black hair, etched lines on his patrician features, added a slight paunch to his trim form. Yet he had not changed, not really. Superiority still frosted his gray eyes. Disdain still curled his noble lip. Arrogance still radiated from his square-shouldered form. He wore a dark blue coat and fawn breeches, tailored at the most exclusive shop on Bond Street. His gold watch fob had come from Locke & Co., his diamond sleeve links from Gray's, his leather shoes from Wilson's.

Drake knew because all these years he had watched Hailstock. He had watched and waited and planned for this moment.

"Name your price," Hailstock bit out. "I'll make it well worth your while to cry off your betrothal to Lady Alicia."

"No."

The marquess took a step toward him. "Knave! You coerced her by setting up her brother for a loss. But she isn't a prize to be won in a wager. You'll only drag her down into your filth."

The cold knot tightened inside Drake. He drained his glass and carefully set it on the mahogany surface of the desk. "Perhaps so," he drawled, his gaze boring into the marquess. "Nevertheless, she will be mine, not yours . . . Father."

The fire on the hearth seethed into the silence. Even the music downstairs had lulled. A strange deadness descended over Hailstock's elegant features. His body went utterly still, the breath hissing out through his teeth. "You are not my son," he said in a brusque tone. "I have but one son. My heir."

Drake had expected that answer. He had heard it before. On one notable occasion that was burned into his memory.

The old pain broke past his self-control and twisted in his gut. He countered it by remembering another moment, the morning when he had knelt by his dying mother's bedside in Edinburgh, a ten-year-old lad faced with the prospect of losing the only parent he had ever known. He would never forget the fear that had strangled his heart. . . .

Muira Wilder had coughed, wiping her lips with the blood-speckled handkerchief. With shaking hands, Drake poured her a cup of water. He had sensed something was wrong, though he'd tried so hard not to believe it. Her once rosy cheeks looked pale as if daubed by white greasepaint. For days, she had been too weak to play any roles with the troupe of actors.

After choking down a sip, she lay back against the pillow and regarded him with haunted hazel eyes. " 'Tis time ye ken I'm dyin'."

"Dinna speak so, Mither. We'll be together always."

She lovingly stroked his hair. "Nay, my son, it canna be. I nivver could carry a bairn, lost so many till ye came along. Ye were my blessin', my gift from heaven. But now ye must go to yer sire."

"I'd rather stay with Fergus!"

"Fergus will go wi' ye, but he is not yer father. Hailstock is a powerful lord whose noble blood will serve ye well." Groping for his fingers, Muira pressed a diamond stickpin into his hands. "Here's the proof. I was to use this fer yer keep, but we scraped by without sellin' it."

"But I wish to stay by ye."

"Och, ye canna. And a lad needs his father. His lordship will love ye when he sees what a braw lad ye've grown up to be. Say ye'll go to him when I'm gone. . . ."

He'd been too stricken to refuse. Only a few weeks later, after burying his mother on a bitter cold autumn day, he and Fergus had set south for England. Drake had spent the long days on the mail coach grieving for his mother and dreaming of the warm embrace of a father. Yet when he found the fine mansion in Mayfair, the butler had refused him entry.

In desperation, he had pushed his way inside, leaving Fergus behind. Pursued by servants, he'd run from room to magnificent room, until he'd dashed into a grand parlor and found the Marquess of Hailstock down on the floor, playing tin soldiers with a handsome, tawny-haired boy, his two-year-old son, James. . . .

Drake's half-brother. The legitimate heir.

Even now, Drake felt a welter of emotions he didn't care to examine. For one prolonged moment, he had fiercely yearned to be a part of that family. He had hurled himself at Hailstock's well-shod feet, blubbered out his naïve hopes. And the marquess had coldly denied him. When Drake had showed him the stickpin, Hailstock's face had turned ugly. He'd called for his servants to haul the scruffy urchin off to the magistrate for thievery. . . .

Gazing again at that haughty face, Drake now focused on the anger that had long ruled his life. "Deny me all you like," he said. "The fact remains that after seeing her perform in Edinburgh, you took a fancy to my mother and seduced her."

"Is that what she told you?" Hailstock let out a contemptuous laugh. "I never even met the bitch."

Consumed by a burst of rage, Drake only just stopped himself from balling his fingers into fists. It would serve no purpose to strike the marquess. There was a better way to rub his noble nose in the dirt.

Drake stalked around the desk and yanked open a drawer. Reaching inside, he pulled out the diamond stickpin in the design of a stylized *H*. "You gave this to her to buy her silence."

Hailstock grimaced. "That only proves her a thief."

"Or you a liar." Drake tossed the stickpin back into the drawer, where it clattered into a corner. "Life hasn't turned out quite as you planned, has it? Your bastard son is a rich man now. And your legitimate heir is a cripple—because of you."

Hailstock turned pale. His hand gripped the back of a chair, and his gold signet glinted in the candlelight. "Riffraff! Should you dare to involve James in our quarrel, by God, I'll ruin you."

Drake couldn't begrudge Hailstock's doting protection of the bedridden twenty-two-year-old. Hailstock had purchased a racehorse for James on his eighteenth birthday, and on that same afternoon, the reckless youth had taken his fateful tumble.

Casually sitting on the edge of the desk, Drake regarded his father. "Luckily for you, my lord, James doesn't concern me in the slightest. I'm far more interested in Lady Alicia Pemberton."

"You aren't worthy of her," Hailstock said. "Your marriage will be a travesty."

"Ah, but she'll be my stepping-stone into society. Henceforth, your by-blow will be invited to the same parties as you."

Those aristocratic nostrils flared. "So that is your plan," Hailstock said scathingly. "Give it up. If you claim a relation to me, no one will accept your word over mine."

"I have no intention of revealing the truth of my parentage . . . yet." First, he would enjoy watching his father squirm.

"The Pembertons aren't even accepted anymore. Lady Brockway is a lunatic, a pariah. She belongs in Bedlam Hospital."

"Are you afraid of one little madwoman?" Privately, Drake admitted he'd enjoyed meeting the dowager. She had a certain elfin sparkle in her eyes that made him wonder if Alicia had possessed such charm before duty and debts had weighed upon her.

Hailstock gave a huff of disdain. "Any association with Lady Brockway will make you even more of a laughingstock."

"That remains to be seen."

Fury glittered in the marquess's eyes, along with something else. Something dark and desperate. His fists clenched, he took another step toward Drake. "For pity's sake, man, choose another wife. A mature widow who won't be hurt by your intrigues. Don't destroy an innocent girl just to indulge this petty delusion of yours."

Was Hailstock truly concerned for Alicia's welfare? Could he, in his twisted way, value her for more than her lofty ancestry? Could he actually love her? As swiftly as the questions struck, Drake saw the advantage in them.

If Hailstock adored her, so much the better.

Chapter Six

"M'lady!" Mrs. Molesworth yodeled up the attic stairs. "Yoo-hoo, m'lady, you've visitors!"

Alicia frowned, her arms full of a billowing blue gown that smelled musty from being shut away for more than half a century. Dust motes danced in the sunlight that came through the windows at either end of the chilly attic. Humming to herself, Lady Eleanor knelt on the bare plank floor and rummaged through a trunk of outmoded accessories. The moleskin cape lay beside her, near the piles of curled wigs, buckled shoes, and tricorne hats.

Alicia had no time to spare for visitors. Until she arrayed herself properly, she intended to postpone the loathesome task of facing the *ton*.

The engagement notice had appeared that morning in the *Post*; Drake Wilder had lost no time in trumpeting their nuptials to the fashionable world. Though most of the nobility would be too haughty to pay their respects to the fiancée of a notorious gambler, there were always those who could overcome their scruples if it meant gleaning a bit of titillating gossip.

Brushing a sticky cobweb off her apron, she picked a path through the jumble of broken furniture and other discards. At the stairway landing, she peered down the steep steps.

Mrs. Molesworth stood at the base of the stairs, a mob-cap perched on her iron-gray hair. She beckoned impatiently to Alicia. "Come quick, m'lady. You mustn't keep these visitors waitin'."

"Send them away. I'm helping Queen Anne find a gown to wear." Alicia also hoped to renovate her own meager wardrobe—not that she'd found many promising prospects yet.

"I won't be sent away." A tall man stepped into view behind the servant, and his familiar deep voice echoed up the narrow shaft. "You should know that by now."

Alicia's heart stumbled over a beat. Drake Wilder wore a grin that deepened the dimples bracketing his mouth. His teeth shone white against his swarthily handsome face. A lock of black hair lay on his brow, creating the rakish illusion of a buccaneer.

He *was* a buccaneer, she thought disparagingly, though not in any romantic sense. He was a robber, a marauder, an exploiter of the weak.

And *she* was no cringing milksop.

"Go back to your club, Mr. Wilder. I'm busy."

Like the uncivilized rogue he was, he ignored her wishes and mounted the stairs two at a stride. "Come, now, that's hardly the proper way to greet your fiancé."

Conscious of her mother at the other end of the attic, Alicia stood guard at the top of the steps. She clasped the antique gown like a shield to her bosom. "Nor is it proper to push your way in, unannounced."

"Then it's good that Mrs. Molesworth invited me." A devilish glint in his eyes, he cleared the last riser and halted before Alicia. "Allow me to teach you how to receive your beloved."

Cupping her head in his hands, he brushed a lingering kiss over her cheek. The freshness of the outdoors swept over her, along with his uniquely male scent. The touch of his mouth conveyed a bone-melting tenderness that sent sparkles of sensation radiating downward, tingling through her breasts and descending to a place so private, she arched backward in alarm.

"Take your vile hands off me."

"As you wish." His fiendish smile still glowed at her. "In matters of intimacy, I am yours to command."

"Then I command you to leave."

"Ah," he said, lowering his voice to a murmur, "but I don't intend to seduce you—yet. Today I'm merely abducting you."

"Abducting?"

"I've come to take you to the shops on Regent Street."

For the barest instant, she felt a yearning so intense that her knees nearly buckled. How wonderful to spend an idle afternoon trying on stylish bonnets and new shoes, inspecting the fine fabrics at the linen draper's, sampling ices at the confectioner's. It was a yearning she ruthlessly squelched. "I've neither the time nor the funds for frivolities."

"That is about to change." Wilder scanned her faded gown with its neatly mended places. "I intend to purchase a new wardrobe for you. My wife must be at the pinnacle of fashion."

His wife. A wave of nausea swept through her. In a matter of days, he would have the right to dictate to her. He would expect her to be his pretty ornament. Reminding herself of the lives he'd ruined, she said firmly, "I won't spend a farthing of your ill-gained fortune."

"You agreed to establish a place for me in society. You cannot entertain the nobility while dressed in tatters."

"I'm clever with a needle. I'll make over some old gowns."

"Like this one?" His eyes laughing at her, he fingered the ancient frock she held to her bosom. "The style must be fifty years out of fashion. And the damn thing reeks."

Alicia allowed he was right about the musty odor. Yet surely the silk could be cleaned and altered, the stiffly boned bodice reworked, the quarter-length sleeves cut to a fashionably short length. Even the lavish, yellowed lace could be bleached and reused on petticoats and chemises—providing it didn't fall apart in the doing.

People will notice, a voice inside her whispered. *They'll snicker behind their hands at you, the prideful Lady Alicia who would adorn herself in hand-me-downs just to spite her rich husband.*

She ought to snatch at the chance to thwart Drake Wilder. Yet somehow, that course of action seemed childish and petty. Would it be so terrible to accept a few gowns? Enough to fulfill her end of their bargain?

"I cannot leave on a moment's notice," she demurred. "I'm spending the afternoon with my mother."

"So I see." His gaze shifted across the attic to Lady Eleanor, who held a fancy fan and twirled as if with an invisible dance parter. He called downstairs, "Mrs. Philpot. You may come up now."

A tall, slim woman with upswept silver hair and surprisingly merry green eyes walked into view. She wore a high-necked gown of gray serge, much like that of a governess or a housekeeper. Exuding an air of dignified competence, she ascended the attic stairs.

Alicia stepped back; to bar the woman from entering would be churlish. She frowned a question at Wilder. His answering smile had the power to devastate a lesser woman.

"My dear Lady Alicia," he said, "may I introduce you to Mrs. Hortense Philpot. She is the widow of one Captain Philpot, a naval hero who died at the Battle of Trafalgar. She will spend the afternoon with Lady Eleanor."

Mrs. Philpot curtsied to Alicia. "Only if you've no objections, my lady."

"I mean no insult, but" —Alicia sent another sharp stare

at Drake Wilder—"such an arrangement is out of the question. I cannot leave Mama in the care of a stranger."

"Forgive me for being presumptuous," Mrs. Philpot said in an anxious tone, "but I understand your hesitation. My own beloved mother suffered from dementia for many years, and I cared for her until her death last year."

The news took Alicia aback. "I'm so sorry."

"Now you will wish to meet Lady Brockway," Drake said smoothly, taking Mrs. Philpot by the arm. "Or shall I say, Queen Anne."

He led the older woman through the cluttered attic before Alicia could retort that *nothing* was settled. Her fingers tightening around the quaint gown, she had no choice but to trail at his well-shod heels. And to watch as he gallantly kissed Mama's hand. "Your Majesty, I've brought you a new lady-in-waiting."

"I am honored to serve my queen," Mrs. Philpot said. She sank into a deep obeisance before Lady Eleanor, who giggled with delight.

"Make haste," Mama said, clapping her hands. "I am preparing for a state dinner."

Rising, Mrs. Philpot picked up a magnificent sack gown of brocaded yellow velvet and held it out for the countess's inspection. "Might I suggest this suitably grand frock?"

They went to an age-speckled cheval glass, where Lady Eleanor held the gown to herself and preened. "Oh, my gracious. I do believe it is perfect for dining with King Louis of France. He is my guest, you know."

"Indeed! We must pay especial heed to your hair, then." Mrs. Philpot whispered conspiratorially, "I hear he means to introduce a new style—the white powdered wig. Perhaps Your Majesty could upstage him?"

Lady Eleanor clasped her hands to her bosom. "Oh, that would be magnificent. We English must lead the world in fashion."

As the two women examined several wigs in the trunk,

Alicia felt a clutch of tenderness in her breast that threatened to overpower her doubts. She so loved seeing Mama happy. It more than made up for the occasions when Mama lapsed into melancholy, weeping for Papa or lamenting some inexpressible fear.

But dare she trust an outsider? The caretaker hired by Drake Wilder? The world knew *his* taste in women.

"Your Majesty," Alicia called, "I would suggest we go downstairs, where *I* will help you don your gown."

Mama lifted her hand in a royal wave. "Your assistance is no longer required. Begone with you now."

"But ma'am—"

"You heard her," Wilder muttered, bending close to Alicia. "The queen has made her choice. She won't even miss you."

His warm breath tickled her ear. Though he crowded her, she refused to budge. He was too large, too brawny, all muscle and masculinity. And she could hardly evict the man who owned the very roof over her head. While she was distracted, he plucked the antiquated gown from her grasp and tossed it over a tailor's mannequin. Placing his hand at the small of her back, he propelled her toward the staircase.

She glanced back to see Mrs. Philpot settle an elaborate wig over Lady Eleanor's golden hair. The trill of Mama's laughter floated through the attic. Perhaps . . . just perhaps if she stole away for a few hours Mama would be safe.

Not that *she* was safe with Drake Wilder.

He held her so close, their hips brushed. His arm encircled her, and she could feel the proprietary pressure of his palm at the base of her spine. His subtle masculine tang enticed her, as did the danger she sensed in him. Whenever he touched her, a melting weakness sapped her strength of will.

Before the Season is out, you'll come begging to share my bed.

At the stairs, she pulled away, ignoring his complacent grin. Head held high, she preceded him down to the second floor.

A patch of sunlight illuminated a faded square on the wallpaper where a landscape painting had hung once. The long corridor showed a forlorn row of closed doors leading to empty bedchambers. No longer did the house ring with frivolous laughter and music from the reception rooms downstairs. Alicia remembered being a young girl, peeking through the balustrade at the elegant guests milling in the foyer below. But after Papa's horrible death and Mama's loss of her senses, the nobility had ceased to visit.

Mrs. Molesworth rushed forward, her hands clasped to her stout bosom. "Mrs. Philpot is a dear," she said. "I couldn't've chose a better companion for 'er ladyship. We 'ad us a nice little chat, that we did."

"Thank you, madam," Wilder said with a flourishing bow. "Your approval will mean a great deal to Lady Alicia."

Then he winked at the servant. *Winked.*

And the stern Mrs. Molesworth blushed!

Alicia stared from one to the other. How had he won over the cook? Just the other day, she had threatened to spit him and roast him for dinner!

"Mrs. Philpot's competence remains to be proven," Alicia pointed out. "Where are her references?"

Her sharp tone appeared to amuse Wilder. "M'lady is a strict one, is she not?" he asked the cook. "Likely, she wouldn't believe me if I said Mrs. Philpot has a glowing recommendation from the Duchess of St. Chaldon. But we know better."

She nodded vigorously, her chins jiggling. "That we do."

"And I trust you'll keep a close eye on Lady Brockway."

"Right-o, sir. And might I say, 'tis a blustery day, so I took the liberty of fetchin' m'lady Alicia's bonnet an' cape." The cook gestured at the accessories, which were draped over the newel post.

"Excellent," Wilder said. "I like efficiency in a woman."

While Mrs. Molesworth tittered in a most ridiculous fashion, Alicia gritted her molars to keep from retorting that he also liked his women vulgar and immoral. "Speaking of *efficiency,* I'd rather go alone. Men have no patience for shopping."

"Then you haven't known the right men."

Taking the bonnet, he settled it over Alicia's head. As he tied the frayed ribbons into a bow, his long fingers brushed the underside of her chin, and his touch set off another quake of sensation inside her. A peculiar breathlessness seized Alicia. It could only be frustration at his high-handed behavior.

"There you go," Mrs. Molesworth said, removing Alicia's apron and then brushing the wrinkles from her skirt. "We can't 'ave you dressin' like a common milkmaid. Besides, you need an outin'. 'Twill put the roses back in your cheeks."

Alicia opened her mouth to protest, but realized it would be her pride talking. Nor could she truly say he was abducting her. Allowing him to purchase a wardrobe for her was the sensible thing to do. After all, she would be entering society again for *his* sake, to promote *his* ambitions. She would be satisfying their bargain, that was all.

Preoccupied, she stood quietly while Drake fastened the cape at her throat. He escorted her downstairs and out into the chilly sunshine, where a sleek black coach waited at the curbstone.

His arm around her, he ushered her into the luxurious interior. The burgundy velvet seat provided a comfortable support for her back. Brocaded trim framed the doors, and pleated damask lined the ceiling. The ivory silk shades were raised, each with a gold tassel hanging at the top of the window.

Instead of sitting in the opposite seat, Drake settled himself beside her, his knee almost touching hers. He looked far too elegant in his dark blue frock coat and buckskin breeches, the crisp white cravat tied at his throat.

Resenting him for his perfection, she edged closer to the corner and folded her bare, chapped hands in her lap. She'd planned to spend the afternoon picking apart the seams of outmoded garments and determining how to refashion them. As much as she felt relieved to be denied that task, she didn't like to contemplate where he had obtained the funds that would pay for her new clothes.

Yet to her shame, she tingled with excitement as the coach started off with barely a jolt. It had been so long since she had ridden in a well-sprung coach with a handsome man at her side. So long since she'd set out on a carefree excursion. She could almost imagine her companion to be an attentive suitor, could almost let herself believe he would be as kind and considerate to his wife as he was to her mother. . . .

"Our wedding will take place on Thursday," he said.

She turned to stare at him. "Two *days*? From *now*?"

"Yes."

"But . . . I will need at least a month to make arrangements, to send out invitations—"

"We're inviting no one outside the family."

"I thought you wished the *ton* to attend."

"And how many would deign to do so?" Wilder aimed an indolent glance at her. "As my wife, you will renew your connections with the nobility and convince them to accept me. That will take time."

Her stomach clenched. She had counted on having weeks to adjust her mind to the reality of this marriage. "The banns must be announced on three Sundays."

"There will be no banns. I've obtained a special license from the archbishop."

"How? You couldn't have bribed the highest official in the church."

"Rest assured, no money changed hands." Those keen blue eyes twinkling, he added, "You see, I confessed to him I'd seduced you, and that you might be with child."

A flush swept hotly from her bosom to her face. "You sullied my reputation? And to a holy man of God, no less."

"Come now, don't get your back up. I made it out to be entirely my fault."

Probing her limited repertoire of curses, she muttered, "*Es barbarus.*"

He chuckled. "I *am* a barbarian. So fling your arrows as you like."

The fact that he understood Latin only fired her resentment. "You can hardly expect society to embrace a woman whose good name has been dragged through the mud."

"You can hardly expect the archbishop to gossip, either."

"He won't need to do so. The very act of marrying by special license will imply that we . . ." She paused, unwilling to finish the statement.

"Succumbed to carnal lust?" Wilder cocked an eyebrow. "Don't tell me you're afraid of what people might think. You're made of sterner stuff than that."

"You just won't listen. You're incorrigible."

He sent her a lazy grin. "You're irresistible."

To her shock, she almost laughed, but caught herself in time. Any mirth she felt could be due only to hysteria. "There is nothing amusing about a scapegrace who makes light of his sins."

"Nor a spinster who cannot speak a kind word to her betrothed." His hand encircled her wrist and brought it to his lips, kissing the sensitive inner skin, his breath warm and tickling, enticing her. "Let's be civil today, shall we?"

She tried—and failed—to tug herself free. "So long as you keep your distance, Mr. Wilder."

"Call me Drake. All the other women do."

"Mr. Wilder," she said with deliberate politeness, "kindly release me."

"Not until you say my name."

She could see the steely resolve behind his jesting smile. And she could not bear his disturbing touch a moment longer. "Let me go . . . Drake."

His grip remained firm. To her chagrin, he examined her fine-boned hand in the light from the coach window, gently rubbing the pad of his forefinger across the rough patches. She felt vulnerable without gloves, ashamed of her broken nails and sandpaper skin. After visiting his club, she'd been so angry that she'd yanked off her last pair, ruining the delicate kidskin.

He fixed her with an intense stare. "How does a lady come to have the hands of a laundress?"

She yanked again, and this time he let her go. "By doing the laundry."

"Have you no other servants but the cook?"

"We also employed a maid-of-all-work and a footman, but I was forced to let them go." Let him think she had done no hard labor before then, that his entrapment of Gerald had caused all her woes.

"One doesn't develop calluses overnight."

"How would you know?" She cast a disparaging glance at his perfectly groomed hands, the long fingers with their square-tipped nails. "All you ever do is deal cards and toss dice."

"And caress women, my other favorite pastime." With his mouth slanted in that infernal smile, he draped his arm across the back of the cushions, toying with the fine hairs at the nape of her neck.

Alicia stiffened to stop the pleasurable sensations that scampered down her spine. How many other women had he touched? How many had he seduced? And why was she even wondering?

He exuded a relaxed confidence, as if he enjoyed letting

her provoke him. He seemed determined today to discomfit her; she was equally determined to ignore his efforts. "How you squander your time matters little to me," she said.

"Yet you continue to harp on my faults."

"Of course. Gamblers don't make reliable husbands."

His face sobered to a watchful expression. "Nor reliable fathers—at least not in your experience."

His words struck the starch from her spirit. She felt defenseless, her painful past exposed to him. But surely he didn't know the whole story. Few did. "Papa was a loving, caring man. I will not hear him criticized."

"He left you and your family near destitute."

"We had enough to live on. Until *you* took the rest."

"Then you'll appreciate having luxuries again," he said without a hint of remorse. "In truth, you'd be wise to spend your days learning how to please me."

Before the Season is out, you'll come begging to share my bed.

"Pleasing you is not part of our bargain," she said with as much dignity as she could muster. "Your comfort means little to me."

As the coach turned into the bustling traffic of Regent Street, he murmured, "You wound me, darling. Don't you know when I'm bedeviling you?"

She didn't know. Nor could she fathom why her heart thrilled to his seductive voice. He was a rake, a scoundrel, a *gambler*.

And in a mere two days, he would be her husband.

Chapter Seven

When Alicia descended the grand staircase on the morning of her wedding, an icy calm numbed her. She had slept fitfully, disturbed by dark unremembered dreams, but with the dawn came an acceptance of her future. Permitting herself to think of nothing beyond the mundane motions of bathing and dressing, she had readied herself for the ceremony.

The elegant new gown rustled with every step. Fashioned of the palest blue satin, it had a gauze overskirt shot through with silver threads that glimmered in the gloom of the rainy day. She shuddered to imagine the many long hours the seamstresses had toiled over the delicate embroidery.

A heavy strand of diamonds and sapphires circled her neck like a noose. From the necklace hung a teardrop-shaped sapphire larger than her thumb. The exquisite piece had arrived the previous afternoon along with matching sapphire earbobs, delivered by a fawning jeweler who said the jewels were a wedding gift from Mr. Wilder.

She had been tempted to send them back. The gems had, after all, been purchased with profits from his gaming club. But rebelliousness would invite his provoking attentions.

She had learned that lesson two days ago, on their shopping expedition.

He had displayed exquisite taste in selecting cloth and trimmings at the linen-draper's, in choosing styles from the latest fashion books at the dressmaker's shop. With cunning finesse, he had charmed the modiste, a tall thin French-woman who at first had decried his request to finish this gown and another in less than forty-eight hours. He had smiled and cajoled her, and the prune-faced woman had melted like whipped cream on a hot tart.

While he and the dressmaker carried on a flirtation—there was no other word to describe it—Alicia had felt like a mannequin. She had been measured and assessed and arrayed with lengths of fabric. And despite her disgust for his money, in a hidden shameful part of her, she had reveled in the delight of owning a new wardrobe.

Her conscience demanded that she accept only the minimum of garments, not the dizzying abundance of morning gowns and walking dresses and ball gowns that Drake had selected. To her mortification, he had ordered underclothing, too, corsets and chemises and petticoats of the finest lawn and lace. A bully with a breathtaking smile, he had insisted, and in the end she had acquiesced.

After all, she had a bargain to uphold. A bargain with the devil.

Alicia paused at the bottom of the stairs, her gloved fingers curled around the smooth twists of the newel post. A prickly awareness pierced her stupor. The dull daylight cast a gray haze over the foyer. Rain tapped against the long windows, mingling with the sounds from the drawing room.

The murmur of voices.

She had no wish to converse with anyone, but earlier, Mama had skipped down the stairs, eager as the schoolgirl she imagined herself to be today, and so Alicia curved her lips upward. It was her wedding day, and by heaven, she would show the world a happy appearance.

Her satin slippers made no sound on the marble of the foyer. But as she entered the drawing room, her smile faltered.

Clutching a posy of white lilies against her rose-pink gown, Mama sat small and forlorn on the lone chaise. For once, she didn't wear the moleskin cape; Mrs. Philpot must have talked her out of it. No longer did Mama chatter in excitement; now she had the demeanor of a chastened child.

Across the empty chamber, Mrs. Philpot stood by the bow window. Her troubled gaze flitted to Alicia before returning to the man who paced before Lady Eleanor.

Lord Hailstock.

Alicia's stomach lurched. Though a close family friend, he was also her rejected suitor. She hadn't invited him to the wedding, so why had he come to call? If he had upset Mama . . .

She hastened toward them. "My lord. This is a surprise."

He strode forward and met her halfway. His silvering hair was rumpled, his posture tense beneath his formal gray coat. "Your servant informed me you were on your way down," he said, nodding grimly at Mrs. Philpot. "My God, Alicia, I heard only this morning that the wedding will take place *today*. What is the meaning of such haste?"

She glanced at her mother. "Let us withdraw to the library," she murmured. "We can speak in private there."

As they walked to the doorway, Lady Eleanor called out, "Please, wait!" Clearly bewildered, she glanced back and forth at them. In a timid little-girl's voice, she went on, "Richard, you never told me why Claire didn't come with you. Is she ill?"

He flinched, his eyes stark. "You know why. She's gone."

"Gone where?" the countess asked, mystified.

"For God's sake, she's d—"

"She's departed on a long journey," Alicia interjected hastily, before Hailstock could reveal the harsh truth of Claire's death. Many years ago, Mama had been best friends with Hailstock's first wife. They had grown up together, Claire a penniless orphan, taken in as a companion for Lady Eleanor, the pampered only child of an earl. This morning, Mama had drifted back to that time and believed herself to be a carefree young lady again.

Mama blinked in confusion. "A journey? Oh, dear, Claire didn't tell me. There is something about her ... something I should remember. . . ."

"You should remember to tell your daughter how foolish she is to marry in haste—" Hailstock began.

"That is quite enough," Alicia said, giving his arm a sharp tug.

Mrs. Philpot hurried forward to sit with the countess. "There, now, I shall keep you company in Claire's absence. Oh, won't we have a grand time at the wedding today?"

A quivering smile touched Lady Eleanor's lips, and she nodded. Over the past week, Mrs. Philpot had proven herself indispensable. She never lost her patience and always displayed a cheerful humor.

Feeling safe to leave them, Alicia led Lord Hailstock into the vacant library, closed the doors, and swung to face him. "Why must you distress Mama? It serves no purpose. And what did you say to her before I walked into the room?"

"I merely reminded her she is no longer a girl just out of the schoolroom. She is a widow, the mother of grown children." His gray eyes keen, he shook his head. "If I may be blunt, Alicia, you are not doing her any service by pandering to her fantasies."

"On the contrary, I'm making her happy. This isn't a game Mama is playing."

"That is precisely why she belongs in a place apart from sane people." He paced with his hands behind his back, his heels clicking on the bare floor. "I'm worried for your sake. Her actions are unpredictable. Remember the time she imagined herself as Joan of Arc? She might have run you through with her sword."

Alicia discounted any danger. "Mama abhors violence. She would never harm anyone."

"And if her condition worsens? You don't always know what she'll do next."

"I know her better than anyone, and she will continue to live with me after my marriage."

Hailstock made a snort of disbelief. "Is that what Wilder told you? You shouldn't believe his pretty promises. He's a cardsharp and a swindler. Honesty isn't his strong suit."

Privately she agreed, yet she felt a strange compulsion to defend the man who would be her husband. "He gave me more than his promise. He signed an agreement granting me sole guardianship of Mama until Gerald reaches his majority." Only yesterday, a sober-faced solicitor had delivered the legal papers for her signature. She had scrutinized the brief statement, satisfying herself that it could not be overturned by any court.

"Wilder won't honor such a contract. He isn't a gentleman. The scapegrace considers himself above the law." His face grim, he added, "Mark my words, he'll find the means to lock Eleanor away."

The knife of doubt twisted in her heart. Was the marquess right? Was she naïve to trust Drake? To put herself and her family at his mercy?

In a low, firm voice, she said, "I must trust in our agreement. I have no other choice."

"You do have a choice. You can wed me."

She shook her head. "I *know* you will lock Mama away forever."

Hailstock came closer and grasped her gloved hands, as if she were a child to be placated. "My dear, I've known you since you were a babe in arms. And I've grown to love and respect you as a woman. I cannot allow you to take this disastrous course of action."

In spite of her resolve, his husky words filled her with warmth. Over the years, he had been both father and friend to her, especially after Papa's death. That was when the marquess had begun to come around more often, offering his assistance, though her father had appointed the director of his bank as executor of the will and guardian. Now Alicia ached to fling herself into Lord Hailstock's protective arms, to breathe in his familiar scent of masculine cologne, to place all her troubles into his capable hands. But she could not.

"It is too late to dissuade me," she whispered.

Though Hailstock gently stroked her hand, his eyes burned with a fervent intensity. "No, it isn't too late. I beg you, do not go through with this wedding. Wilder will bring you to grief. He'll flaunt his affairs and taint you with his vices."

Taking a deep breath, she extracted her hands and willed her voice not to shake. "I know what he is, my lord, and I'm entering this marriage with open eyes."

"You and Wilder come from utterly different worlds. Better you should wed me, a gentleman who will cherish you as a lady." He paused, his face grave and his gaze hooded. "As to Eleanor . . . I am willing to allow her to live with us, so long as she remains confined to her rooms."

His offer surprised Alicia, and at one time, she might have accepted it. Yet into her memory flashed the image of Drake Wilder, bowing to her mother with courtly regard, playing along with her mad fancies, purchasing all of her flowers. . . .

Why, oh, why couldn't Lord Hailstock treat her so well?

She sharply shook her head. "Locking her up won't do. Mama needs to be a part of her family. She needs *me*."

"If you won't heed your own welfare, then consider your brother's. Wilder will corrupt Gerald to the ways of a gam-

bler. No doubt the boy will end up in an early grave, the
same as your father."

The knife took another painful turn. Yet Gerald had
promised to stay away from Wilder's Club, and didn't she
owe him her faith? "My mind is made up. There is nothing
more to say."

Hailstock studied her with a tightly drawn intensity, as
if gauging the strength of her resolution. "As you wish,
then," he said in a clipped tone. "But you must take this."
He brought forth something from an inner pocket of his
coat and pressed it into her hand.

It was a ring, the gold band studded with sapphires and
diamonds. A stunned confusion flooded her. "I can't accept
this."

"You must. It was to be your betrothal ring from me."
On that, he turned and stalked out of the library.

As the raindrops drummed a lament on the windowpanes, Alicia leaned against a barren bookshelf and stared
down at the ring in her hand. She shouldn't accept such a
token from another man. And yet how could she refuse
Lord Hailstock? She felt as if she'd lost a dear friend.

Heartsore, she eased off her glove and slid the ring onto
her finger.

His bride was late.

Though tension gripped his chest, Drake forced himself
to stand calmly by the altar. Rain drizzled down the tall
windows. In the loft, a choir of white-robed boys sang a
hymn, accompanied by the stoop-shouldered curate on the
pipe organ. The damp air smelled of beeswax from the
many candles burning in the chandeliers and on the altar.
A few of Drake's most trusted employees occupied the
front pews of St. George's, and someone coughed, the
sound echoing through the church.

On one side of him stood the vicar with his mousy wife,
who would stand witness to the nuptials. On his other side

lurked Fergus MacAllister, clad in his stiff Sunday best. Drake could feel that disapproving glower burning into his back.

Or maybe Fergus was gloating.

The ceremony had been scheduled to begin a quarter of an hour ago. Drake silently cursed his decision to obey custom and arrive separately from his bride. He had sent his coach when he ought to have gone to her house—*his* house—and brought her here. He wouldn't have judged Alicia craven, yet her cool blond beauty concealed her thoughts, and for once in his life he distrusted his ability to read a woman.

What if she never appeared?

The galling possibility festered in his stomach. For years, he had schemed for this moment. He had plotted his revenge ever since he'd been a grieving boy, denied by his father. Driven by bitterness, Drake had studied elocution and etiquette, finance and commerce. He had used his talent with numbers to amass a fortune at the gaming tables. Then he had lured Gerald, Lord Brockway, into a game of chance.

All so that Drake could claim the woman Hailstock wanted.

Now Lady Alicia Pemberton might thwart him at the altar.

The notion filled him with unholy rage. Before God, he would never again permit any member of the aristocracy to humiliate him.

Never again.

The clergyman cleared his throat, and Drake cast an aggravated glance at the Reverend Lord Raymond Jeffries, who leaned on the ivory knob of his cane. While arranging the nuptials, the haughty cleric had made it clear he was the brother of a marquess.

If only the snob knew how much they had in common. But Drake wasn't yet ready to proclaim his parentage.

First, he must secure a position in Hailstock's world. If Alicia dared to play him for a fool by canceling their wedding . . .

A brown curl dipping onto his brow, the cleric leaned closer and whispered, "Your bride, Mr. Wilder."

Drake snapped his gaze down the aisle. Mrs. Philpot assisted Lady Eleanor into a pew near the front, Mrs. Molesworth trotting behind them. Then his attention flashed to the couple who waited at the rear of the church.

Holding her brother's arm, Lady Alicia Pemberton stood half hidden in the shadows of the double doorway. Drake's anxiety dissipated in a surge of unmanly relief. In his mind, he muttered a prayer of triumphant thanksgiving.

As if by divine answer, the clouds parted and a ray of sunlight gilded her in splendor. A halo of white rosebuds crowned her golden hair, and the pale blue gown skimmed the form of an angel. Her hands were folded around a bouquet of white flowers. He spared only a glance at those outer trappings; her purity and beauty struck him breathless. He could hardly believe her chaste perfection soon would be his.

At Gerald's side, she glided down the aisle. Her eyes were cool and steady, her face pale and composed. She might have been a martyr on her way to the scaffold. Instead of pleasing him, her passivity scorched a path to his gut. He didn't want her to be resigned to her fate, as if he were her executioner. Damn it, he wanted her to fight him, to show her spirit.

Cold sweat broke out on his palms; he resisted the urge to rub them on his dark blue frock coat. What the devil was wrong with him? She was no more to him than an instrument of revenge.

Brother and sister reached the altar railing. Lord Brockway paused, his gaze fierce on Drake. Despite his boyish features and scrawny physique, he looked every inch the earl in his finely tailored coat and buff knee breeches. The aggressive tilt of his jaw said that he would defend his sister if the need arose. Drake nodded sardonically. A pity the tadpole hadn't been more protective when he'd risked all at the gaming table.

Then Gerald gave Alicia to him, and Drake drew her close, tucking her gloved fingers in the crook of his arm. With her other hand, she held the bouquet of lilies at her slender waist. Her subtle feminine scent cast a veil of bewitchment over him, and even here in church, he felt himself tighten with lust. Keeping his hand firmly over hers, he drew her a few steps closer to the altar.

The clergyman opened his leather-bound prayer book. "Dearly beloved, we are gathered together here in the sight of God . . ."

The commencement of the marriage service barely penetrated Drake's keen awareness of his bride. He felt a grudging admiration that this small and dainty woman could possess such flawless self-control. Her fine, alabaster profile displayed no trace of emotion. She gazed straight ahead as if pledging her life to a bastard gambler were nothing out of the ordinary.

He'd half expected her to shun his gifts, the gown and the necklace. The diamonds matched the luster of her skin, the teardrop sapphire nestling in the shadowed valley between her breasts. He wanted to put his mouth there . . . and elsewhere. He wanted to peel off her gown and lay seige to her composure.

The explicit fantasy seared straight to his groin.

"If any man can show just cause why they may not lawfully be joined together, let him now speak, or else hereafter forever hold his peace."

The Reverend Lord Raymond Jeffries paused. His squirrelly eyes darted left and right as if he fully expected someone to step forth and stop this scandalous wedding. On the altar, the candle flames danced in the silence. A gust of wind rattled the windows. Fergus noisily shuffled his feet, and for one uneasy moment, Drake feared the old man meant to voice an objection.

He clenched his teeth to keep from snapping at Jeffries, *For Christ's sake, get on with it!*

At last the clergyman began to read again, droning on for several more interminable minutes before indicating they should join their right hands. Drake spoke his vows quickly and felt no tremor in her slim fingers, no hint of agitation as Alicia murmured her vows. Even then, she did not lift her eyes to his, and her voice was smooth, her movements mechanical. She might have been a marionette worked by invisible strings.

It was done. He'd sealed his fate. And hers.

At his prior request, there was no blessing of the rings, for Drake saw no need to bother with such romantic indulgences. While the cleric spoke the final prayers, Alicia's ladylike reserve continued to rub on Drake. It was as if he didn't truly own her—she kept a part of herself inviolate. The primitive desire to put his brand on her swept through him.

She was *his* wife. His to use as he willed.

He crushed her to him and claimed her mouth. Her soft lips parted in startlement. He seized the advantage, capturing the back of her head in one hand to hold her steady while his tongue plundered her in a deep, demanding kiss. She tasted of innocence, of a sweetness he had never before known. As if from a distance, he heard a gasp from the clergyman, a muttered protest from her brother.

The onlookers made no difference to Drake. Only a lightning bolt from the heavens could have stopped him.

He kissed her long and hard and deep. She clung to his shoulders, and her quickened heartbeats fluttered against his chest. The scent of crushed lilies blended with her light feminine fragrance. With skillful strokes of his tongue, he caressed her sensitive inner flesh until the woodenness left her body and she gave a little sigh and melted in his arms.

The victory left him only marginally satisfied. He wanted more than a kiss. He craved her complete surrender.

And he would have it. By God, he would.

Later.

He forced himself to draw back. Alicia stood looking at him, her breasts rising and falling, her breath coming in little panting gasps. Wisps of fair hair framed the soft beauty of a well-pleasured woman. Her eyes were dazed blue pools of desire—but only for a moment.

Then a mask of cool disdain once again smoothed her noble features.

Fumbling with his prayer book, the clergyman concluded the service. No doubt he was accustomed to witnessing more sedate kisses. The civilized kisses of aristocratic couples.

To hell with the aristocracy.

Drake grasped her slender waist. He and Alicia would have no civilized courtship. Their bedsport would be wild, uninhibited, lusty. He was not at all discouraged by her coldness. Whether she would acknowledge so or not, a strong current of passion flowed beneath her serene surface.

We will have a chaste marriage. . . .

He smiled. How wrong she was. He would have his pleasure of Alicia. He would charm her into his bed and make his claim on her complete and irrevocable. She was his now.

His wife.

Chapter Eight

Her husband.

Descending from the coach with the aid of Drake's hand, Alicia struggled to assimilate the reality of their marriage. His firm grip threatened her hard-won control. They had ridden together from the church, just the two of them. Determined to appear calm, she'd filled the silence with polite comments on the weather, her mother, the delay in their arrival, anything but the ceremony and that earthshaking kiss. While she'd chatted away, he'd watched her, his eyes a dark, disconcerting blue in the gloomy daylight.

She hadn't known a kiss could be so private, so intimate. He had invaded her with his tongue. *His tongue.* And she had *enjoyed* it.

The daring embraces she'd experienced during her first Season now seemed tame and lackluster, those gentlemen mere schoolboys. Drake Wilder, however, had seen the depths of depravity. He had done acts so wicked she could not even imagine them. In that kiss, he had shown her a glimpse of his erotic skills, subjecting her to an intimacy that stirred a shockingly carnal desire inside her.

No wonder he'd been amused by her naïve attempt at seduction that day at his club. Unknowingly, she had made a fool of herself. Worse, she had underestimated his power over her.

She wouldn't do so again.

She stepped down onto the wet drive. A freckle-faced footman held an umbrella to keep off the rain. As they walked, Drake's arm circled her back and his fingers splayed over her hip, as if to claim ownership of her. She would not cause a scene by flinching from him.

His mouth curved into that smile of lethal charm. "Welcome home . . . Mrs. Wilder."

Mrs. Wilder.

His keen gaze unnerved her as much as her new status, and she turned away to view Number Ten, Swansdowne Crescent. Her new home was not the vulgar monstrosity she had expected of an upstart gambler. The magnificent four-story house had the fluid grace of a Greek temple. Tall white columns supported the carved pediment of the portico. The many windows shone with a warm golden light, and Alicia seized on the distraction. "Do you always burn so many candles in the middle of the day?"

"It's a paltry expense."

"If you're a spendthrift."

"Better a spendthrift than a skinflint." He arched an amused eyebrow. "Besides, if ever I run low, there are always vast funds to be won from aristocratic gentlemen."

On that outrageous remark, he drew her up the broad marble stairs to the porch. Once they reached the shelter of the overhang, the footman sprang ahead to open the large front door. Alicia slowed her steps, glancing down the drive and past the dark green iron fence with its opened gate. A few pedestrians hurried along the quiet, curved street, their heads bent against the drizzle.

"Mama and Gerald should be arriving soon," she said.

"Afraid to be alone with me?"

She wouldn't admit to the grain of truth in that. "I am

concerned about their coachman. He seemed a trifle . . . slow-witted."

The massive man with the battered face had had an almost vacant look in his beady eyes. He had made several wrong turns on his way to the church, and Gerald had been forced to redirect him.

"Big Bill was once a pugilist, so perchance his brain is rattled." Under his breath, Drake added, "He should never have taken the reins today."

"What's wrong?" she cried out. "If he causes an accident—"

"He won't," Drake said, though he flashed a frown at the street. Then his expression smoothed. "Ah, there they are now."

Moving at a sedate pace, the fine black coach trundled around the far curve of the crescent, with Big Bill hunched on the coachman's box. Relieved, but still perturbed, Alicia wrinkled her nose. "A prizefighter. Why would you employ such a brute?"

"Ask my steward. He handles the outside staff." Drake applied pressure to the base of her spine. "Come, they'll be a few minutes yet. There's no sense standing out here in the damp."

The chilly air made her shiver—there could be no other reason for her sudden tremor—and she glided past the liveried footman who held open the door. The soaring beauty of the entrance hall took her breath away. A chandelier sparkled from the high-domed ceiling. The rich brown pillars against the buff-colored walls gave the vast room an understated elegance, while the mahogany chairs and side tables lent an air of comfortable grace.

Hard-pressed not to gawk like a bumpkin, Alicia lowered her gaze and noticed the long line of servants who awaited the customary introduction to their new mistress, the grooms and footmen in dark blue livery with silver buttons, the maids in matching blue gowns with white

aprons. The sight brought a measure of calm to her. Before
Papa had lost his wealth, she had been trained to oversee
a large household. Though her marriage was not the love
match she'd once dreamed about, she would make a place
for herself here. She would forget her despair in the per-
formance of her duties. . . .

Realizing that Drake was leading her to the grand staircase, she murmured, "The staff has assembled to meet me."

His handhold restrained her from veering toward the servants. "That won't be necessary," he said in a low-pitched
voice.

"Not necessary?"

"You heard me. Wait here." He strolled toward the
group; Alicia ignored his edict and followed him.

At the head of the line stood a stoop-shouldered, elderly
man in the garb of a butler, and beside him, a voluptuous,
red-haired woman who wore a ring of keys at her waist. In
her daringly cut bodice, she looked more like a female of
ill repute than a housekeeper.

"You disobeyed my order," Drake said.

"I tole her you shed not to gather here," the old man
slurred. He blinked his rheumy eyes at the housekeeper.
"Din't I, Yates?"

"Oh, hush up, Chalkers. Everyone will know you've
been tippling in the cellar again." Yates smiled coyly at
Drake. "We merely thought to offer our congratulations,
sir, on your marriage."

The butler was *drunk*? Alicia wondered in outraged surprise. And why would Drake permit such a wayward manner in his housekeeper?

She stepped out from behind him. "I should be pleased
to meet each and every one of you—"

"No," Drake said. Raising his voice to address all the
servants, he added, "Mrs. Wilder and I thank you very
much. You may return to your duties now."

While Alicia stood rigid with shock, the staff dispersed

toward the rear of the house, though a plump, dark-eyed girl continued to gape at the master's bride until a skinny footman tugged at her arm. Uttering a gasp, she darted away with him, disappearing through a doorway at the end of the corridor.

Alicia rounded on Drake. "For heaven's sake, I need to learn their names. And to establish my authority here."

"You're not to bother with the servants. Mrs. Yates will handle them."

"Indeed? She arrays herself like a bawd and disobeys your orders. And your butler was inebriated!"

"That is no concern of yours."

"I beg to differ. The head servants should act as examples of propriety for the lower staff. They are in need of firm guidance from the lady of the house."

"*I* shall have a word with Yates and Chalkers. *You* shall concentrate on renewing your connections in society."

His steely-soft voice left her cold. So that was how he intended their marriage to be. He would deny her any prestige in his house. He would treat her as unworthy in front of his employees. Even the most downtrodden wife controlled the domestic affairs. But he would strip her of that right.

She hid her anger behind a chilly mask. Let him give her orders. She would do as she saw fit. "Never fear, Mr. Wilder. I shall fulfill my part of our bargain."

"You agreed to call me Drake."

"*You* agreed I would be your wife. Not your chattel."

He chuckled, guiding her toward the staircase that soared upward in a sweeping curve. "I'm giving you every luxury. You won't have to lift a finger. That's hardly the life of a slave."

In a show of dignity, she drew off her gloves. "Yet you refuse me the freedom to make my own place here."

Their eyes clashed in a battle of wills. It was a battle that had little to do with the trifling issue of names—and everything to do with her determination to command respect from him.

A wicked warmth entered his eyes and he grasped her by the waist. Leaning closer, he said, "Hellcat."

"Hell-hound."

"Touché. And if you wish to be treated like a wife, I'll be happy to oblige." He crowded her against the newel post. His voice soft and silken, he said, "There's no shame in desiring your husband, Alicia." His thumb rubbed her inner wrist. "Tonight is our wedding night. Invite me to your bed, and I'll show you pleasures beyond your wildest dreams."

Her senses surged with the heat of his body, the hint of masculine cologne, the alluring blue of his eyes. His snowy cravat made a striking contrast to his coal-dark hair and swarthy skin. He stood so close she could see the faint black stubble on his jaw, and she wanted to touch him there, to learn every hard angle of his face. Her heart beat faster, making her dizzy. She wanted—she *craved*—another taste of that beautiful male mouth. . . .

"What the hell's this?"

Jolted to her senses, she realized he held her hand up. The sapphire and diamond ring glinted in the watery light from the windows.

"I didn't buy this for you," he said.

She ought to tell him a half-truth. But still shaken by his nearness, she felt the irrepressible need to punish him. "Didn't I tell you?" she asked airily. "This is Lord Hailstock's wedding gift to me."

A darkness descended over Drake's face, and a muscle worked in his jaw. Abruptly he plucked the ring off her finger. "I'll return it to him."

Angered, she reached for the gold band. "It's mine."

"No," he stated, thrusting it into his pocket. "You will never, ever accept gifts from any other man. Is that understood?"

His aura of barely restrained violence startled Alicia. She hadn't known a man could be so possessive. She could better understand his jealousy if theirs was a love match. . . .

Then the sound of voices and tramping feet intruded from the porch. Into the entrance hall stepped Mama, clinging to Gerald's arm, Mrs. Philpot behind them.

Mama spied them and giggled like a schoolroom miss. "Oh, my," she said, lifting her gloved hands to her cheeks. "We've caught the bride and groom in a private moment. Isn't it romantic?"

Her face hot, Alicia stepped away from Drake. It was on the tip of her tongue to say that they had been quarreling, not embracing. But a glance at Gerald's grim features stopped her. His green eyes asked a probing question: *Are you all right?*

Her breast tightened. She had always been the strong one in the family. Yet today she wanted to run to her brother, to beg him to rescue her from this circumstance of his making. With all her effort, she forged a smile of greeting.

Gerald strode forward, his heels clicking on the marble floor. "I'll have a word with you, Wilder." His imperious voice cracked, and he cleared his throat in a rasping cough. "Immediately."

Alicia sprang toward Gerald and patted him between his bony shoulders. "You'll tend to yourself," she chided. "The damp weather isn't good for your lungs. You must sit and rest—"

"All he needs is a brandy," Drake broke in. "You ladies will wish to freshen up before luncheon. Yates will escort you upstairs."

As if she'd been eavesdropping, the housekeeper glided around the corner of a long corridor. Her expression almost smirking, she folded her hands beneath her buxom bosom. "Shall I show Mrs. Wilder to her suite, sir?"

Drake gave a curt nod. "And Lady Eleanor as well."

Alicia stubbornly shook her head. "I'll see to my brother first. His cheeks are flushed. He might have a fever." Reaching up, she placed her hand on his brow. It was cool, but then, he'd just come in out of the rain.

"For pity's sake, Ali," Gerald said, squirming away from her. "You needn't coddle me. I'm perfectly fine."

"Dear me, you're quarreling again," Lady Eleanor said. Tilting her head to the side, she blinked her china blue eyes beneath her pink straw bonnet. "You two have quarreled often, haven't you?"

Gerald hung his head and muttered, "She's too bossy, that's why."

"I'm the eldest," Alicia felt compelled to point out. "Of course I'm in charge."

Looking even more befuddled, the countess rubbed her temples. "The eldest . . . Oh, dear, it seems we *have* met before today. Yet why can I recall no more?"

"Don't worry yourself over it," Alicia said, stricken by a helpless love. "You'll remember—"

"We'll puzzle it out over luncheon," Drake said. Taking Lady Eleanor's hand, he guided her to Mrs. Philpot, who stood decorously to the side. In a voice far more gentle than he'd ever used with Alicia, he added, "Go upstairs now, my lady. The earl and I will join you in the dining room shortly." He nodded to her brother, and the two men walked away.

Watching them cross the hall to a pair of opened double doors, Alicia felt a tremor of misgivings. Gerald looked like a schoolboy, his slender form and honey-brown hair a striking contrast to Drake's powerful, dark physique. They might have been Gabriel and Lucifer.

She bit her lip. If only Gerald hadn't witnessed that passionate kiss in church. In a rash attempt to protect her, he might challenge Drake, and heaven knew, her sickly brother was no match for a cunning rogue who had grown up on the rough-and-tumble streets of London.

It was even more frightening to think that Drake might influence Gerald. Drake was a silver-tongued serpent who could talk a saint into selling his soul. What if he led her brother further down the path of destruction? What if . . . Gerald ended up like Papa?

"M'lady? Will you not accompany us?" Mrs. Yates stood on the stairway, staring back over her shoulder, Mama and Mrs. Philpot behind her.

Alicia gathered her composure and gave a crisp nod. Lifting the hem of her rich gown, she trailed the other women up the curving steps. She took only peripheral notice of the fine statues in niches and the gilt moldings of her new home.

Wilder will corrupt Gerald to the ways of a gambler. No doubt the boy will end up in an early grave, the same as your father.

Was Lord Hailstock right? Had she made a dreadful mistake?

Drake closed the doors to the library and led Gerald to a pair of comfortable leather chairs arranged near the black marble mantelpiece. He was still furious about that ring. Damn Hailstock for his insult! He'd like nothing more than to smash his fist into that arrogant face.

Deliberately Drake took a deep breath. For now, he had Gerald to pacify. He would deal with Hailstock later.

Beads of rainwater slid down the outside window. A fire burned on the hearth, dispelling the damp chill, and a branch of candles flickered on the nearby desk. Here Drake liked to read in the dark, predawn hour after returning from his club. And here he liked to plan.

An alabaster vase on the mantelpiece held a tuft of white ostrich feathers. No one but him—and Fergus—knew the feathers were the remnants of a fan his mother had carried long ago, playing the part of an Egyptian princess in some long-forgotten drama. She'd delighted in recounting how he'd made his theatrical debut as baby Moses in the bulrushes, squalling with indignation until she'd picked him up and cuddled him close.

He needed that reminder now. Muira Wilder had raised him with the fierce devotion of two parents. She hadn't deserved to be used and abandoned by a haughty English lord.

Stalking to the sideboard, he lifted a crystal decanter. "Brandy?"

The Earl of Brockway flexed his puny fists. "I didn't come here to drink, Wilder. I demand to know your intentions toward my sister."

"That is a private matter."

"You promised her a chaste marriage. She told me so herself. If you've gulled her, you'll answer to me."

"Have a care whom you call a liar."

Like a foolhardy pup, Gerald took a step closer. "I witnessed that unmannerly embrace at the altar. You mean to use her ill, to force your attentions on her."

Drake curbed his angry impatience and splashed amber liquor into two glasses. In any other situation, he would put an end to such insolence in no uncertain terms. But Gerald was family now.

Besides, coercion of Alicia would be unnecessary. Drake had only to bide his time—and charm his bride. "I've never forced myself on any woman. And I don't intend to start now." His footsteps silent on the Turkish rug, he walked over and handed Gerald a brandy. "Sit down."

The young earl accepted the glass, but didn't drink—or sit. "I shan't let you play the devil with my sister."

"May I remind you, she is my wife now. By the laws of God and man." Moderating his stern tone, Drake placed a hand on Gerald's shoulder. "Rest assured, I will not harm her. You have my word on that."

Gerald blinked uncertainly, and at a slight push from

Drake, plopped down into one of the leather chairs. He took a gulp of brandy and coughed deep in his chest, his eyes watering. All the fight seemed to drain out of him. He slumped with his elbows perched on his bony knees, his head bowed over his glass. " 'Tis my fault. I've been a cork-brain, and Ali's the one to pay for it."

Drake settled himself in the opposite chair. Stretching out his legs, he crossed them at his ankles. Against his will, he felt a tug of kinship with the young earl. His brother now.

He had seen his own half-brother James close up on only one occasion, as a cherubic two-year-old toddling toward his father. And he had witnessed the pride on Hailstock's face. He wondered if Hailstock still felt such pride now that his heir could walk no more.

Taking a tasteless swallow of brandy, Drake regarded Gerald's glum face. "What's done is done," he said. "Don't flog yourself over that game we played."

"But only a hen-hearted knave would risk his mother's home, his sister's happiness. I was a fool to think I'd win, just because I held two bloody aces."

Drake had known Gerald's cards that night. Not by sleight of hand, but by cold calculation. The earl was like most men, relying on luck, hoping for fortune to turn, rather than analyzing the odds.

Nagged by restlessness, Drake rose from the chair and went to the gleaming mahogany desk. From the top drawer he extracted a paper, which he carried to the fire and dropped into the flames. The I.O.U. curled and blackened, turning to ash.

He pivoted on his heel. "There, your vowels are paid in full. Twenty thousand guineas."

"It might as well have been thirty pieces of silver," Gerald said morosely.

"Nonsense. Alicia and Lady Eleanor will lead a far more comfortable life here. You haven't betrayed them."

"Alicia ought to have had a choice. Women set great store by love."

"Women have married for monetary reasons since the beginning of time. This is no different." Gerald didn't look convinced, and it was pointless to argue. Now that she was irrevocably his, Drake had other concerns. "What will you do now?"

"I'll seek my fortune, perhaps in trade." Placing his glass on a side table, the earl pushed to his feet and straightened his coat. "I'll find lodgings elsewhere, too. I ask only for a day or two to clear out my belongings."

"For Christ's sake, sit down. I've no intention of tossing you out of Pemberton House."

Gerald stiffened. "My pockets may be at low tide, but I won't accept your charity."

"I don't expect you to do so. There is a way for you to pay me back." Cursing himself for a softhearted fool, Drake hoped he wouldn't regret the offer. Alicia certainly wouldn't approve—not that she had any say in the matter. "Tomorrow, you'll report to me at my club."

Chapter Nine

Four days later, Alicia stood in the drawing room of a grand house in Grosvenor Square while a snooty footman went to inquire if Her Grace was at home. Too nervous to sit on one of the many chairs and chaises, she paced the beautifully appointed chamber, her gaze sliding over the colorful tapestries on the walls, the fine porcelain figurines on the tables, the mantel carved of pure white marble. She stopped at a tall window framed by blue brocaded draperies and gazed unseeing into a garden.

Usually she waited in the coach while her footman delivered one of her newly printed calling cards. But that made it too easy for the mistress of the house to be conveniently unavailable.

Since the wedding, she had worked her way down a list of the most venerable hostesses of the *ton*. She had visited every acquaintance with whom she'd once had a connection. Thus far, everyone had refused to receive her. The reason was bitterly clear. No one wished to associate with the wife of a baseborn gambler. Or the daughter of a madwoman.

But this time she would not be put off. This time she would try an act of desperation. She would wheedle an interview with her former friend—and long-ago rival.

The tap of measured footsteps came from the foyer. She turned from the window, expecting a servant with a message of refusal. Instead, a young woman strolled into the drawing room.

Sarah. The Duchess of Featherstone.

Alicia was immobilized by a confusing flood of affection and resentment and surprise. The liveliness had vanished from that exquisitely beautiful face, and there was a hint of strain around Sarah's mouth. Faint shadows lent a fragility to her violet eyes. But it was more than her countenance that had changed. A black gown skimmed her slender form, and a widow's cap crowned her shining sable hair.

Hastening forward, Alicia only just remembered to curtsy. "Pray forgive me for intruding, Your Grace. I didn't realize you were in mourning."

"There's no need to apologize. It's been nearly a year since Timothy's passing."

Her husband was dead. That tall, vigorous nobleman who had always had a droll remark. "Sarah . . . I'm so sorry. I've been away from society and hadn't heard."

"I quite understand." With a smile that didn't reach her eyes, Sarah waved a slender hand at a grouping of chairs near one of the long windows. "Do sit down. We can have a cozy chat while we await our tea."

Her aloof manner invited anything but coziness. Seating herself in a straight-backed chair, Alicia pondered how much they had both changed in the past five years. They had been inseparable friends from their first meeting, two starry-eyed girls enjoying the pleasures of their first Season. They'd giggled over silly suitors and exchanged confidences about ardent admirers. Until Alicia had fallen in love with the dashing Duke of Featherstone.

At first, Sarah had been strangely silent whenever Alicia sighed over the handsome duke. Then, one fateful evening, Alicia caught Sarah kissing him in a darkened garden, and a bitter rivalry ensued. Harsh words were spoken. On learning of their betrothal, Alicia had wept angry tears. She had stubbornly refused to receive Sarah, even departing town before the wedding.

Her youthful anguish now struck her as uncomfortably like sulking. She hadn't really loved the duke; she'd been enraptured with the *idea* of love. Her behavior seemed especially petty in light of Sarah's bereavement.

Looking far too young to be a dowager, the Duchess of Featherstone arranged her skirts on the chaise. The black silk made a striking contrast to her pale skin. "So," she said, her voice politely frosty, "this is most unexpected— you calling on me after all these years."

"I've been out of touch with everyone," Alicia murmured. "Papa died not long after your wedding, so I never did have another Season. Oh, Sarah. I do regret what happened between us. I behaved badly when I ought to have been more gracious. Can you forgive me?"

Sarah lifted one slim shoulder. "The past is of little consequence anymore. If that is all you have come to say . . ." Her regal tone clearly stated she would hear no more about it.

Swallowing her regrets, Alicia focused on her purpose. Was there any hope of inveigling herself back into Sarah's goodwill? She felt ashamed of her plan, knowing Sarah's loss. But she had no alternative. "I've thought about you often," she said, putting warmth into her smile. "It's wonderful to see you again. How is your family?"

"My parents are quite well, though they prefer the quiet of Oxfordshire to the bustle of town."

"And your elder brother?"

"He's wed now, with a son a year younger than mine."

"You have a son?" Alicia felt a pang of longing so sharp it hurt. She would never cuddle a baby of her own. It was a fact she hadn't considered when she had made her pact with Drake. "Please, tell me about him."

"William is four years of age, a rather solemn child."

Sarah's mouth formed a brittle smile. "I daresay, it is fortunate I bore Featherstone an heir. I shouldn't have liked Timothy's penny-pinching cousin to have inherited the title."

Her callous manner disturbed Alicia. And yet . . . hadn't there been a faint softening in her eyes when she'd spoken of her son? "Is William here?" Alicia asked. "I should very much like to meet him."

"He's at his lessons in the schoolroom and cannot be disturbed." Sarah cast a dispassionate glance at Alicia's fashionable gown of pale blue muslin. "But enough about me. How is your family?"

"As I said, Papa died a few years ago, and Mama . . . went into a decline for a while. But she's happy again, as dear and sweet as ever."

Keeping her gaze steady, Alicia wondered if Sarah would make a snide remark about Mama's demented state. If she dared . . .

The duchess merely said, "And your little nuisance of a brother? I hope he isn't still peeping through keyholes."

"No," Alicia said, relieved at the turn of conversation. "He outgrew such nonsense, thank heavens. He's eighteen now."

"Yet I hear you've been rather busy of late, tidying up after the earl."

"Gerald is no different from other young gentlemen who must learn their way in the world." And Gerald *had* learned his lesson. Just yesterday, she had called on him at Pemberton House, but he had been absent. Later, he'd sent her a note explaining that he'd found a post at a financial institution and she wasn't to fret about him anymore. He sounded so sure of himself—yet it was difficult *not* to fret.

Sarah released a well-bred laugh. "My dear, you really cannot expect *me* to swallow such a milk-and-water tale. The *ton* is agog with the scandal."

"What have you heard?" Alicia said cautiously.

"Why, the truth about your marriage. Everyone knows Brockway's gaming habit forced you to wed that common scoundrel."

Alicia caught a sharp breath. Just then, a white-wigged footman entered the drawing room carrying a silver tea tray, which he placed on a wheeled trolley beside the duchess. Sarah dismissed him with a majestic wave. As coolly as if she hadn't just plunged a knife into Alicia's pride, she said, "I trust you still take sugar in your tea."

"Yes."

While Sarah poured, Alicia fumed. Sarah's lofty status must have eradicated her finer qualities. At one time, she had wept at the sight of a beggar child and she had taken baskets to the infirm. Now there was a cynicism to her so different from the sweet, spirited debutante. If it weren't for that loathsome bargain, Alicia thought, she would walk out and end this visit.

Sarah handed her a dainty porcelain cup, then offered a plate filled with an array of pastries. "Would you care for a cake? The poppy seed is quite delicious."

"No, thank you." Their politeness seemed ludicrous considering the ugly words that hung between them. *That common scoundrel.*

Though it was the truth, Alicia bristled at the label for reasons she couldn't fathom. She must accustom herself to such nasty remarks. She must convince Sarah that Drake was worthy of acceptance. "Odd that you would have such a mistaken notion about my husband," she said lightly. "He is a fine, respectable man. Someone undoubtedly misled you, perhaps one of those gentlemen who have lost their fortunes at his club."

Pursing her lips, Sarah lowered her teacup to its saucer. "I am not referring to the nature of his *trade,* but to his philandering. Mr. Wilder is a notorious rake. He carries on with actresses and ladybirds."

"That is nothing more than mean-spirited gossip," Alicia

said glibly, her smile fixed, the lies tasting sour on her tongue. "You shouldn't believe everything you hear."

"My dear, you've been tucked away at home with your mother. *I* am more experienced in the ways of the world. For your own good, you must realize such men hold women in the lowest regard."

"Perhaps so, but my husband is a gentleman. He has the utmost respect for me."

"So it seems now. But once the honeymoon is over, he'll return to his doxies. I've seen it happen in many aristocratic marriages." Her movements coldly precise, Sarah lifted the cup to her lips and took a sip. "And for you, with a husband of low birth, the shame will be all the worse."

That superior tone grated on Alicia. She gritted her teeth and counted to ten, reminding herself that Drake's position would be secured if the *ton* saw him in the company of the Duchess of Featherstone. "Why don't you judge his character for yourself?" she said with a brilliant smile. "We could all go for a drive tomorrow afternoon in the park."

"Quite impossible."

"Then another day?" Alicia said doggedly. "I would like for us to be friends again, as we once were."

Sarah gave her that frigid, unfathomable stare. "I'm sorry, but those days are long gone. And might I add, back then, you'd never have married so far beneath yourself."

That final jab infuriated Alicia. Her cup rattled in its saucer as she rose to her feet. "Not all of us have the leisure to marry for love. You might show a little kindness toward those less fortunate than yourself."

Sarah turned her head away as if to pretend Alicia wasn't there. Her beautiful face might have been carved from the purest alabaster, her hair dark and gleaming in the light from the window.

Alicia would not be ignored. She had to speak, to rid herself of the old hurt and the new resentment. "I once envied you your happiness, Sarah, and I'm truly sorry for your loss. But I don't envy the smug and condescending person you've become."

She set down the teacup. Her throat burned, but at least she could leave with her self-respect intact. She cast one last look at the duchess, and the icy farewell melted on her tongue.

A tear sparkled down that perfect cheek. Then another. Those firmly pressed lips trembled ever so slightly. Sarah made no other move, and an impression of something so private, so *unhappy* about her reached past Alicia's anger.

"Sarah? Are you all right?"

Without taking her gaze from the blue brocaded draperies, the duchess spoke in a thready whisper. "Just . . . go."

Had she been wrong to think Sarah frigid and unfeeling? Alicia stepped closer. Hesitantly, she touched Sarah's arm, the black silk sleeve warm beneath her fingertips. "You must still be grieving for the duke. It was wrong of me to remind you."

With surprising suddenness, Sarah turned on Alicia, the tears flowing freely now. "Yes, I *do* grieve. But not for Timothy . . . never for him."

The angry agony in those watery violet eyes stunned Alicia. She sank down on the chaise and drew a handkerchief from her pocket, pressing it into that cold hand. "There, now. You needn't hold back your tears. I'm here for you."

While Sarah sobbed into the scrap of embroidered linen, Alicia wondered at the source of her pain. Had she endured a troubled marriage? Surely she and the duke had been a fairy-tale couple, young and handsome and blissful. Or had Alicia been mistaken all these years?

At last Sarah's weeping slowed, and she dashed at her wet cheeks. "I never meant to bawl like a silly child. I haven't done so in a long, long time."

"There is nothing childish about sadness. I've wept, too, about my mother . . . and other sorrows."

"Oh, Ali, how can you bear to sit here with me? I've behaved like a shrew. I despise what I've become—sour and angry at the world." Sarah gripped Alicia's hand. "The truth is, I've missed you. I've missed confiding in you. So many times I've wanted the courage to tell you—to tell *someone*. . . ."

"To tell me what?"

"That I grieve . . . for the happiness I knew before Timothy came into my life."

Confused, Alicia fumbled for words. "I—I thought yours was a love match."

"Love." Saying the word like a curse, Sarah shook her head, her eyes haunted. "I deluded myself. . . . I didn't see his true character. All his pretty words . . . they were lies. *Lies*."

"I don't understand."

"Nor did I . . . for too long. After getting me with child . . . after I *gave* myself to him with all my heart . . . he would have nothing more to do with me."

Alicia's heart wrenched. "But why?"

"I was too highborn, he said, too virtuous and naïve . . . and he . . . he preferred his doxies." A breath shuddered from her. "He died of a heart seizure . . . in the bed of his mistress."

Horrified, Alicia understood so much now. "That's why you despise my husband. You believe he's like the duke."

"All men are the same," Sarah said derisively. "I've yet to meet one who can resist temptation. And we women are blind to their faults . . . until it is too late."

Alicia wasn't blind to Drake's faults. She knew he'd had many paramours before their marriage, and she didn't harbor any illusions about his fidelity. Yet Sarah's pessimism disturbed her in some elemental way. "So let the men do as they will. You shall do as *you* will, too. You can't allow one rotted apple to spoil the rest of your life."

"I haven't done that. . . ." But she looked dubious, thoughtful.

"Listen to me," Alicia said, wanting fervently to help. "You mustn't let Timothy defeat you even from the grave. You must forget about him and go out into society again."

Sarah's expression slowly lightened. "How right you are. You always did have such good sense."

Trying for humor, Alicia said, "A number of my former suitors would disagree with that."

"We did have a lot of admirers, didn't we? Remember how we would divide the gentlemen?" A smile spread over the duchess's face, transforming her beauty with a wistful humor. "You would have first choice of the fair-haired ones—"

"And you would have the dark-headed men."

"The ginger-tops and graybeards and bald pates—"

"We'd leave for the other ladies."

"How generous of us not to charm them *all*." Sarah gave a laugh reminiscent of the girl she'd once been. "Oh, I do wish I could go back to those days. I miss the parties, the amusements, the light-hearted fun."

"You *can* go back," Alicia said, the tug of nostalgia as strong as her vow to a dark-haired knave. She was married now. But oh, how carefree they'd been, before Papa's death and Mama's illness. If only she could forget the need to use Sarah for her own purpose.

No, for Drake's purpose.

"Once your mourning period is over," Alicia added, "you can dance and flirt to your heart's content."

"Perhaps so. Perhaps it's past time I shed my widow's weeds." A calculating excitement in her violet eyes, Sarah squeezed Alicia's hands. "And if *I* am to set society on its ear, then *you* shall be at my side."

Returning to Swansdowne Crescent, Alicia went in search of Drake on the chance that she might find him still at home. Though their paths seldom crossed—she made sure of *that*—she had learned his schedule from hearing his footsteps in the corridor or the rumble of his voice in the foyer. For a short while in the afternoon, he often worked at his desk in the library. Then he would leave for his club, spending the evenings there and not returning until near dawn. She would awaken at first light to hear him moving about the suite of rooms adjacent to hers. He seemed to require very little sleep.

She handed her wraps to the butler, who waited at the front door. "Thank you, Chalkers. You're a dear."

The stoop-shouldered old man blinked his rheumy eyes at her. "Mishish Wilder? Good evenin' . . . er, good day, that ish."

The odor of spirits drifted from him. He was drunk again, Alicia realized. Though annoyed that Drake hadn't dealt with the problem, she wondered briefly what would happen to the elderly servant if he were let go. For that reason alone, she wouldn't pursue the issue with her husband. Drake would undoubtedly throw him out on the streets.

Deciding that she couldn't bear for that to happen, she hastened through the foyer to the library, where one of the double doors stood ajar. She tapped on the oak panel and without waiting, stepped inside and paused.

The rich perfume of leather and paper greeted her. She breathed deeply, savoring the quiet joy of being surrounded by books. The walls held floor-to-ceiling shelves, stained a deep brown and filled with row upon row of bound volumes. There was an amazing variety of literature and scientific studies, plays and mathematical texts. She already had made a habit in the evenings, after Mama was abed and the house was silent, of curling in one of the comfortable chairs here, warmed by the fire and reading to her heart's content. It was the single most glorious advantage to being Mrs. Drake Wilder.

And the most baffling. Did he own these books for the sake of appearances, because he believed all gentlemen possessed a fine library? Or because he truly had a keen interest in many divergent topics? He professed to know Latin. That meant he must have pursued academic studies at some point in his life. . . .

She ventured farther into the long chamber. "Drake?"

Beyond the door stood his desk, broad and shining with polish. The empty chair was pushed back as if he'd only just left. A tidy pile of papers lay on the blotter. Beside an inkpot, a silver cup held a collection of quills.

Disappointment needled her. She had so wanted to tell him of her success. That she had procured the sponsorship of the esteemed Duchess of Featherstone.

"What a pity you missed the master," someone said behind her.

Startled, she pivoted to see Mrs. Yates standing in the back corner, half hidden by the spreading green fronds of a fern. A white servant's cap was perched jauntily on her red curls. She held a closed book in one hand and a feather duster in the other.

The smirk on those cosmetic-enhanced features raised a prickle over Alicia's skin. "What are you doing in here?"

The housekeeper gave the volume two swipes, then returned it to the shelf. "Tending to my duties, of course."

"Housemaids should do the dusting. You must have more important tasks to see to."

"By the master's order, *I* am the only servant allowed in here, and I must do my cleaning in his absence." With the wrong end of the feather duster, Yates flicked a speck off her low-cut bosom as if to draw attention to its generous proportions. "He trusts me, you see."

Her implication of intimacy left Alicia cold with shock. Was Drake carrying on an affair with this hussy? Was that why Yates felt free to show such insolence? Alicia wanted to believe that even a scoundrel like him would show more discretion. Yet she could not be certain. . . .

"Finish your work, then. Henceforth, you will also have to answer to me."

Ignoring the housekeeper's scowl, Alicia turned to go. How she did miss Mrs. Molesworth, who had remained at Pemberton House. They had been like a close-knit family, she and the cook and Mama and Gerald. Mrs. Molesworth had shown them respect, and so would this impertinent housekeeper, if Alicia had her way. But she hadn't walked three steps when she heard Yates mutter something under her breath.

"Too high and mighty to share the master's bed."

Alicia spun back around. Although she'd heard the brazen words clearly enough, she snapped, "What did you say?"

Yates widened her long-lashed brown eyes, then lowered them. "Nothing, m'lady."

"Really?" Alicia said in her haughtiest tone. "Do bear in mind, it would be no trouble to run an advertisement for a new housekeeper."

To her surprise, the boldness vanished and the housekeeper appeared genuinely alarmed. She dipped a curtsy, the feather duster hiding her bosom like a penitential scourge. "Please don't tell the master. He's been so good to me."

It was on the tip of Alicia's tongue to ask precisely *how* he'd been good. But she wouldn't reveal her secret uncertainties to this upstart. "Because I am feeling charitable, I will give you a second chance—this time."

Yates fixed her gaze on the red and blue pattern of the Turkish carpet. "Bless you, m'lady."

Walking to the door, Alicia looked back to see her diligently dusting the shelves again. She couldn't dismiss a lingering suspicion about the housekeeper, that her sudden meekness was merely an act.

Too high and mighty to share the master's bed.

Alicia's cheeks burned. How did Yates know that she and Drake had a chaste marriage? Had he gone tale-telling to his doxy? The thought seared her with renewed fury.

Her first impulse was to go storming to his club. But she forced herself to stop outside the library and take several deep breaths. There would be gentlemen congregated there, gambling and drinking. It wouldn't do to make a scene in public. She would behave like the lady she was, not lower herself to *his* level.

The papered wall felt cool to her fevered cheek, as chilly as her resolve. She would bide her time. And when Drake returned home, she would confront him.

Chapter Ten

Drake stood for a moment in the darkness, staring up at his father's house. The grand facade built of Portland stone featured Palladian columns and tall, corniced windows. The ground floor was dark, but lamplight glowed in a chamber above. He wondered what his life would have been like if he'd grown up here. If he had been raised as the son of a powerful lord. . . .

To hell with it. He'd done better for himself without a father at all.

Reaching into his pocket, Drake fingered the slender gold band encrusted with sapphires and diamonds. The reminder of Hailstock's audacity filled him with rage.

Though the hour was late, he knew the marquess had just returned home from a dinner engagement. Drake had instructed his coachman to wait around the corner. He didn't intend for anyone to see him here. The time was not yet right for him to reveal his paternity.

He strode up the broad steps and rapped on the front door. A footman clad in black and silver livery admitted him. As Drake stepped into the entrance hall with its marble archways and soaring staircase, an eerie sense of familiarity came over him. He remembered standing here as a boy of ten, his neck craned in awe at the magnificence of the place.

And his chest aching with hope that he would at last know his father.

Addressing the footman, he said coolly, "Tell his lordship that Drake Wilder is here to see him."

"Yes, sir." After casting him a curious glance, the servant mounted the grand staircase.

As soon as he vanished out of sight, Drake followed. He didn't intend for Hailstock to refuse to see him.

At the top of the stairs, Drake glanced around at the fine statuary in niches and the passageways leading off in several directions. He strode past the shadowed gallery and toward a short corridor that led to the front of the house. Sure enough, he saw the footman conferring with a silver-haired man out in the corridor.

Hailstock.

Controlling a surge of loathing, Drake walked toward them, and the marquess pivoted on his heel to stare. The footman scuttled off in the opposite direction. Swiftly, Hailstock marched away from a large salon, where lamplight glowed and a fire glimmered on the hearth.

"How dare you invade my house," he said through gritted teeth, his voice low. "I'll have you tossed out like the rabble you are."

Ignoring him, Drake frowned into the salon. On a chaise by the fireplace, a young man reclined, his crippled legs covered by a blanket. The firelight glinted off his tawny hair and petulant profile. His eyes closed, he appeared to be dozing.

Drake felt a sharp twist inside himself that could only be anger. James, Lord Scarborough by his courtesy title. His half-brother.

He swung to Hailstock. "What's the matter?" he jeered. "Are you afraid your other son might hear?"

Alarm flashed into those frosty gray eyes. His face ashen, Hailstock glanced into the salon. "Damn you," he muttered. "Keep your voice down. Now go on downstairs. We can talk there."

Drake held his ground. "There's no need to talk. I merely wish to return this." Reaching inside his coat, he drew out the ring and tossed it to Hailstock.

The older man caught it reflexively, gripping the small circle in his hand. "This ring belongs to Alicia."

"My wife doesn't accept gifts from you." Savoring a cold triumph, Drake took a step toward the man he had abhorred for so many years. "And if you dare to come near her again, I'll kill you."

In the salon, James lay with his eyes closed.

It amused him at times to pretend slumber while his father entertained guests. James knew how to concentrate his attention, blotting out distractions. He had garnered juicy tidbits of gossip that way, and a few times he'd had difficulty restraining laughter while an old dowager flirted with his widowed father. No one realized the keenness of his hearing. They seemed to think that being crippled had somehow impaired his other senses, too.

When he'd heard the footman out in the corridor announce Drake Wilder, James's ears had perked with interest. Wilder was the baseborn gambler who had married Alicia. James had known his father was furious about the wedding, but had attributed it to the fact that he liked to control those around him, a trait James had noticed more since he'd been crippled and had so much time on his hands to watch people. But never had James imagined anything like this.

What's the matter? Are you afraid your other son might hear?

A chilly dampness prickled his palms. He felt as if a knife had been thrust into his gut. He had a *brother*. His father—his priggish, principled father—had sired a *bastard*.

His father stepped into the salon. Forcing himself not to tense, James detected the faint rasp of his breathing and imagined him standing over the chaise. If he hadn't been irked with Father for going out after promising him a game of chess, if he hadn't pretended to be asleep when his father had returned home, he would never have learned the staggering truth.

What's the matter? Are you afraid your other son might hear?

"James," his father said very quietly.

James didn't respond. But he let himself stir a little against the pillows as if the sound had disturbed his slumber.

After a moment, he heard his father walk away. James burned to confront him, but knew bitterly that he would only deny it. The almighty Marquess of Hailstock could never admit to siring a bastard. And so he had denied his legitimate son the knowledge that he had a brother.

What's the matter? Are you afraid your other son might hear?

James felt betrayed, furious, shaken. He needed time to think, to absorb the shock, to find out more about Drake Wilder.

And he needed time to decide what to do.

Chapter Eleven

A sound lured Alicia to the surface of sleep. Lingering in a limbo of warmth, she snuggled deeper into the nest of pillows and blankets. She longed to drift back to her dream, back to that splendid ballroom, back to the arms of a most fascinating man with midnight-blue eyes. . . .

The noise came again. A faint scraping. Metal.

She opened her eyes to the pearly shimmer of dawn and the high arch of a canopy overhead. A gilt bird perched atop each bedpost, wings spread, beak trailing a ribbon that twined downward to the cream and gold bedcurtains. Groggy, she wondered where she was, why Mama wasn't sleeping beside her.

Mama.

Even as Alicia raised herself on one elbow, she remembered. This was Drake Wilder's house. Mama was safe. She now shared a chamber with Mrs. Philpot across the corridor.

So what had caused that sound?

Though the chilly morning air made her shiver, Alicia sat up and glanced around her richly appointed bedchamber with its gold watered silk on the walls and the magnificent gilt moldings. Night still lurked in the corners. The first fingers of daylight crept over the dainty writing desk with its pens and stationery, caressed the lush Aubusson carpet, touched the blue and cream chaise by the ivory marble mantelpiece . . . and pointed to a maidservant quietly cleaning the hearth.

The scrape of her shovel had awakened Alicia.

This was the first time she had caught the maid at her work. Always before she would awaken to the cheery whisper of the fire, though once she'd glimpsed the girl as she'd darted out of the chamber, ignoring Alicia's call to wait. Most of the servants acted just as wary.

As if they'd been instructed to avoid her.

"Good morning," Alicia said.

The servant made no response. Crouched on her knees, she tilted the last scoop of ashes into her pail, then silently placed the brush in her box and reached for the kindling.

"Good morning," Alicia called louder.

The maid paid no heed, laying the sticks of wood on the grate. Her every move was noiseless, efficient, almost furtive.

Had Yates told the staff to pretend the mistress of the house didn't exist? The very thought angered Alicia.

"It's quite all right to speak," she said, pushing off the counterpane and sliding out of bed. She shivered as her warm bare feet met the cold rug. She reached for her dressing gown, lying on a chair. "I merely wish to know your name."

Still the housemaid ignored her.

Gritting her teeth, Alicia donned the robe and knotted the sash. This impertinence could not continue. She stepped quickly to the hearth.

The maidservant was a stout young woman with a mobcap perched on her dark hair. And she looked vaguely familiar. Wasn't she the one who had lingered in the foyer on the morning of the wedding, staring at her new mistress until a footman had pulled her away?

It *was* her. And Alicia would tolerate no more disrespect. Leaning down, she placed her hand on that rounded shoulder just as the maid reached for the bucket of coal.

The girl yelped. The bucket tipped over with a loud clatter. Black chunks tumbled over the hearth rug, rolling onto the fine carpet and disappearing under chairs and footstools. She cringed, wide-eyed, her grimy hands pressed to her apple cheeks.

To her chagrin, Alicia realized the servant had heard neither her approach nor her words. Had she been deep in thought? Or was she stone deaf?

"I didn't mean to startle you," Alicia said, sinking to her knees. "Truly, I didn't."

As she spoke, the girl watched her lips. Deaf, then. The knot of anger inside Alicia unraveled into amazement. A rich household like this one could afford to hire the most able-bodied servants. Yet Drake employed a deaf housemaid, a misfit who would be denied a post by the nobility.

It couldn't be out of kindness. He was a ruthless, selfish man. So that left only one explanation. He must not be aware of her impairment.

The girl's brown eyes brimmed with tears. Remorsefully, Alicia patted that soot-smudged hand. "Don't weep," she said, taking care to form her words slowly. "It was an accident. My fault."

The maid scrambled to right the bucket. "Nay, m'lady. 'Twas my clumsiness."

Her voice had a nasal flatness, but by a miracle, she wasn't mute. Touching the girl's shoulder to get her attention, Alicia said, "What is your name?"

"Kitty." Her lower lip trembled. "Don't put me out on the street, mum, please. I'll clean up in a jeffy."

"You won't lose your post. I promise you that."

On hands and knees, Alicia gathered the black lumps, dropping them with a tinny bang into the bucket. Kitty scrambled to work faster, glancing cautiously at her mistress, as if unable to believe her reprieve. Alicia vowed to

make her believe. In time, Kitty—and the other servants—
would realize the lady of the house was no ogress to be
feared.

Spying one last piece beneath a gilt chair, she crouched
low and stretched out her hand to retrieve it. Her fingers
closed around the hard chunk just as a soft rap sounded on
the door.

The door connecting her chamber to Drake's.

Alicia's heart skittered over a beat. He couldn't walk in,
she reminded herself. The door was locked. Her first night
here, she had hidden the key in one of her gloves and
tucked it away in the farthest corner of her wardrobe. Every
night since, she had tested the bolt before going to bed.

What could Drake Wilder want with her at this hour?

She had a few words to say to him, too. But not until
she was fully clothed. If she pretended to be asleep, he
would go away in a moment.

The lock rattled. The door swung open. Her husband
appeared.

She froze. Like a sultan surveying his harem, he lounged
against the gilded frame, his hair mussed and his tall form
in an alarming state of undress. He wore no cravat or coat,
only dark breeches and a plain white shirt, the tails hanging
loose. The unbuttoned front showed a wedge of naked
chest. Even his feet were bare.

In his hand he held a ring of keys. She should have
guessed he had a spare.

He frowned at the maid, then at Alicia. "Someone cried
out," he said. "What happened here?"

Kitty cowered by the fireplace. Alicia scrambled to her
feet, tossed the lump of coal into the bucket, and stepped
forward to block his view of the hearth. "Nothing happened," she said coldly. "And I did not give you permission
to unlock that door."

"I heard sharp words spoken. I won't have you berating
my servants."

"You misunderstood," she said quickly, before he could address a question to the maid. "Now give me that key." She held out her hand.

He twirled the iron ring on his forefinger and caught the keys in his palm with a metallic chink. "I keep the master set."

"I don't want the whole ring. Just the key to my door."

"No," he said flatly. "Now, I saw Yates this morning. She said you were looking for me."

Her suspicions about the housekeeper added to her furious tension. Alicia had lain awake half the night, listening for his return, rehearsing the recriminations she would hurl at him. Yet she couldn't challenge him here, for fear he might perceive Kitty's affliction. Heaven help her, he'd send the poor girl packing.

Alicia hastened forward and drew him into his chambers. "We'll talk where there's more privacy."

He went quite willingly, closing the door behind them. It was a mistake to touch him, to feel the heat of his flesh through the linen shirt. Stopping a few steps into the room, she snatched back her hand, but she could still feel the hard smoothness of muscle imprinted on her palm.

Feigning indifference, she swung away and surveyed the large chamber. For all its size, it was surprisingly inviting, with books piled on mahogany tables and wild landscapes decorating the walls. The shutters were closed against the dawn. The only light came from a low fire on the hearth and a branch of candles on the bedside table.

Her gaze fixed on that broad bed. The linens were rumpled, and the pillow bore the imprint of his head. He must have been lying there. Odd that he wasn't clad in nightclothes.

Sauntering to the foot of the bed, he leaned against the post and idly jingled the ring of keys. His mouth slanted into a grin more wicked than that of the devil himself. "Well, well. I did predict you'd come to me in my chamber before the season was out." He studied her from her sleep-tangled braid down to her small bare toes. "And here you are, all ready for bed."

Her cheeks went hot. His scrutiny made Alicia aware of herself as a woman—his wife. He could do with her as he willed. He could force her onto the bed, kiss her, subdue her with his superior strength. Uneasiness lurked low in her belly, a feeling she scorned. Irksome man. The high-necked white robe covered her more completely than a ball gown.

"I am here to have a word with you," she began.

"If you mean to confess your unrequited passion, my darling, then pray proceed."

Such conceit. She would relish knocking him off his high perch. "It is not *I* we are here to discuss, but you. *Your* behavior."

He slapped a hand to his bare chest. "I've been a paragon of propriety. A veritable vision of virtue."

"Not with Yates."

"Yates?" A faint annoyance crossed his features. "I told you not to pester her. She'll do her job, and you do yours."

Alicia clenched her fingers into the silk of her robe. She would not allow him to rob her of her rights in this house. Nor to pretend ignorance. "The true question is, what will *you* do with her?"

His black eyebrows lowering, he tossed the ring of keys onto the bed. They landed in his blankets. Right where Alicia was loath to venture. "For pity's sake," he said, "stop speaking in riddles. If you've something to say, then say it."

Her gaze snapped from the keys to his face. "All right, then. Yates is your doxy."

He stood unmoving, his face blank. She could see the peppering of whiskers along his jaw. His untidy state made him appear even more depraved. Abruptly, he burst out laughing, the hearty sound filling the chamber. "So that's what you imagine while lying in your virgin's bed."

"It is no flight of fancy." Annoyed that he could make purity sound like a fault, Alicia stepped toward him. "The woman has been nothing short of insolent. And there can be only one reason why she feels safe to voice her unbridled opinions to the lady of the house. Because she knows the master will not reprove her."

"Tell me exactly what she said to you."

"It is not worth repeating."

"I will hear what she said. So that I may judge for myself if you are too quick to take offense."

A flush stung Alicia's cheeks. "She said . . . I am too high and mighty to share your bed."

His dimples deepened, though he didn't precisely smile. "I see."

"No, you don't see." Prodded by resentment, Alicia edged toward the bed, the carpet soft beneath her bare soles. "The only way she could know that we have a chaste marriage is by *your* telling her."

"Bosh. The servants can guess we don't engage in marital relations. They change the linens, don't forget."

Alicia aimed a mystified frown at him. What in the world did *that* mean? She suspected he would laugh at her again if she asked him to explain.

She inched a little closer to her goal. "Well. I won't tolerate your philandering in this house—with Yates or anyone else. If you wish to carry on your affairs, then do so elsewhere."

The wretch smiled, as if she were a child to be humored. It was now or never. Darting to the four-poster, she scooped up the ring of keys. With the cold hard metal clutched to her bosom, she turned to leave.

Only to discover that he'd moved with catlike stealth to block her path. "If the truth disturbs you," he purred, "then make her a liar. Come to bed with me."

He extended his hand to her. She could only gape at him in breathless agitation. One black lock dipped onto his brow, giving him a rakish air. The strong line of his throat widened to the contoured muscles of his chest. Behind her loomed the tousled sheets, the counterpane in a shade of blue as deep and mysterious as his eyes.

"I haven't slept yet," he went on in that husky, hypnotic voice. "Lie down with me. Let me hold you, kiss you."

Defying the dictates of her mind, her body softened. He was her husband. And yet she did not know the intimacy of cuddling in the darkness with him. She could detect his faintly smoky scent, the hint of brandy. He had been at his club all night, gambling, drinking, carousing. She had every reason to despise such a rascal. So why did she feel the bite of temptation?

"You're violating our agreement," she snapped, appalled to hear a wobble in her voice.

"Nonsense. We agreed I could charm you. If only you'd let me, I'd show you the sweetest pleasure any woman could know." Catching her wrist, he brought it to his lips, planting a kiss on her tender inner flesh.

A flurry of gooseflesh raced up her arm and into her bosom. She wanted to succumb, and her weakness horrified her. The keys rattled as she snatched back her hand. "We also agreed you'd stop when I told you so."

"Which you have yet to do."

She backed away from the dangerous intent on his face. "Profligate. I'm telling you to stop right now."

"Puritan," he murmured. "You can't deny me forever."

As if he had all the time in the world, he strolled after her. She retreated until her bottom met the hard edge of a table near the connecting door. She longed to take refuge in her own bedchamber, but Kitty might still be coaxing the coals into flame.

Gripping the keys like a weapon, Alicia glared at him. "Once I've fulfilled my end of our bargain, you'll leave me be."

"Once I've had you, I'll leave you be."

Did he mean it? That he would cease tormenting her if she allowed him a husband's rights just once? If she could believe that . . .

Alicia wrenched her mind from that appalling path. How could she even consider giving an inch to this scoundrel? "This discussion is absurd," she said icily. "Especially since our agreement is nearly fulfilled."

He stopped, all playfulness vanishing. "You've found a way for me to enter society."

She nodded, and her heart slowed its frantic beating. The approval of the *ton* was what he really wanted, the reason he had wed her. How foolish of her to have forgotten that. "Yes, I have."

"Tell me how," he said.

"Sarah, the Duchess of Featherstone, has agreed to give us her nod of approval."

His eyes narrowed to a secretive expression. Or perhaps it was a trick of the firelight. "When will this event come about?"

"Lord and Lady Cuthbert are giving a ball next Tuesday. Sarah intends to bring us along as her guests."

They had spent the afternoon making plans, laughing together like old times, though a certain wariness lingered, perhaps because they each knew they were using the other. But that didn't seem to matter. Alicia could only think of how amazingly wonderful it was that she and Sarah had overcome their animosity. They had chatted for hours, filling each other in on the joys and sorrows of their lives, although, of course, Alicia had confessed little about her marriage. It was enough for Sarah to know of Gerald's debts and the necessity of accepting Drake Wilder's offer.

"Who is she to you?" Drake asked.

"I beg your pardon?"

"The duchess. You had a wistful look on your face."

Reluctant to share her private thoughts with him, she schooled her features into a cool expression. "We were friends once. A long time ago—during our come-out Season."

"If she scorned you after your father's ruin and your mother's illness, she isn't much of a friend."

"That wasn't the case. We had a disagreement about . . . something else."

"What?"

Alicia compressed her lips. From the force of his stare, she knew he would dig until he uncovered the truth. Wasn't it better to fob him off with a brief explanation? From the table behind her, she picked up an enameled snuffbox, one of a collection on display. "It was silly, really," she said, pretending to admire the mosaic design. "We both favored the duke."

"You would admire Featherstone."

The wealth of disdain in his voice caught her attention, as did his stern expression. "You knew him?"

"I make a practice of knowing the character of every man who frequents my club. And Featherstone didn't know a moral from a mudhole." Drake paused, his mouth twisted sardonically. "But of course he did have that impeccable pedigree."

"He was a gentleman."

"Then why did he live openly with his mistress, even after his marriage? She bore him three children."

Alicia slowly set down the snuffbox. Sarah had known of his paramour, but was she aware of his second family? That her young son—the present duke—had natural half-siblings? "I don't believe it," she whispered. "You must have been misinformed."

"I heard it from the duke himself. He was proud of his prowess." Drake strolled closer. "So you see, my lady, you're better off wed to me. At least I haven't spawned any bastards."

"Yet." On that scathing remark, Alicia headed toward the connecting door and turned the knob.

Drake flattened his palm on the gilded panel. "The keys, my lady."

He stood mere inches away. She could feel his body heat. How easily he could overpower her. Tightening her fingers around the ring, she refused to show any vulnerability. "I will have the one that fits this door."

His eyes narrowed, concealing his thoughts. For a moment, she feared he would refuse, and she would be forced into an undignified tussle.

Then he gave a nod. "As you wish, then." He took the ring, unscrewed the clasp, and extracted a key, which he passed to her. "But you're a coldhearted woman, Mrs. Wilder."

"You're a tiresome devil, Mr. Wilder."

She considered testing the key, then decided that might be pressing her luck. Entering her chamber, she glanced toward the hearth, where a fire now burned. The maid had gone.

Relieved, Alicia turned to shut the door. "Good day. Or shall I say, good night."

His smooth expression took on a hard edge. "One more caution, dear wife. I doubt that Kitty fits your exacting standards. But you will not discharge her. That is an order."

Then he closed the door on Alicia's startled face.

Chapter Twelve

A short while later, Alicia stepped out of her bedchamber and encountered another surprise.

Intending to spend the day acquainting herself with the household, she had donned a gown of ice-blue muslin that fell in a straight line from her bosom. For the sake of modesty, she had tucked a length of Brussels lace into the bodice. She felt armored and calm again, ready to face the world.

Though she couldn't forget Drake, presumably asleep next door.

This morning, when he'd entered her bedchamber, he had shattered her sense of security—a false security, she now knew. Though she had hidden the second key beneath the papers in her writing desk, she was uneasily aware that he could procure another if the mood suited him. That meant she must never lower her guard.

Not even his defense of Kitty proved him trustworthy. Granted, he knew the servant was deaf. But compassion hadn't prompted his protectiveness toward the maid. Like the autocrat he was, he enjoyed exercising his power over his wife.

Let him. She would do as she saw fit—

That was when she noticed the army of footmen trooping in and out of her mother's bedchamber. They carried towering piles of boxes.

Puzzled, Alicia joined the procession into the bright, yellow and white chamber. The curtains had been drawn back to a view of the green park, and both beds had been tidied. Mama and Mrs. Philpot were nowhere to be seen.

Directed by a short, barrel-chested man in a cherry-red coat and blue pantaloons, the footmen marched into the dressing room. "Have a care, you clumsy oaf," he proclaimed in a startlingly deep, dramatic tone. "This is no delivery from the ragman."

Alicia hurried toward him. "Sir? What is going on here?"

"Ah, the lady of the house." He swept a bow so low she could see the bald circle crowning his skull. When he straightened, he rocked back and forth on his heels and regarded her with an air of self-importance. "Permit me to introduce myself, my lady. I am Signor Renaldo, master of wardrobes for the Royal Theatre."

"Theater?" Perplexed, she peered into the dressing room, past the footmen depositing the boxes and the maidservants unpacking them. Garments and shoes and gloves littered the green carpet with its pattern of yellow ribbons. The armoires and cupboards and clothespresses stood open like great mouths waiting to consume a feast.

At the far end of the long room stood Mama, a voluminous red cloak enveloping her delicate form and a plumed cavalier's hat perched on her head. Spying Alicia, she waved. "Ahoy, there. Climb aboard my pirate ship. We're about to give chase to a Spanish galleon."

"Dear heavens," Alicia murmured under her breath.

Abandoning Signor Renaldo, she picked her way through the clutter, aghast to see piles of wigs and mounds of costumes, from Roman togas to medieval tunics to witch's robes. On the dressing table, a chest full of paste jewelry glinted in the sunlight. Had Mama, in a moment of mad indulgence, ordered these theatrical props and charged them to Drake's account?

Mrs. Philpot straightened up from the trunk she'd been rummaging through. She handed Lady Eleanor a black silk sash. "For you, my captain."

The countess tied the sash around her slender waist. She tucked a toy dagger into the belt and planted her feet wide as if she were balancing on the deck of a ship. "Beware, ye fainthearted dastards. I am Anne Bonny, queen of the high seas."

Humoring her, Alicia snatched up a small cask brimming with fake coins, which she presented to her mother. "A tribute of gold doubloons, O Great Pirate Queen."

"Ye may consider yerself under my protection," Lady Eleanor said grandly, settling down on a chair to examine her treasure.

While her mother was preoccupied, Alicia drew Mrs. Philpot beyond a stack of boxes. "Did Mama order these things?" she whispered. "I fear they will all have to be returned before Mr. Wilder finds out."

"Nay, my lady," Mrs. Philpot said, her green eyes sparkling as she patted Alicia's hand. "Everything you see here is a gift."

"A gift? From whom?"

"Why, your husband, of course. Mr. Wilder knows how your mama likes to playact, and so he purchased these costumes from a theatrical company. They are your mama's to keep. Is it not wondrously kind of him?"

"Oh . . . yes."

Her legs weak, Alicia sank down onto a footstool and regarded her mother. Lady Eleanor had abandoned the coins to explore the contents of another box. She lifted out a gaudy crimson scarf and draped it around her neck. The delight on her gentle face warmed Alicia's heart.

Drake had done this. He had brought joy into Mama's life.

It was difficult to believe such generosity of a man who cared only for himself and his own pleasures. Yet she could find no selfish reason for his benevolence. The more she learned about her husband, the less she understood him. He was fast becoming an enigma to her. And she resented him for making her question her assessment of his character.

Alicia lifted her chin a notch. He was the villain who had lured Gerald to the gaming tables. He had used that debt to force her into marriage. He had stolen even the roof over their heads. With cold-blooded intent, he had manipulated their lives to his own purposes.

So let him have his little secrets. She didn't care to unravel the mystery. Better she not think of him at all.

The crimson carpet muffling his footsteps, Drake strode down the wide passageway on his way to the staircase. The pale glow of the lamps enhanced his irritable mood. He had overslept. He should have left for the club hours ago.

Of course, Fergus would handle the bank, and his well-trained staff would cater to the whims of those members who arrived early, primed for a night at hazard or faro. But Drake prided himself on overseeing the play. Keen attention to detail had given Wilder's a reputation for luxury and refinement.

After tossing and turning for hours, he had been plagued by restless dreams. He had awakened hard and frustrated, obsessed by his wife. The Lady Alicia. How soft and touchable she'd looked this morning, tousled from sleep. She had been naked beneath her nightdress, her breasts unbound. Though she'd pretended indifference, she'd wanted him; he'd seen the desire in her eyes, heard it in the way her breath caught whenever he touched her. He burned to strip away that cool superiority, to awaken the earthy passion she kept locked inside. He wanted her lying beneath him, moaning in ecstasy. . . .

Ah, hell. What he needed was a long, lusty session with

his mistress. A pity he had discharged her with the gift of a diamond necklace. He could have been enjoying her eagerness to please instead of suffering the scorn of a woman who regarded him as dirt beneath her aristocratic feet.

She had accused him of carrying on with Liza Yates. The thought was darkly amusing. Of course, Alicia couldn't know the real reason why the housekeeper was so possessive of him.

Rounding a corner, he took a shortcut through the darkened gallery, his heels ringing on the pale marble floor. Here he kept many of his acquisitions, the paintings and statues that proved his wealth. But tonight he took only peripheral notice of his surroundings. He reminded himself he should be reveling in the closeness of success.

Already Alicia had finagled an invitation to a ball. In a week's time, he would insinuate himself into the *ton*. But not for the purpose she believed. He smiled grimly to think of Hailstock's face when he realized he could no longer bar his bastard son from society.

"Oh!"

The quavering gasp came from the shadows. He turned sharply. In an alcove, a pedestal diplayed an alabaster statue of Diana the huntress. Behind the sculpture, a small cloaked form peeked out from the gloom.

A plumed cavalier's hat topped the pale oval of a face. He recognized the costume from a production of *Blackbeard, or The Captive Princess.*

"My lady," he said, executing a deep bow. "Forgive me for startling you. Where is Mrs. Philpot this evening?"

Lady Brockway tiptoed out to regard him quizzically. Through the dimness, those fine-boned features bore a haunting resemblance to Alicia.

"Mr. Wilder?" Lady Eleanor asked, obviously in one of her saner moments. Ignoring his question about her companion, she stammered, "Oh, dear . . . for a moment there I thought . . . I thought you reminded me of someone. . . ."

Drake went ice cold. *Hailstock.*

He had lulled himself into believing the similarities were too subtle to notice. Certainly Alicia had never seen a resemblance. But Lady Eleanor had known Hailstock for many years; she would remember him in his younger, more vigorous days, when he'd been closer in age to Drake.

The last thing Drake wanted was for anyone to guess the truth.

Stepping closer, he took her hands; they nestled like dainty birds in his palms. "Who, my lady?" he asked urgently. "Who do I remind you of?"

"Someone . . . years ago . . ." A quiver stirred the cloak around her small shoulders. "Oh, I'm so afraid."

"Afraid of what?"

"Afraid . . . to remember . . ." Pulling her fingers free, she groped underneath the cloak, and he realized she wore that shabby moleskin cape. Her eyes brimmed with tears and she swayed, weeping as if her heart were broken.

Drake acted without thought. Sliding his arm around her, he held her close, and she burrowed into him, the cavalier's hat tumbling to the floor. He drew out a clean handkerchief and pressed it into her fingers. He didn't know how to soothe her. The crocodile tears of a mistress he could handle, but not the profound anguish of the dowager countess. His mother-in-law. Strange to think that.

Was she weeping because she feared Hailstock? Did she know that he had threatened to lock her away in Bedlam Hospital?

His jaw clenched, he said, "I assure you, my lady, you've no cause for distress. You're safe in this house. Safe with me."

Huddling her face against his chest, she took a shuddering breath, her sobs slowing. "Oh, but it is not I who needs protection."

That jolted him. Who could she mean? Alicia?

"Look at me," Drake said. Placing his forefinger beneath

her chin, he nudged up her face. Silvering strands of blond hair framed her guileless features. Her eyes, like bruised pansies, blinked slowly, as if she struggled to place him. He sensed her withdrawing into herself, into her secret sorrow. Willing her to remain rational, he went on, "You must tell me who requires protection. It's the only way I can help."

Dabbing at her cheeks with his crumpled handkerchief, she mournfully shook her head. "No one can help. Alas, it is too late."

"I don't understand, then. Why are you still afraid?"

She gazed blankly at him. Then she patted his hand as if he were the one who needed comforting. "I like you," she said in a musing tone. "You are a very kind man."

He curbed his impatience. "My lady, please try to think. If someone has made a threat to you or to anyone dear to you, I should like to hear of it."

Lady Eleanor reached inside her cloak and drew a toy dagger from her sash. "Threaten me? Why, no one would dare, sirrah. I am Anne Bonny, queen of the high seas."

Frustration churned in Drake. The dreamy look in her eyes told him he would coax no more out of her. Hissing out a breath, he picked up her hat and presented it to her. "I believe this is yours, Madame Pirate."

Lady Brockway donned the too-large hat, unmindful that the tapered ends lay low over her ears or that the white plume drooped over her eye. "Why, bless ye, sir. How do I look?"

"Fierce enough to terrorize Blackbeard himself." He held out his arm. "Allow me to escort you to the lower deck. We'll see if we can't locate your shipmates."

Giggling, she accepted his assistance, and they strolled out of the gallery and down the grand staircase to the formal rooms. Contentment radiated from her, a peace of mind quite opposite to the alarm that had troubled her only moments ago. He had the uncanny impression that fantasy was her refuge from unhappy memories, that perhaps her madness was the result of an unbearable event she had witnessed.

Who had frightened her into weeping? Hailstock? And who else did she believe to be in danger? Drake intended to find out.

They approached the tall, arched doorway of the drawing room. Alicia and her brother had made a custom of taking tea at this hour, and sure enough, the chatter of anxious voices emanated from within.

Halting outside the door, he saluted Lady Eleanor. "It sounds as if the crew is about to mutiny," he said in a low voice. "You had better go assume command."

"Will ye not accompany me? Ye would make a fine navigator."

Smiling, he shook his head. "Regrettably, I have my own seas to navigate tonight."

Affording him a crisp nod, she swaggered into the drawing room like a pirate down a gangplank. He heard Alicia's cry of relief, Mrs. Philpot's concerned murmurings, Gerald's fond scolding.

Drake intended to walk away. Instead, he found himself stepping to the doorway, where he paused in the shadows of the threshhold. The joyful group stood at the far end of the long, lamplit room.

Slender and graceful in pale blue, Alicia embraced her mother. Mrs. Philpot dabbed at her eyes. The plumed hat once again had toppled to the floor, and Gerald scooped it up, grinning foolishly at his mother in her pirate's costume.

None of them noticed Drake.

Alicia guided Lady Brockway to an intimate grouping of chairs by the mantelpiece. They all gathered around, fussing over the dowager, fetching her tea and cakes from a silver tray. Their excited voices drifted to him.

"We were organizing a search party," Gerald said, settling a damask cloth on his mother's lap. "By gad, Mama, you gave us a fright, wandering off like that."

"I wasn't lost," Lady Brockway objected. "A captain always knows her directions."

"Of course," Alicia said, touching her mother's shoulder, smiling tenderly down at her. "We love you, and we were worried, that's all."

Drake felt a pang unpleasantly close to envy. They were a family, close-knit and happy. He was the outsider. An outsider in his own home.

He stepped back out of sight, his face a grim mask. The course of his life had been set long ago, and he would not rest until he had achieved his purpose. Nothing else mattered.

Especially not his highborn wife.

Chapter Thirteen

On the evening of the ball, Alicia was ready nearly an hour before the appointed time for departure. She had intended to visit awhile with her mother, but Mrs. Philpot sat reading *Gulliver's Travels* aloud by the fireplace, and Mama was so engrossed in the story that she gave Alicia a vague smile and waved her out of the bedchamber.

At loose ends, Alicia wandered downstairs to the library in search of a book of her own. A distraction might dampen the restless anticipation that had troubled her all day. Too many times, she'd had to reprimand herself for looking forward to this night. Likely, she would suffer snubs; not even the duchess's influence could force everyone to accept her. And she reminded herself that she did not reenter society for her own pleasure, but to fulfill a bargain.

A business arrangement with a heartless gambler.

Yet not even the bitter purpose behind her marriage could spoil her excitement. She felt a dizzying thrill much like the night of her come-out party long ago, when she had been eighteen and buoyed by dreams.

She wore a ball gown of embroidered gold-on-white muslin with short, puffed sleeves. A daily regimen of salve had made her hands smooth and white again. No one would

guess from looking at her that only a fortnight ago, she had
scrubbed floors and washed laundry.

Her dancing slippers made a whisper of sound in the
empty entrance hall. She remembered the swarm of her
admirers, the exhilaration of having so many choices. She
imagined gliding to the music again, laughing, feeling carefree and joyful. Caught up in fantasy, she performed a little
twirl through the doorway of the lamplit library.

And danced right into the arms of Drake Wilder.

His hard-muscled form drove the air from her lungs.
With her next breath, his alien scent of cologne and masculinity flooded her. His keen blue eyes gazed down at her
in faint amusement.

"Dreaming of me?"

His taunting voice completed the rude jolt of reality. She
stepped back, bumping into a leather chair. "You shouldn't
be here so early," she accused.

"Neither should you." Turning, he slid a book into place
on a shelf.

Against her will, she noticed how tall and magnificent
he looked in a form-fitting coat of deep blue with silver
buttons, cream-colored breeches, and dazzling white linen
at his throat. An uneasy warmth awakened within her, a
feeling that was part attraction and part resentment.

Ever since their disturbing encounter in his chamber, she
had seen little of her husband. They each had adhered to
their own routines. At dawn, he returned home from his
club and slept all morning. Then he left again sometime
during the afternoon, while she was out shopping, helping
Sarah select a new wardrobe to replace her drab black
mourning. The arrangement suited Alicia well. The less she
saw of her husband, the better.

He turned to study her with a brooding intensity, his
gaze wandering the length of her body before lingering at
her deep, scooped neckline. She resisted the urge to cover

the daring display of bosom. He would only chuckle in that irritating way of his.

She assumed a mask of icy hauteur. "A word of advice," she said. "If you stare in such an ill-bred manner at any lady tonight, you are certain to brand yourself a profligate."

"And if you speak in that waspish manner to any gentleman, *you* are certain to brand yourself a prig." With his mouth curled into a sardonic smile, he subjected her to another leisurely survey. "A very lovely prig, nonetheless. Though you do need the crowning touch."

He strolled to the desk and picked up a palm-sized leather case, which he opened to display the contents. Against the cream velvet interior lay a glittering suite of diamond and pearl jewelry. The lavish artistry wrested a gasp of pure feminine awe from Alicia.

Just as swiftly, she jerked her gaze away. "You already gave me jewelry for our wedding. I can't accept another such expensive gift."

"You can, indeed. My wife will be admired by everyone tonight."

His steely tone reminded her that she was his pawn, taken as payment for a gambling debt. Tonight she must flaunt the wealth he had gained at the expense of weak, foolish men. She had no choice. And deep inside her, she felt a shameful gladness.

She stood stiff and silent while he adorned her in diamonds . . . the exquisite tiara . . . the dainty earbobs . . . the extravagant necklace with its network of pearls from which hung a sinfully large solitaire.

Then he propelled her out of the library and into the corridor, stopping before a gilt-framed mirror. He stood behind her, his hands resting on her bare shoulders. Their eyes met in the mirror. An almost palpable spark flashed in the shadowed air.

"Look," he commanded. "See how beautiful you are."

The satisfaction in his tone shivered through her, and

she rebelled to think that he viewed her as a pretty possession. Rather than admire herself, she was struck by how
perfect they looked together, she in her white ball gown
with diamonds glinting at her throat and in her blond, upswept hair . . . and he all lean masculine perfection, his
roguishly dark features displaying a dangerous allure.

"It is merely an illusion," she whispered, speaking more
to her own private thoughts than to him.

"But you are *my* illusion." He bent closer, holding her
gaze in the mirror, his breath stirring the downy hairs at
the nape of her neck. "You are mine alone."

They arrived early at Sarah's town house. A balding butler
led them down a gilded corridor and through a doorway,
where he intoned their arrival. At Drake's side, Alicia entered a cozy yellow sitting room.

Sarah stood as if frozen by surprise, her fine dark brows
winged upward. The vibrant green silk of her ball gown
enhanced her sable hair and long-lashed eyes. An heirloom
emerald necklace adorned her throat.

Alicia hurried forward to place a kiss on that smooth
white cheek. "Oh, Sarah, do forgive me. We've arrived too
soon. I hope we haven't inconvenienced you."

"It's quite all right."

There was a stiff formality to her that belied their friendship of the past week. A thought dismayed Alicia more than
she cared to admit. Did Sarah regret her offer? Would she
scorn Drake?

"May I present my husband," Alicia said, stepping back
and watching the two of them. "Mr. Drake Wilder."

He raised Sarah's hand to his lips. "Your Grace. It's a
pleasure to meet so dear a friend of my wife's."

"Mr. Wilder," Sarah said with cool hauteur. "You're
quite the mystery man. Alicia has divulged little about
you."

"As she has done with you. I look forward to becoming better acquainted."

His mouth slanted into that smile of practiced charm, the one that too often caused a disgraceful weakness in Alicia's knees. But Sarah seemed impervious to his masculine allure. She cast her gaze toward an arrangement of chairs by the night-shrouded window. Only then did Alicia notice the small boy standing at attention there.

Her heart turned over. Sarah's son.

The duke had his mother's hair, falling in soft brownish black curls below his ears. But there the resemblance ended. Solemn of face, he looked like a miniature adult in knee breeches and tailored gray coat, lace at his throat and cuffs.

Her skirt swishing, Sarah went to his side, placing her hand on his shoulder. She glanced rather anxiously at Alicia and Drake. "I was just saying good night to my son, William. Take a bow to our guests, darling."

Obediently, the four-year-old bent at the waist, one small arm clasped to his front, the other in back.

Alicia walked forward and curtsied to him, holding the pose for a moment so that she could look into his sober brown eyes. "Your Grace," she said. "I am Lady Alicia, your Mama's friend. I do hope we can become friends, too."

Saying nothing, he lowered his gaze to his polished black shoes.

"I'm sure he is delighted to meet you," Sarah said quickly. "It is just that . . . he isn't easy with strangers. Since his father's passing, we've not gone out much."

Alicia's heart ached for him. This past week, Sarah had made excuses for not introducing him, saying he was at his lessons or taking a nap. She had been protecting the timid boy, Alicia realized. Aside from his mother and the nursery staff, William would encounter few other people. It must be difficult for an only child to lose his father, however negligent Featherstone had been. And it would be daunting for one so young to shoulder the position of a duke.

"Perhaps we might go on a picnic sometime with your mama," she suggested. "Would you like that?"

William lifted his shoulders in a noncommittal shrug.

"If you were to fashion a little boat," Drake said, "I daresay we could find a pond on which to sail it."

Alicia rose quickly to her feet. She hadn't realized he stood behind her. But his attention wasn't on her; he watched William.

William watched the floor.

"That's very kind of you, Mr. Wilder," Sarah said with a concerned glance at her son. "But really I wouldn't dream of troubling you—either of you."

"It's no trouble," Drake said. He hunkered down in front of William. "Perhaps you would prefer a visit to the circus to see the acrobats, the clowns, the trapeze artists. There is even a magician who can perform the most amazing tricks."

The boy slid a cautiously interested glance at him.

"What's this?" Drake reached behind William's ear and produced a sparkling guinea. "I think you must wash better behind your ears."

William's eyes rounded. Almost reverently, he took the gold coin, turning it over and over as if to discover its secret. "Please, sir, how did you do that?"

"Magic. Shall I make it disappear again?"

William gave a vigorous nod.

Drake placed the guinea in one palm, closed his fingers into a fist, and turned it over. He tapped the back of his hand and paused for dramatic effect. When he opened his palm, the coin was gone.

William crowed with delight.

Sarah stood watching, smiling, as Drake performed his sleight of hand again, and Alicia was amazed not so much by the street urchin's trick as by his willingness to entertain a little boy. It was a side she had never seen of him—nor would have believed he possessed if she weren't witnessing it right now. Had he ever wanted children of his own? Had he felt the same longing for a family that she had once felt, before Mama had taken ill?

She shook off the intrusive questions. Marriage served only one purpose for him—to satisfy his social-climbing ambitions. Besides, she had sworn to deny him his rights as a husband, and for a reason aside from his unsuitable character. It was best that she never bear children. No matter how much she craved a son or daughter to love, she must not risk having a child who might inherit Mama's weakness of mind.

And yet as they left for the party, her heart still ached for the girl who had dreamed of love and a family of her own.

"Gerald?" Alicia said in astonishment.

Stopping with Drake and Sarah on the steps to the Cuthberts' stone mansion, she stared at her brother. He rode on horseback, bypassing the long procession of carriages waiting to discharge their noble occupants. Strains of music drifted from inside the house, and the torches along the drive cast a golden glow over the young earl. Looking uncommonly smart in a peacock-green coat and yellow knee breeches, he swung down from his mount and handed the reins to a waiting groom.

"Let's hope no one tosses a tomato at me for cutting in line," he said, grinning as he made a bow to the ladies. "Ali. And Your Grace of Featherstone, is it?"

"Why, is this the little brat who dared to spy on his sister and her friend?" Sarah said, her eyes glinting in the torchlight. "I daresay you've grown a bit since then."

"Tell that to Ali," Gerald said on a dramatic sigh. "She

would have me still confined to the nursery, well away from this glorious event."

Alicia barely heard their exchange. Her gaze was fixed on the sleek reddish mare that a groom led away by the reins.

Heedless of the scandalous stares from the arriving guests, she picked up her hem and dashed after the groom. She took hold of the bridle and stroked the horse's neck. Those liquid brown eyes held a spark of recognition, and the velvety mouth nuzzled her, looking for a treat. "Pet," Alicia murmured. "I'm so happy to see you again."

Dazed with delight, she returned to her party. "Oh, Ger. You didn't tell me about Pet. However did you manage to get her back?"

Her brother shrugged. "The feisty old girl kept tossing Chesterfield. So I persuaded him to give her up."

"You returned the two hundred guineas?"

"More or less."

The answer might have satisfied her had she not intercepted a telling glance between the two men. Then Drake turned to her. "Come," he said. "There'll be time later to chat."

Prodded by suspicion, Alicia took his arm as they joined the elegant throng gliding up the steps. Gerald and Sarah led the way through the opened front doors, past the poker-stiff footmen standing at attention, and into an enormous entrance hall crowded with guests. They joined a receiving line wending toward their host and hostess, who were stationed by the grand staircase.

A multifaceted crystal chandelier sparkled like a thousand stars. Enormous vases of lilies perfumed the air. The hum of genteel conversation echoed to the vaulted ceiling. Sarah and Gerald walked ahead, engrossed in teasing each other like brother and sister.

Alicia seized the chance to interrogate her husband.

"Tell me," she murmured for his ears alone. "Have you encouraged Gerald to gamble again?"

He raised an eyebrow in the perfect imitation of innocence. "Of course I haven't."

"Well, I don't believe for a moment that Viscount Chesterfield would give up Pet unless it was worth his while. He's coveted the mare for years. So where did Gerald procure the additional funds?"

Drake shrugged. "I heard he found employment."

"Fiddle-faddle," she said under her breath, fixing a smile on her face for the benefit of anyone who might be watching. Gerald claimed to have procured a post in a financial institution, but he had refused to elaborate. She suspected he was too proud to admit he labored for a pittance as a lowly bank clerk. "He cannot squander two hundred guineas on a horse. How will he pay his bills?"

"You needn't mollycoddle him. That is his concern, not yours."

"It *is* my concern," she hissed. "He's my brother. Not that *you* could ever understand the close ties of family."

The moment the words were out, she regretted that last remark. It was unkind and uncivil. Regardless of Drake's provocation.

An unreadable darkness flickered in his eyes. "I'll tell you, then," he said, crowding closer to her, "if only to cease your badgering. I gave him the funds." He bared his teeth in a smile. "So that no one would think ill of me for allowing my brother-in-law to go about London on foot."

His nearness raised the fine hairs on Alicia's skin. She shouldn't feel this softening toward him; she should be affronted that he'd further indebted her to him. By his own admission, he had acted for a selfish purpose. Money had paved his path to respectability, and he would have the nobility believe him a gentleman.

Yet . . . he had given a wonderful gift to Gerald. And

not just any horse. He had purchased the prize mare that her brother had raised from a filly.

Before she could sort through her confusion, Sarah turned, her eyes flashing with determined gaiety. "Make ready," she whispered. "The fun is about to begin."

Alicia's palms felt damp inside the white kidskin gloves. Already, she noticed the stares, some hostile, others merely curious. She assured herself that few would recognize a young lady among so many others making their come-out five years ago. Yet some women were putting their heads close, raising their fans to hide their scandalized whispering. One lady turned to her neighbor, then another and another as the news spread.

They reached the stairway, where a rather stout lady in pink silk curtsied to Sarah. "Your Grace, you honor us. Your first appearance in society since your untimely loss."

Sarah acknowledged her with a regal nod. "Lady Cuthbert, allow me to introduce my guests. My dearest friend, Lady Alicia Pemberton, now Mrs. Wilder. And her husband, Mr. Drake Wilder."

Lady Cuthbert's fawning smile sagged. Swaying as if on the verge of a swoon, she raised her jeweled lorgnette, and the circles of glass magnified her eyes into huge brown orbs. "The Wilders? Here?" she said faintly. "Good gracious. I—I don't know what to say. . . ."

Her teeth gritted, Alicia dipped the obligatory curtsy. "You might say you are delighted to have us as your guests—"

"*We* are delighted," Drake broke in. He kissed Lady Cuthbert's plump hand and gazed into her enlarged eyes. "*You* are a saint for braving the scandal, a woman of open mind and warm heart. People will admire your generosity of spirit."

Looking rather dazed, she lowered the lorgnette. "Oh . . . do you really think so?"

"Without a doubt, my lady. You are kindness personified."

While she blushed and blustered, they moved on to his lordship, a creaky old gentleman who cupped his ear as if he couldn't quite make out their names. "Carry on, carry on," he said, waving them past.

Then they were walking up the broad, curving staircase to the reception rooms, Alicia on one side of Drake, Sarah on the other. Gerald had gone ahead to greet a friend.

Sarah's eyes sparkled. "There," she whispered, "I knew we had a chance to get past the Cuthberts. But I didn't realize it would be so simple. Mr. Wilder, I do believe you could charm the stripes off a tiger."

He graced her with that devil-may-care grin. "I far prefer to charm the ladies."

"I can see that," she said tartly.

With a wary smile, the duchess gazed at him as if only just realizing his attractiveness. A pair of young ladies glided by, casting coy, appreciative glances.

A fierce heat twisted in Alicia. It was mostly irritation at Drake for his effect on women—but also resentment of Sarah, too. Mortified, Alicia realized she was jealous. *Jealous.* She might have once lost a suitor to Sarah, but it was unworthy even to think that her dearest friend could have designs on Drake. Or that she herself could care!

They strolled through the crush, Sarah introducing them to anyone she could corner, blatantly using her exalted position to quell any snubs. Drake knew some of the gentlemen by name, presumably from his club. More than one gave him a wary nod or a surprised greeting. And of course Alicia encountered former acquaintances, too. Some acted friendly, others seemed embarrassed, and a few turned away, pretending not to recognize her. She held her chin high, determined to appear the picture of serenity.

In the ballroom, the guests mingled near the dance floor, waiting for the first set. Their conversation and laughter made a pleasant buzz in the long room with its high, gilded ceiling. The mirrored walls reflected the dazzling brilliance of the chandeliers.

Sarah had excused herself to chat with an acquaintance. Leaning against a pillar festooned with gold ribbons, Drake watched the crowd. Despite his casual stance, he appeared alert, almost tense in a way that puzzled Alicia. Was he looking for someone in particular? Before she could ask, a man sauntered toward them.

A thatch of muddy-brown curls capped his long-nosed features, and a dark burgundy coat with gold buttons topped a green waistcoat and tan breeches. "Wilder," he said with a sniff. "Haven't you toddled into the wrong place tonight? This is a party for respectable folk."

"If *respectable* is the measure of a man, Mountjoy, I must question your presence, as well."

Those thin lips curled. He focused his pale eyes on Alicia. "I understand this is the new Mrs. Wilder?"

She remembered Baron Mountjoy. Long ago, when she was still in the schoolroom, his mother had befriended Mama, dropping hints about a match between their families, though even then, Alicia had never liked his shallow pretensions. Politely, she said, "My lord. What a pleasure to see you again. Is your mother well?"

"Quite so. She is visiting with the Marchioness of Bancroft." He inclined his head toward a grouping of gilt chairs occupied by the matrons of society.

"If you will excuse me, I must pay my respects to her."

She took a step. He neatly blocked her path, regarding her and Drake with an almost triumphant conceit. "Spare yourself the humiliation. She would never acknowledge *you*."

Alicia held on to her smile. "Surely she can accept my marriage for the sake of an old family friendship."

"Ah, but it is more than your unfortunate marriage—far more." He gave a nasty chuckle. "There is also the matter of your mother. She has . . . how shall I say it? Bats in her belfry."

The breath left Alicia's lungs. The music faded to a dull echo. Before the heat of rage could unfreeze her tongue, Drake took hold of Mountjoy's arm. Only Alicia was near enough to discern the pressure of that grip, to see the baron's face whiten.

"Apologize to the lady," Drake said in a pleasant tone.

"You . . . oaf . . ."

Drake's fingers moved slightly, squeezing all the tighter. "I'm waiting."

Mountjoy's desperate gaze flashed to Alicia. He babbled, "F—forgive me, my lady. I spoke out of turn."

Drake released him. "Not very prettily done, but we'll overlook your lack of manners."

Mountjoy rubbed his arm. "How dare you," he whined. "You nearly broke a bone."

"A pity I didn't. One must behave oneself when out in public."

The two men exchanged a look, Mountjoy glaring, Drake unsmiling. With a huff of contempt, the baron turned on his heel.

"I haven't yet dismissed you," Drake said in a low-pitched voice.

The nobleman glanced over his shoulder. "Do not speak as if you have any rights over me—"

"I expect your vowels to be paid in full. Tomorrow."

That narrow face grew even paler. "Cad! You agreed to wait. You know I haven't the funds till next quarter—"

"Tomorrow," Drake repeated in that firm, civil tone.

Mountjoy's thin lips opened and shut; then he slunk away, disappearing into the throng of people.

Alicia fought the unladylike urge to gloat. She shouldn't be glad he owed Drake a gambling debt. She shouldn't rejoice to see another person defeated. It wasn't charitable of her. But he had voiced the one insult she had feared to hear tonight.

"He has no right to mock Mama," she said murderously. "Even in a fit of madness, she is far sweeter and more genteel than he or his mother could ever hope to be."

Large and comforting, his hand settled at the back of her waist. "Don't give Mountjoy another thought. He is a pompous ass."

"He is a prune-faced weasel," she corrected, seeking a more demeaning image.

"A hen-hearted coxcomb," Drake offered.

"A ham-fisted clodpate."

"A brainless sapskull."

"A pudding-headed" —she scoured her mind for another slur—"nincompoop."

Drake chuckled, his fingers stroking lightly over her back. "Running out of insults, are you? I never thought to see the moment."

She tried to hold on to her anger. But his eyes crinkled at the corners and his dimples carved an attractive humor into his rogue's face. A smile nudged at her mouth; then she laughed so gaily that a cluster of ladies aimed outraged glares at them.

Alicia didn't care. Let the *ton* spread their petty gossip. They wouldn't dampen her spirits tonight.

"Thank you," she murmured. Then, lest he think she needed him to fight her battles, she added, "For defending Mama."

"I did it for you."

Her heart gave a little jump, and she had to remind herself not to trust that lazy smile of his. He was more interested in fighting for his own respect than for hers. Still, his protectiveness pleased her somehow.

She felt suddenly alive, her senses attuned to the magic of the night. In the candlelight, the ballroom glowed like a fairyland. The orchestra played softly, though the dancing had not yet begun. The tension weighing on Alicia lightened and lifted, floating away on the lovely notes. Until this moment, she hadn't realized how much she had missed going to parties. Their penury and Mama's illness had required her to remain at home, though she had done so as much out of love as necessity.

But tonight she could revel in the festivities, and oh, she might dance again. The hours ahead stretched out like a sparkling strand of diamonds. With the toe of her slipper, she tapped out a rhythm on the polished parquet floor.

She noticed Drake scanning the assemblage again. His gaze moved in a slow, systematic survey; then he watched the door for new arrivals. His vigilant manner piqued her curiosity. For a man who had plotted so nefariously to raise his social consequence, he didn't seem inclined to mingle with the nobility.

"Are you looking for someone?" she asked.

"Anyone in skirts." On that outrageous remark, he lifted two glasses of champagne from the tray of a passing footman and handed one to her. "However, you'll be pleased to hear you are the belle of the ball."

It was the second time tonight he'd flattered her, and just as with the first, an insidious softening swept her body. "Save your charm for someone more gullible," she said, taking a sip from her glass. The sparkling wine slid down her throat in a burst of tiny bubbles, and she released an involuntary sigh of pleasure. "Mmm."

"It's been a long time, hasn't it?"

"I beg your pardon?"

"Since you've drunk champagne. Or accepted a compliment from a man."

She had the dizzying sense that he could see straight into her soul. She took another reckless swallow. "Swaggerer. You know nothing about me."

"Sweetheart. I'm ready whenever you'd like to change that."

His carnal suggestion should have shocked Alicia. But she felt a guilty pleasure that he found her desirable. She was aware of his fingertips tracing down her spine, brushing the curve of her bottom. He made the movement seem casual, yet his touch ignited a rush of sparks beneath her lace-trimmed undergarments. The smoldering intensity of his eyes held her enthralled.

It was useless trying to fathom why her mind failed to dictate to her body. Useless to wonder why she felt no inclination to seek out other company. For some mysterious reason, she had even enjoyed trading insults with him tonight. It had become a game with them, this matching of wits.

"You two have been hiding for quite long enough."

Sarah's quiet scolding broke the spell. Alicia spun around to see the duchess regarding them. The too-quick motion of her fan, fashioned of green silk with ivory spindles, betrayed her irritation.

"We haven't strayed from the ballroom," Alicia protested.

"What Her Grace means," Drake murmured, a glint in his eyes, "is that we seemed unaware of anyone else present."

A blush tingled up Alicia's throat and into her cheeks. "*I* am well aware of our surroundings. The music is starting for the first set."

"Just so," Sarah said. "Hurry along, now. You must dance and mingle and be seen by everyone."

In the middle of the room, lines were forming, one for the men, the other for the ladies. Alicia slipped into position opposite Drake just as the lilting tune commenced. She lifted her gloved hand to his, and as their fingers touched, she wondered wildly if he even knew how to dance. He hadn't, after all, had a gentleman's upbringing.

But her fears proved ungrounded; he performed the intricate steps with flawless grace. All the while he watched her. The light from the chandeliers cast a sheen on his coal-black hair and made shadows beneath his cheekbones. He looked as arrogant as any nobleman present. And she realized with jolt how easily he fit into this glittering world.

The lines shifted, forcing them apart, and she found herself partnered with a portly man with side-whiskers. Drake squired a young miss in virginal white, who simpered when he smiled at her. Alicia forced her gaze away. Let him enchant every woman he met. *She* certainly didn't care.

She concentrated on the dance, on being pleasant and giving no one cause to gossip. And she reveled in the joy of gliding to the music, letting the notes guide her feet as if on air. She spied Gerald dancing in another line, and couldn't help smiling when he winked at her.

All the while, she was keenly aware of her husband as they moved farther apart down the long lines. When at last the steps brought them back together, the tune ended, and Sarah appeared with a timid, freckle-faced gentleman in tow. He stammered an invitation to dance, and Alicia lacked the heart to refuse him.

Drake gallantly relinquished her. As he walked away, he scanned the assemblage again, and again she had the odd impression that he sought someone in particular. Who? A member of his club? Someone else who owed him money?

As the evening progressed, she caught sight of him from time to time. He had no trouble finding dance partners. The ladies congregated nearby, drawn by his notoriety and the suggestion of wildness behind his civilized appearance. Time and again, Alicia saw him leading a woman onto the dance floor, conversing with her, flattering her no doubt, using his charm to demolish the barriers that had barred him from this exclusive circle.

He had made himself a social success. The thought was

oddly dispiriting. He had needed his wife only to get him through the door.

So be it. She was glad to be rid of any obligation to him. Glad to have discharged her debt. So why did she feel this confusing jumble of fascination and longing?

Her face began to ache from smiling. She sat out a set and sipped champagne. There were only so many sprightly comments that one could make to gentlemen who were either too snooty to acknowledge the bride of a gamester or too preoccupied with their own conceits. Had they been so dull five years ago? Had she been so impatient for the company of one man alone?

She lost sight of Drake. He wasn't anywhere among the colorful lines of dancers. Champagne glass in hand, Alicia left the ballroom and glanced into the other reception rooms. She felt pleasantly woozy, unable to lie to herself. In all good conscience, she couldn't say that she sought a respite from the press of people. No, she was looking for her husband.

Downstairs, tables had been set up in the drawing room and guests sat playing cards. The library echoed with the voices of gentlemen discussing politics. The dining room rang with the clatter of china and silver as footmen carried in platters from which eddied the aromas of roasted beef and fresh-baked bread. Supper would be served at midnight. But Alicia had no interest in food.

Then she saw him.

In a dimly lit room toward the rear of the house, Drake stood in the shadows, speaking urgently to someone behind the partly closed door. The lamplight from the passageway cast his profile into sharp relief. A concentrated intensity kept his attention focused on his companion. He spoke in a voice too low for her to discern the words.

A sickening possibility lurched in Alicia. Was he alone with a woman?

Fury eradicated the brief stab of pain. Blast him. She

would not be shamed by his philandering. Not here, in front of the entire *ton*.

Marching forward, she thrust back the door. And stopped, struck by recognition of the tall, familiar figure standing in the gloom. His haughty facade radiated hostility.

Lord Hailstock.

Chapter Fourteen

Drake had been too impatient to choose another dance partner. They held no interest for him, these women of privilege who would condescend to flirt with a man of ill repute only in the safety of a crowded ballroom. He had borne their insipid company for one reason alone. So that he could watch the arched doorway for a late arrival.

But the Marquess of Hailstock did not appear.

His absence gnawed at Drake. He had been certain his father would attend this gathering. Hailstock prided himself on being a pillar of society. He liked to prowl his exclusive territory—and Drake burned for the moment when his lordship came face-to-face with his bastard.

Intending to look elsewhere, Drake strolled restlessly toward the door. He scanned the ballroom one last time. And spied, through the resplendent swarm, the one lady who could rivet his attention.

Alicia. His wife.

Her slim back to him, she walked alone toward the refreshment tables. The candlelight cast a halo on her fair hair. With each sinuous movement, her gown brushed womanly curves. She held her chin high as if to mock anyone who might dispute her right to be here.

This had been an ordeal for her, to face disapproval and

scandal. Yet she comported herself like a queen.

For one mad moment, the pull of his wife's attraction surpassed his need for vengeance. He was tempted to go after her, to make lewd remarks so that he could enjoy her reaction. He wanted to touch her, to remind her that she belonged to him, to see that spark of defiance in her eyes. He wanted to lure her into a darkened room and make long slow love to her. The craving shook him with its intensity.

Turning toward the door, he ruthlessly banished her from his mind. Lady Alicia meant nothing to him—nothing beyond his means to get back at Hailstock.

The familiar acid of anger burned inside him. He walked through the crowds, ignoring the murmurings as he passed. Though he'd had no dearth of dance partners, these snobs didn't truly accept him. They would tolerate an outsider in their midst only because he had been forced upon them. Little did they know, their petty animosities merely amused him.

Descending the grand staircase, he glanced around. A quick accounting of the card players in the drawing room elicited no success. A red-haired dandy gave a languid wave, inviting him to join their game, but Drake politely shook his head. His heels rang out as he rounded the corner past the staircase. There must be a library where the politicians would gather. It was a likely spot to check.

The rumble of male voices grew louder as he neared a doorway. Then a man walked out, his movements jerky and fast. The light from the wall sconce fell on his thickly silvered black hair and arrogant features.

No surprise widened those frosty gray eyes. Hailstock didn't so much as flinch. He merely regarded his son with cold contempt.

Someone had told him. He already had heard that an infamous commoner had invaded his privileged circle.

Drake wanted to drive his fist into the wall. He'd been cheated. Cheated of the moment he had anticipated for twenty years. And the more fool he for not anticipating this turn of events.

Wheeling around, Hailstock stalked down the corridor and thrust open a door. He stood waiting, his face stern, his hands pushing back his finely tailored coat. He looked like a father intending to thrash his son.

"Get in here," he growled.

Drake had never hated him more than in that moment. He was forced into the position of either obeying like a chastened child or refusing to accede, thereby flouting his own plans. Cursing under his breath, he strode forward. The supercilious tyrant would not direct the course of this confrontation.

As befitting his self-importance, Hailstock led the way into a dimly lit chamber. He made a move to shut the door.

Drake caught the panel and stopped it. "Afraid someone might see us together and guess the truth, *Father*?"

The marquess's lips thinned. "Desist in this fantasy of yours. I am no more your father than the Prince Regent himself."

"Deny it all you like. But you did have an affair with my mother in Edinburgh thirty years ago."

"You have no proof beyond that stickpin she stole."

Once, just once, Drake wanted to hear Hailstock acknowledge his paternity. And by the devil he would. "Tell me, my lord, if your net worth is presently four hundred sixty thousand pounds—"

"Wretch!" Hailstock broke in angrily. "Where did you come by that knowledge?"

"—and through various investments, you earn a tidy four percent annual interest, what size will be the fortune that you leave to dear James, should you die in, say, eighteen years' time?"

Those eyes narrowed slightly in calculation. He made a sharp, dismissing motion with his hand. "So that's what this is all about—you're planning to blackmail me. Name your price, then. Tell me how much it will cost to send you back to the sewer out of which you crawled."

Drake's chest muscles tightened. "Keep your bloody fortune. I have my own. Just answer my question."

"I'll not discuss my personal finances with the likes of you."

"Then *I'll* solve our hypothetical problem. Your worth will be precisely nine hundred forty-three thousand, nine hundred eight pounds." Tasting triumph, he went on in a low tone, "But you already knew that, of course. Because you, too, have the ability to figure complex sums without resorting to paper and pen. It is a talent I inherited. From you."

Hailstock said nothing. He stood, shoulders stiff, fists clenched at his sides.

"Go on, test me if you like," Drake said softly. "Give me any combination of numbers and I'll give you the answer."

"I've no interest in parlor tricks. Now step aside."

"No. You can't walk away and pretend I don't exist. Not any longer." He focused the full force of his will upon this man who had abandoned him to poverty as an infant. "Know this, my lord. Every time you enter a ballroom, you will see me. Every time you attend a dinner party, I'll be sitting there. Every time you talk politics in the library, I'll challenge your opinions."

"You're playing games. You'll soon tire of this charade."

"It's only a matter of time before people begin to notice the resemblance." A steely edge to his voice, Drake added, "It's already happened."

"Liar. No one has seen us together."

"Lady Brockway knows us both. She told me I favor someone she once knew."

For one tension-filled moment, Hailstock stared, his face as still and pale as a death mask. Then he scoffed, "And you believe that madwoman? She seldom knows her own name."

Drake remembered her weeping, the dread she had been unable to articulate. "Did you frighten her?" he said in a harsh whisper. "Did you threaten to lock her away forever?"

Before Hailstock could reply, a movement flashed in the corridor. Someone pushed open the door.

Alicia stood there, her slender form limned by lamplight from the passageway. A frown creased her brow as she stared from Hailstock to Drake. Then she curtsied to the marquess.

"My lord, pardon me for intruding. I thought . . . you were someone else."

Resenting her obeisance, Drake hooked his hand beneath her elbow and brought her to her feet. In a conversational tone, he said, "Hailstock and I were renewing our acquaintance. I was just commenting on the resemblance between him and his son."

The marquess made a strangled sound deep in his chest.

Alicia glanced at him in confusion, then returned her gaze to Drake. "I wasn't aware that you knew James. He's an invalid. He seldom leaves the house."

"So his lordship has informed me. Yet he must be the young man I saw riding in Hailstock's carriage not a fortnight ago."

"He does go for the occasional drive in the park," Hailstock said rigidly. "Attended by his physician, of course."

Drake considered making him squirm further, but reluctantly decided against it. He was skating too close to the truth, and Alicia had the intelligence to catch him. "Ah, that explains it," he said. "A pity he doesn't get out more often."

Stepping toward Hailstock, Alicia touched his sleeve. "How *is* James?"

"Quite melancholy these days, I fear." The marquess settled his hand over hers. "You should know, he's asked about you. He misses your visits quite dreadfully."

"Please convey my apologies and tell James I'll call on him soon. If that is permissible to you, my lord."

"Certainly, my lady. You are always welcome in my home."

Drake clenched his jaw, fighting the fury inside him. Presumptuous noble. He touched Alicia as if he had the right to do so. He probably believed in *droit du seigneur*.

Drake would kill him first.

Sliding his arm around her waist, he pulled Alicia against him. He splayed his fingers over her hip in an unsubtle sign of ownership. "You will excuse us now, Hailstock. *My wife* requires my attentions."

The marquess glowered balefully as Drake steered her out of the room and into the corridor.

"Why were you rude to him?" Alicia said in a chiding whisper. "I didn't realize you even knew his lordship. Has he been to your club?"

"Yes." But only once. To warn Drake away from her.

"Is he indebted to you, then? Is that why you two were snapping at each other like dogs?"

Seized by a dark humor, he ran his fingertip down the dainty slant of her nose. "Money is irrelevant. You see, we both want the same bone."

She stared uncomprehendingly. Then she pursed her lips and tried to twist away. "How flattering to be compared to a bone."

He kept a firm hold on her, securing her lithe form to his side. With lingering anger, he stated, "You're damn beautiful, and well you know it. The crux of the matter is, my wife will not go calling on other men."

Her steps slowed. Her glare pierced him. "Are you forbidding me to visit a friend of my family? A helpless invalid who cannot walk?"

Her logic made him feel uncomfortably like a cur. Still,

he despised the notion of her straying into Hailstock's territory. Befriending Hailstock's legitimate son—the half-brother Drake had never known. Without thinking, he said, "You may visit James, but only in my company."

Alicia released a huff of displeasure. "And when will that be?"

Never. "Soon. When I'm not busy at the club."

"I'll remember you said that."

She gave him a hard look of concentration. A look so intent that her heel caught on the long carpet runner in the corridor, and she stumbled. As he tightened his arm to steady her, he savored the inward bend of her waist, the ripe curve of her hip. He was struck by the fantasy of following those contours to hidden places, to moist womanly heat and soft inner flesh. To a place that belonged to him alone, though Alicia didn't accept that fact.

Yet.

The sounds of conversation and music drifted from the reception rooms. Spying a doorway beneath the staircase, Drake steered her into a small, darkened chamber. The cloakroom, he knew by the scents of wool and leather, the brush of fabrics against his coat sleeve.

Alicia's face formed a perfect oval in the gloom. He could just see the innocent blue of her eyes. "Why are we in here?" she asked.

"Because I prefer privacy when I kiss my woman."

He dipped his head and claimed her mouth. She was warm and velvety, sweet and feminine. Her lips parted in surprise, and he took swift advantage, tasting the tang of champagne on her tongue as he caressed her with his mouth. Her fingers caught at the front of his coat. He expected resistance. But instead of pushing him away, she leaned into him, releasing a little sigh. Heat surged hard in him, spreading fast, igniting the need to delve deeper into her mysteries.

Cupping her bottom, he lifted her against him, and she

quivered, her arms wreathed around his neck. Her eagerness enflamed him. *His wife.* He wanted to plunge into her, to brand her as his once and for all.

The barrier of clothing frustrated him. He grasped her skirt, intending to draw it to her waist, but the trill of female voices intruded through the fog of passion. Out in the corridor, two women passed by, chattering.

Hell. What madness to take her here. In the midst of a party.

She would enjoy it, of course. But she would never forgive him.

Raising his head, he gazed down into her dreamy eyes. She clung to his shoulders, her breasts crushed to him, her submissiveness utterly unlike the prickly puritan he'd married. Though he knew his effect on women, he had the sudden suspicion that something more had caused that dazed look.

"You're drunk."

"I'm not!"

"The truth, now. How many glasses of champagne have you had tonight?"

Her brows drew together as she considered. "Only two. No, three. Oh, bother . . . perhaps four at the outside."

His mind leapt to a nefarious plan. He fought—and won—a brief tussle with his conscience. Bargain or not, she was his wife. His by the laws of God and man.

Inhaling her heady scent, he caressed her cheek. "Find the duchess and see if she can't ride home with someone else. I'll fetch our carriage."

"We're leaving?"

"You're in no condition to remain here."

"But . . . we should mingle. There's still the supper dance—and hours of dancing afterwards." She tilted her head as if confused. "You do wish to be accepted by the *ton,* don't you?"

He couldn't admit he had already accomplished his purpose here. Brushing a kiss over her moist lips, he told her a version of the truth. "I've had my fill of the aristocracy for one night. I'm taking you home."

As the coach pulled away from the Cuthberts' mansion, Alicia watched the torches slide past in a blur of brilliance. Then there was only the light from the colza oil lantern mounted on the inside wall of the coach, the enclosed flame flickering with the motion of the vehicle. The intimacy of the setting made her heart beat faster. She felt giddy, and from more than a few glasses of wine.

You're damn beautiful, and well you know it.

Drake sat beside her on the plush velvet seat. His leg brushed hers. She should be offended by his vulgar cursing, by his aggressive behavior, by his high-handed insistence on leaving the ball. Yet his mastery fed fuel to the banked fire within her.

That kiss. It had been even more wonderful than the first time, at their wedding. He had tasted her deeply, and she had done the same to him. Taking shocking license, he'd pressed their bodies together, and she had *liked* it. His touch had aroused an almost frantic ache deep within her. The memory made her breathless—but not with indignation. She yearned to feel his hands on her again.

Was this love?

As quickly as the intolerable thought flitted into her mind, she rejected it. She couldn't possibly love a gambler, a man so disreputable he'd forced her into marriage. He was a cad, a knave, a scapegrace. Though, granted, he wasn't *entirely* wicked. He had done a few worthy acts. . . .

Baffled by the contradictions in him, she turned her head to study her husband. He lounged against the cushions like a debaucher in his lair . . . no, like an aristocrat confident of his place in the world. The lamplight etched shadows beneath the slash of high cheekbones. He looked sinister . . . and as seductive as sin.

Who was the real Drake Wilder?

His hand descended over hers. Intense and caressing, his gaze burned into her. "Are you dizzy?"

Only from you. She should freeze him with an icy remark. Instead, a question tumbled out. "How can you be an unprincipled rogue if you do good deeds?"

His eyes widened ever so slightly. Then he smiled that oh-so-charming smile. "I always have a contemptible reason for everything I do. You should know that by now."

"So what was your reason for purchasing cartloads of theatrical costumes for Mama?"

He shrugged. "They keep her occupied so that you may go out in society with me."

Alicia conceded the logic in that. "Then why were you kind to William? Why would you bother entertaining a little boy with magic tricks?"

"I wanted to win the approval of the duchess, of course."

Of course. "And what about Kitty? Any person of rank would have discharged her. In fact, a deaf maid would never have been hired at all."

"And because she values her post, she works twice as hard as anyone else," he countered. "So you see, I benefit from increased productivity. It is merely good business practice."

He made it all sound so tidy and reasonable. Yet Alicia suspected a flaw in his smooth explanations. A flaw that touched a tender place inside her. "I wonder," she mused, "if you *want* me to think badly of you."

For a heartbeat, something flashed in his eyes. Something that came and went so quickly, she couldn't be sure if it was surprise or annoyance. Or something else entirely.

"And I believe you're being far too serious," he said. "Better we should celebrate our success tonight." So saying, he leaned down and pulled out a long drawer from beneath the opposite seat. He straightened up, brandishing a tall green bottle and two glasses. "Behold, the bubbly."

"Champagne?" Alicia glanced down in shock at the array of decanters and glassware tucked into the padded lining of the drawer. "You carry spirits in your coach?"

He shoved the drawer shut with the toe of his leather shoe. "No maidenly swoons, please. And this"—he brandished the bottle—"I snitched from the butler's pantry. Don't tell the Cuthberts."

He winked at her, and an involuntary smile demolished her attempt at disapproval. "You can't really mean to open that here."

"I do, indeed." He handed her both glasses. "Hold these, if you will."

Turning his attention to the bottle, he tugged off the metal closure. With an explosive whoosh, the cork popped out and champagne sprayed the interior of the coach.

Gasping, Alicia ducked from the mist that prickled her face and arms. "Drake! You shouldn't have—"

"The glasses," he urged.

She thrust them forward, and he diverted the foaming stream into them, ending the shower. Laughter bubbled in her like the champagne in her glass. She shouldn't find humor in his lack of restraint. A puddle soaked into the expensive velvet covering the opposite seat. Damp spots marred her expensive gown. A droplet trickled down her cheek.

Catching it with her gloved fingertip, she fought against an appalled, incredulous delight. "For heaven's sake! You've stained the upholstery."

"It can be cleaned."

"And my dress. The silk is *ruined*."

"I'll buy you another."

"You are utterly uncivilized."

"I beg to differ." His grin incorrigible, he lifted his glass and toasted her. "There is nothing more civilized than fine wine in the company of a lovely woman."

Pleasure curled deeply within her. She felt dazzled by

his gallantry, dizzied by the admiration in his eyes. *Caution*, she told herself. *You're only a game to him. Take care to resist his charm.*

Summoning a semblance of calm, she sipped her champagne, relishing the tingling sensation over her tongue and down her throat. "You are a decadent man."

"Decadent? I'm depraved." Holding the bottle between his knees, he unknotted his cravat and yanked it free, exposing his strong male throat. Then he did something else shocking. He touched the strip of linen to the bare skin above her bosom.

Her hand shot up to grip his wrist. "Drake . . ." His name sounded more like a plea than an admonition. "Don't."

"I'm merely tidying up." He flashed her a bland smile, his white teeth gleaming. "Champagne leaves a sticky residue."

Imprudently, she let her hand drop to her lap. The gently rocking coach enclosed them in a bower apart from the world. His gaze lowering, he dabbed at her, starting at her shoulders and moving methodically downward, taking care around her necklace. The starched linen felt strange and masculine, oddly alluring. Her breasts felt taut and heavy. With every breath, she inhaled the warm, distinctive scent of him. Her fingers curled around her champagne glass, but she lacked the strength to lift it to her lips.

She told herself to be outraged by his boldness. Any other man would have offered her the use of his handkerchief while he discreetly looked in the other direction. Any other lady would have slapped Drake's face.

Or perhaps not. Perhaps this sort of intimacy was nothing unusual between husband and wife. What exactly did wedded couples *do* in the privacy of the bedchamber?

Remembering that lewd statue in his office, she squeezed her eyes shut. She mustn't think about straddling him, their naked limbs pressed together. She mustn't wonder how he would touch her, and where. For her, marriage could never follow a conventional path. And she'd known that long before she'd met Drake Wilder.

A sudden stimulating pressure at her bosom snapped Alicia to attention. She looked down at his dark head. He was kissing her. On her *breasts*.

A thrill of almost frightening intensity coursed through her. She threaded her fingers into the rough silk of his hair. "Please . . . you can't do this . . . you *mustn't*."

"Tell me you don't like it and I'll stop." He flicked his tongue into the valley between her breasts. "My God. You taste of champagne and roses."

His frank pleasure robbed her of breath. Surely he must detect the quickened beat of her heart. She pushed her hand beneath his jaw and turned his head to the side. "I don't like it. Don't you understand? I *loathe* you."

Drake scowled at her. She wanted to retract her cruel harshness, to explain the fears that strangled her. But she said nothing.

Slowly he straightened, the silence filled by the muffled clop-clop of hooves and the rattling of the wheels. His midnight-blue eyes seemed to penetrate her innermost secrets. She wanted to look away, but feared that any concession would weaken her resolve.

"This reluctance of yours," he bit out. "It isn't just that ridiculous agreement. Or your distaste for my character."

"I don't—" She bit down on her lip, unable to fully understand why her feelings toward him had undergone a subtle softening. Then, with cool deliberation, she lifted her glass and took a swallow of champagne. "I don't wish to discuss it," she said loftily. "Suffice to say, it's best you find your pleasure elsewhere."

"Best for whom? You?" He leaned closer, crowding her into the corner, a brooding harshness in his features. His fingers pressed almost painfully into her shoulder. "Tell me, my lady. Are you in love with Hailstock?"

"Certainly not!" she blurted out. "Why would you imagine *he* has anything to do with *us*?"

"He was your fiancé."

"He was never my fiancé. Granted, he'd asked me to marry him, but I couldn't because . . ." She stopped, her throat constricting.

"Because of your mother. The wretch wanted to lock her away." His taut expression growing more thoughtful, Drake continued to regard her, his grip easing, his fingers gently massaging her collarbone. "But you're not telling me everything."

Could he see the quiet torment in her heart?

Of course not. Men were dense creatures, too caught up in their own selfish pleasures to understand a woman's deeper emotions.

"There's nothing to tell. I've fulfilled our bargain, and that should suffice." Glaring at him over the rim of her glass, she drank defiantly and then added, "You must go away and leave me alone."

His expression took on a faint calculation. "You desire me. But you're afraid—"

"I'm *not*."

"I wonder . . . if you're afraid you might bear a child who will inherit your mother's madness."

His shrewd perception plumbed the sorrow buried within her. She wanted to deny it, to shield her private thoughts and feelings from him. By exposing her vulnerabilities, she would be placing herself into his power.

But perhaps he *should* know the truth. Perhaps then he would leave her be.

Concealing the ache inside her, she regarded him with a level gaze. "All right, then, I *am* afraid. It would be cruel to bring such a child into the world."

"You were ready to take that risk when first you came to me. You offered to be my mistress."

"I had no other choice." Then, her decision had been a

matter of life or death. Gerald would have been imprisoned for his debts. She and Mama would have been thrown out on the street to starve.

Drake refilled her glass, his hand steady despite the movement of the coach. "Has your mother always been addled?"

"What has that to do with anything?"

"Has she?"

Regarding him warily, she sipped her champagne. "When I was younger . . . she had spells where she behaved more like a sister than my mother. She would climb trees with me. And help me dress my dolls. . . ." A smile wavered and died on Alicia's mouth. "She also had episodes of melancholy, where she wept for days on end."

"Did she ever tell you what disturbed her?"

Alicia shook her head. "Papa forbade me to visit her chambers during those times. He said she needed rest and quiet."

"Her condition worsened after your father's death."

"Yes. She became . . ." —Alicia's throat constricted with pain and helpless affection—"as she is now."

Drake leaned toward her. "Did Lady Eleanor suffer a shock in her youth, something so unbearable that it could have overwhelmed her?"

Alicia blinked. "If you're suggesting that Mama's illness *isn't* inheritable—"

"I am, indeed. Your mother is a gentle, sensitive woman. It is conceivable that her condition was brought on by a trauma of some sort. I saw a similar reaction once—" His voice broke off abruptly.

"What do you mean?" she asked, intrigued in spite of herself.

Turning his gaze to the carriage window, he said, "I once found a woman lying by the roadside in Whitechapel. She'd been beaten by her husband and left for dead."

"Dear God," Alicia whispered. "What happened to her?"

"While she recovered from her wounds, she would sit staring for hours, day after day. Then slowly she regained her senses. Some people, you see, are more resilient than others."

She was touched that he would give aid to a stranger. Then her thoughts went to his theory, and she wanted to reject it. How could he know her situation better than she did?

Yet Alicia found herself wondering. Was it possible her fears were unfounded? That Mama's condition was the result of unusually distressing events? Certainly, her mind had snapped after she'd witnessed the horrible circumstances of Papa's death. But even before then, she had been a bit otherworldly. . . .

Alicia frowned into her glass, watching the bubbles rise to the surface and pop. It was absurd to imagine anyone had ever harmed her mother in her youth. From the tales Mama had once told, she'd enjoyed an idyllic childhood. And yet . . . Alicia had never known her grandparents; they had died in a cholera epidemic when Mama was sixteen. Shortly thereafter, Mama's dearest friend Claire had perished as well. Were those losses enough to unbalance an impressionable girl?

"Tell me what you're thinking," Drake said.

Looking up to see him watching her, the lamp casting shadows on his hard features, she shivered against an impossible rise of optimism. "I'm thinking it's merely conjecture to suggest that my child wouldn't be like Mama."

"You're perfectly sane—if maddening—and so is your brother. That proves I'm right." His black lashes lowered slightly, veiling his thoughts. "And should you have any reservations about my suitability as a father, know this: I would never, ever forsake my child."

Again, she sensed grim secrets in him. Had Drake lost his parents at a young age? His mother had been an actress. He had been born on the wrong side of the blanket, that

much Mrs. Molesworth had divined from gossiping with
the neighborhood servants. No one knew much about him
beyond that he had come from the vast ranks of the London
poor before winning his fortune and building his club.

His expression took on a subtle seductiveness, and his
gaze moved lazily over her bosom. The promise in his
rogue's eyes held her enthralled. Never had she seen such
raw resolve directed at her, a purely sexual intent that both
frightened and fascinated her. How she longed to be a dis-
ciple to his erotic knowledge. . . .

"Alicia—"

The coach swayed and turned. His gaze flashed to the
window. "We're home," he said, an alluring roughness in
his tone. "Finish your champagne."

What had he meant to say? That he wanted her beyond
all reason?

She ought to dash the contents of her glass in his too-
handsome face. That would cool his ardor.

Instead, she tilted back her head and recklessly drained
every drop.

Chapter Fifteen

It was inevitable that he escort Alicia to her bedchamber. Inevitable that he dismiss her maid, a shy little mouse who bobbed a curtsy and darted from the room. Inevitable that he close the door and turn the key.

A lamp glowed on the bedside table, and a fire burned on the hearth. The muted lighting wrapped the room in cozy intimacy. In the canopied four-poster, the linens had been turned down and the pillows lay plump and white against the gilded headboard.

Alicia felt caught in a strange dream. She watched, helpless with longing, as Drake set the champagne bottle on a rosewood table, then unbuttoned his frock coat and shrugged out of it. All the while, his dark and determined gaze held hers.

Controlling a tremor, she picked up the bottle and poured champagne into a glass. For one night, she wanted to forget all the reasons he was wrong for her. She wanted to forget the past and pretend they had a real marriage, the happiness her parents had known long ago.

Before she could lift the glass to her lips, Drake caught her wrist. "You've had enough of that."

"I thought you wanted me tipsy," she said, lifting her

chin in dignified defiance. "So that I would do as you willed."

"I did," he admitted. "But I've changed my mind. I want you to be fully aware of who I am."

Her brief rise of rebellion died. It would serve no purpose to delude herself. He was the man who had forced her into marriage. Tonight she would give herself into the power of Drake Wilder, gamester, scoundrel, pirate of noble fortunes.

He took the glass and set it on the table. Then he moved his hands to her upper arms, caressing lightly over her bare skin. "Alicia," he murmured. "There is but one way to rid ourselves of this obsession we have for each other. One way to be done with it."

She couldn't answer. She could only stare mutely at him.

"I am going to make love to you," he went on, and the confidence in his voice raised an inexplicable pleasure along her nerves. His fingers left a trail of sparks down her arms and over her breasts. "I will touch you and kiss you as I please. And when it is over, you will no longer be a virgin."

She felt incapable of denying him. The bargain that had been so vital to her pride and her self-preservation seemed unimportant now. She could think only of the need burning inside herself, the need that made her lie awake in the darkness, her mind and body too restless for sleep. If one night with him ended this torment, then it would be well worth the price.

And she might conceive a child. A healthy child. A child to hold and love and guide. The possibility shone like a bright beacon in the dark turbulence of her desire.

I would never, ever forsake my child.

Did Drake want an heir to his fortune? Most men did. Yet she knew little of his thoughts, his dreams, his past.

He unbuttoned his silver-striped waistcoat, tossing the garment onto a chair. As he shed his shirt, the firelight bronzed his broad, muscled chest with its dusting of dark hairs. His abdomen looked hard and trim above the waistband of his breeches. He had the robust physique of a workman.

She stared, dazed by his splendor, stunned by his lack of modesty. Did he expect her to disrobe, too? Right here in front of him?

He must.

Turning unsteadily around, she took a deep breath and tugged off her gloves. He was a stranger to her. They had been wed less than a fortnight. A month ago, she hadn't even been aware of his existence. And now she would surrender herself to him in a manner so private, no lady ever spoke of it. Yet she *wanted* to know the passions of the flesh; she craved him with an unladylike hunger.

Faintly horrified at herself, she stepped to the bedside table and arranged her gloves in a neat pile. She leaned down, but before she could extinguish the lamp, Drake caught her from behind and pulled her away.

"Leave it," he said, his voice rough and low. "I wish to look upon you."

Glancing back at him, she was relieved to see that he still wore his breeches. She couldn't yet reconcile herself to shedding her clothes in front of him. The notion seemed shameful . . . and furtively exciting.

Standing behind her, he undid the buttons of her gown. She stood quietly, bemused by the shivers that prickled her skin. How extraordinary, to be tended by a man, to feel his fingers brush her undergarments in so familiar a fashion. He pushed the small cap sleeves from her shoulders, and the silk slithered downward in a whisper of sound.

With a stately calm that belied her inner agitation, she stepped out of her skirts. She intended to reach down and pick up the gown, but he slid his arms around her waist and drew her back against him. He kissed her bare shoulder, tasting her with his tongue, nipping her with his teeth.

When he lay his palm over her corseted bosom, chills flashed down her spine.

"Alicia," he said. "How composed you appear. But the swiftness of your heartbeat betrays you."

Her skin tingled with heightened sensitivity. Awareness of him penetrated to her innermost depths, intensifying the secret pulsebeat between her legs. She said coolly, "I will not behave like one of your hussies."

He rubbed his cheek against her hair, and she sensed his smile. "What do you know of how a hussy behaves?"

"I know how she *doesn't* behave. With propriety and restraint."

A full-fledged chuckle stirred the fine wisps along her neck. "My dear wife, manners don't belong in the bedchamber."

She didn't believe him, of course. He had known only doxies, not a lady of good breeding. She held herself perfectly still as he removed her necklace, then untied her corset strings and the bindings of her petticoats. Her undergarments fell away until she wore only her white lawn shift. Before she could feel more than a twinge of embarrassment, he turned her to him and kissed her.

His lips moved with gentle pressure at first, his hands cradling her head, his thumbs stroking her temples. Their tongues met in a leisurely kiss, a kiss that was almost sweet, as if he controlled the wildness inside himself. He tasted of champagne and darkness, secrets she could not fathom. Placing her hands on the sweeping breadth of his shoulders, she succumbed to temptation and leaned into him, liking the pressure of her breasts against his hard chest.

Muttering something unintelligible, he caught her closer, his arms flexing around her. His hand sought her breast with a warmth that penetrated the flimsy shift. This time, she couldn't stop a quiver of longing. Their mouths melded with increasing urgency, the thrust of his tongue growing more demanding and hungry. He slid his hand inside her loose bodice and cupped the heavy globe of her beast. When his thumb brushed the tip, she whimpered, unprepared for the rush of intense pleasure that radiated throughout her body. She raised herself on tiptoe, straining against him, wanting to be closer and frustrated by the limitations of the flesh.

He groaned deep in his chest, and his mouth crushed hers with a need so fierce she could scarcely draw a breath. Her senses swam with giddiness, and she moved her hands over his form, unable to get enough of his brawny contours, his steely muscles. He was stunningly hewn, utterly male. With a wild willingness that faintly appalled her, she welcomed his caresses, leaning back a little to let him lower one shoulder strap and take her naked breast in his palm.

Appreciation burned in his gaze as he looked down at her. "You are exquisite," he muttered harshly. Then, to her shock and delight, he bent his head and suckled her.

His mouth was hot and hungry. An insidious softness weakened her limbs and strengthened her desire. Unable to silence her gasps of pleasure, she could only hold fast to Drake. He was right, she thought hazily; she could not pretend indifference. She longed for him, body and soul.

He raised the shift to her waist and moved his big, masculine hand over her bare thighs and bottom. Too enraptured to protest, she hid her face in the musky hollow of his shoulder, while he brought his hand between them and touched the tight curls between her legs. In some distant part of her, Alicia knew she should be mortified by his unthinkable liberty. But as he stroked her with expert fingers, a maddening pleasure leapt in her, a passion that made her twist and arch against him. Need built and coiled in her until she thought she might die from it.

"Drake, stop . . . please . . . I can't bear it . . ."

Then she felt the sharpness of loss when he *did* stop, walking her backward until her legs met the edge of the bed. As he sat her down, she clung to him, her insides still knotted from his wondrous caresses. He removed her hands from around his neck, and as he stepped back, dismay flashed through her.

"Is that all?" she asked. "Are you leaving me?"

His teeth clenched into a hard grimace of a smile. His gaze scorching her, he unfastened his breeches. "I'm far from done, my lady."

Alicia's mouth went dry. She knew she oughtn't stare as he stepped out of his breeches, but she couldn't look away from her first view of a naked man. The sheer size of him awed her, even as she felt a frisson of alarm.

He caught her chin in his hand and tilted her face up for a tender, compelling kiss. "Say that you want me," he whispered against her mouth. "Say it."

"I want you," she said in a weakening rush of feeling. "Oh, Drake, I do want you."

His breath hissed out between his teeth. He tugged at her shift, the fragile fabric tearing as he jerked it over her head. As her last vestige of modesty vanished, a mindless sensuality swept over Alicia. She slid into bed, the linens cool to her fevered skin. *Now.* Now he would draw her onto him like that couple carved in stone. . . .

He pressed her back onto the pillows and came down on top of her, letting her feel the power of a man's body. She knew the shock of flesh on flesh, and then he kissed her again with a violence that surpassed her most romantic dreams. All the while, he stroked her intimately, fondling her in ways that made her twist and moan, pushing her again to the edge of a precipice.

He parted her legs with his knees, caught her hips, and held her still. Through the cloud of ardor, she felt a probing invasion, too thick and hot to be his finger. She knew his intent, then, and she gloried in it. Bracing her feet against the mattress, she arched to receive him. A feral groan broke from his throat and in one swift thrust, he breached her last defense.

A brief stab of pain melted into an amazing sense of fullness. He held himself on his forearms, his chest sheened with sweat in the candlelight. His eyes glittered against the harsh handsomeness of his face.

"You're mine," he muttered. "Mine alone."

"As *you* are mine, too."

The fierce vow escaped her without forethought. They stared at each other, both of them panting. Something flashed in his eyes, a starkness she couldn't read. She didn't understand herself, either; she knew only that a bond had been forged between them, a link that connected them by more than the flesh. If she belonged to him, then he also belonged to her. It was as simple and as complicated as that.

Stretching up her hand, she caressed his cheek, and his expression darkened with passion. He turned his head and kissed her palm; then he began to move. She closed her eyes to savor the incredible intimacy, the unimaginable pleasure. The heat inside her flared into a frantic, mindless urgency, and she cleaved to him, writhing, reaching for something she could not name. She cried out and he did, too, in the moment before she plunged, breathless, into great waves of ecstasy. An impossible rapture rolled through her, and she sensed him there with her, as if they were one being, one heart, one soul.

The flash of heaven faded, leaving her limp and replete. For a long while they lay entwined as their breathing slowed and their bodies cooled. She drifted in the sweetest peace she had ever known. His arm rested on her bare middle, and his fingers curled against the side of her breast. The weight of him was heavy, yet infinitely comfortable. She wanted to lie with him forever. . . .

She must have drowsed, for the next thing she knew, he was leaning over the bed, sliding his arms beneath her pliant form. She squirmed in protest, loath to leave her warm nest, but he merely chuckled and swung her up into his arms.

As she wreathed her arms around his neck, a distant noise puzzled her momentarily. Then she realized the connecting door stood ajar.

"The key," she murmured. "How did you find my key?"

A self-assured smile slanted his mouth. "I didn't," he said. "I had another in my coat pocket."

So, he could have entered her chambers at any time he chose. An uneasy sense of vulnerability crept into Alicia. She was at his mercy; she had always been at his mercy. And now that he had won the high-stakes challenge and seduced her, would he come through that door every night?

To her shame, she wanted that. She blushed to remember all they had done together, all the ways he had touched her. Like a slave to passion, she had lost control, moaning and twisting beneath him, her dignity abandoned in the heedless need to couple with him, to appease the hungers of the flesh.

"Don't," he growled.

Tilting her head against his collarbone, she regarded him warily. "Don't what?"

"Don't retreat into that prim, prudish lady. Tonight, she doesn't exist." Shouldering open the door, he carried her into his room.

Alicia thrilled to his masterful manner, though a part of her longed for the safe and familiar trappings of pride. "Beast," she muttered.

"Beauty," he countered in the seductive tone that raised chills over her skin. "You shan't escape me tonight."

His dark promise nestled warmly within her. As he strode across his bedchamber, the background noise grew louder. It sounded curiously like . . . flowing water?

He carried her through another doorway and into a room bedecked like a grotto with statues tucked among the ferns and pillars. Candles flickered in niches, adding a subtle glow to the scene, and water poured from a wall spout shaped like a dolphin's mouth. As the liquid cascaded musically into a circular pool, steam rose in a fine mist that dampened her skin.

"A Roman bath?" she said in wonderment. "With piped-in water?"

"For my lady's pleasure."

He bore her down the steps and settled her on a shelf carved into the marble below the waterline. Little waves lapped at the undersides of her breasts. Heat enveloped her, relaxing her muscles and soothing the slight ache where he had made them one.

Unashamedly naked, Drake waded toward the spout and shut off the levers that controlled the flow. With a suddenness that startled her, he dove head-first below the surface and emerged at her feet like Neptune rising from the sea. Droplets rolled down his magnificently muscled chest, over his taut midsection, to vanish into the pool, where the surface of the water blurred the most intriguing portion of his anatomy.

Feeling flushed from more than the bath, she looked up to see a cocksure smile on his face. He knew his effect on her, the wretch. But she smiled anyway, beset by a wave of utter happiness. She let her doubts float away on the gently rippling water. She wouldn't let herself think tonight. She wanted only to bask in his virile presence.

He combed his fingers through his wet hair, the slick strands gleaming like black silk in the candlelight. Then he sat beside her and leaned closer to tuck a few strands back into her drooping chignon. His action held a curious tenderness.

How astonishing to recline naked in a pool with her husband. *Her husband.* They were truly wed now, their union consummated. Her heart full, she said lightly, "What a marvelously decadent life you lead, Mr. Wilder."

"What a marvelously decadent life you will lead, too, Mrs. Wilder."

His gaze held the pledge of more pleasures to come. No wonder young ladies were kept in ignorance of lovemaking, she thought dreamily. If they were to learn of physical joy, they would crave it all the time.

A glint in his eyes, he picked up a cake of soap and lathered his hands. Slowly he massaged her bosom, sliding over slick skin, his thumbs teasing the sensitive peaks until her breasts felt heavy and aching. As longing swelled in her, she braced her palms on the marble seat to keep herself from melting into the pool.

His hands moved lower, washing her belly and thighs with scrupulous care. "How soft and delicate you are," he mused. "I must have hurt you."

"No, I'm fine," she assured him. "Truly I am."

He raised an eyebrow. "My dearest lady, I took you like a savage. I'll be gentler next time. Now lie back and relax."

A droplet of water trickled down his chiseled face. On impulse, she leaned forward and caught it with her tongue. He tasted faintly of salt, and she breathed in his damp, exhilarating scent. "I liked what you did to me," she said. "I wouldn't change a moment of it."

His eyes gleamed a dark mysterious blue against his swarthy skin. "Alicia."

Then he moved his hand exactly where she wanted it, his gaze holding hers while he aroused her. Soft sounds of enjoyment rose from her throat. She reveled in the lazy stroking of his finger, the slow rise of tension, the warm lapping of water against her breasts. She hadn't known herself to be a creature of sensuality, or that a woman could feel such delight. In a fever of impatience, she brought her leg over so that she straddled him, her breasts moist against his chest, her aching center meeting his hardness. At last she understood the ecstasy of this position; it gave her the freedom to move against him.

Groaning out her name, he caught her hips and in a wild upward surge entered her. Water sloshed around them. Their lips met in an urgent kiss, their bodies straining, reaching for the pinnacle of pleasure.

When it was over, she lay spent and weak in his arms. His mouth drifted along her brow, leaving a trail of languid kisses. After a few long moments, he lifted her from the pool, holding her upright while he wrapped her in a soft towel. He bent his head to her hair and breathed deeply. "You've driven me half mad with wanting," he said in a rough undertone. "I can't get enough of you. You'll sleep with me tonight."

"Yes," she said, her voice husky, her throat tight.

He took her up into his arms and walked to his bed, laying her down. The linens felt cool against her deliciously flushed skin. He blew out the bedside candle and settled himself beside her, bringing her close to the hearth fire of his body.

Drowsy and contented, she cuddled to him in the darkness, her head tucked onto his broad shoulder. His arm lay heavy and possessive over her stomach. As if in a dream, she felt his mouth against her brow, his lips gradually searing a downward path until he parted her legs for the most intimate kiss of all. His lovemaking was slow and sweet and strangely unreal, and she nearly wept from the beauty of it. He wielded a mastery over her body that was almost frightening in its intensity.

And in the quiet aftermath, as she drifted toward sleep, he held her within the strong circle of his arms as if he, too, could not bear for the night to end.

Chapter Sixteen

A streamer of sunlight awakened Alicia. The brightness crept through a narrow crack in the closed shutters.

She sat up, taking in her dim surroundings at a glance. A broad bed with a rumpled blue coverlet. Dark masculine furnishings. She had slept for the first time with her husband. Where had he gone?

The room lay in shadow, and the pillow beside her held a trace of his scent. Hugging it to her breasts, she let the memories of the previous night wash over her. Never had she imagined that she could behave with such unbridled ardor. An inner ache gave testament to the wildness of their couplings. Drake had made love to her three times, his caresses shattering her usual reserve. She blushed to remember how swiftly her defenses had fallen under his sensual assault. In his arms, she had become another woman, a creature of carnality, no longer a lady.

The troubling memory brought her fully awake. She blinked at the softly ticking clock on the marble mantel. Then blinked again. Two o'clock?

She had slept the entire morning away and nearly half the afternoon. And she wore not a stitch of clothing.

Disoriented, she rose from the warm linens, her muscles protesting. Could she steal back into her own chamber without being seen? A maidservant might be there, sewing or cleaning. Or gathering up the garments that lay strewn over the carpet, the evidence of seduction.

She quickly reached for a blanket to cover herself. Then she saw something lying at the foot of the bed. Her white silk robe. And on top of it, a perfect red rose.

A sweet pressure caught at her throat. *Drake.* He must have left them here before departing for his club. Picking up the flower, she closed her eyes and breathed in its rich scent. The velvet petals brushed her skin like the echo of a caress. *His* caress. Did he still desire her after their night together? Or now that he'd had her, would he turn to another woman?

Her heart aching, she donned the robe. She mustn't forget that vows meant little to him. He was a charmer, this man she had married to avert disaster. He was a rake who knew how to please a woman. But he wouldn't remain true to his wife. He believed this spark between them to be mere sexual obsession.

You've driven me half mad with wanting. I can't get enough of you.

Her doubts wavered beneath a reckless rush of longing. How could lust explain the turmoil inside her, the yearning to fathom all his secrets? She wanted to know his thoughts, his hopes, his feelings. And therein lay danger. The last thing she wanted was to give him her heart.

All her life, Alicia had taken her troubles to one person. Today she needed to talk to someone who knew Mama well, to find out if her condition had been caused by traumatic events. But the moment she walked into the foyer of Pemberton House later that afternoon and hugged Mrs. Molesworth, all thought of her own worries vanished.

Exuding a familiar floury scent, the housekeeper stepped back, her sturdy fingers bunching her apron in a distraught manner. "M'lady! 'Tis time you've come to see me, and today of all days."

Guiltily, Alicia said, "I should have brought Mama to visit, I know. And I promise I shall very soon—"

She paused, noticing for the first time the canvas that covered the floor of the drawing room. Scaffolding stood against the wall, and a painter balanced on the high platform, his brush whisking up and down, leaving swaths of yellow against the dull gray plaster. The acrid scent of paint hung in the air, and a distant hammering echoed from somewhere upstairs. "What's going on?" she asked. "Gerald can't afford to renovate."

" 'Tis your Mr. Wilder who's payin' the bills, m'lady. Fer fixin' that rickety stair rail, and all the other repairs. An' there be tables an' chairs an' all manner of furniture comin', too."

Softness crept into Alicia's heart. This was another of Drake's good deeds. Though, of course, *he* would claim to be merely protecting his property. "Where is Gerald? Has he returned home yet?"

"Why, 'e's gone, m'lady. Slept till noon an' rode off not thirty minutes ago."

"I don't understand. . . ." If her brother held a position in a bank, then why would he be sleeping late? Had he been discharged? Another possibility distressed her. "Is he ill? You should have sent word immediately."

Mrs. Molesworth shook her head so vehemently, her mobcap slipped slightly askew. "Nay, 'e's been right as rain. But there be other trouble brewin', I fear." Taking Alicia's arm, the housekeeper urged her into the empty library. She glanced around as if half expecting a spy to pop out from behind the faded draperies. In an nervous whisper, she said, " 'Tis Lord Hailstock."

"What do you mean?"

" 'E's 'ere, m'lady. 'E arrived a few minutes ago." Setting her hands on her broad hips, Mrs. Molesworth pursed her lips. "An' 'e's pokin' through the earl's study."

The oak-paneled room was situated at the rear of the house. Here, many generations of earls had tended to business matters. The study belonged to Gerald now, though with their family holdings vastly reduced, Alicia knew there was little but bills left to occupy him.

She had been unable to bring herself to sell these furnishings. The chamber held too many memories of sitting on her papa's lap while he told her a tale of knights and dragons, or running to him when she'd been hurt so that he could soothe her tears. Pain thrust into her. Of course, she hadn't realized back then his ineptness for managing money. Or his weakness for playing cards. . . .

The door stood ajar, and she pushed it open. Dust motes danced in the late afternoon sunlight, and the air held a haunting trace of her father's pipe tobacco. The study looked as it had always been, spartan and masculine, with comfortable leather chairs and dark brown draperies.

Lord Hailstock crouched before the oak desk. He had his arm thrust to the elbow into an opened drawer, as if he were feeling for something stuck far in the back. His gaze met hers, and he went still.

His unorthodox pose stunned Alicia, as did his odd air of furtiveness. She advanced toward the desk. "My lord! What on earth are you doing?"

He stood up, brushing at his fine gray coat. His debonair smile seemed forced as he rounded the desk and walked to her. "My lady. You gave me quite a start."

Still baffled, she dipped a curtsy. "May I help you find something?"

"As a matter of fact, no." The marquess laughed a trifle self-consciously. "There were some letters I wrote to your father a long time ago. I wondered if he had kept them."

"I went through his papers after his death, and I don't

recall seeing any letters from you." Though Lord Hailstock had been a family friend for as far back as she could remember, Alicia somehow mistrusted his explanation. Why would such a principled man lower himself to snooping?

"I would be happy to look again if you like."

"Please don't trouble yourself. And do pardon me. It was a silly, sentimental impulse that brought me here."

"Of course." Politeness kept her from pursuing the matter, and perhaps she was making too much of it, anyway. "Would you care to stay for tea?"

"Thank you, but I mustn't impose on you any further." As he studied her keenly, from the slim-fitting spencer down to her pale green skirt, a subtle darkness shadowed his face. "May I say, you're looking exceptionally fine today. There's a softness about you that wasn't there last evening."

The ball. She had nearly forgotten it after the tumultuous events of the night. The searing memories delivered a flush to her cheeks, and she glanced away, as if he could guess that she had behaved like a wanton. "It was pleasant to see you at the Cuthberts'. I do wish we'd had more time to chat, but Drake and I—"

"It's Wilder, isn't it?" Hailstock grasped her by the arms. "He's won you over."

"Please!" she chided. "You're hurting me."

Compressing his lips, he relaxed his hold, letting his arms fall to his sides. "Forgive me, my dear. It is just that I'm concerned he will misuse you. The man is a common rogue."

"He is a gentleman," Alicia said, surprising herself with her fierceness. She could not bear for this haughty aristocrat to belittle her husband. He must have done so at the ball; that would explain the animosity she had sensed between them. "Oh, I cannot deny that Drake coerced me into marriage. But the deed is done. And ever since, he has been nothing but kind and generous to me and my family."

"I see." The marquess raised a cold eyebrow at her. "Clearly, you have no inkling of what your kind and generous husband has done for Gerald. Or where your brother spends his time these days."

Through her anger, Alicia felt a niggling of alarm. "Don't speak in riddles. Tell me."

"As you wish, then, though I would have preferred to shield you from such an indelicate matter." His mouth curled in distaste. "You see, my dear, Drake Wilder has lured your brother back to the gaming tables."

As was his custom, Drake strolled through the club at six o'clock in the evening to survey its readiness. In the drawing room, most of the round tables were empty at so early an hour. He nodded to a croupier who counted gambling discs, for no coin was permitted in here. To minimize distractions, all debts and credits were settled in an office down the corridor, jokingly known as the Devil's Exchequer.

The room was tastefully elegant with its tall columns of Sienna marble and the forest-green draperies over the arched windows. To keep attention focused on the game, no paintings or mirrors adorned the pale green walls. Fires burned cheerily at either end of the chamber. The well-padded leather chairs encouraged gentlemen to linger at the tables. Wine would flow freely, another inducement to deep play.

Under normal circumstances, he would have enjoyed making the rounds. But today, he gave the room only a cursory glance. In his mind, he kept seeing Alicia as she'd been that morning, cuddled against him in slumber, all soft and rosy, a woman well pleasured. Her tousled blond hair had felt like silk to his fingertips, and he'd had the fierce desire to bury himself inside her so that she would awaken to his possession.

Instead, he had eased out of bed. He had used her

enough already. And there could be no other reason to stay.

How she had surprised him, his lady wife. Beneath her cool elegance lived a warm, sensual woman. She had been a virgin, and he had intended to tame her gently. But her eagerness had made him react with all the finesse of a rutting bull. Never before had he experienced such a driving need to mate with a woman. Passion for her had controlled him, when he was accustomed to being the one in control. Even now, he felt the violent urge to stake his claim in the most primitive way possible. He wanted to impregnate Alicia, to get her with child, *his* child.

"Ho, there, Wilder."

Drake jerked his attention to a pair of gentlemen, one tall and gangly, the other short and rotund, who stood by a table near the drawing room door. Though most of the crowd would arrive at a fashionably later hour, a few members already had straggled into the club. Unfortunately, these two were imbeciles.

Hiding his irritation behind a congenial smile, he strolled toward them. "Keeble. Duxbury. I trust the both of you have been staying out of trouble."

Viscount Keeble patted his stout belly. "We were about to toddle into the dining room for that fine roast beef your chef prepares. That is, until Ducks here put me to a wager."

"I bet fifty guineas that he'd be leg-shackled before I am," Duxbury said, towering over his crony, a fool's grin on his baby face. He gestured at the open betting book, where members of the club recorded such wagers. "If you will stand witness, Wilder."

"This makes me want to find an heiress to feather my nest," Keeble said, rubbing his hands in glee. "And if I do, you'll have your fifty, Ducks, and I'll have my thousands."

Duxbury poked him in the ribs. "Mayhap we'll both find a plump pigeon. We'll be *birds* of a feather."

" 'Tis better than being *bird*-witted."

Looking at each other, they chortled with laughter.

God pity the woman who married either of these idiots, Drake thought. Picking up the quill, he dipped it into the silver inkpot and scrawled his name beneath theirs in the betting book. "If you gentlemen will excuse me now."

"One moment," Keeble said, his eyes avid beneath his thinning brown curls. "We hear you're to be congratulated, Wilder, for moving up in the world."

"By snaring yourself a lady*bird*," Duxbury added.

Both men hooted with mirth again.

Gripped by an icy tension, Drake fisted his fingers into each man's coat sleeve. Their merriment ground to a halt, and they gaped at him, Keeble short and plump-cheeked, Duxbury tall and slack-mouthed.

"Never describe my wife with a name reserved for whores," Drake said in a tautly pleasant tone. "Is that understood?"

"Right-o," Keeble blurted out. " 'Twas only a jest, old boy."

"No need to fly off the handle," Duxbury added.

Drake released his grip. Like rats fleeing a tomcat, the two men scurried toward the dining room.

They were cork-brained fools, Drake knew. Still, he resented their implication, that Alicia had lowered herself by marrying him. She had benefited from their union as much as he had—and in more ways than wealth. Were it not for him, she would still be a sour-mouthed spinster instead of a well-satisfied woman. Remembering her carnal awakening, he wanted to strut with all the pride of a conquerer. But he had the uneasy sense that she had conquered him, too.

Oh, Drake, I do want you . . . I liked what you did to me . . . I wouldn't change a moment of it . . .

Those soft words still had the power to blot out reason and logic. One night had not sated him. His loins still burned for his wife. He wanted her with a maddening urgency that defied comprehension. And there was no reason not to indulge himself.

Striding into the deserted foyer, he headed for the front door. The club could function without him for a few hours. No doubt Fergus would glower and grumble about the extra work, but he'd survive.

Drake was the master now. And there was no one he wanted to master more than his wife. Would she welcome him into her bed this time? Or would she act the prickly puritan again? He couldn't wait to find out.

As he neared the door, the frosted glass panel swung open. Reacting fast, he caught it with his hand. "What the devil—?"

He bit off the curse and stopped in his tracks. As if summoned by the dark force of his fantasies, Alicia walked into the club.

Or rather, *marched* would have been a more apt description, he thought, admiring the swish of her skirts as she spun around to face him. A close-fitting jacket outlined her bosom and defined her slim waist. Her lips were pursed, her gaze icy, her manner stiff. Ah, the puritan.

So much the better. He would enjoy seducing her all over again.

The epitome of an arrogant aristocrat, she lifted her chin and raised one eyebrow. Without preamble, she asked coldly, "Where is my brother?"

So she had found out. With deliberate nonchalance, he kissed her soft cheek. "Good evening to you, too, darling."

She turned her head away. "Don't waste your charm on me. I know what a villain you are beneath all that male posturing."

"And I know what a beauty *you* are beneath all that feminine outrage."

He reached out to caress her, but she slapped his hand away. "Don't try to work your wiles," she said in a low-pitched voice. "I've found out that you've been corrupting Gerald."

Drake was so struck by her first statement that he almost didn't hear the second. Work his wiles? His *wiles*?

In a swift move, he caught her arm and escorted her up the broad staircase, down a corridor, and into his office, where he slammed the door behind them. "I don't play a woman's coy games," he stated. "You should know that by now."

She twisted away from him. "No, you play a man's game of enticing the unwary into your club."

"Your brother is old enough to know what he's doing."

She scowled, a very pretty scowl that made him want to kiss her senseless. "So you admit that you lured him back here."

"I offered him a position on staff here. He had the intelligence to accept it."

"A position?" she scoffed. "That isn't what Lord Hailstock told me."

A burning tension seized his chest, and he cornered her against the desk. She tried to wriggle free, but he held her by the arms and snapped, "When did you see Hailstock?"

"Get away from me," she said, pushing ineffectually at him. "I will not be bullied."

"Then answer my question."

"I happened upon him at Pemberton House."

"What the devil was he doing there?"

"He came to . . . to fetch some old papers from my father's study." Her gaze faltered slightly, a sure sign that she was hiding something.

A murderous edge to his voice, Drake demanded, "Did he dare to touch you?"

"Of course not. *He* treats me like a lady." She cast a pointed glance at Drake's fingers on her arm, and her blue eyes flashed with contempt. "And I wonder at your animosity toward his lordship."

He forced himself to ease his grip. He must be careful, lest she guess the truth. "I will not share you. Remember that."

"And I will not abide my brother's gambling in this club. You will bar him from the premises immediately."

"He isn't here to lay wagers. He holds a respectable position."

"Respectable," she huffed. "This is a gaming hell. What is he doing, collecting overdue debts from those you've fleeced?"

That set his teeth on edge. "May I remind you, madam, this *gaming hell* pays for your wardrobe, your house, your carriage. My wealth kept your mother out of Bedlam and your brother out of Fleet."

"And he'll land in prison if you encourage him to sink into debt again!"

"I gave him a purpose in his life. If you don't believe me, then ask him. He should be downstairs in the dining room."

"And thence to the gaming tables he'll go," she said bitterly. "How will he repay you this time? He hasn't any more sisters for you to procure."

He felt the violent urge to stop her insults in the best way he knew how, by thrusting her flat on the desk and mounting her. "A pity, that. I might have negotiated a trade when I tired of you."

Alicia took a sharp breath that lifted her bosom enticingly. "You are vile."

"And you are beyond reason. If you had any sense at all, you'd let Gerald make his own decisions."

"He isn't deciding for himself, he's listening to you," she flung back. "Like any man, he'll follow the path of temptation."

"And women know nothing of temptation?" Goaded, Drake pressed himself to her, letting her feel his arousal. It angered him that she could tie him in knots while belittling all that he had worked to build. "I'm afraid it's too late to persuade me that ladies are angels, pure and ethereal, incapable of lust."

A delicate flush stained her cheeks. She tilted her head back and met his gaze squarely, her gloved fingers clenched at her sides. "We were speaking of wagering, not bedsport."

"Ah, but lechery is a far more fascinating topic."

He would show her who was her master. He brought his hands to her breasts, kneading her through the layers of spencer, gown, and corset. Though she stood rigidly, she lowered her lashes slightly and parted her lips.

"Bully," she said, a betraying catch to her voice. "Let me go."

"Beloved," he taunted. "I'll never let you go."

Trapping her against the desk, he took her mouth with deliberate sensuality, using all of his skill to wrest a response from her. She brought her hands up as if to push him away, but instead her fingers caught at his shirt and she arched up on tiptoe, straining against him, opening her mouth to him. She tasted sweet and luscious, and he kissed her deeply, stroking her with his tongue until she moaned with pleasure and he burned with need. Her swift surrender drove him mad. He wanted to feel her, flesh to flesh. He wanted to thrust inside her. He wanted to rid himself of this power she held over him. *Now.*

He pulled at her skirts, only to stagger backward under the force of her shove. Disoriented by passion, Drake grabbed for her, but she slipped beneath his arm and darted across the office.

He stalked after her. When she tried to wrest open the door, he planted his palm on the oak panel. "For Christ's sake, Alicia—"

She spun to face him. Her distraught expression silenced him. His gaze riveted to the unshed tears in her eyes.

"I can't resist you," she said in bitter bewilderment. "Not even knowing what you've done to my brother."

Drake felt unmanned by her tears. Wanting to comfort her and despising her effect on him, he bit out, "I've done nothing. If you would understand that—"

"No, *you* try to understand," she said wildly, her gaze stark. "My father shot himself. He fell so far into debt from gambling that he could no longer face his family. And I fear . . . I fear Gerald may someday do the same."

Chapter Seventeen

Alicia maintained the pretense of calm all the way to the back staircase. Her footsteps echoed in the narrow shaft. A wall sconce on each landing provided light for the servants, but thankfully, the place was deserted.

Wilting onto the wooden steps, she buried her face in her hands and released her bottled-up tears. She could not understand herself. How could she desire a man who preyed upon the weaknesses of others? How could she have let passion overshadow her hatred of gambling?

She hadn't meant to hurl the truth at Drake. Few people knew the nature of her father's death. It had been Lord Hailstock's idea to conceal the horrifying reality, and grief-stricken, she had allowed him to handle the matter, to sort through her father's affairs and pay off his ruinous debts. The shooting had been attributed to a thwarted robbery. If people whispered, she had heard none of it. She had kept busy caring for Mama, who had gone out of her mind with grief, and consoling Gerald, a bewildered thirteen-year-old.

She sat there for a while, weeping. Then, on the floor above, a door clicked open. Heavy footsteps descended the stairs. *Drake?*

She sprang up, sniffling, scrubbing at her damp cheeks.

She must not let him see her weakness. He would use it to his own purposes.

But the man who came into view wasn't her husband.

He was a tall, rangy giant clad in sober black. The leather patch over one eye made him appear sinister. The butler, she remembered. He had escorted her up to Drake's office that day she had come to make her desperate offer.

She averted her head and waited for him to pass. But he stopped two steps above her. When he didn't proceed, she tilted her head back to see him regarding her with faint horror.

"Wilder didna say he'd driven ye to tears."

Making a final furtive brush at her cheeks, she forced a polite smile. "You spoke to him?"

"Aye. The dastard ordered me to find ye and take ye to yer brother."

In spite of her distress, she felt oddly cheered by his disapproval of Drake. "Thank you, Mr. . . ."

"MacAllister," he said gruffly. "Fergus MacAllister." He thumped down the steps and awkwardly patted her shoulder. "Dinna fret over yer husband. He's a braw heart beneath all his manly blustering. His mither raised him well."

Alicia wasn't sure what *braw* meant, but she did know that Drake had nothing resembling a heart. Biting her tongue, she asked, "Did you know his mother?"

"Aye. We met in Edinburgh long ago, when she was a puir actress, struggling to support the wee bairn." On that stunning statement, he went past Alicia and tramped down the stairs.

Holding on to the wooden rail, she hastened after him. "Drake was born in Scotland? He never told me so."

MacAllister snorted. " 'Tis no surprise. The lad's a close-mouthed one."

"He doesn't speak with a brogue."

"Nay. After his mither died, we came to London and he set himself to learning the fancy ways of the nobility."

"How old was he?"

"Ten, m'lady. And alone in the world save fer me. Times were wretched fer him, then." He regarded her with a piercing stare. " 'Twill take patience to earn his love, ye ken."

Alicia stiffened. Did he think she *wanted* Drake's love? Or that she needed advice on her marriage?

She should be offended by MacAllister's presumption. But he had known Drake since childhood, and she supposed that gave him a certain prerogative. Besides, she couldn't spoil this rare opportunity to learn more about her husband. "Please tell me about Drake's mother. And his father."

Halting on the next landing, the servant shot her a one-eyed scowl. The kindness fled from his grizzled face so that he looked dour and dismal. " 'Tisn't fer me to say. Ye should ask yer questions of yer husband."

MacAllister opened the door and stalked out. Her lips pursed, Alicia followed him into a broad passageway decorated in muted greens with a tasteful touch of gilding on the arched ceiling. What had she said to make him turn uncommunicative? Was it the mention of Drake's father?

Perhaps she should not have been so bold. Drake had, after all, been born out of wedlock. He might not even know who had sired him.

Sympathy stirred in her, but she pushed away the sentiment. A lack of paternal guidance did not excuse his faults. He was a conscienceless exploiter. And she would not allow him to get past her guard ever again.

Yet those words sounded hollow to her. She knew he had only to touch her, and all of her good sense vanished. . . .

At the end of the corridor, the butler held open a door, and she stepped into a vast kitchen filled with delicious smells. Great pillars stretched to the high ceiling, and huge, hanging oil lamps illuminated the cooking areas. The room was a beehive of orderly activity, with a white-coated chef directing an army of helpers who sliced and chopped and kneaded. A stoop-shouldered man drew trays of fragrant loaves out of a tall bake oven. In the center of the kitchen, a table held many silver platters with gleaming domed lids.

Alicia turned to MacAllister. "Is my brother here?"

"Nay, but there's time aplenty to see the earl. Right now, ye need a wee cuppy."

A cuppy?

Mystified, she followed him through another doorway and into a chamber dominated by a long table. At the far end, a small group of servants sat laughing and talking, eating their supper. One fell silent, then another and another, as all eyes turned to Alicia.

"Here be Mrs. Wilder, sister to Lord Brockway," Fergus MacAllister said ominously. "Come make yer bows to the lady."

The servants quickly gathered their plates. Cutlery clattered. Chair legs scraped the flagstone floor. As a mobcapped maid stood up, Alicia stared at an unmistakable mound beneath the girl's white apron. Drake employed a pregnant servant?

"Please stay," Alicia said quickly. "I don't mean to interrupt your meal."

Silence reigned for a moment. Five pairs of eyes looked from her to MacAllister and back again.

"We are finished, my lady," intoned a man at the head of the table. "So it is no imposition."

Stout and balding, he alone remained seated. With an abrupt push against the table, he moved backward—or rather, *rolled* backward. His chair had *wheels*.

Wide-eyed, she watched him advance the chair, capably turning the large wheels with his hands. He stopped in front of her, pressed his hand to his plain coat, and inclined his head in a bow. "The name's Lazarus Cheever," he said, enunciating each word. " 'Tis a pleasure to meet the lady who tamed our Wilder."

"Oh . . . thank you. Though I fear he is hardly tamed yet."

A nervous giggle escaped the two maidservants standing behind him. Alicia hid her chagrin. It wasn't like her to speak so familiarly to strangers. The encounter with Drake must have addled her senses.

MacAllister cleared his throat. "Cheever tallies the accounts here," he grunted. "Oftimes he still fancies himself a thespian."

"You were once an actor?" Alicia asked Cheever.

"As true and dedicated a performer as ever trod the boards. Until one fateful night when a vigorous sword fight sent me tumbling off the stage." He jabbed an imaginary blade into the air, then dropped his hand to his lap. "Alas, I lost not only the use of my legs, but my livelihood as well. No one would hire a cripple. That is, no one but the esteemed Drake Wilder."

"God bless Mr. Wilder," the pregnant maidservant whispered fervently.

"Go on," MacAllister prompted her, "tell m'lady yer tale."

She bobbed an awkward curtsy to Alicia. "Wot 'appened is, Mr. Wilder were the only bloke who'd gi' me a place after me master used me ill, then tossed me out on the street."

A freckle-faced footman took her hand. "Y-y-you're safe now," he stammered. "W-w-with us." When she smiled shyly at him, he ducked his head, his cheeks beet-red.

The two giggling maids were orphans, Alicia learned, sisters who had been rescued from a hard life in the workhouse. While they spoke of Drake with a worshipful admiration, Alicia smiled politely.

But deep inside, she felt shaken, unable to withstand a flood tide of confusion. Drake had provided employment for these desperate souls who might have starved otherwise? The conniving rogue who had led Gerald astray also played the philanthropist? How could she reconcile two such divergent sides in one man?

"Go awa' wi' ye now," MacAllister told the servants. "An' bring the lady her tay."

The servants hastened out, leaving Alicia alone with the butler. She sank into the nearest chair and frowned down at the burled pattern in the oak table. "Who is he?" she mused aloud.

"M'lady?"

She looked up to see MacAllister sitting across from her, and she searched his gloomy features for answers. The tangle of her emotions stifled her natural reticence. "My husband," she said in a rush of frustration. "He's like two utterly different people. The ruthless gambler . . . and the generous benefactor who helped Cheever and the other servants here. And at home, too." She paused, faintly astonished to realize the extent of his munificence. "There's Kitty, our deaf housemaid. Chalkers, the drunken butler. And the coachman—the one who made me late to my wedding."

"Aye, Big Bill. A braw pugilist in his time, till his brains got rattled a bit too much." MacAllister tapped his skull, then leaned forward, bracing his elbows on the table. "And dinna forget Mrs. Yates."

Alicia stiffened. "What about her?"

" 'Tis the most dire tale of them all," he said. "Wilder found her half dead from a beatin'. Many's the man who'd've driven on by an' left the puir soul lyin' in the ditch. But he brung her home, fetched the physician, and had her nursed for months till she recovered."

Alicia stared, dumbfounded. The woman from Whitechapel who had been battered by her husband. Drake had said the shock had caused her to lose her wits for a while. That defenseless invalid was . . . Mrs. Yates?

Impossible. But there could be no reason for MacAllister to lie. Not when she could easily find out the truth.

Resentment and understanding warred within her. Against her will, she realized that the impertinent house-keeper must view Drake as her savior. As such, she would feel a certain possessiveness toward him.

Shaken by her own violent jealousy, Alicia wanted to believe she didn't care if Drake took a mistress. But she couldn't fool herself. If he dared to kiss and caress any other woman, to do with her that profoundly intimate act that should belong to married couples only. . . .

Holding fast to her anger, she said, "If Drake likes to help people so much, then how can he encourage my brother to gamble?"

"To gamble?" Regarding her blankly, MacAllister shook his head. "The master didna tell you?"

"Oh, he mentioned something about Gerald having a po-sition here. As a croupier, no doubt. But if my brother so much as puts his hand on a pair of dice or deals a deck of cards, he will be drawn into the game."

"Nay, the earl isna here for his own indulgence." MacAllister gestured in the direction of the main rooms at the front of the building. "He's here to save those auld fools out there from ruin."

"I don't understand."

"His duty, m'lady, is to watch over the tables, to make certain no one wagers beyond his means. Ye must ken, the master canna abide the notion of penniless wives and starv-ing bairns."

Disbelieving, Alicia stared into his weathered face. "Drake was certainly willing to let *my* family starve. He stole the very roof over our heads. He forced me to marry him."

"Aye, that he did." Avoiding her eyes, MacAllister squirmed uncomfortably in his chair. "He's a hard man at times. But dinna fret. He has a softness well hidden inside him. In time, he'll come to love ye."

Love. That was the second time the servant had used the

unthinkable word. Clearly, he overlooked the fact that she had been Drake's stepping stone into society. Drake had wanted a noble wife, and he had stopped at nothing to achieve his purpose. And if gentlemen could not play beyond their means in this club, that meant that Drake had coldly and deliberately beggared Gerald. He had turned her life upside down by forcing her into marriage. The thought caused an icy shiver around her heart.

So how could she still feel such a yearning inside her? Why did she long to lie in his arms again, to feel the hard weight of his body on hers? Why did she ache to hear him whisper words of love?

She must not soften toward him again. Yet if she could believe MacAllister, Drake had offered her brother a worthy role. He had given Gerald the chance to redeem himself. And she couldn't overlook the fact that Drake directed at least a portion of his illicit profits to aiding those in need. It pained her to admit that her husband did far more to help the indigent than she did.

So who was she to think herself better than him?

Yet who was he to reorder her life? To risk her brother's life?

Back and forth, her thoughts tumbled until she wanted to scream with frustration. Granted, Drake did have a core of decency. But he wielded too much influence over Gerald. She shuddered to think of her brother anywhere near a betting table. If he were to end up like Papa . . .

The freckle-faced footman trotted in with a tea tray, setting it on the table before scurrying out again. MacAllister closed his massive paw around the delicate porcelain pot and poured the steaming liquid into a cup. "Here's a wee cuppy fer ye, m'lady."

"A cuppy," she said faintly. "So that's what you meant."

Taking the cup from him, she attempted a mannerly smile, but a sob choked out instead. To her chagrin, tears blurred her eyes again.

MacAllister groped in his pocket for a folded handkerchief. "Dinna weep, lass. I didna mean to distress ye."

He looked so alarmed, Alicia couldn't help laughing through her tears. "You've been more than kind," she told him. "It's just that . . . I don't know what's wrong with me today."

But she did know. And his name was Drake Wilder.

Women were barred from the exclusive rooms of the club, where gentlemen dined and wagered and drank in an atmosphere of opulent splendor. So when Alicia finished her tea, Fergus MacAllister sent Gerald back to the servants' hall. Her brother sheepishly apologized for misleading her.

"I've touched neither dice nor cards, I swear it." He drew himself upright, his thin shoulders squared beneath his peacock-green coat. "I'm far too busy prowling the floor, watching so that no one plays deeper than his means. Already I've kept Lord Witherspoon from wagering away his sister's marriage portion. And Captain Lord Rogers would've been done up if he'd lost at hazard."

"That is all fine and good, but let someone else do the job. I cannot approve of you being here." Her throat tight, she touched his sleeve. "You know why."

He glanced away, his Adam's apple bobbing above the white cravat. Then he returned his determined gaze to her. "I am not like Papa. And I have to stay, Ali. Don't you see? I must keep other coves from ruining their families as I did."

His altruistic purpose filled her with unexpected pride. She ached to protect her brother as she'd always done. Yet she was forced to concede that perhaps the responsibility would be good for him. Perhaps Drake was right; perhaps Gerald should make his own decisions.

But why, oh, why could he not assert his independence anywhere but in this gaming hell?

*   *   *

More confused than ever, she returned home to spend the evening pacing her bedchamber. Sarah had left her calling card that afternoon, but Alicia couldn't bring herself to see anyone. The turbulence of emotion she felt for Drake was something she had to sort through alone.

He wasn't the well-bred aristocrat she had been raised to marry. Orphaned at ten, he had grown up under the dour guidance of Fergus MacAllister. Times had been wretched, MacAllister had said. Drake had led a rough-and-tumble life on the streets, a hard existence she could only imagine. Though she herself had faced poverty, at least she'd had Mama and Gerald and Mrs. Molesworth as her family. She'd had a roof over her head and food on the table. She'd had love.

Had she wed a nobleman, she would have led a more genteel life with a husband who knew how to treat a lady. But would such a marriage have guaranteed her happiness? She had to admit it would not. Sarah had made a brilliant match, yet she had been miserable, tormented by the duke's devotion to his mistress.

Papa had been flawed, too. Though he had adored Mama, he had indulged his weakness for wagering. In the end, the cards had destroyed him.

Sinking onto a chaise, Alicia propped her chin on her cupped hands. Her long-ago dreams of a fairy-tale prince had been just that . . . dreams. For better or for worse, Drake was her husband. Wishing wouldn't change that fact.

Did she even *want* to change it?

A ridiculous question. Of course she wouldn't *choose* to be wed to a gambler. Especially not a man who owned a gambling club, a man who was aggressive, blunt-spoken, domineering. Yet Drake also had a surprising decency beneath all his masculine swaggering. He could be generous to those in need, kind enough to return Pet to her brother, patient with her befuddled mother.

And he could be seductive. Oh, yes, he could make his wife burn with desire.

A wave of intense longing swept over Alicia, bringing with it a realization that shone brightly in the maelstrom of her emotions. She wanted to feel the warmth of Drake's arms around her. She wanted to learn the secrets of his past, to share his innermost thoughts. Though her mind rebelled at the notion, her body reveled in anticipation.

Whether it be foolishness or folly, she wanted to make the best of their marriage.

Chapter Eighteen

Stretched out naked between the sheets, Drake pillowed his head on his crossed arms and listened for sounds from the adjoining chamber. He could hear only the hissing of the coal fire. Except for a faint, reddened glow from the hearth, the bedroom was black as night, though beyond the closed shutters, dawn was lighting the sky.

Scowling up at the darkened canopy, he told himself to forget about Alicia. He had no wish to invite her scorn. Although he couldn't purge her from his mind, he felt reluctant to face her. Now he understood the depths of her hatred of him.

No wonder she had fought against their marriage. She had told him that wealth wouldn't make him a gentleman, and he had seen it as proof of her snobbery. But her coldness hadn't arisen from a belief in her own superiority; rather, she'd despised his profession. For good cause.

Damnation! He ought to have investigated her past. He would have discovered the truth about her father.

And had he known, would he have desisted?

Drake had to admit he'd have gone through with his plan regardless. She was the one woman Hailstock wanted. And stealing her for himself made Drake's revenge all the sweeter.

Remembering her tears, though, he felt a sour distaste for himself. He told himself he shouldn't care how miserable she felt. He had given her wealth and a comfortable life, when most women had to scrabble to put food on the table. But he did care, and that angered him.

He wanted to hold her close and comfort her. *Hell.* Soft embraces were for milksops. He wanted her for one purpose, and one purpose alone. If he wasn't so certain she despised him, he would join her in bed and awaken her for his pleasure. She would be sleepy and warm, her silken blond hair streaming over the pillow. He would push the nightgown to her waist and come down on her. Even as awareness darkened her eyes, he would touch her and tame her—

The connecting door opened.

He lifted his head, his heart jolting, his gaze narrowing. Alicia stood in the doorway. The pale light of dawn outlined her slim figure, and her flimsy nightdress hinted at womanly curves. His desire turned to hard, pulsing arousal. She couldn't resist him, after all.

"Drake?" she called softly. "Are you awake?"

For a moment, he didn't answer. He wanted her too fiercely for words. Curse this obsession. Alicia was no different from any other woman he'd bedded. He would slake his lust and be done with her.

"Come in," he said.

She ventured inside and shut the door. The room plunged into darkness again. His eyes still dazzled by the light, he couldn't see her in the dense black shadows. Yet he was keenly aware of her presence . . . and the erotic thrill inside himself.

He pushed up against the pillows, raising one knee and resting his arm on it. By the faint glow of the fire, he found her. She stood at the foot of the bed, a ghostly shape in the gloom. He hadn't even heard her move.

"I need to speak to you," she said, her voice too firm and too restrained for a seductress.

Perhaps he was wrong. Perhaps she had another purpose. She could have a knife in her hand, ready to cut off his ballocks.

He felt an involuntary twinge in that part of his anatomy. Annoyed with himself, he nonetheless felt compelled to say gruffly, "I'm sorry about your father. I didn't know."

The rasp of his own breathing answered him. Then she spoke, so low he had to strain to hear. "Not many people did," she whispered. "You see, he went out to the mews . . . it was late at night . . . very dark . . ." She paused, a little catch in her voice. "His death was . . . attributed to a thwarted robbery."

He had to ask, "Who found him?"

"A groom . . . and by ill fortune Mama awakened . . . she went out there and saw . . ."

Hell. He could sense the pain in Alicia. Every fiber of his being urged him to go to her. But she wouldn't welcome his comfort. She viewed him as a villain who bled men dry. Men like her father.

There was nothing he could say in his own defense. Nothing that would ease her grief and anger. Did she hate him enough to do something rash? Uneasy again, he peered through the darkness, seeking a glint of cold steel. "Why did you come in here?" he asked bluntly.

"I've a few questions for you," she said, her voice brisk and sharp again.

She wanted to talk? He'd humor her. "Ask away."

"Why didn't you tell me about Mrs. Yates?"

He tensed, sitting up straighter. "What about her?"

"*She's* the woman you rescued in Whitechapel. Had I known, I might have been more understanding toward her. So why did you not identify her from the beginning?"

The question made him uneasy, so he dodged it. "How did you find out?"

"From Mr. MacAllister. He was most informative."

Damn Fergus. What else had he told her?

"Yates doesn't like people to know the story," he said glibly. "So naturally I respected her wishes."

"Naturally." Her cool, patrician tone, faintly sarcastic, floated through the darkness. "Nor did you wish me to take notice of Kitty or Chalkers or Big Bill—among others in this house. *That's* why you denied me any authority over the servants. You feared I would realize the truth."

"What the devil is that supposed to mean?"

"You didn't wish me to know . . . that you have a soft heart."

A cold sweat broke out on his skin. "On the contrary," he snapped, "I didn't want you to get any ideas about discharging my servants—you with your haughty ways and highborn standards. It's a well-known fact that ladies can't abide the seamier side of life."

Alicia rounded the bedpost. He tensed, half expecting the flash of a blade toward his groin. But she halted just out of his reach. "*Most* ladies," she said mildly. "You forget that for the past five years, I haven't led the typical life of a lady."

He could say nothing to that. After her father's violent death, she had cared for her dotty mother and her profligate brother, all the while struggling to make ends meet. Drake felt a surge of anger at the elder Lord Brockway. No man should subject his family to such horror and grief.

Yet all too often, wagering was a sickness in some men. He had witnessed it himself many times and exploited the weakness for his own profit. Damn her for making him doubt his actions.

"I will have authority in this house," Alicia stated.

"What?"

"I promise not to discharge any of the servants, but I *am* taking over my rightful duties as mistress here. You will agree to that."

Again, he found himself searching through the darkness for that knife. "Fine," he muttered. "Do as you please."

A silence stretched out. Shifting restlessly against the sheets, he braced himself for another slew of questions. Had Fergus mentioned anything about Hailstock? Surely not. By God, if Alicia found out that he had wed her for revenge on the man she regarded so highly—

"I will also take over my rightful duties as your wife."

Drake's attention snapped to her. "Duties?"

"I will have you in my bed," she said, a husky note entering her voice. "Or in yours, if you prefer."

His mouth went dry. She glided closer, a pale wraith in the shadows. Silk rustled, torturing him with the knowledge of what lay beneath it. She reached up as if to adjust her gown. Then she wriggled her shoulders and the garment slithered down to her feet.

At once he felt a desire so fierce it shook him. She stood naked, and he cursed the darkness that prevented him from seeing more than the glow of creamy flesh, a hint of ripe breasts. God! Despite all that had happened, she still desired him.

"Your duty," he murmured, "is my pleasure."

"No," she corrected, "*my* pleasure is *your* duty."

He chuckled at that, his body reacting with animal readiness. When she slipped into bed, he pulled her atop him so that her soft slim body draped his. He knew she could feel his arousal, thick and hard against her belly. He wanted her so much his fingers trembled as he cradled her head in his hands.

She sighed, lifting herself slightly so that the tips of her breasts brushed tantalizingly close to his mouth. He drew one into his mouth and suckled her until her hips undulated, rubbing his hard length, torturing him with anticipation. The darkness fired his blood and heightened his other senses. The faint rosy scent of her skin. The warm silk of her breasts. The sweet taste of her nipples. He slid his hands down her smooth spine and over her shapely backside, touching her thighs before bringing his hands back up to lace his fingers with hers.

"No knife," he murmured into her fragrant hair.

"Knife?"

"Darling, I thought you'd come to skewer me."

"Mmm." Reaching down, she caressed his throbbing arousal. "I'd far prefer you do the honors—to me."

He sucked in a sharp breath. Where had she learned her sultry playfulness? He must be corrupting her. And he ought to regret it. But he could only anticipate all the endless depravities he wanted to teach her. Subjecting her to a hungry kiss that roused a demon in him, he slid his hand between them and found the warm, slippery elixir of her passion. Alicia moaned and arched to him, and he needed no further encouragement. Rolling her onto her back, he mounted her, plunging deep enough to touch the mouth of her womb.

A primitive exultation stilled him for a moment. Her wet silken heat surrounded him. No other woman had ever fit him so tightly, so perfectly. He could get no closer to her than this, yet irrationally he wanted more. Rubbing his unshaven cheek against her soft skin, he muttered her name and moved slowly, torturously inside her.

Her lips sought his in little stinging kisses. Like a blind person in the darkness, she touched his face with her fingertips, tracing the contours. "Drake ... oh, Drake ... I love you. ..."

Something strange and powerful gripped his throat. *No.* She didn't love him; she loved *this.* He thrust hard and deep into her sheath, honing the tension with his sword, determined to prove her lust by carrying her to new heights of rapture. He relished her soft sounds of passion, the eagerness of her hands on his body. Panting, she locked her legs around his waist. He felt her begin to convulse around him in delicate inner shivers that pulled him deeper inside her, driving him wild. *His woman. His wife.*

In the moment before he spilled his seed in a violent rush, he had the illogical sense that they had ceased to be two separate beings. As one, they cried out with the explosion of ecstasy. As one, they held fiercely to each other through the long waves of pleasure. As one, they sank into the peaceful aftermath.

Grateful for the darkness, Alicia rested her cheek against Drake's sweat-dampened shoulder. His heavy weight pinned her to the bed, and he lay with his face tucked into the crook of her neck. His breathing was slow and deep, and she wondered if he'd fallen asleep. A terrible tenderness caught at her throat. She was glad of the reprieve, for it gave her a chance to face her newfound feelings.

In the throes of passion, she had voiced words of love. She had spoken ardently, without thought, the disclosure rising from a hidden place in her heart. And she feared it was true. She loved Drake Wilder.

The knowledge left her feeling vulnerable and shaken. Never could she forget what he had done to her, taking merciless advantage of her desperate situation. Never could she overlook who he was, a man who had made his fortune off the weaknesses of others. Those facts shone as clearly in her mind as the admirable charity he bestowed on other people. He was a complex, ruthless autocrat, and she had wed him because she'd had no other choice. But she did have a choice in matters of the heart.

Or did she?

Beset by a helpless yearning, she savored his sheltering closeness. She could not ignore the deep river of emotion that flowed inside her heart. Her long-ago attraction to the Duke of Featherstone had been mere infatuation; her regard for Lord Hailstock, only affection for an old family friend. Then fate had brought Drake into her life. He had wanted a wellborn wife, and he would stop at nothing to have her.

She had been a pawn to his ambitions. He might have lured another nobleman into debt, then taken his sister or his daughter as payment. But by a twist of fate, he had chosen Alicia. And to her shame and chagrin, she could no longer lament what had happened.

She had decided to make the best of her marriage. She had wanted to wring a bit of happiness from a circumstance she could not change, to find some comfort in the physical. She had never meant to fall recklessly in love.

Drake lay over her, dominating her even in sleep, his arm slung beneath her breasts. He didn't love her; he felt only lust. It served no purpose to delude herself about that. Though she felt cozy and protected in his embrace, it was all an illusion. And she knew she mustn't lie here all morning, pining for his heart, while he slept.

Easing away, she gasped when his arm tightened, trapping her against the bed. He turned onto his side to face her, though she could barely see him. "Stay," he mumbled, his voice raspy and deep. "It's early yet."

"I thought you were asleep."

"Almost." As he idly stroked her breast, a slumberous seductiveness crept into his tone. "This was an unexpected pleasure. I expected you to be angry . . . about your brother."

"I . . ." How could she explain the torment that still lurked inside her? How could she *think* while he was touching her? "I cannot like Gerald working in such a place. But you were right to say that I shouldn't make his decisions for him. We must all make our own choices."

"Except you," he mused, as if too relaxed to guard his words. "You had no choice but to marry me."

She swallowed hard. "I'm here now by choice," she said steadily. He might not love her, but by heaven, she wouldn't share him. "And you will have no need for any other woman. Should you stray, I might just get that knife."

He said nothing to her bold assertion, and Alicia wished she could see more than the faint black outline of him against the shadows. Would he remember her declaration of love? But perhaps he hadn't even heard it. Perhaps he had been too lost in passion to heed her. Another thought pierced her. Or perhaps he was accustomed to women proclaiming their love in bed.

He seemed suddenly like a stranger. She knew so little about him, and she felt the jealous need to share more than just lovemaking. To make their relationship special compared to the women in his past.

"Will you tell me about your childhood?" she asked, laying her hand on his broad chest. "I understand you were born in Scotland."

His muscles tensed beneath her fingertips. "Fergus told you."

"Yes." She wouldn't let him keep a wall between them. She would break it down, brick by brick. "He said you were born in Edinburgh, and your mother was an actress. What was her name?"

The dark silence seemed alive. She could feel the strong pulse beating in his throat. Slowly, almost reluctantly, he said, "Muira Wilder."

"What was she like?"

"Why do you want to know?" he countered.

"You've met my mother. Now I'd like to know at least something about yours."

"It was a long time ago. I've forgotten." Shaping his hand around her breast, he fondled her so that she gasped with involuntary pleasure.

But Alicia wouldn't be distracted. Seizing his wrist to still his caress, she said firmly, "Then I'll ask Mr. Mac-Allister. He'll tell me."

She feared Drake wouldn't answer. But he did finally, his voice flat and emotionless. "She sang like a nightingale.

She baked bannocks that would melt in your mouth. And she would give her last pence to the poor."

"But *you* were poor."

"And now I'm not. Thus ends my rags-to-riches tale."

Bracing himself on his forearms, he slid his body back and forth with slow eroticism so that springy hairs on his chest teased her breasts and his masculine flesh touched her between the legs. She clasped his lean waist and struggled to keep her mind focused. Not even for lovemaking would she relinquish this opportunity. "You were only ten years old when you came to London. Why didn't you stay in Edinburgh?"

For a moment he paused, his big body hovering over hers. She sensed a peculiar tension emanating from him, but the darkness kept her from reading his expression. "Can't you guess?" he taunted. "Scotsmen are notorious misers. So I came to where the pluckings are richer."

"You can't have decided to be a gambler at age ten," she said logically. "There had to have been another reason to uproot yourself."

"Fergus and I wanted a grand adventure. So we joined a theatrical troupe here in London."

"The theater? You were an *actor*?" How strange to imagine him in the artificial life of the stage. Yet it made sense. He would follow in his mother's footsteps; he would gravitate to the world he knew.

"I wasn't an actor," he said. "I worked behind the scenes, doing odd jobs. I hardly even remember what."

He spoke dismissingly, as if his rough childhood years were of no consequence. He settled onto her, heavy and hot, his hands gliding up and down her body. But she wasn't ready to acquiesce. "Is that where you met Lazarus Cheever?" she asked.

"Yes—" Drake bit off his words, and through the gloom, she felt the force of his stare. "How the devil do you know him?"

"We were introduced at your club, of course. Yesterday evening."

"Fergus," he said through gritted teeth, "has some explaining to do."

With her fingertips, she tenderly soothed his clenched jaw. "You truly do dislike for anyone to know of your generosity," she murmured. "But I'm pleased by it. So tell me, *is* that how you know Mr. Cheever? From the theater?"

"I used to help him and the other players learn their lines by reading one of the other parts." The admission sounded pulled from him.

"Is that how you lost your accent?" she prompted. "By reading aloud from plays?"

His exasperated breath gusted warm against her ear. "Och, dinna go on so," he muttered. "Ye're too bonny a lass to blether like an auld fusspot."

His low-pitched brogue made her toes curl, and she couldn't stop a delighted laugh. "Oh, Drake. I can see you as a mischievous lad, with your black hair and blue eyes . . . and your beautiful smile." She traced his mouth with her fingertips, then the slight indentations on either side that deepened when he smiled. Her voice lowered to a yearning whisper. "I hope . . . that someday we have a son who looks just like you."

He pulled in a harsh breath, his chest expanding against her bosom. With quick aggression, he pushed his hand between her thighs and stroked her. This time, she let herself respond with all the passion in her heart and body. Their differences ceased to matter in his arms. He made her feel desired, almost cherished, and she would seize every moment of happiness he offered her.

When it was over and they lay sated, their bodies cooling, she could sense his weariness. Gently she stroked back a lock of his hair and kissed his brow. Drake guarded his privacy, but this morning he had let her see a glimpse of himself. She felt as if he had finally become a whole man to her, a man with a past. Could she ever mean more to him than an obsession that would burn itself out?

She ached to know, to coax more answers out of him, but she had slept last night and he had not. Reluctantly she wriggled out from under him, only to feel his fingers curl around her wrist.

"Leaving?" he asked in a voice thick with exhaustion.

"Yes," she whispered. "I've things to do today."

She half wished he would draw her back down, but after a moment he loosened his grip. Rising from the bed, she groped on the floor for her nightgown.

The linens rustled as he shifted position. His voice rumbled out of the darkness. "What things?"

"Well . . . I'll spend the morning with Mama. . . ." Gathering her thoughts, Alicia slid the gown over her head, the silk cool on her sensitized skin. She knew one act she must accomplish today. She would visit Lord Hailstock's son, James.

But she couldn't tell Drake. Their accord was too wonderful, too new, to risk destroying it with a squabble. Though he had stated his intention to accompany her, she suspected his loathing for Lord Hailstock would cause him to put her off for days, for weeks, possibly longer. In the meantime, a disabled young man would do without the cheering visit of a friend.

Despising the need for subterfuge, she added lightly, "And Sarah came to call yesterday. Likely she'll want me accompany her to the shops."

Drake mumbled incoherently. He sounded halfway to slumber already. She could hear his breathing, slow and deep.

Alicia hesitated in the darkness, wishing she knew how to end his hostility toward the marquess. The rivalry between them was ridiculous. She belonged to Drake, and that was that. But men were possessive, territorial creatures who seemed to thrive on competition. Perhaps in time Drake would mellow.

And perhaps in time she would feel easier about loving him.

Chapter Nineteen

A footman led Alicia upstairs, although from previous visits she already knew her way around Lord Hailstock's house. As she entered the sitting room, she frowned in dismay. Though it was early afternoon, the blinds were down, the lamps unlit, the air stuffy. James must be in one of his more melancholy moods today.

By the meager light from the hearth fire, she could see him reclining on his favorite chaise longue, watching her as she picked her way past the lumps of French gilt furniture to the window, where she drew up the blinds and threw open the casement window, letting the balmy spring air eddy into the chamber. "Good afternoon, James," she said in her cheeriest voice. "For heaven's sake, why were you sitting here in the dark?"

He squinted against the invading sunshine. "There's nothing else to do," he grumbled. Then he aimed a scowl at the doorway. "The duchess didn't follow you, did she?"

"She's waiting downstairs, in accordance with your request. But I must say, she would like to visit with you."

"No. I don't care to entertain strangers."

Alicia had expected such an answer. She had warned Sarah, but her friend had insisted on accompanying her, anyway. Not that Sarah was a complete stranger to him.

Their first Season, Alicia had introduced her two friends. Though he was a year their junior, allowed to join society at seventeen by his indulgent father, James had wooed Sarah with the impudent arrogance of a privileged only son. They'd spent most of their time sparring, and for a time, Alicia had thought their teasing might develop into something deeper. As heir to the Marquess of Hailstock, James would have made a fine match for the daughter of a viscount. But then Sarah had set her sights on the Duke of Featherstone.

And soon thereafter, James had suffered his fateful fall. It had happened that summer at Hailstock's country estate. James had been riding a horse his father had given him on his eighteenth birthday, charging recklessly over the moors when the stallion stumbled, throwing him to the hard ground. The fall had caused permanent damage to his spine—and an even more tragic injury to his spirit. His legs useless, the once-cheeky boy had grown sullen and irritable, angry at the world.

That same summer, Alicia had lost Sarah's friendship and then her father had died. Perhaps because they'd both endured tragedies, Alicia had always felt an affinity with James, a bond as strong as if they were brother and sister.

Lost in memories, Alicia sat down near him. An odd thing happened then. For a fleeting second, as she met his narrowed blue gaze, it was like looking into Drake's angry eyes. The impression vanished when she blinked, taking in the younger man's rumpled tawny hair, the sour slant of his mouth, the cheeks pale from too little sunshine.

She gave herself a mental shake. She mustn't allow thoughts of Drake to preoccupy her. James deserved her undivided attention.

"It's good to see you again," she said, flashing him a bright smile. "It must be nearly a month since last I visited."

One arm propped on the back of the chaise, James reclined like a fallen archangel. His face bore a petulant handsomeness, and his shoulders were broad beneath his dark blue coat. A fine cashmere blanket hid his withered legs. "*More* than a month," he complained. "And don't bother to comment on how well I'm looking. My aunts and cousins feel compelled to fabricate compliments whenever they visit. As if I'm blind as well as crippled."

"You *are* a handsome man," she protested. "And I've missed your company—"

"Now, there's another lie," he broke in, his gaze more watchful than reproachful. "I understand you've been busy. And that felicitations are in order. You now have that bastard gambler to occupy your time."

She dug her fingers into the arms of the chair. Not even from James would she tolerate disrespect. "My husband's name is Drake Wilder," she said icily. "And he is as much a gentleman in his manners as you are not."

James did a mock wince. "I do beg your pardon, my lady."

"You are forgiven. Only if you will judge Drake for himself, not for what you may have heard about him."

James narrowed his eyes. "So tell me, where does he hail from? Who are his parents?"

"He's from Scotland originally, though he came to London after his mother died when he was ten. I know nothing of his father." She frowned at James. "And if you dare to make any more snide remarks about his low birth, I shall never come to visit again."

"Ah, how prettily you defend him. Could it be a love match, then? Not the forced marriage that has so enraged my father?"

She felt a flush climb to her cheeks. "I'm content with Drake, and we shall leave it at that. I would have brought him here to meet you, but—"

"But the old man would have aimed the wrong end of

a dueling pistol at him." James leveled his finger at her and pretended to pull the trigger.

"Don't exaggerate," Alicia said, though she felt uneasy. "I know the marquess doesn't approve of my husband, but I can't imagine him reacting in violence."

"Yet wouldn't it be interesting to find out for certain?" James eyed her with a sly, almost secretive smile. Then he shrugged, picking at the fringe on his blanket. "Ah, well, it's a pity you didn't bring Wilder, after all. Father had an appointment with his tailor this afternoon."

"Be sure to give him my greetings when he returns."

"He'll be sorry to have missed you. He hasn't been very happy about losing you to a man like Wilder. As for me . . . I've been disconsolate over losing you as my stepmama."

Was he teasing? He must be. "Well," she said lightly, "the only person I brought with me, you don't wish to see."

His brief playfulness vanished and his mouth settled into a sullen line. "Poor duchess," he said with biting sarcasm. "It must be trying for her, having to wait downstairs when she wanted to glean a few juicy tidbits of gossip."

"Nonsense," Alicia said, not bothering to hide her annoyance. "Sarah came with me because we're going to Bond Street."

"Ah, shopping. That bubble-brained ninny will be in her favorite milieu."

"Sarah is an intelligent woman. She'd probably enjoy our literary discussions." Unwilling to tolerate another nasty comment, Alicia changed the subject. "Tell me, have you read any more of Carter's *Epictetus*?"

His wide shoulders lifted in a moody shrug. "What's the use of studying the opinions of dead philosophers?"

"It's a challenge that will exercise your mind."

"It's a waste of time and energy."

"But it's better than brooding in the dark." Rising, she went to a circular bookstand near the chaise longue and plucked out a leather-bound volume. "I'll read to you for a while if you like. There's a passage here about the free will of man—"

Before she could find the page, he grabbed the book. "Everyone is always wanting to read to me. As if I'm a bloody idiot."

Heedlessly, he tossed the volume over his shoulder and hit a vase behind him. The porcelain shattered against the wall. Purple irises flew in all directions, and water dripped onto the opened book.

Alicia gasped. "James!" As she hastened to pick up the book, she caught a flash of movement through the doorway.

"You *are* a bloody idiot," Sarah said. "In addition to being an ill-natured boor."

She glided into the sitting room, looking very inch the duchess, with her upswept sable hair and gown of primrose muslin, the deep scooped décolletage revealing her creamy bosom and swanlike neck. James sat utterly still. His upper body was rigid with shock, his legs lying useless on the gold-striped cushions.

Sarah stopped at the end of the chaise and regarded him. "Are you over your tantrum yet?" she said, languidly removing her gloves. "Or shall I fetch your nursemaid?"

"How dare you presume to come in here," he snapped. "And to insult me in my own house."

"Oh, is that privilege reserved for you, then? Am I to stand here meekly and let you take your shots? Well, I am no *bubble-brained ninny* to do so."

Setting down the book, Alicia hastened to her side. Though privately she agreed with Sarah, she also understood that James's anger rose partly from embarrassment. "Please, let's go. I'll return tomorrow—alone."

"Oh, but I should like to visit with my dear friend," the duchess said, sitting on a gilt chair and serenely arranging her skirt. "I must say, James, you've changed. You never used to be so rude and unmannerly."

"Nor did you, Sarah," Alicia chided.

But neither of them were listening.

James glowered at the duchess. "Of course, I'm no longer the man I was," he bit out. "Look at me. I'm crippled."

"Look at me," Sarah retorted. "I'm widowed. We all have our tragedies in life."

"At least you can go about as you please. Rather than lie here all day with nothing to do."

She lifted an elegant shoulder in a shrug. "Then find something to do."

His mouth twisting with fury and frustration, he leaned forward and growled, "Blast you, there's nothing. Nothing but reading and thinking and remembering."

Sarah looked unmoved. "Tell me, when was the last time you left this house?"

"I go for a drive now and then. But it's a trial to be carted around like an invalid with servants and hangers-on. So don't be suggesting I get out more."

The duchess tilted her head. "Do you know what I think?" she asked softly. "I think you're afraid."

His compressed lips blanched with rage. Anxious to avert disaster, Alicia stepped between James and Sarah, giving voice to the idea that had just sprung into her mind.

"James, will you go somewhere with us right now?" Alicia asked.

He made an impatient gesture. "I can't get around the shops. You know that."

"Please," she said. "It isn't shopping. I've somewhere else in mind."

A cautious interest lit his blue eyes. "Where?"

Anticipation flashed through her. Why hadn't she thought of this before? Knowing Drake wouldn't leave the house until midafternoon at the earliest, she took a deep breath. "We're going to Wilder's Club."

*　*　*

Drake headed down a pathway through Green Park, his steps brisk and energetic. Sunlight dappled the grass, and the afternoon air held the rare promise of summer. He felt relaxed and sated, invigorated after making love to Alicia at dawn. He had slept deeply and awakened refreshed after only four hours. Rejuvenated, he'd decided to walk to the club rather than take his carriage.

He hadn't expected to find satisfaction in marriage to a noblewoman. He had believed Alicia to be cold through and through. He'd wed her solely for revenge, and their compatibility in bed was a bonus. He smiled to himself, anticipating the long sessions of sex in the weeks to come. It would take quite a while to purge so strong a need from his blood. And by her eagerness, Alicia would be willing for whatever pleasures he had in store. She had even claimed to love him.

Aware of a gathering tension inside himself, he filled his lungs with a deep breath of fresh air. She was mistaken, of course. Having a lady's delicate sensibilities, Alicia needed to justify the raw nature of her passion. So she had swathed her lust in the pretty illusion of romance.

So be it. If it kept her hot for him, he'd let her enjoy her fantasies.

Leaving the park, he strode down a footpath between two mansions and emerged in the mews at the rear of his club. He relished the tall edifice of Portland stone before entering through a plain green door. In the kitchen, several maids were at work, two polishing the silver, another cleaning the big Bodley range. They curtsied to him, even Molly, the pregnant girl, whom he ordered to sit down and rest. Their obeisance made him uncomfortable, but he had long ago given up trying to forbid it. They viewed him as their lord and master. And he supposed it was true; the club *was* his castle.

As he went into the corridor, his sense of satisfaction grew. Until he saw Fergus MacAllister hovering outside the door leading into a suite of small offices. The Scotsman spied Drake and froze for a moment, his bushy eyebrows lifted in surprise.

Then he came loping like a giraffe down the passageway. "By jings," he said a shade too heartily, "I dinna ken ye'd arrive here so early."

"I'd had enough sleep. So I thought I'd go over last month's accounts." He stepped toward the door. "Is Lazarus in?"

Fergus surged past him and planted himself like a tall oak in front of the door. "Cheever's feelin' puirly. Go on up to yer office, and I'll bring the books to ye."

Something in his manner roused Drake's suspicions. "I'll get them myself."

As he reached for the door handle, Fergus thrust out his arm to block him. "Ye mind yer manners, now. Else ye'll have me to answer to."

Even now, that stern gaze could reduce Drake to a scrappy lad of ten. Refusing to quail, he gave the old man a challenging look. "Move aside."

Fergus scowled at him for another long moment, then stepped out of the way. Leaving him standing in the outer passage, Drake pushed open the door. A long corridor stretched out with several doorways leading to the club offices. Here, no carpet softened the stone floor, so the bookkeeper could negotiate his wheeled chair more easily.

The hum of voices eddied from the farthest room.

Wondering what—or who—Fergus was trying to hide, Drake walked quietly toward the back office. The door was cracked open, and he could see only a slice of blue-painted wall and a low filing cabinet. He raised his hand to knock when the conversation inside stopped him.

"How do you get around in that contraption?" A stranger's voice, a man, his question spoken with cultured disdain.

"The upstairs is unquestionably a problem," said Lazarus

in his mellifluous tone. "But Wilder installed a ramp at the rear of the building. I can maneuver in and around the ground floor quite on my own."

"There, you could move your chambers to the ground floor." That cool female voice sounded familiar. *The duchess?* "At least you wouldn't have to rely upon footmen to carry you about like a baby."

"And I could get away from the likes of you," the stranger snapped. "That is the greatest advantage to such a chair."

"Please, no quarreling. You two are worse than children."

Alicia. Drake's heart surged against his rib cage. What the devil was she doing here? And why was Fergus protecting her?

Thrusting open the door, he stepped into the office. All conversation halted. Four heads turned to stare at him. Behind the desk, Lazarus Cheever leaned back in his wheeled chair, his hands folded over his stout belly. Across from him, Sarah, the Duchess of Featherstone, perched on a plain wooden chair as if it were a throne. Beside her, Alicia sat slim and pretty in bronze silk, her fair hair soft around her pale features, a familiar stubborn firmness to her shapely lips.

And the stranger—not a stranger at all.

A band of tension tightened around Drake's chest as he stared at the man. He reclined in a sort of litter that was gilded and cushioned, as if he were a damned Egyptian prince. His eyes were a piercing blue, his shoulders broad beneath a finely tailored coat, his hair a rich tawny hue. And his mouth was curled into a thin smile.

For the barest flash of time, Drake thought he saw a spark of recognition on those haughty features. And he was aware of something like a bond stretching between them. An affinity, a kinship.

Impossible. This pampered aristocrat could know noth-

ing of a bastard's existence. And Drake didn't intend for
him to know . . . yet.

Focusing his mind, he felt the rise of a familiar hatred.
At last, he'd come face-to-face with his half-brother, James.

Hailstock's heir.

The favored son.

Chapter Twenty

Alicia turned in her chair to see Drake looming in the doorway of the office. The air felt suddenly suffocating. All belligerent, overbearing male, he afforded her and Sarah only a passing glance. His gaze riveted to James.

With a sinking heart, she knew he had recognized Lord Hailstock's son.

"What the devil's going on here?" he demanded.

Until now, she had been pleased with the meeting. Once James had seen the rolling chair, the light of interest had entered his eyes and things had proceeded well. She wouldn't allow Drake to interfere. "We're visiting with Mr. Cheever," she said coolly. "James, this is my husband. Drake, Lord Scarborough."

"I'm heir to the Marquess of Hailstock," James drawled, his mouth twisted into a sly, superior smile. "My family and Alicia's share a longtime closeness."

"I'm aware of that," Drake said. "So perhaps it's time for my wife to broaden her horizons."

Sitting back against the cushions of his litter, James cocked a sardonic eyebrow. "Indeed? Will you have her seek her acquaintances from among the lower orders? I hardly think that worthy of a lady."

"Your opinion doesn't matter. She is *my* lady."

Good heavens, must she contend with this hostility again? Alicia sprang to her feet. "I am quite capable of choosing my own friends," she said firmly. "James, have you any more questions for Mr. Cheever?"

James shook his head, his attention still narrowed on Drake.

The bookkeeper cleared his throat. "I am happy to assist as I can," he said. "But Mr. Wilder can better answer any questions about the chair's construction. He saw one like it in Rome, determined how it was made, and then ordered one for me."

Sarah had been watching the exchange with avid interest. "How enterprising of you, Mr. Wilder. You must direct us to whomever did the workmanship. We shall be ordering one posthaste."

"There is no *we* about it," James said, casting her an irritated glance. "I daresay I can handle the details myself."

"But you're helpless," the duchess said blandly. "You said so yourself."

"And you're impertinent. Run along now, Your Grace. At least the shopkeepers will be happy to see you."

"How will you get home?" she asked.

"I'll send for my coach." Dismissing her with a wave, he studied Drake with a strangely secretive interest. "Have a seat, Wilder. I'm interested to hear how you managed to build this gambling club from nothing."

"Sorry, I'm too busy for idle chatter," Drake said flatly. "Cheever, I'll need the account ledger for last month."

His rudeness angered Alicia. Where was his generous spirit now?

As the bookkeeper wheeled around and plucked a leather-bound book from the shelf behind the desk, she bent to James and murmured, "Please wait for me in Sarah's coach. I need a word with my husband."

"You must promise we'll return here very soon." That cunning smile hovered about the younger man's mouth.

"Perhaps I'll even bring Father next time. I'm sure that once he gets over his little fuss, he'll want to become better acquainted with your husband."

James knew that Lord Hailstock had no such desire. Was it boredom that made him so determined to stir up trouble? Alicia could only hope that once the wheeled chair gave him more mobility, he would develop other interests.

A pair of footmen carried the litter out to the coach, and Sarah followed, giving Drake and Alicia a droll glance as she departed. "Take your time," she murmured. "It will annoy James exceedingly."

Then Lazarus Cheever discreetly exited the office, leaving Alicia alone with Drake.

As she closed the door, intent on remonstrating him, his strong arms enfolded her from behind. The feel of his hard body caused a traitorous leap in her pulse, and the aroma of his shaving soap tantalized her. Without subtlety, his fingers spread over her belly. As he rubbed his cheek against her hair, his warm breath tickled her ear, raising a flurry of goose bumps over her skin.

"I thought they'd never leave," he said in a husky growl.

"I thought *you* were busy today," she said, holding herself rigidly.

"I'm never too busy for you, my lady." His lips brushed the nape of her neck and his hands roamed to her bosom. Shivery desire swelled in her, threatening to obliterate her anger.

She twisted away, pivoting to face him. "Enough," she stated. "I wish to know why you were so uncivil to James."

"*Was* I uncivil? Perhaps my mind was on other matters." Stunningly handsome in a dark blue coat and buff-colored breeches, he stalked her with aggressive sensuality. "I could think of nothing but being alone with my wife."

Her heart beating faster, she retreated behind the desk. "And I can think of nothing but how rudely you treated my guest—my longtime *friend*. James deserves your compassion, not your contempt."

"If he wanted my compassion, *he* ought to have behaved better."

"You despised him before he even said a word. Why is it that you can show sympathy toward Cheever but not toward James?"

"Cheever is a hardworking man. His lordship is a vain, self-serving aristocrat."

"That isn't why. You dislike him simply because he is Lord Hailstock's son."

Drake's eyes glittered with an intensity that had little to do with physical passion. His features darkly compelling against the white of his cravat, he braced his palms on the desk and leaned toward her. "Speaking of Hailstock, I'd like to know why you disobeyed me and went to his house."

"Because I won't abandon my friends just to suit your whims."

"You were to wait for me to escort you there at my convenience."

"And when would it suit your convenience? Next year? Or perhaps five years from now?"

His mouth quirked into a tolerant smile. "You're right," he admitted. "I've no wish to associate with those who think themselves superior to me."

That confused her. Did his bitterness extend beyond Lord Hailstock? "You're contradicting yourself," she said slowly. "You married me in order to seek acceptance by society. You knew that many in the *ton* would view themselves as your better. And now you're saying that you *don't* wish to associate with them?"

His eyes narrowed to a deep, impenetrable blue. Again, she sensed mysteries in him that eluded her understanding. If he despised all the nobility, then where did that leave her?

In a flash of movement, he rounded the desk and caught her to him, locking her in his embrace. Putting his face to her hair, he inhaled deeply. "I scorn any man who dares to touch you. And Hailstock *has* dared. He is determined to woo you for himself."

His fervent tone softened her as no amount of badgering or blustering ever could. Didn't he realize that no other man could ever tempt her? Yet she wouldn't voice her love again, not until he had earned it. "You must think I'm a hussy who would leap into another man's bed!"

"I'm merely saying that Hailstock is an arrogant snob. He's not to be trusted."

"And you *are* to be trusted?" she said tartly. "The circumstances of our marriage prove otherwise."

His gaze burned down to her breasts, then back up to her face. "Our marriage was your salvation, Alicia. Were it not for me, you'd still be an untried spinster."

With unbridled confidence, he lowered his mouth to hers in a hungry kiss that laid siege to her resistance. How could she love a man who insulted her and enticed her all in one breath? But she did; there was no denying the longing that flowed deep within her, the ache that tempted her to surrender to his caresses. He tasted her deeply as if he couldn't get enough of her. Then he kissed a path down to her throat, licking and nibbling, casting delicious shivers over her skin.

He wanted to distract her. He wanted her to forget that Hailstock's son waited outside in the coach. This was his way of resolving their differences, to use his power over her body.

Flattening her palms against his coat, she pushed at him. "I won't be seduced," she said. "Not until we settle this quarrel."

"There's nothing to settle," he said in a roughly stirring tone. "We want each other. That's all that matters."

"No, you just want to distract me. There's more to marriage than making love."

"Ah, but making love is the best part."

His mouth claimed hers in another ravenous kiss, and his hands clasped hard to her backside, lifting her against him so that she felt the strength of his arousal. Her tenuous hold on her control began to slip. She clung to his neck, her entire being focused on holding still, not moving, not succumbing to his lethal charm.

But when he moved his hand to her breast, caressing her through her bodice, she couldn't restrain a moan. Through the haze of her passion, she sensed him reaching down, pushing up her gown and petticoat.

Shock clashed with forbidden longing. Furiously, she squirmed against his iron embrace. "Drake, no!"

"Yes," he muttered, his hand beneath her skirt, heavy on her bare thigh where garter met silk stocking. "Let me touch you. Just touch you."

He slid his finger into her cleft, and the exquisite pleasure of it blotted out rationality. *Oh, sweet heaven.* She pressed deeper into his hand, instinctively seeking gratification. His clever strokes wrested another moan from her, and she hid her face in his cravat to muffle her uninhibited cries. Yet even as her desire soared, she held to a vestige of discipline. She wouldn't let go. She wouldn't let him win.

Seeming to sense her resistance, he held her firmly, one arm strong against her back, his other hand plying its slow, relentless magic. He whispered naughty, indecent phrases that should not arouse her, but did. Against her will, she felt the gathering tension and could no more stop it than she could halt an approaching storm. With his touch, with his voice, with his skill, he lured her to the pinnacle and compelled her over the edge, so that she shattered into a thousand falling stars.

Dazed and drained, she came to an awareness of their surroundings. Daylight streamed into the office through a high window. She clung weakly to him, her skirts hiked to her waist. His hand still cupped her between the legs.

"Send the carriage away," he murmured against her mouth. "There's a bedroom upstairs, connected to my office. We'll spend the afternoon there."

She couldn't think. "Drake, I . . ."

His hand applied a persuasive pressure. "My darling Alicia," he said in tone so raspy it made her toes curl. "I've imagined making love to you up there. Having you waiting for me each night, my love slave, ready to fulfill my every command."

Distracted by the fantasy, she burrowed her fingers inside his coat. "No, *you* would be *my* slave. Pleasuring me as *I* command."

"I am yours, then, O exalted mistress." Stepping back, he placed his palms together and bowed low. "Pray tell, what is your delight?"

Entranced, she stared down at his dark head, his mock submissive pose. Temptation again threatened her better judgment. In a few minutes, he could be undressing her in private, indulging her desires, pleasing her with his leisurely love play. Oh, would it not be exciting to have him do as *she* commanded?

She put out her hand, but stopped short of touching him.

Only moments ago, he had shown a forceful disregard for her wishes. Now she sensed a practiced quality to his seduction. Rather than a true warmth of feeling, he exuded a cold ruthlessness of purpose. Did he see lovemaking as a convenient way to keep her from James . . . and Lord Hailstock?

He must.

Drake kept his emotions locked in a place where she could not venture. No matter how hard she tried to probe deeper, he wanted only physical pleasure from her. Perhaps because she was a member of the hated nobility, he could admit only to an obsession for her, nothing more.

How long would his infatuation last?

Willing strength into her wobbly legs, she stepped away and adjusted her gown. "I must go. You know why."

"The devil you say," he bit out. "You can't walk out now."

His eyes were dark with unslaked passion. She could see the turgid outline of his manhood straining against the placket of his breeches. His unsatisfied state stirred a wicked satisfaction in her.

The balance of power had shifted, she realized. It might prove useful to keep her husband at a disadvantage. To find some way to make him view her as more than an object of lust.

Walking to the door, she turned and smiled at his angry features. "You said you would do whatever pleasures me. Well, it pleasures me to wait."

Chapter Twenty-one

Holding a large map of England against the wall, Sarah stole a glance at Alicia, who used a hammer to tack down the corners. In the morning sunshine that lit the study at Pemberton House, her friend looked fresh and pretty. The periwinkle gown enhanced her blue eyes and golden hair, and a serene strength shone on her delicate features.

Sarah saw nothing of her own jaded bitterness there.

She breathed deeply to dispel the tightness in her breast. If only she could be so caught up in life again. She would relinquish her title, her wealth, her standing in society, if only she could eradicate the unhappiness inside herself.

Her gaze strayed to the far end of the study, where several rows of little desks stood empty, except for the last one. There, William sat in a desk beside James in his new wheeled chair made of caned beechwood. The two of them had their heads together in conversation, her son small and dark-haired in contrast to James with his vast shoulders and even vaster conceit.

Sarah burned to know what he found to talk about with her quiet son. If he dared to speak an unkind word to William . . .

Alicia stepped back to survey the map. "There. Do you think the place looks ready?"

"I suppose so." Still baffled by her friend's unorthodox plan, Sarah glanced around the study at the plain oak desk with its piles of primers, the standing globe, the slates and chalk. "But I cannot approve of this eccentric whim to open a school for servants."

Alicia set her chin in a stubborn pose. "Opening a school isn't a whim. I wish to do my small part to help those in need. It's a worthy occupation, instructing the less fortunate so they may better themselves."

Sarah couldn't deny Alicia's kindness. She wished she herself could be so unselfish. But this school went far beyond the charitable works appropriate for a lady of the *ton*. "If anyone in society finds out, you'll be ostracized. Need I remind you, you're barely accepted as it is."

With a shrug, Alicia walked to the desk and set the dictionary on its stand. "The good opinion of the nobility doesn't concern me."

"But why not hire a staff to run your ragged school? Why would you and *James*"—Sarah scowled to see him chuckling at something William said—"teach the hired help?"

"Why, to help them, of course," Alicia said serenely. "I've several in my household who would benefit from learning their letters. Perhaps you might wish to send a few pupils as well. It's only for a few hours each day."

Sarah pursed her lips. "Servants are paid to serve, not to shirk their duties. And somehow I have the feeling there's more to your determination than you're telling."

Alicia's blue eyes widened; then she turned her attention to tidying a pile of spelling primers. "It's quite simple. Mama doesn't need me anymore. Nor does Gerald. And Drake . . ." A subtle husky quality entered her voice. "Drake sleeps during the day, so I'm free to do as I please."

"Ah." Her curiosity pricked, Sarah sank onto the window seat and studied her friend. "Does your husband know about this school?"

Alicia hesitated, then firmly shook her head. "I shall tell him when the time is right. He *will* approve."

"I wouldn't be so certain. He seems fixed on making his way in society. He'll forbid you to spend your time with the lower classes."

"Oh, but you're *wrong*. Drake has given employment to many poor souls. He helps the needy, and I must, too. I am determined to show him that we're compatible in more ways than . . ." Alicia's voice trailed off. There was a softness about her mouth, a delicate flush to her cheeks.

"Bedsport," Sarah murmured, struck by understanding. "He pleases you in the bedchamber."

Her eyes dreamy, Alicia twirled the globe on the desk. "That does seem to be a time when we're in perfect accord."

Sarah felt a sharp stab of something remarkably like . . . *jealousy*. She tried to deny it. Charming though he might be, Drake Wilder walked the wicked path of a rake, and she didn't envy Alicia the heartache that surely lay in store for her. Yet through the wall of her bitterness, Sarah yearned to feel a man's touch again. To wear a look that bespoke private pleasures in the bedchamber. To be adored, cherished. . . .

For no reason she could fathom, her gaze strayed to James. The sunlight gilded his tawny hair, and she wondered how different her life would have been if she had chosen him five years ago, if he had been with her instead of out riding that unruly stallion—

She banished the useless fancy. It served no purpose to harbor regrets. If she'd married anyone else, she wouldn't have William.

Her heart clenched sweetly as she gazed across the study at her son. Not for all the adoring swains in the world would she give him up.

What *was* James saying to him?

William sat straight at the desk, his small face sober and

attentive. For a four-year-old he was far too still. He didn't swing his legs like other children or fidget on the wooden seat. Perhaps she oughtn't have brought him here. But they spent so little time together, and she'd wanted to make up for all the times she'd been too mired in her own unhappiness to give attention to him. He was so reserved, Sarah hardly knew what to say to him anymore.

She pressed her fingernails into the window seat. James didn't appear to be having any such trouble. The deep murmur of his voice drifted the length of the study, and though she strained her ears, she could not discern his words.

"I'm so glad James has agreed to help," Alicia said. "It's been good for him to get out of his house. He'll make a fine instructor for the school. Don't you agree?"

Sarah assumed an indifferent expression. "He won't last beyond the first day. He'll succumb to his cantankerous nature."

"He hasn't acted cantankerous this past fortnight. I do believe that having the wheeled chair has changed him for the better."

Sarah didn't agree. All too often, she'd skillfully parried the sword of his sarcasm. If he had grown more tolerant with others, it was only because he'd focused the full force of his resentment on *her*. She opened her mouth to say so when something astonishing happened.

William hopped out of the desk and onto James's lap. The two of them rolled toward the doorway, James deftly turning the large, iron-shod wheels with his hands. He wore no coat and his shirtsleeves were rolled to the elbow, displaying the strong muscles of his forearms.

Alarmed, Sarah hastened across the study. "Where do you think you going?"

James shot her a look of supercilious amusement. "Calm down, Duchess. I'm merely taking Will for a ride up and down the corridor."

Irrationally angered by their rapport, she curled her fingers into fists. "His name is William. And he is staying here with me."

"Nonsense. He wants to help me test this contraption." He glanced down at the boy clinging trustingly to his neck. "Don't you, Your Grace?"

"I would, sir." William lifted his hopeful gray eyes to her. "Please, Mama, may I?"

The ice in her melted a little. "Well . . . if you hold on tightly . . . and promise to be very careful—"

"A little less mollycoddling, if you please," James broke in.

The impertinence of him, Sarah fumed, to criticize her maternal concern. But before she could retort, he rolled the chair away, picking up speed far too quickly. Worried, she hurried out of the study to see the chair careening down the corridor toward the front of the house. The wheels clattered over the bare marble floor. As they neared the foyer, a workman stepped out of the library.

He spied them and leaped back. The chair swerved.

Sarah's heart surged into her throat. The scene seemed to freeze into agonizing slowness. They would crash. . . .

Then James glided into a neat turn. They came racing back, and a squeal of laughter barely registered through her petrified senses.

William's laughter.

They were both laughing, man and boy, as the chair rolled to a smooth halt, the wheels caught by James's deft grip. But Sarah barely noticed him.

With a strangled cry, she snatched her son up into her arms, hugging him close, kissing his soft cheek, touching his small form to reassure herself of his safety. With each shaky breath, she drew in his little-boy scent. Awash with a numbing relief, she glanced over his head at James.

The wretch was smiling at Alicia, bantering with her as she delivered a good-natured scolding.

Sarah had forgotten his smile. She had forgotten that

flash of white teeth, the dimpling of his cheeks, the twinkle in his blue eyes. And she had forgotten how her insides could twist into a knot at the sight.

"Mama, you're squashing me," William complained, wriggling in her arms.

She loosened her grip. "I'm sorry, darling," she said, giving him another kiss before reluctantly letting him down and smoothing his rumpled hair. "It's just that . . . I'm glad you're happy."

James looked at her, and his smile vanished. By the sardonic curl of his lips, she knew that he had seen her unguarded emotions. She loathed him for exposing that vulnerability in her. Fury welled up in a choking flood, and she pressed her lips together, determined to hold her temper in front of her son.

Alicia glanced at both of them, then took hold of William's small hand. "How would you like to go down to the kitchen with me? Mrs. Molesworth, our cook, has baked a chocolate cake."

Obediently, he took her hand and they walked away, disappearing through a door that led down to the basement rooms.

James cast her a hooded glance. "He was never in any danger, Duchess."

"*Never in danger?*" Beset by rage, she curled her fingers into fists. "Is that all you can say? You nearly killed my son."

"Don't be theatrical. Will enjoyed it. You oughtn't shelter him so much."

"His name is *William*," she said again through gritted teeth. "And I'll be as theatrical as I bloody well please. After all, he is *my* son, not yours."

A granite stillness descended over James's features. Into the silence came the faraway sound of workmen pounding somewhere upstairs. Then James swung his chair around and rolled into the study, leaving her standing alone in the corridor.

In spite of her anger, Sarah felt ashamed of her thoughtless cruelty. Of course, *he* would never have a son. Why had she not considered that?

She marched after him. "I'm sorry," she said stiffly. "I didn't mean to offend."

Flanked by bars of sunshine from the windows, he sat watching her. His lips curled ever so slightly as if he contemplated a scathing riposte. But he said the last thing she'd expected. "You really ought to marry again, Duchess."

"I beg your pardon?"

"Will needs a father." James paused, his blue eyes intent on her. "So why don't you run along to one of your social events and bedazzle the gentlemen?"

A dozen retorts sprang to her tongue. But she could only sputter, "Are *you* telling *me* to leave?"

"How perceptive of you," he went on in that biting tone. "And before you go, let me give you some friendly advice. This time, try to choose a man who won't leave you for another woman."

A wallop of pain rendered her speechless. "How dare you . . . presume to pass judgment on me—"

"It's Will I'm thinking of. You need a husband who will give him the attention he needs."

Restless with anger, she paced before James. "What can you know of my son's needs? You'd never even met him before today. I've cared for him since he was born." She remembered that day, the agony . . . and the joy of holding him to her breast for the first time. . . .

"Tell me, Duchess, do you know what Will wants to be when he grows up?"

She scowled at the insolent, godlike expression on his handsome face. "He is the duke, of course," she said frostily. "What else can he be?"

"He wants to be a coalman. He wants to drive a dray and deliver the coal—"

"I know what a coalman is," she snapped. "And you're making up this Banbury tale."

"Ask him, then. Each Tuesday morning, Will sits by the nursery window and sees the coalman down in the courtyard. Apparently he's a jolly fellow, always whistling, always giving a friendly wave." James paused, a faint grin showing a hint of his dimples. "Besides which, the coalman is very dirty. That part does appeal to small boys."

The image jolted Sarah. Against her will, she pictured her son kneeling on the window seat in the nursery, waving to a filthy tradesman. In the midst of a very proper horror, she had to repress a strange, aching desire to smile. "How do you know all this?" she scoffed.

"By talking to him. It took a little coaxing, but Will has quite a lot to say."

He did? Again, Sarah had that disconcerting sense of inadequacy. The sense that she had failed as a mother. In less than an hour, James had learned something about her son's innermost dreams.

"Don't look so stricken," James said in a neutral tone devoid of cold mockery. "There are things a boy won't tell his mother. He needs a father in his life, that's all."

Did he? Was she, in her bitterness toward men, cheating William of a normal life?

She caught James watching her as she paced, his gaze narrowed on her, following her every movement. There was something in his scrutiny that caused her breasts to tighten. To ache with the need to feel his hands . . .

No. Appalled at herself, she denied the feeling. She wasn't attracted to this man. She *loathed* him.

"Go," he taunted softly. "Begone from here, Duchess. Go to the park or to the shops or wherever else you can flirt with the gentlemen."

She had the perverse desire to stay right here, to show

him that he could not dictate her life. Seeing a crate filled with geography primers, she walked to it, sinking down to her knees, graceful despite her slim orchid skirt. She reached inside and took out a book. "I told Alicia I'd help her, and that is what I intend to do."

James wheeled closer, angling his chair beside the crate. He cast a derisive look at her fine muslin gown with its daring décolletage. Any other man she would have suspected of enjoying the display of her bosom. But not this man.

"Now, there's a sight I never thought to see," he said in his disparaging tone. "Her Grace of Featherstone kneeling before me."

Immediately she realized her mistake. From this perspective, she was forced to look up at him, to endure his sulky attractiveness at too close a range. "Go away," she said, reaching for another book. "I've work to do."

"I'll unpack here. Your admirers await you." He reached for the primer in her hands.

She held tightly to the book. "What makes you so certain I have admirers?"

"Fishing for compliments?" he jeered. "You know you're beautiful, with those violet eyes and kissable lips. You can't resist flaunting your breasts at any man you meet. Even me."

A strange fierceness in his eyes made her heart beat faster. Did he really find her beautiful? And why did she care? "I've done nothing of the sort! So leave me be."

"I want you gone from here."

"That is your misfortune, then. I am not yours to command."

He yanked again at the book, but she refused to let go. For a moment they engaged in a silent tug-of-war. Aware of his superior strength, she clenched her teeth, her fingernails biting into the leather cover. She wouldn't let him win this battle of wills. She wouldn't—

Abruptly he gave a pull so powerful and unexpected that she followed the book into his lap. Sprawled ungracefully, her bosom pressed to his chest, she could only stare at him in shock.

His eyes glittered back at her. "Damn you, Sarah," he growled. *"Damn you."*

The extreme frustration in his voice startled her. Through his shirt, she could feel the heat and strength of his upper body. Breathlessness assailed her. "What . . . what have I ever done to you?"

"This." Seizing her hand, he brought it down to his breeches, forcibly shaping her fingers around his male member.

Speechless, she couldn't move. He felt long and thick and hot, a man in full arousal. *For her.*

Excitement rushed over her, reckless and irresistible. She couldn't catch her breath. "James," she murmured shakily. And she brought her mouth to his in a kiss.

Chapter Twenty-two

"Now, there's a sight," Drake said, surveying the audience at Astley's Amphitheatre. "Lady Markem's lover just pinched her bottom."

Alicia had been enthralled by the amazing fire-eater in the center ring. She had been enjoying little William's delight as he stood with his mother at ringside, too excited to sit. Seeing Drake's lazy grin, Alicia couldn't help but smile back. "Lady Markem?" she scoffed. "Impossible. She's the doyenne of propriety."

"Have a look, then." He handed her the opera glasses. "First balcony over there."

Unable to resist, she peeked through the magnified circles. To the left, leaning over the wall of the balcony, stood the buxom, middle-aged lady with a gangly young man who was definitely not the staid Lord Markem. The man tickled her beneath her fleshy arm. Even above the din of the crowd, Alicia could hear her squeal as she playfully slapped his hand.

Aghast, Alicia let the opera glasses fall to her lap. The fire-eater took a bow and left the ring. Amid cheers from the crowd, she murmured to Drake, "It *is* Lady Markem. How can she behave so immodestly in public?"

"Her iron underdrawers must have finally rusted through."

Working her features into a severe expression, she whispered, "Mind your tongue. And behave yourself."

Drake flashed her a grin, his teeth white against his swarthy skin, his blue eyes full of the devil. "Never. This is a night made for amusements."

A shivery awareness danced over her skin. He sat beside her, his leg brushing her skirt, his coat sleeve pressed to her arm. As he turned his attention back to the entertainment, she reveled in the excitement of his presence. He took genuine enjoyment in the spectacle, laughing easily, clapping with vigor.

She was especially impressed that he had kept his promise to William, procuring excellent seats for the early evening show almost within touching distance of the performers. Barely tall enough to see over the side, William stared agog as an acrobat rode into the ring, standing on the backs of two white horses. They cantered side by side around the huge ring, kicking up sawdust, passing so close that Alicia could see the slender man's straining thigh muscles and hear the faint jingle of the harness. The man did a back flip, followed by a handstand, and the onlookers roared their approval.

With undukelike abandon, William jumped up and down. Sarah crouched to say something to him, her eyes sparkling in the brilliance of the magnificent glass chandelier. They laughed together at a roly-poly clown who skipped into the arena.

Alicia's heart overflowed with a yearning delight. How much happier Sarah had been this past fortnight. She and James had flirted rather than fought, and Alicia suspected a romance, though neither would admit to it. With a pang, she wished that James could have accompanied them tonight.

But Drake didn't yet know about the school, let alone that Lord Hailstock's son was assisting her.

The horses rode out of the ring, and a surge of music from the orchestra drew attention to the adjoining stage. The green velvet curtains lifted, and a barrel-chested announcer proclaimed the next act. He made a sweeping gesture at a man in a red-lined black cape, who removed his tall hat and bowed to the audience.

William ran to Drake. His brown eyes large in his small face, he said with reverent awe, "The magician."

"So it is," Drake said, smiling as he tousled the boy's dark hair. "I told you he'd be here."

His easy affection toward the child warmed Alicia's heart. She hoped someday they would have children, for Drake would be a wonderful father. They would be happy together, and he would surely love her.

In a haze of dreamy contentment, she watched as the magician pulled endless scarves from his sleeve and then drew a rabbit out of his hat. The finale of the evening was a mock battle between performers dressed as the French and British cavalry. The clash of their swords, the leaps of their horses, made a grand spectacle that had William cheering his country and booing the enemy.

Afterward, in their coach, the young duke talked enthusiastically, asking Drake questions about the training of the horses and how many hours the acrobats must practice. Then, in the midst of one of Drake's answers, William gave a great yawn, tucked his head against Sarah's side, and fell promptly to sleep.

Though it was not yet ten o'clock, Alicia stifled a yawn, too. She found herself wishing the night would not be over yet. . . .

The coach slowed to a halt in front of Sarah's mansion. Sarah whispered a good night to Alicia and accompanied Drake as he carried the slumbering boy inside. When he returned alone a few moments later, the coach started off again. Relaxed and happy, Alicia debated with him the merits of the various acts, trying to agree which was their favorite. Upon reaching home, he stepped out of the coach, then turned to assist her.

His firm grip stirred her pulse. She hoped he shared her longing to continue their evening together. But to her disappointment, he told the coachman to wait.

Escorting her up to the torchlit portico, he bent to kiss her cheek. "Until later," he said.

Alicia ached for him to kiss her, though they stood only a few yards from the footman stationed by the front door, and in plain view of any pedestrians or carriages along Swansdowne Cresent. She yearned for him to come up to her bed. She wanted to feel his arms around her and his mouth on her bare skin. She wanted him inside her so that she could savor the sweet illusion that they were one heart, one soul.

"Must you go to the club tonight?" she murmured.

Standing in the shadow of a pillar, he gazed at her, his sinfully handsome features revealing nothing of his thoughts. But with a thrill, she knew he desired her. She knew because he held her gloved hand, and the increased pressure of his fingers gave subtle indication of his interest.

With a subtlety of her own, she took a step toward him, so that her breasts touched his dark gray coat. "Please, Drake," she whispered, curving her lips into a provocative smile. "Stay with me."

The night breeze stirred his black hair. His eyes glowed through the gloom. Then he released her hand and stepped back. "I'm afraid you must excuse me," he said. "I've duties to attend to."

Disappointment needled her. Ever since that torrid encounter at his club, they had been playing a sensual dance of power, she alternately tempting and rebuffing him, and he subjecting her to his seductive skills, then drawing back. But perhaps the time had come to force him to view her as more than a physical need or an engaging companion at the circus.

She took a deep breath. "Will you come to Pemberton House tomorrow afternoon? At two o'clock?"

"Why?"

Giving him a deliberately mysterious look from beneath her lashes, she shook her head. "I'm afraid I can't tell you. This is something you'll have to see for yourself."

His gaze made a slow sweep from her face down to her low-cut bodice and back up again. For a moment she feared he would refuse her. Then he smiled, his dimples deepening. "I'll be there."

With a final caress to her cheek, he strode down the steps and entered the waiting carriage. The coachman touched his whip to the pair of horses and with a clattering of wheels and hooves, the vehicle set off into the darkness.

She was alone.

Shivering, Alicia noticed for the first time the damp chill in the air and an overwhelming weariness in herself. She walked slowly into the house, her footsteps echoing in the vast entrance hall with its tall brown pillars rising against the buff-colored walls. In the quiet, her ears still rang with the sounds of the amphitheater. As she climbed the grand staircase, she let her thoughts center on Drake.

In the weeks since she had given him her innocence, he had taught her many inventive ways to make love. Often he would enter her bed while she was still asleep, and she would feel his touch like an erotic dream come true. Sometimes she would awaken to him already inside her, and with only a few strokes he transported her to ecstasy. Other times, he would torture her with a slow building of pleasure. In turn, she would tantalize him in the afternoons, playing the valet as he dressed until they would end up in bed again or making love in the Roman bath.

But even when he was at his most aggressively charming, she could never be certain he felt any more than an infatuation. He seemed determined to keep their relationship light and amusing.

And she was just as determined to make him love her. That was why she wanted him to see her school. Perhaps then he would realize they had more in common than bodily pleasure.

Several wall sconces lit the upstairs corridor, and her slippers made no sound on the plush carpeting. Lost in thought, she didn't notice her mother's door partly open until she was almost upon it.

Mrs. Philpot hovered in the doorway. The lamplight glinting off her silver hair, she made an urgent beckoning motion. "Thank heavens you're here, Mrs. Wilder."

Her heart jolting, Alicia hastened to her side. "What's wrong? Has Mama run off somewhere?"

"Never fear, Lady Eleanor is well," Mrs. Philpot whispered. "Though she has been terribly distraught this evening. Perhaps I ought to have administered her nightly posset, but I thought you might wish to speak to her first."

She stepped back to allow Alicia into the bedchamber. Across the candlelit room, her mother sat curled up on a chaise, her favorite cape tucked around her shoulders as she stared out the darkened window. She appeared to be unaware of their presence.

"You were right to wait." Not for the first time, Alicia appreciated Mrs. Philpot's devotion to her mother. Her throat taut, she asked, "Has she been remembering Papa?"

"No, it is something else entirely. You see, while you and Mr. Wilder were gone this evening, Lord Hailstock paid her a visit."

Alicia frowned. What could the marquess have said to Mama? Like many people, he loathed her illness and went out of his way to avoid her. Not only that, she couldn't imagine why he would deign to set foot in Drake's house. "Do you know what they spoke about?"

Mrs. Philpot shook her head, her lips pursed. "He ordered me out of the drawing room. But afterward, your dear mama was weeping, and she kept going on about some letters."

Letters? Alicia's heart clenched painfully. Mama never received mail anymore. When the madness had descended on her after Papa's death, all of society had forsaken her.

Then a peculiar memory struck Alicia. Lord Hailstock in the study at Pemberton House, his hand in the drawer of the desk. He'd said he was looking for letters . . . letters he'd written to Papa.

"I am sorry," Mrs. Philpot murmured. "I fear I should not have left them alone."

"Don't be troubled. You couldn't have known." Alicia patted the older woman's hand. "Please give us a few minutes alone. I'll put Mama to bed."

"As you wish, my lady." With one last concerned look at Lady Eleanor, Mrs. Philpot left the chamber, quietly shutting the door.

The yellow and white bedchamber had a cozy aura with a fire burning cheerily on the hearth. A fanciful painting of clouds and cherubs danced across the ceiling. On the four-poster bed, the snowy-white counterpane had been turned down to the soft linen sheets and feather pillows.

Alicia hurried to the chaise, where her mother huddled in cape and nightdress, her feet curled beneath her, a braid of silvering fair hair draped over her shoulders.

"Mama, it's Alicia. I've come to visit."

For a moment her mother continued to gaze blankly out into the night. Moisture matted her eyelashes, though no tears fell. Then slowly she turned her head. Her blue eyes blinked and focused, growing lucid with awareness. "My daughter. I haven't seen you in ever so long."

Clearly she didn't remember that Alicia had taken tea with her that very afternoon. Mama had been dressed as a fairy princess in gauzy, flowing robes, insisting they use a child's tiny tea set while sampling morsels of cake.

But thank heavens, now must be one of her moments of sanity.

Aching with bittersweet relief, Alicia perched on the edge of the chaise and took hold of her mother's thin, cold hand. "Mama," she whispered. "Oh, Mama, I heard you were sad, so I came to see what was wrong."

"You're a dear girl to worry about me." Her gaze took in Alicia's gown of muslin over a lavender slip, the gold silk spencer over her bare shoulders. "Are you going out for the evening? I mustn't keep you."

"Drake and I have just returned from Astley's circus. Then I heard what happened and—"

"Is your husband here?" Her eyes bright, Lady Eleanor straightened up and looked toward the door. "I should so like to visit with him."

Alicia shook her head. "I'm afraid he had to go back out."

"Oh," her mother said on a sigh of disappointment. "He is such a gallant gentleman. He sometimes stops by to see me, you know." Frowning, she tapped her chin with her forefinger. "I have been trying to remember of whom he reminds me. . . ."

There was no one like Drake. A sweet softness curled in Alicia's breast. Surely any man who could take the time to humor her befuddled mother had to be capable of a deep, abiding love. . . .

She wrenched her thoughts back to the present. "Mama, you had a visitor this evening. Can you tell me what Lord Hailstock wanted of you?"

"Richard." Her eyes glazed as if her thoughts turned inward. "Now that you mention it . . . I believe he *was* here."

"He inquired about some letters," Alicia prompted.

A starkness came over the countess's face. Sinking deeper into the cushions of the chaise, she moved her head in a violent shake that stirred her braid. "I don't know anything about any letters."

"Could he mean letters he'd written to Papa long ago?" Alicia asked gently. "Do you know where they might be?"

"I know nothing of it. Nothing at all."

It? Was there one letter in particular that he'd wanted? "Did Lord Hailstock tell you why he needs this letter?"

"I can't say. Truly, I *can't*." Lady Eleanor hunched into her bedraggled moleskin cape, the satin lining rustling. "Oh, he is a cold man. But I never dreamed he would break Claire's heart."

"Break her heart?" Hailstock's first wife had died very young, but this was the first Alicia had heard of an unhappy marriage. "But I thought . . . they were in love. They ran off together to be wed."

"Richard never believed her good enough for him. The dear girl couldn't help it she was born of common blood." Pressing a crumpled handkerchief to her face, the countess lapsed into piteous weeping.

Anger nudged at Alicia as she hugged her mother, patting her back through the bedraggled cape. "I know, Mama. I know."

She wasn't entirely surprised to hear that the marquess had looked down on his first wife. Noble bloodlines meant everything to him. Was it possible Drake was right to despise him?

Over the past weeks, they had encountered the marquess at a number of society events. Each time, he disdained Drake; each time, Drake insulted him back. And Lord Hailstock had even made *her* bristle by insinuating that she had married far beneath herself.

The memory of her own prejudice troubled Alicia. She, too, had thought herself superior to her husband. She had condemned Drake as a good-for-nothing gambler—until she had witnessed the extent of his generosity, a munificence he strove to hide behind the dynamic charm of a scoundrel.

He had done far more than she for those in need. But tomorrow, he would come to Pemberton House and see her school. He would realize that she shared his goodwill toward less fortunate souls.

She pressed a kiss to her mother's brow, her skin bearing the faint, familiar scent of lily of the valley. It would do no good to question her further. The next time Alicia saw Lord Hailstock, she would ask him about the letter and insist that he come to her with his questions, rather than badger Mama.

Lady Eleanor lifted her head, blinking her tear-wet eyes. Like a veil lifting from her face, the anxiety and grief vanished, and a wondering quality illuminated her gaze. She gently cupped Alicia's cheek. "My dear girl," she said musingly. "I do believe . . . you have that look about you."

Mystified, Alicia frowned at her mother. "What look?"

"Why, that certain softness. Your papa said he could tell simply by gazing at me."

"Tell what?"

Lady Eleanor smiled very tenderly. "Why, that I was breeding, of course. As *you* must be."

Alicia drew an astonished breath. *Had* she conceived a child? Had that marvelous intimacy with Drake wrought the miracle of a baby? An awed happiness rose in her, but she held it at bay. She mustn't hope too much. No one could look at her face and *know* she was pregnant. This had to be another of Mama's mad fancies.

Lady Eleanor patted Alicia's hand. "It is too wonderful to believe, isn't it? But there are certain signs in a woman. Have you been exceedingly weary of late?"

Alicia couldn't deny the fatigue dragging at her. "Yes . . . but I've been teaching the servants to read during the day and that could account for it."

"When did you last have your monthly?"

"Right before . . . before my wedding. Nearly six weeks ago."

Alicia wasn't used to discussing personal matters with her mother. And for many years, she hadn't had a circle of friends from whom she might have gleaned knowledge. Consequently, she had only a vague understanding of the changes that pregnancy could cause in a woman's body. But now she realized the significance of her delayed cycle.

Gently placing her hand over her flat abdomen, she breathed deeply as an indescribable joy blossomed within her. A baby. In less than nine months, she would give birth to Drake's son or daughter. She would hold their child to her breast, and they would be a family.

Now she had an even more compelling reason to win his heart.

The following afternoon, his head bent against the pouring rain, Drake strode up the steps at Pemberton House. He didn't bother to knock; this town house belonged to him. He couldn't feel any regrets about how he'd acquired the place, either. Winning that deed had assured him of Alicia's hand in marriage.

Alicia.

In the dimly lit foyer, he removed his damp overcoat and flung it over a chair. She would not be expecting him quite yet. He'd arrived early, wild to learn what surprise she had in store for him. It would be an erotic interlude, he hoped. She had been hot for him when they'd parted company the previous evening. What a delight she had been at the circus, her eyes shining, her face animated with unguarded enjoyment. He'd wanted to see a similar joy on her face while he bedded her, and he'd had the very devil of a time resisting her invitation to make love. It wouldn't do for her to think him too taken with her.

His obsession for his wife showed no sign of abating. Indeed, though he would never admit so to Alicia, he'd had to fend off the urge to follow her around like a besotted mooncalf. He didn't understand himself. He had always been able to separate his physical needs from the rest of his life. He would take his satisfaction of a woman and then be done with her. But he couldn't forget Alicia.

Since that one dawn when she had come to him, she hadn't spoken of love again. Not even in the throes of ecstasy. She'd acted both aloof and alluring, slowly driving him mad. It wasn't enough to possess her hand in marriage. He wanted to own her, body and soul.

Perhaps today he would.

Anticipation seared him. He would take a quick look around here on the ground floor. Then he would go upstairs and search the bedrooms. Perhaps he'd find her naked, ready for him. Or perhaps she would titillate him by wearing a sheer gown with nothing on underneath.

Yes. He looked forward to undressing her, kissing every inch of her body, hearing her sweet sounds of pleasure, her whispers of love.

Running his hand through his rain-slicked hair, he stepped into the drawing room. The painters had completed their work, and the pale yellow walls glowed behind the mahogany furnishings. But he took only cursory notice. Alicia wasn't lying on the chaise, waiting to seduce him.

He crossed the foyer and looked into the library. The shelves had been filled with books, and the scent of new leather bindings filled the air. Tables and chairs were arranged on the blue and gold rugs. But Alicia wasn't beckoning to him from the desk, where he might have pressed her down on the flat surface, lifted her skirts, and slid into heaven.

He walked down the long corridor, glancing into a morning room, the dining chamber, and a butler's pantry. She must be upstairs, then. So much the better. They would conduct their little tryst in complete privacy. There would be no one at home but a few servants, who would know better than to disturb the master and his lady. . . .

As he neared the back of the house, he heard the rumbling of a man's voice. The sound came from the chamber at the end of the passageway. From Brockway's study.

He cursed under his breath. If Gerald hadn't yet left for the club, his presence would put a damper on Drake's plans. He'd have to get rid of the stripling, think up an errand to occupy him.

He was considering various excuses when he paused at the partly open door, arrested by a curious sight inside the study. In place of the leather chairs there were rows of desks occupied by an assortment of servants, both male and female.

Before them, his back to the door, sat James in his wheeled chair.

The heat in Drake's veins chilled to ice. In a rush of angry understanding, he realized the truth. There would be no idyllic afternoon spent in his wife's arms.

Alicia had tricked him. Again.

Chapter Twenty-three

James shook his fist at the group. "You will never be welcome in my home," he railed at them. "Do you understand me? Never!"

That venomous tone enraged Drake. Damned haughty blueblood. The servants quailed in their desks, their fearful eyes focused on James.

Drake thrust back the door so hard it banged against the wall. The room fell silent. In a swift glance around, he spied the Duchess of Featherstone seated in a straight-backed chair near James. Across the chamber, Alicia sat with her legs tucked beneath her on the window seat, her rose-pink gown bright against the gray day.

Her eyes widened on him; she sprang to her feet. Her lips formed his name, though no sound emerged.

He gave her a scathing glance. She condoned this injustice?

Furious, he strode toward James. A sea of startled faces turned to Drake. With a jolt, he recognized some of them: Kitty, the deaf girl; several grooms from his stables; Molly, the pregnant maid. The room was quiet except for the patter of raindrops against the windowpanes.

He swung toward James. "How dare you presume to chastise my employees? This is *my* house, not yours."

The silence lasted a heartbeat. Then giggles swept the gathering, the pupils covering their mouths to hide their mirth. Their reaction left Drake nonplussed.

James grinned briefly, then returned his attention to the group. "Quiet, now," he commanded. "It isn't polite to laugh. Mr. Wilder didn't realize I was reading you a story."

The tittering subsided. For the first time, Drake noticed the notebook propped open in James's lap. And he felt a rare moment of utter foolishness.

The duchess glided toward James, placing her hand on the back of his wheeled chair. "James is an eloquent reader as well as a gifted writer."

A faint flush colored his fair skin. "Enough, Sarah," he muttered.

She ignored him. "You should know, Mr. Wilder, that James penned this tale of knights and dragons, of evil sorcerers and fair princesses. The class has enjoyed hearing his stories. Is that not so?"

As one, the pupils eagerly spoke their assent.

Drake looked at their bobbing heads and felt more off balance than ever. James, a writer of fairy tales? A benefactor who entertained the underprivileged?

Drake couldn't reconcile that image with the snobbish lord who had been raised as a privileged only son. This must be a ruse of some sort. But to what purpose, he couldn't imagine.

While the younger ones begged James to read another chapter and he laughingly refused, Alicia pulled Drake to the side of the room, where a large map of England was tacked to the wall. His senses were attuned to the brush of her soft breast, the seductiveness of her subtle scent, the delicacy of her features.

Somehow, she looked especially fragile today, her skin translucent and her eyes shadowed as if she needed a nap. "I thought you'd be arriving in half an hour," she murmured. "I'd meant for you to see the class at their lessons."

"Class?" he repeated numbly.

"Yes, I've organized this school for those wishing to learn their letters and sums. That way, a maid can aspire to the post of housekeeper someday. And a groom might prove adept enough at numbers to become a steward. They can better their lot in life."

A school for the poor? He'd thought she'd been spending her days shopping and socializing, the usual activities for a lady of wealth. He struggled to assimilate her actions.

She'd been here at Pemberton House. With *James*.

Feeling betrayed, he gripped tenaciously to his anger. "What the devil is Hailstock's son doing here?" he said under his breath. "The wretch is toying with these commoners, playing the Good Samaritan. He hasn't any true interest in them."

"You're wrong about that," she whispered back. "And before you pass judgment, I ask only that you listen while the pupils show you what they've learned this past fortnight."

He despised being gulled. Yet he couldn't refuse her. Not when she gazed at him so hopefully with those clear blue eyes. Not when she curved her lips into the soft smile that could turn him into a babbling idiot.

Compressing his mouth into a thin line, he took up a stance by the hearth, propping his elbow on the mantelpiece. She walked toward the class, her hips swaying, all graceful, beguiling woman.

While Sarah and James sat watching, Alicia clapped her hands for attention and called the beginning pupils to the front. Scullery maids and grooms alike assembled in a circle on the large rug while she seated herself on a stool. One by one, they proceeded to draw their letters on their slates. After that, they did a little game using marbles to count their sums. Some of them were remarkably quick; others struggled with the simplest numbers. But Alicia showed patience toward them all, giving a word of encouragement or a quiet correction as needed.

Fascinated, Drake watched her. He shouldn't be surprised to see that she was an excellent teacher. After all, she'd been responsible for her family these five years, and she had exhibited a serene tolerance for her mother's most eccentric impersonations. But he had always viewed Alicia as a *lady*. And ladies did not associate with the lower classes.

He was still trying to adjust himself to seeing this new side of her when she dismissed her group. Expecting her to call on the more advanced pupils, he tensed when James did the honors.

The students filed to the front and stood at attention. Taking turns, each recited a sonnet by Shakespeare. Then James quizzed them on geography, and they used a pointer to indicate the counties of England on the map, naming the noteworthy sights of each region.

Drake flexed his fist. It was all he could do to keep from breaking that damned pointer in two. Right on top of his brother's privileged head.

James had to be trifling with these servants. They were a curiosity to him, a game to dispel his boredom. From his life on the street, Drake had known other do-gooders like James. When he lost interest—and undoubtedly that would happen soon—he would leave them heartbroken, disillusioned.

"Class is dismissed," Alicia said. "Please return tomorrow morning at our usual time."

The students put away their slates and walked out of the study, casting surreptitious glances at Drake. The clatter of their footsteps sounded in the corridor as they dispersed through the back door.

James wheeled his chair around to give Drake a challenging stare. "So what do you think of our little school?"

"Oh, not quite *our,*" Sarah said on a laugh. "I've done naught but bedevil these two at every turn."

"One man's bedeviling is another man's bewitching," James murmured.

He and Sarah exchanged an intense glance that struck Drake as overtly sexual. He frowned, seized by curiosity about his crippled brother. He'd assumed the accident had rendered James impotent, that he'd been forced to survive without life's greatest pleasure.

But perhaps he was able to engage in sexual activity, after all. Did Hailstock celebrate the fact that his legitimate son could sire the next heir?

Drake gritted his teeth. Hell, why was he even wondering? He didn't give a bloody damn about his brother's love affairs—or lack thereof.

Edgy and restless, he snapped, "I can admire those with a sincere desire to aid the less fortunate. But I condemn those who would merely amuse themselves with charitable diversions."

James gave a faint smile. "And pray tell, into which category do I fall?"

"Among the dilettantes who seek to ease their ennui."

Alicia stepped between them. "Drake! Is that all you can say?"

Her hands were folded primly at her waist. She looked angry and hurt, disappointed in him. He fought the urge to drop his gaze like a chastened child. The truth was, he admired her willingness to help others. Most aristocrats cared nothing for those who served them.

But Alicia cared. And he had ridiculed her efforts.

"Forgive me," he said gruffly. "I don't mean to disparage your achievements here. There's a great need for schools like this. And you're an excellent teacher."

A fledgling warmth illuminated her eyes. It stirred a yearning in him that somehow transcended the physical. The light on her face drew him. . . .

"James did much, too," Sarah said, poised like a champion beside him. "I shan't allow you to think otherwise, Mr. Wilder."

"Let him think as he will," James said with a shrug. "Eventually, he'll be forced to face the truth."

Abandoning leniency, Drake growled, "I very much doubt that. You'll be gone from here soon enough."

"Are you forbidding me to enter this house?" James taunted.

"I'm saying that you don't belong here—"

"Enough." Alicia marched toward Drake. "This is a schoolroom, not a boxing ring. If you will excuse us, James and Sarah. My husband and I need to speak in private."

She slid her arm through Drake's and pulled firmly. He was half tempted to stand his ground. But if he did, he might awaken her suspicions. She would start asking too many questions.

And if ever she guessed that James was his brother, there'd be the devil to pay.

Controlling her temper, Alicia led the way into the morning room and closed the door. She leaned back against the gilded panel, wanting to stay as far from Drake as possible. She didn't need his touch distracting her. The air smelled faintly of wallpaper paste and the new flowered carpet. The greens and yellows of the decor lent a natural brightness to the gloomy day. But she could feel only the agitation of anger.

Going to the window, he propped his shoulder against the woodwork and scowled out at the rain. His hard features had a pensive quality that crept past her pain. Heaven help her, she wanted to be enveloped by his warmth. She had envisioned a far more romantic scenario in which she would tell him he would be a father. . . .

Guarding her heart, Alicia crossed her arms. "Well. You

managed to turn the afternoon into a disaster. Have you nothing to say?"

"I do, indeed. What's going on between those two?"

His keen gaze scattered her thoughts. "Sarah and James?" Her voice softened. "I believe they are in love."

"Or in lust," Drake said. "Is he capable of consummation?"

Alicia huffed out a breath. She oughtn't be surprised he could ask such an indelicate question. "How should I know?"

"Women talk to each other."

"There are some things a lady doesn't discuss, not even with her best friend. I wouldn't betray a confidence, anyway." Watching him, she tried to fathom his deep dislike. "And why do you wish to know? So you can reassure yourself that James finds no pleasure in his life?"

"Of course not. I'm curious, that's all." Leaving the window, he sauntered toward her, stopping mere inches away. "Don't look so dubious, my lady. You should know that, of late, my thoughts have been centered on"—he looked her up and down—"intimate matters."

An involuntary thrill eddied through her. In direct opposition to her will, her breasts tightened and her pulse surged. Keeping her voice steady, she said, "I know that you've carried on a ridiculous rivalry with Lord Hailstock. And you've let that absurdity extend to his son."

"He doesn't belong here with you. It isn't proper."

"Since when have you cared about conventions? Besides, James and I have been operating a school, not conducting an affair."

"And it's a fine school, indeed." All charming scoundrel again, Drake placed his warm hands at her waist and gave her the smile that could turn her into a helpless ninny. "I'm proud of you, Alicia. I'll admit, you surprised me today. I'd never imagined you had any interest in teaching—especially those less privileged than yourself."

His praise soothed the wound within her heart. She wanted to melt against him, but she also wanted to make her point. Placing her hands on his chest, she held him back. "James is my partner in the school. As such, I insist that you cease this hostility toward him and his father."

For a heartbeat, Drake stared at her. Then he nuzzled her mouth again. "Never mind them. Kiss me."

She turned her face away. "No. I will have your promise."

"Don't be a scold. Be my lover."

"Don't be a scoundrel," she countered. "I know you're capable of better than that."

Their gazes clashed. He scowled as if determined to conceal his worthy side from her.

She was just as determined not to back down. "I mean what I say, Drake. I cannot abide this constant strife. I want your pledge to be civil. I can't imagine why you'd refuse me that."

His jaw clenched; he glanced away for a moment. "If it means so much to you," he said grudgingly, "then I'll try."

"You'll do more than try. You'll give me your *vow*."

His fingers pressed into her waist. He looked so fierce, Alicia felt a sinking expectation of his refusal. Then he ground out, "All right, then. You have it."

The breath left her lungs in a sigh of relief. At once her anger dissolved and she wrapped her arms around him, relishing the beat of his heart against her breasts. She trusted him to keep his word. The realization warmed Alicia down to the tips of her toes. He was a difficult, complex man, but beneath his hardened exterior, he had a core of integrity.

Standing on tiptoe, she pressed her lips to his smooth-shaven cheek. She breathed deeply, smelling the freshness of rain on his still-damp hair. No longer could she quell the feelings inside herself. "Oh, Drake. I do love you."

His dark lashes dipped slightly over his midnight-blue eyes. She could not read the expression in his shuttered gaze. Moving his hands to cup her neck, he lowered his mouth to hers. She parted her lips, welcoming his deep exploration, offering him all the affection in her heart. With patience, she could bend him, change him, make him a better man. In time, he would realize how foolish he'd been, how unimportant were his petty resentments. And their child would look up to him as a man of honor.

He pressed his hand against her back, urging her across the room to a chaise. Though she felt the shivery anticipation of his intent, she set her heels. "Wait. I've something to tell you. Something very important."

"Nothing can be as important as this." He nuzzled her breasts, the tip of his tongue dipping into the shadowed valley. His hands reached back to release the buttons of her gown.

"Please, Drake, *listen*." Catching his upper arms, she wrapped her fingers around his hard muscles. "I'm going to have your baby."

His gaze searched hers as he slowly straightened. Into the silence, the rain dripped from the eaves and tapped on the windowpanes. His rakish charm altered subtly into a look of intense concentration. In a gruff voice, he said, "Do you know this . . . for certain?"

She nodded, her throat choked. She wanted so badly for him to be pleased, to share in her happiness. "The physician examined me this morning. Shortly after the new year, we're to have a child."

He drew a raspy breath. Then he brought his hands up to lightly caress her shoulders. As if she were made of the finest porcelain, he drew her against him, pressing his cheek to her hair. "A baby," he said in a roughened undertone. "My God."

She laughed at his dazed tone. "I found it hard to believe at first, too."

"You should have told me straightaway. I'd have guarded my damned temper. And I certainly wouldn't have pawed you." As if to verify that, he reached between them and very gently cradled her belly.

More than words, the tenderness in his touch bespoke the power of his emotions. She felt the bond between them strengthen and grow. Though he hadn't voiced any words of affection, she felt certain he would in time. He would conquer his prejudice against the nobility and love her for herself.

She teased him, brushing her breasts against him. "I happen to like the way you touch me."

He set her back firmly. "Have you been ill? You're pale."

"I've been overly weary, that's all—"

"Then you ought to be lying down." His arm around her waist, he walked her to the door. "I'm taking you home. As for your school, I'll hire another instructor. You mustn't overtax yourself."

Rather than irk her, his masterful manner gave her hope that he truly cared for her. As he opened the door, she looped her arms around his neck. "I'm perfectly healthy. The doctor said I may continue *all* my normal activities."

His eyes gleamed with a banked fire. "I'll consult with him myself and see about that—"

Abruptly he bit off his words, his dark brows lowering. He turned his head to peer down the passageway in the direction of the study.

At the same moment, Alicia grew aware of the sound of raised voices. Holding on to him, she strained to see over his broad shoulder.

Just then, James wheeled out of the study. Sarah marched stiffly beside him. At first, Alicia thought they were quarreling. Until she saw the tall, distinguished gentleman who stepped out of the study after them.

Lord Hailstock.

Chapter Twenty-four

"Stay here," Drake said in a low-pitched voice. "I'll deal with him."

Alicia had no intention of meekly retreating into the morning room. "No," she murmured. "Something tells me they'll need a mediator."

Ignoring his impatient exclamation, she hastened down the passage. James and his father faced each other like two snarling dogs. Each time James attempted to wheel away, Lord Hailstock stepped out to block him. Their sharp voices echoed against the green-painted walls.

"I am not finished," the marquess snapped. "You will have the courtesy to remain still and listen."

James met his gaze without flinching. "I've heard quite enough. Whether you will admit so or not, I'm of age and no longer under your jurisdiction."

"I cannot condone this willfulness," Hailstock said, his hands held stiffly at his sides. "I was pleased you'd discovered that wheeled contraption. You seemed quite happy, going off every day with the duchess. But you led me to believe you were at the park or visiting at her house. And all that time, you were *here*."

"I'm under no obligation to report my activities to you, Father."

"I must concur," Sarah said, placing her hand on the back of James's chair. "There is no point to this quarrel."

"Your Grace," Hailstock said, lifting his angry gaze to her. "As a leader of the *ton,* you of all people should see the folly in consorting with the lower classes."

Arching an eyebrow, she regarded him with cool majesty. "It is not for me to gainsay James. Nor for you, for that matter."

Alicia stepped quickly to the marquess. Despite the foul weather outside, his greatcoat bore not a drop of rain and his hair was perfectly groomed as always. "My lord, I didn't realize you were coming to call." Hoping to diffuse the quarrel, she forced a gracious note into her voice. "If you'd care to go to the drawing room, I'll order tea."

"Thank you, my lady, but this isn't a social call." His frosty gray eyes studied her accusingly. "I understand *you* are a party to this preposterous school."

Though he'd been like a father to her, she held her chin high, unwilling to let him chasten her. "Yes, I organized the school. We are helping people who would otherwise have no opportunity to better themselves—"

"No doubt it was your husband's idea," Hailstock broke in. "He would seize any chance to bring down disgrace on my family. He would have my son—my heir—associate with lowborn rabble."

"That isn't true. He didn't even know about the school until today."

But the marquess wasn't listening. Rounding on Drake, he clenched his fists at his sides. "If I hear so much as a breath of scandal, I will hold you personally responsible."

Drake fixed him with a hard, impassive stare. "Do as you will," he said. "I've given my approval to the school. If my wife and your son choose to educate these servants, then I shall not stand in their way."

He stood close to Alicia, a warm and solid presence. He had not lost his temper, thank heavens. Yet dislike radiated from him, and she knew he must be tempted to forget his vow.

Turning to Lord Hailstock, she felt a pang of regret. Why couldn't he and Drake set aside their differences? Quietly, she said, "Though it pains me to say so, my lord, I must ask you to leave."

A dull flush suffused his face. His lips thinned, he glanced from Alicia to Drake and back again. "My lady, if you wish to throw yourself into the gutter with Wilder, then so be it. But you will not include my son. He is going home where he belongs."

Striding behind the chair, he gave it a hard push.

Drake made a move as if to stop him. But without any help, James grabbed the wheels, his knuckles whitening from the effort of holding the chair still.

"Blast it, Father! You're treating me like a child."

"Leave go. So long as you live in my house, you will obey me."

"Then I shan't live there anymore," James said through gritted teeth. "I'll move in with my brother."

Lord Hailstock froze, his face pale as chalk, his fingers like claws around the caned back of the chair.

Certain she'd misheard, Alicia frowned at James. "Your brother?"

"But you haven't any siblings," Sarah added.

"I do, indeed," James said in a hard voice. He whipped his head around, a strangely savage light in his eyes as he stared up at the marquess. "Tell them, Father. Tell them that Drake Wilder is your bastard."

A moment of silence spun out. Alicia felt paralyzed, aware of the thumping of her heart, the coldness of her palms. It couldn't be true. *It couldn't be.* Yet a chaos of impressions whirled though her mind. Drake. Lord Hailstock. No wonder she'd never fully understood their hatred. *Until now.*

Desperate for him to deny it, she clutched at Drake's

sleeve. For no reason, she noticed how smooth and fine the dark blue cloth felt to her fingertips, how his heat penetrated her chilled skin. "Please," she whispered. "Tell me it's a lie."

He gazed at her with the blank face of a stranger. His features were etched in granite, his eyes inscrutable. The moment stretched out into eternity. Then her worst fears were answered when, in lieu of reply, he turned his attention to James. "How did you find out?"

"You came to our house a few weeks ago, to return a ring that Father had given to Alicia," James said, gazing intently at him. "I was in the salon. Father believed me to be napping, but I heard you out in the corridor. You said . . . you were his other son." He glanced searchingly at the marquess. "Then he threw you out of the house."

"Wilder was lying," Lord Hailstock said, his voice hoarse as he stepped out from behind the wheeled chair. "*You* are my son, James. My only son. He's a swindler who wants to steal your inheritance."

"If I'd wanted your money," Drake said, "I'd have blackmailed you. And you'd have paid me, too."

Lord Hailstock's face twisted in a grimace of fury. "You are determined to besmirch my good name. I warn you, I won't tolerate it."

Their angry voices swirled around Alicia. She let her hand fall to her side. She couldn't think; she could only stare with a shocked fascination at the three men. Never had she thought to look for similarities, but she looked now. And now the slight resemblance struck her: Though Drake had darker coloring than James with his tawny hair and pale complexion, they had the same piercing blue eyes, the same cleft in their cheeks that deepened when they smiled. And they both shared Hailstock's muscular build, his noble bone structure.

"I'll admit to hating you, Wilder," James said, his gaze tight on Drake. "I resented your power over my—*our*—

father. So I flaunted my rank at every opportunity. But I've since had reason to believe I was wrong."

Drake said nothing. He merely returned his brother's stare.

"If it's no inconvenience," James went on, "I'd like to stay with you and Alicia for a short time. Until I'm able to settle certain matters."

He glanced obliquely at Sarah, who had been listening nearby, her violet eyes wide. Now she stepped forward. "That is an excellent notion." She frowned severely at Drake. "Don't you agree, Mr. Wilder?"

"Of course," Drake said in a voice devoid of emotion. "My housekeeper can handle the arrangements."

"No!" Hailstock ground out. His face stark, he sank down on one knee in front of his younger son. "Think, James. You cannot claim kinship to a common scoundrel. People will talk. What reason will you give for staying with him?"

"There is always the truth."

"But he is a knave, a gambler. You have noble blood—"

"So, it seems, does he," James said acidly.

The marquess took a deep breath, his nostrils flaring. "Don't do this, I beg you. Wilder has no proof of his allegations. You're making a disastrous mistake."

"I rather doubt that," James said. "And regardless, I will know the brother you've kept from me all these years."

He maneuvered around his father, leaving Lord Hailstock crouched on the floor, his head bowed and his eyes closed.

"My carriage should be waiting out front," the duchess said. "I told the coachman to return at precisely half past two."

James nodded, then moved to Alicia, gathering her hand in his. "I'm sorry," he said with a trace of regret. "I never meant to blurt out the truth that way. This must have been quite a shock."

A shock? The shattered numbness inside her felt like the devastation after an earthquake. She could not assimilate her thoughts beyond one fact. Drake had lied to her. All this time, he had prattled excuses for his antagonism toward Hailstock.

And she had been fool enough to believe him.

James released her hand; then Sarah touched Alicia's arm in a offering of support. "We'll talk later," the duchess murmured.

Alicia gave a wooden nod and the pair headed down the passageway toward the front of the house.

Hailstock rose slowly, his shoulders slumped. Rather than aim another venomous look at Drake, the marquess subjected Alicia to a probing scrutiny. She could think of nothing to say to him. He, too, had lied to her.

Then he turned on his heel and strode after James and Sarah.

As the front door opened and closed, a draught of damp air eddied down the long corridor. Shivering from a deeply penetrating chill, Alicia wrapped her arms around herself. She was aware of Drake's presence beside her. But no longer did she feel an affinity for him. The connection between them had been severed.

Perhaps that closeness had never really existed.

"You're too pale," Drake said, sliding his arm around her back. "You need to rest."

In a daze, she let him guide her down the corridor to the foyer, their footsteps echoing on the marble floor. But when he would have urged her up the staircase to the bedrooms, she balked.

Her disjointed thoughts came together in a cohesive whole.

Drake had known the marquess was his father. That meant he had not chosen her at random. With sinister intent, he had exploited Gerald's weakness for gambling, then forced her to be his bride. All because Lord Hailstock wanted her.

And Drake had wanted revenge.

With that horrifying realization died all of her naïve hopes to win his love. He possessed no capacity for tender emotion. He was poisoned by hatred.

Alicia twisted away from him, backing up until her spine met the hard column of the newel post. Afraid she might break down in tears, she buried her pain beneath a bitter cold dignity.

"You used me for vengeance," she stated. "You never cared about being accepted by society. You married me to spite your father."

Drake wanted to flinch from those blunt words, enunciated in her cool, patrician voice. What a fool he'd been for believing he could keep Alicia in the dark. He was furious with himself for being so careless in letting James overhear him. Yet he couldn't gull himself, either. Deep down, he felt a certain gloating satisfaction that James knew they were brothers.

As for Alicia, there was nothing to be done now but take his knocks. And hope that, later, he could charm her into forgiving him.

"Yes, that is why I married you," he admitted. "Hailstock had been courting you. And I also wanted to enter society, so that he'd be forced to see the bastard he'd never acknowledged."

The mere thought of that set Drake's teeth on edge. Welcoming a surge of rage, he paced the foyer. None of this would have been necessary if Hailstock had accepted him long ago. If the wretch hadn't threatened a defenseless boy—

"Why didn't he acknowledge you?" Alicia asked. "Perhaps you really aren't his son."

Stunned, Drake pivoted toward her. "It's the truth, damn it. My mother wouldn't have lied to me."

"You needn't curse," she said icily. "I merely wish to know if she offered you any proof."

He tamped down his unreasoning anger. She didn't know the whole story. "Yes," he bit out. "She gave me a diamond stickpin bearing his coat of arms. That and her word are enough for me." He didn't mention his unusual skill with numbers, a trait he shared with Hailstock. He wouldn't beg her to believe him.

"How it must gall you to be denied the title by an accident of birth."

"It galls me that he used my mother, then refused to support his child."

Alicia merely raised an eyebrow. "She died when you were ten. Then you came to London—not in search of a grand adventure. And not to join a theatrical troupe. To confront Lord Hailstock."

She made him uncomfortable, reminding him of all his half-truths. "I did join a theatrical troupe," he muttered.

"But only after you'd seen his lordship. Only after he'd rejected your claim."

"Yes."

"Tell me what happened when you went to see him."

Loath to reopen that scar, Drake prowled around the foyer, stopping to peer out a window. Raindrops slid down the glass panes in an endless stream. "It was a long time ago. Suffice it to say he would have nothing to do with me."

"But you did show him the stickpin, didn't you?"

"Of course I showed it to him." What had happened then had been the most painful experience of his life. He disliked exposing that vulnerability to anyone. But if it helped him to win Alicia's sympathy . . . "He denounced me for a thief and a swindler. Then he called for his footmen to haul me off to the magistrate, and thence to Newgate Prison."

Alicia didn't even gasp. The blue eyes that had glowed with love only half an hour ago now regarded him as if she'd enjoy seeing him chained in a dank cell. "*Did* you go to prison?"

He shook his head. "I'd lived on the street long enough to learn a few tricks. I ducked past his men. We were on the ground floor, so I jumped out an opened window."

She said nothing to that. In the murky afternoon light, she stood as straight as the newel post behind her, the rose-pink gown skimming womanly curves that he never tired of touching. He wished to hell he knew what she was thinking. Did she feel even a scrap of understanding?

What an ass he'd been to hurt her. He wanted to make it up to her, to hold her in his arms again, to hear her whisper words of love. Extending his hands, he walked toward her. "Alicia, I'm sorry—"

"Do not presume to touch me," she said in that frosty tone.

He stopped, uncertain for one of the few times in his life. She regarded him with chilly composure, reminding him of the poised and remote Alicia of their wedding day. She might have been gazing at a despicable stranger.

And he *felt* despicable. "If you'll give me a chance, we can discuss this reasonably—"

"Do not presume to question my reasoning, either." She folded her arms beneath her bosom. "Everything is clear to me now. You kept watch at that first ball we attended. You were looking for Lord Hailstock. Waiting for him to appear so that you could flaunt your presence there."

"He'd tried to bar me from his world—"

"You forbade me to associate with James, too. Not, as you claimed, because he is a vain, self-serving aristocrat. Because he is your half-brother."

"Both facts influenced me. He is a haughty snob."

"You were quite inventive in your efforts to keep me away from him," Alicia said, continuing the litany of his faults. "You used your charm to manipulate me. You even resorted to seduction that day at your club."

He had reached beneath her skirts and stroked her to climax. She couldn't regret *that.* "You enjoyed what I did."

"You gave me no choice," she countered. "Everything in your life has been founded on revenge. I wouldn't be surprised if you even see my child as yet another way to taunt his lordship." She moved her hands to her waist as if to shield the baby from his unscrupulous character.

That single accusation stupefied Drake. He couldn't find the words to express his exultation at learning about her pregnancy. A man shouldn't admit to emotions so sweet and tender. Or to so intense a romantic attachment to his wife.

He took another step toward her. "Alicia . . . you're wrong. My happiness about our baby has nothing to do with Hailstock."

"Am I to believe you? After all the lies you've told?" She shook her head, as if appalled by her own gullibility. "You never meant that vow, either."

"Vow?"

"To cease your hostilities."

"I did mean it," he muttered. He'd made that pledge out of the irresistible wish to have her believe him a man of honor. "I intended to make more of an effort to conceal my hatred of him."

She made a small sound of derision. "And what if I had visited Lord Hailstock or James? Would you have set aside your petty hatreds then?"

"There is nothing petty about this," Drake snapped, his footsteps loud in the foyer. "Of course I wanted to keep you away from Hailstock. He would have turned you against me."

She regarded him with cool contempt. "No, Drake. You have managed to do that all by yourself."

Then she walked past him and into the library, shutting the door.

Chapter Twenty-five

Alicia had a question to ask her mother.

Stepping down from the carriage that evening, she assured herself that was her sole reason for coming home. She needn't brace herself for an encounter with her husband, either. At this hour, Drake would be at his club.

Her throat tightened with unshed tears. After his departure, Mrs. Molesworth had fussed over Alicia, bringing her tea and toast with jam, wrapping her in a warm knitted blanket, making a fire in the library hearth. Alicia had curled up in a wing chair and stared out at the endless rain. She'd spent the remainder of the afternoon alternately weeping and brooding, hurt and angry at Drake for using her to such a foul purpose.

And through it all, she'd had the nagging sense that she'd missed something vital. Something that nagged at the edge of her awareness. Pondering that puzzle, she'd dozed off there in the library, and she had awakened at dusk, remarkably clear-headed.

And with an astonishing question in her mind. Only Mama could provide the answer.

Though the rain had slowed to a drizzle, a footman held an umbrella over Alicia's head as she walked across the drive, heedless of the puddles. Gazing at the house, she felt caught by a bittersweet sense of homecoming. How she had grown to love this magnificent four-story mansion with its tall white columns and the many windows glowing golden with lamplight through the darkness. How she had grown to love its master, the most deceitful, heartless, obstinate, domineering, *stupid* man who had ever lived.

As she walked up the marble steps to the portico and entered the front door, Mrs. Yates stood in the foyer arranging red tulips in a Grecian vase. She whirled around, her sensual features alight with an uncommon interest. "Good evening, m'lady."

With a polite nod, Alicia headed straight for the grand staircase. "Is Lady Eleanor in her chamber?"

"Nay, she's in the ballroom with Mrs. Philpot." The flame-haired woman smiled a trifle indulgently; Alicia wondered if the housekeeper could actually show compassion for Mama. "She is Queen Eleanor of Aquitaine tonight."

Alicia considered going to the ballroom, but she hesitated, her foot on the first step. Perhaps before she questioned her mother, she should take advantage of this opportunity. If Mama was deep in fantasy, she wouldn't be able to tell Alicia where to search, anyway. . . .

Mrs. Yates cleared her throat. "You should know, m'lady, that the master had the morning room made into a bedchamber for Lord Scarborough so that he may get around more easily in his wheeled chair. They are both there right now, putting things in order."

Surprise struck a painful jolt to Alicia's heart. Drake was *here,* only a few steps down the corridor.

An impossible yearning lured her. She could go to him, forgive him his monumental faults, tell him that she would stay even if he couldn't give her his heart. He would take her upstairs and love her with his body at least.

But he was with his *brother.* Lord Hailstock's son. That was enough of a reminder of his perfidy.

"I shall inform the master that you're here," Mrs. Yates said.

She turned to go, but Alicia spoke sharply to stop her. "Please don't. I won't have him interrupted."

"But he wished to be told at once if you returned. He was quite insistent on that point." Mrs. Yates eyed her with blatant curiosity. "To that purpose, he ordered me to tarry here all evening to watch for you."

Alicia tightened her fists at her sides. He wanted to ply his charm on her again. She was nothing more to him than a body, nothing but the woman his father had wanted. "You are not to say a word," she said, her voice taut. "Is that understood?"

She feared the housekeeper would refuse. Mrs. Yates had an unswerving loyalty to Drake, a loyalty based on gratitude toward her savior.

But she gave a slow, considering nod. "As you wish, m'lady."

Did she no longer regard her mistress as an interloper? Or had she guessed the truth and would seize the chance to bar a reconciliation? Alicia no longer cared to know.

By way of dismissal, she started up the grand staircase.

Mrs. Yates called after her, "I must say, the master has been stomping around here like an angry bull. If something is amiss between you two, perhaps I could relay a message to him."

She wanted gossip, that was all. Alicia forced a nonchalant smile. "I'll have a word with him myself . . . later."

Unwilling to think beyond her quest, she lifted her skirts and hastened upstairs. When she reached the second floor, she walked down the elegant passageway with its familiar gold wallpaper, the framed landscapes, the gilding on the woodwork. She must order her belongings packed and sent to Pemberton House. Mama's, too.

But not now. Not yet.

Stepping into her mother's room, she closed the door.

On the bed, the embroidered coverlet had been turned down to show the feather pillows. The yellow draperies shut out the darkness, and a lamp burned on the small writing desk.

Alicia hurried there, her shoes making no sound on the leaf-green carpet with its pattern of yellow ribbons. Stifling her misgivings at invading her mother's privacy, she opened each desk drawer in turn. A pile of blank stationery. A few extra quills. A collection of buttons in a shallow dish. And in the bottom drawer, a sketch of hearts and flowers with labored lettering: *To my deer mama, with love, Alicia.*

Smiling in spite of herself, she picked up the sheet. Mama had amassed a veritable fortune in old papers. Alicia sorted through the stack, glancing at compositions, arithmetic exams, history essays, half in Alicia's progressively neater handwriting and an equal number in Gerald's scrawling penmanship.

But she didn't discover what she sought.

Going to the bedside table, she examined the contents: an embroidered handkerchief, the stub of a candle, a prayer book. Nothing of significance. Then she carried the lamp into the dressing room to explore the clothespresses and armoires, methodically moving aside the many costumes Drake had given to her mother.

Her heart clenched anew with the pain of his treachery. How could a man capable of kindnesses allow himself to be ruled by hatred and vengeance? And how could she still long for him?

But she did. Deep within herself, love still burned, a flame too stubborn to be extinguished. She had known Drake could be ruthless, and she had allowed herself to become vulnerable to him, anyway. She should never have convinced herself that he could return her love, that his carnal passion for her might grow into true affection.

Blasted gambler. She should have realized that a scoundrel like him was never to be trusted.

Blinking back angry tears, she shoved aside gown after gown, determined not to overlook any nook or cranny. She focused her mind on reaching into drawers, checking on top of cabinets, her fingers probing in the deepest corners.

At last, dejected, she plopped down on a stool and tried to think of where she hadn't looked, where Mama might have concealed something she considered to be a treasure. There was no other possible hiding place—

Then her gaze alighted on the cask of fake gold coins, the ones Mama used when playing pirate.

Hardly daring to hope, she rushed to it and dug into the pile of painted tin circles. The metal made a tinkling noise, some of the coins spilling onto the floor. Near the bottom of the cask, her fingers brushed a small bundle.

Alicia pulled it out. Letters, a dozen or so, the paper yellowed and tied with a bedraggled pink satin ribbon. She had known Mama had saved these letters. She'd stumbled across them before, hidden beneath a loose floorboard in the bedroom they'd shared at Pemberton House. Attributing Mama's secretiveness to eccentricity, Alicia had replaced the letters unread. She had believed them to be a sentimental keepsake of no significance to anyone but her mother.

Until today.

Closing her eyes, Alicia held the packet to her breast. Heaven help her, she shouldn't look. She didn't want to read the letters Mama had saved all these years. The letters that she now knew Lord Hailstock had been anxious to find.

For if her suspicions proved correct, she would be giving Drake the means for a far more enduring revenge.

Having busied himself for the past hour directing a bevy of servants, Drake felt an uncustomary awkwardness when he was finally alone with his brother.

A team of footmen had brought down a mahogany four-poster bed and reassembled it here in the morning room. Several maids had fixed the linens, made a fire in the hearth, and closed the varnished wood shutters. The rug had been rolled up and taken away so that James could roll freely across the pale marble floor. Behind the closed door of a small antechamber, a valet was unpacking several trunks full of James's clothing.

Watching him pick up a lamp and move it to the bedside table, Drake wondered why he'd agreed to this damned fool arrangement. He should never have allowed his noble younger brother into this house. It was a revenge Drake had never conceived, to steal the marquess's heir. And he felt no triumph, only a curious sense of unreality.

He'd gained a brother today. And lost a wife.

He tossed back a flavorless swallow of brandy. Though he'd downed half a decanter already, the liquor hadn't dulled the sharpness of loss. If anything, it had made him maudlin.

Leaving Alicia at Pemberton House had gone against his every instinct. He didn't know how long he'd stood there in the foyer, staring like a lovesick fool at the closed door to the library. He'd felt the desperate need to bring her back home where she belonged. She would have resisted, but he could have picked her up in his arms and carried her to his coach. She wouldn't have kicked and screamed; Alicia had too much dignity for that.

But it was that very dignity that had stopped him. He couldn't forget the look of chilling contempt in her eyes.

His wife despised him. Even more than she had at their forced wedding. And he had the discomfiting fear that this time, he might not succeed in charming her into his bed. He might never again trade witty barbs with her. He might never see her smile at the circus or get tipsy on a few glasses of champagne. He might never hear her soft voice whispering words of love.

His chest tightened with a restless, unfamiliar panic. Why was he dallying here when he ought to be trying to convince her? He had to *do* something. Having already exhausted his repertoire of excuses, he had no idea of what he'd say to her. Scouring his brain, he started toward the door.

"Hold there," James said, rolling swiftly forward. "You can't bring me a brandy and then leave."

"I'm going to the club," Drake lied.

"Take the evening off. And sit down, blast it. I'm getting a crick in my neck from looking up at you."

He'd probably like Drake to bow and scrape like a damned servant.

Wearing a white shirt and dark breeches, his brother stared at him challengingly. Had James been able to stand, they'd be of a similar height. The muscles in his arms and chest were well developed from exercise. Drake had seen a footman bring in several barbells in various sizes.

For some reason, he had the sudden impression that James was lonely for company. He knew no one in this house, except perhaps Lady Eleanor, who might not recognize him. Even Alicia was gone.

Alicia.

Damn. Why was he letting her turn him into a lapdog who would go sniffing at her heels, whining for her favors?

Angry with himself, he went to fill his glass from the decanter he'd left on a table. After taking a long drink, he sank into a comfortable leather chair by the fireplace. It couldn't hurt to stay a few more minutes, to lay down some rules.

As James wheeled closer, his glass tucked between his thighs, Drake said without preamble, "I'll assign a manservant to assist you as necessary. Confine your orders to him alone."

"I won't need help," James said. "I brought along Tilford, my ever-faithful valet."

"I'll leave it to you, then, to make sure he doesn't interfere belowstairs." Drake wouldn't allow either of them to harangue the staff, misfits who wouldn't conform to a nobleman's exacting standards.

"Tilford is no instigator. He'll keep to himself."

"If you've any special requests for Cook, give at least half a day's warning. I won't have my servants sent off to the market on a moment's notice."

James raised his glass in a mock salute. "Strict bugger, aren't you?"

"Tomorrow, the servants will remove the rugs in all the ground-floor rooms," Drake went on tonelessly. "Then you can roam about as you please. The library is just down the corridor. My housekeeper will take you on a tour tomorrow—"

"I'll find my own way around," James said, his mouth tightening. "I'm more interested in you. Who, may I ask, is your mother?"

Drake had been expecting the blunt question. Much as he hated revealing his past to this self-serving aristocrat, James should know the truth of his father's neglect.

So Drake gave an abbreviated version of the story. All the while he watched James, daring him to cast any slurs on Muira Wilder's honor. Crippled or not, he'd get a fist in his face.

But James didn't jeer. He merely shook his head as if amazed. "I can't imagine Father having an affair. He's a stickler for convention."

Drake thought Hailstock capable of any perfidy. He said nothing, though. If James wished to cling to his illusions, let him.

"To the best of my knowledge, he never strayed from his marriage vows," James went on, lifting his glass to study the amber liquor in the firelight. "I've often wondered if he would finally take a mistress after my mother's death. That was a year ago. . . ."

"He hasn't."

His brother looked up sharply. "How the devil would you know?"

"I've had the both of you watched."

James gave a low whistle. "You really do despise us."

Drake took a long swallow from his glass. Though the fine French brandy slid like silk down his throat, he grimaced. What the devil had possessed him to come in here, to sit down, to converse as if they could one day know the true camaraderie of brothers? They shared the same blood, but little else.

"He's rigid-minded and controlling, but he really isn't as awful as you think," James said, leaning back, his face earnest. "We'd play chess of an evening or argue politics. He's as well read as any lecturer at Oxford, and he has an amazing grasp of numbers. He's published treatises on mathematics."

Drake had read those papers. He'd never admit to anyone—least of all this pampered nobleman—that he'd felt a sharp craving to debate those complex theories with the genius who had written them. But James had been the sole recipient of their father's attentions.

Searching himself for resentment, he found a hollow longing, a sentiment that annoyed him. "So if you two get along so well," he asked in a brusque tone, "why the hell did you leave?"

James fixed him with a lordly stare. "As I said, I wish to know my brother. And I shall."

"We're too different to be friends," Drake said, finishing off his drink. "Let's leave it at that."

James gave a taunting laugh. "Don't get your back up, Wilder. And I shan't impose on you for very long. It's past time I set up my own household."

Seizing the chance to change the subject, Drake asked, "Have you asked her to marry you?"

A faint flush mottled James's cheeks. "The duchess?"

"Who the hell else?" Reaching for the decanter, Drake

refilled his glass. "Surely you'll want her in your house."

In one quick swallow, James emptied his glass. His voice mocking, he said, "She deserves better than to be shackled to a cripple for the rest of her life."

"I've a suspicion she doesn't look at it that way."

"We'll have our affair and nothing more," James muttered, wheeling forward to pour himself another drink. "Then she can walk away whenever she likes."

Drake couldn't let Alicia walk away. *Fool!* Why did she have such a stranglehold on his heart?

"Don't be an arrogant ass," he snapped, with the uncanny suspicion that he meant himself. "You shouldn't make that decision for her."

"And you're the expert on women? If you had half as much brains as conceit, you'd have gone on your knees to Alicia, begging for her forgiveness."

"I don't kneel before any woman."

Snorting, James pointed to the doorway. "Then you should tell her so yourself."

Drake turned in his chair to see Alicia standing on the threshhold. *Damn.* Had she heard him?

The lamplight from the corridor limned her slender form and haloed her golden hair. One of her hands clutched the doorframe as if she needed support. She wore the same rose-pink dress, though now it was rumpled as if she'd slept in it. Her face was too pale, her breathing too fast, her expression too anguished.

She *had* heard him.

Cursing himself, he sprang up and strode across the room to take her arm. Her skin felt chilled and her body trembled. "You look as if you're about to swoon," he said.

To his surprise, instead of recoiling or lashing out in anger, she merely stared at him as if trying to see into his soul. In a low voice, she said, "Drake, I must talk to you."

"We'll go upstairs." This might be his chance. If he could get her alone, he could soften her, charm her, convince her that besting his father no longer mattered to him. *She* mattered.

"No." Pulling away from him, Alicia walked into the chamber. "This involves James, too."

James?

In baffled anger, he strode after her. What had James to do with that stupid remark about not kneeling before any woman? Unless something else had upset her. . . .

She glided to his brother and touched his hand. His brow furrowing in concern, James took her hand in his. "Alicia? What is it?"

"I must read something to both of you. This."

For the first time, Drake noticed the paper she clutched in her other hand. He craned his neck to view it—a letter, the ink faded, the handwriting feminine with fancy curliques. Burning to know what had put her in such a state, he reached for the letter, but she held it to her breast.

"I must ask you to listen while I explain certain matters," she said. "Ever since this afternoon, I've been thinking, remembering. And one of the things that came to my mind was a packet of old letters that Mama has always kept hidden. They were written by her childhood friend, Claire."

Alicia paused, gazing at him with that strange seriousness. Drake hardened his jaw to subdue his impatience. "And?"

She walked slowly back and forth. "Claire Donnelly was a poor Irish orphan, a maidservant in the country house where Mama grew up. When the girls became fast friends, Mama convinced her parents to relieve Claire of her duties and raise her as their own daughter. And so the two girls studied together, learned etiquette and the ways of a lady. Then when they were sixteen, Claire fell in love with Lord Hailstock. They eloped to Scotland to be wed."

James blew out a breath. "Father's first wife. He certainly never told me she was a commoner."

"So much for his exacting standards," Drake muttered.

His brother flashed him an annoyed glance. "Save your comments. Alicia is distraught enough as it is."

She was, and Drake couldn't understand why. He couldn't see how reciting family history had any benefit to either James or himself.

"Lord Hailstock and his wife remained in Scotland for a time," she went on. "They lived there for nearly a year—until her death." Stopping in front of Drake, she let her fingertips brush his lapel, the brief touch having all the substance of a butterfly's wing. "It was the same year that you were born."

Something in her purposeful tone caused a stirring of disquiet in him. He glanced at James, who leaned forward in his chair, his gaze intent on Alicia.

"So the wretch cheated on his bride," Drake said, forcing a laugh. "That doesn't surprise me."

"It does me," James said, his face serious. "I tell you, it isn't like him."

"Well, clearly he did so at least once," Drake said flatly. He took hold of Alicia's elbow. "This is all very interesting, but you needn't distress yourself over a tragedy that happened a long time ago. You should lie down and rest."

She pulled away. "Will you cease your patronizing remarks and listen?" she said sharply. "What I'm trying to tell you . . . what this letter *confirms* . . . is that you are *not* Lord Hailstock's bastard."

Her words struck Drake like a blow. Did she trust his word so little? Through gritted teeth, he said, "We've already discussed this point. He *is* my father."

She glanced worriedly at James, then back at Drake. "I know," she said in an urgent tone. "What I'm saying is . . . you are his lordship's *legitimate* son."

Chapter Twenty-six

Her heart beating in her throat, Alicia watched Drake. He stood unmoving. His narrowed eyes showed only the blankness of shock.

Silence shrouded the chamber. The coals hissed on the hearth; a clock ticked on the bedside table. James wore a stunned expression, too, his brow furrowed, the glass forgotten in his hand.

"Give me that letter," Drake said, his voice tight.

She handed it to him. Her legs as weak as a newborn kitten's, she sank into a chair and watched him scan the girlish penmanship. The small square of paper looked flimsy in his big hands. Yet it carried a weighty revelation.

"What does it say?" James asked in a low, shaken tone. "For God's sake, read it aloud."

Drake thrust the letter back at Alicia. "You do the honors."

She wished to heaven she could spare James. Before coming here, she had given serious thought to burning the letter. But there had been enough lies already. Enough secrets.

Wetting her dry lips, she lifted the paper and gave voice to the words that were already burned into her mind:
" *Two nights ago, at midnight, I bore Richard a healthy*

son. Oh, my dearest Eleanor, I do wish you could see my precious boy! He is a wee mite, black of hair and blue of eyes, and I fancy I can hear you say he looks so like his mama. Richard cares not what I call him. So I have named him Drake, for my da, God rest his soul.

"Yes, it pains me to write that Richard has no interest in his son. In my letters these past months I have hidden my unhappiness, but now I must reveal the sad state of my marriage, for I am dying. And I fear Richard will deny our son.

"He accuses me of having lain with another—not true!— and declares that my vulgar blood caused a wantonness in me. This he would say, though I did guard my innocence until we plighted our troth at Gretna Green. From the start, he was jealous of every man I might speak to, whether he be footman or cleric. We were not wed a month when he returned home early from his business ventures to find a tradesman in my bedchamber, having just finished repair-ing the flue in the chimney. I was there, too, paying the man. Richard railed at me, and thenceforth he suspected me of the worst possible betrayal.

"Ever since, the coldness of his gaze chills me. To no avail have I begged my husband to give his blessing to our darling son. But he will neither hold Drake nor look at him. Though I will plead to my last breath, I cannot protect my child much longer. With each passing hour, my life-blood ebbs and with it, my strength. Being alone in the world, I have no recourse but you, my dearest Eleanor. You must hide these documents, let no one see them, in particular not Richard. Safeguard them for my son, so that if the need should arise, he may prove his claim to Hailstock.

"Bless you, my lady, for helping me in my most desper-ate hour.' "

Alicia slowly lowered the paper to her lap. The an-

guished words haunted her. "The letter is signed, '*Claire,
Lady Hailstock.*' "

Drake stood staring, his chest rising and falling beneath
his linen shirt. For once in his misbegotten life, he looked
too confounded for words.

No, she thought with a giddy sense of unreality. Drake
was *not* misbegotten. He was Lord Hailstock's *true heir.*

James braced his arms on the chair. "So where are these
documents?" he demanded, his face ashen, his voice harsh.
"A marriage certificate, I presume? And proof of birth?"

"I don't know," she said with a helpless shake of her
head. "Mama is . . . not herself this evening, so I doubt
there is any purpose to asking her."

Drake prowled the chamber, his footsteps loud on the
bare marble floor. He tunneled his fingers through his hair,
mussing the black strands. "This must be a hoax. Muira
Wilder bore me. She wouldn't have lied about that."

"Perhaps she was warned to keep silent," Alicia suggested. "Perhaps she'd been told you would be taken from
her if ever she revealed the truth."

"Warned," he said through clenched teeth. "By whom?
Hailstock? If he'd wanted to get rid of Claire's child, he
could have smothered him."

James brought his fist down on the arm of his chair.
"My father is no murderer," he flared. "He wouldn't kill a
baby."

"We seem doomed to disagree about his character."

The two men glared at each other. As if they would
come to blows rather than help her find a way out of *their*
dilemma.

"Stop, both of you," Alicia said sharply. "Your quarreling only makes matters worse. Drake, did Muira Wilder
ever say anything at all that might verify this story?"

"No. Nothing." Then he stopped pacing, his gaze un-
focused, as if he were looking inwardly at his past.

"You've remembered something," she said.

"It doesn't mean anything."

"Tell us anyway."

Drake paced to the window, opening the shutters to stare out into the night. "On her deathbed . . . when she told me to go to London and see my father, she said, " 'I nivver could carry a bairn, lost so many till ye came along. Ye were my blessin', my gift from heaven.' "

His husky Scottish lilt caused a prickling over Alicia's skin. As did the message . . . *I nivver could carry a bairn.* "There, you see?" she said, a tremor in her voice. "She raised you, but she *didn't* give birth to you."

He shook his head. "She meant I was her only surviving pregnancy. She'd suffered a few miscarriages before I was born, that's all."

But Alicia saw the doubt in him. The subtle change from disbelief to cautious acceptance. Would he rejoice now? Would he seize his chance to exact the most punishing revenge of all?

She prayed he would not be so cruel to his brother.

James made an impatient sound. "We must find the documents proving the validity of this claim. Is Lady Eleanor truly so unbalanced that she cannot remember where she put them?"

"She has moments of sanity," Alicia explained. "We shall have to wait for one of those times."

"God!" With an angry push, James sent his chair careening across the chamber. He caught the wheels and spun to face her. "I cannot sit idly by, wondering if my father did such a deed. Have you searched your mother's chambers?"

"Yes. I did so when I looked for the letters." To steady her nerves, Alicia took great care in refolding the letter. "You should know, James, that your father has been seeking these documents, too."

He wheeled closer. "What do you mean?"

Before she could reply, Drake pivoted. "Alicia came

upon him poking through the study at Pemberton House. He *said* he was looking for some old papers that belonged to her father."

"That isn't all," Alicia added. "Yesterday evening, while Drake and I were gone at the circus, his lordship came here and badgered Mama about a letter. I'm sure it was *this* letter—"

"The wretch came into my house? He upset your mother?" His hands clenched, Drake took a step toward her. "You ought to have told me so immediately."

"I have had other things on my mind today," she said, enunciating each word to keep from shouting back at him. "And I was about to say that I didn't realize his purpose, or why he was so concerned about finding some old letters. Until . . . this afternoon."

When she had found out that Drake was the marquess's son. When she'd had enough time to ponder and consider and realize . . .

Unable to sit still any longer, she surged to her feet. "I am going to find Mama. If she has a lucid moment, I'll ask her to show me where she hid the papers."

With quick decisive steps, Drake strode toward her. "I'll go with you. I'll convince her that I'm"—he grimaced as if still fighting the truth—"Claire's son."

"No." Alicia didn't care if he saw the raw pain in her eyes. "I don't want you with me. I will do this alone."

He stopped as if struck. That look of fathomless intensity hid his thoughts from her. It would always be that way with him, she reflected bitterly. He would close his mind and his heart to her.

She glanced at James, who watched, his eyebrows raised. A lump in her throat, Alicia turned swiftly and left the chamber.

She clutched the folded letter to her bosom. Claire . . . Drake's real mother. The reality of it still stunned her. In less than half a day, the world had turned topsy-turvy. No longer would her husband be a disreputable, baseborn scoundrel. By virtue of his birth, he would be elevated to the position of heir to one of the most powerful men in England. The doors of society would open wide to him; he would no longer need his aristocratic wife to gain entrée. She had given him the means to defeat Lord Hailstock once and for all.

And James. Drake's triumph would strip James of his honored rank as heir to the title. That realization stabbed into her anew. All of his life he had known he would some-day become the Marquess of Hailstock.

She wondered what they were saying to each other now, if Drake at least had the good grace not to gloat.

As for her, there was nothing to be done but to follow this task through to its bitter conclusion. Her slippers made a faint scuffing sound on the marble tiles, and the wall sconces cast a shadowy light over the empty passageway. Unerringly she found her way through the maze of corridors to the ballroom, situated in the opposite wing.

She would see if Mama was there, still engaged in her playacting. She might coax an answer from her tonight. And if not, tomorrow she would take Mama back to Pemberton House and wait until the right moment presented itself.

A glimmering of light shone from the huge archway of the ballroom. She had toured this chamber once, to inspect the housekeeping. The floors were kept polished, the woodwork pristine, the windows gleaming. Mrs. Yates had said the room had never been used.

But now Drake could host parties here. He could invite all of the *ton*. He would do so alone. He didn't need her, and Alicia didn't need *him*.

Marching through the doorway, she saw that gloom shrouded the Venetian-blue walls and the tall pillars, the ornate plasterwork on the high ceiling. The faint illumination came from one end of the ballroom, where magnificent gold draperies framed a dais for an orchestra. There, two oil lamps sat at opposite ends of the raised floor. Between them, a wing chair substituted for a throne. On a table, a silver tea service gleamed in the meager light.

Her footsteps made a whispering noise that vanished into the vast darkness. Beyond the throne, her mother's diminutive form stood in the shadows cast by the curtains. Beside her loomed a tall, black form in the garb of a man. Had Mama convinvced Mrs. Philpot to dress as a courtier?

Alicia felt a faint smile penetrate her unhappiness. But as she approached, her brief humor dissipated.

Something lay curled on the floor beside the dais. She strained her eyes to make out what it was. In growing horror, she recognized the glint of silver hair, the paleness of a face, the body lying motionless.

Mrs. Philpot.

Alicia's gaze snapped to her mother. Mama was struggling against . . . a *man*. They weren't playacting, either. Alicia could hear their panting breaths, his low curses.

She rushed to the dais and hastened up the short steps. "Mama!"

In that same moment, the man turned to look. Recognition struck. Alicia stopped dead, her heart beating so fast she felt on the verge of a swoon.

For through the darkness, she spied the glint of metal as he pressed a dueling pistol to her mother's head.

"Come closer, my lady," Lord Hailstock said. "You've saved me the trouble of going in search of you."

Chapter Twenty-seven

The marquess prodded his prisoner into the lamplight. Resplendent in a medieval gown of richly embroidered crimson, Lady Eleanor carried herself like the queen she fanced herself to be. She wore the tattered moleskin cape like the finest ermine stole. A circlet of gold held a flowing blue veil over her silvering flaxen hair.

She raised her arm in an imperious gesture. "Send for the guards, my lady! They must arrest this treasonous knave! He would dare to put his hands upon my royal person."

Lord Hailstock gave her a shake. "Hush your mouth, Eleanor. Lest I stuff a gag into it."

Glaring at him, she pressed her lips shut.

To give herself a moment to calm her frenzied fear, Alicia sank into a deep curtsy. "Greetings, Queen Eleanor," she said, willing her voice not to quaver.

If she shouted for help, Lord Hailstock might shoot Mama. If she rushed at him, both she and her mother could be injured. He was far stronger than either of them.

Oh, why had she not allowed Drake to accompany her?

Because he had deceived her. Because he had destroyed her trust in him. And now she had only her own wits to rely upon.

"What have you done to Mrs. Philpot?" she asked, hoping to distract Lord Hailstock.

"The beldam suffered a little knock on the head. After she ordered me out of here."

Her belly clenched. To think she had once believed him to be an honorable man. "Put the pistol away, my lord," she said, striving for composure. "You're frightening me."

"As well I should. Perhaps you will convince this madwoman to reveal her hiding place."

"Hiding place?" Alicia stalled.

"She has something in her possession that I want. And I believe you know what I mean."

In the lamplight, his menacing gaze bored into her. Instinctively wanting to back up, she held her ground. "You shall have to explain yourself. You are being very obscure."

"And you are being deliberately obtuse." He pushed his captive closer, making Mama circle around the chair. "I suspected you might piece the puzzle together once you found out about Wilder's claim," he added. "You know too much of Claire's story."

"Claire?" Mama said sharply. "What have you done with my lady-in-waiting? If you've harmed her, sirrah, I shall have you thrown into the darkest of dungeons!"

He ignored her, his frosty gray eyes intent on Alicia. "What is that paper in your hand? That looks like Claire's handwriting."

Alicia clutched the folded letter to her bosom. Lord Hailstock would destroy it. With the documents missing, it was the only proof of Drake's claim. She had to preserve it, to let him make his own choices.

Wracking her brain, she stepped closer, keeping Lord Hailstock within her sight. Then, out of the corner of her eye, she caught a flash of movement near the shadowed doorway to the ballroom.

A twitch of black skirts. A white mobcap on flame-red hair.

Her heart leapt. *Mrs. Yates.* Would the housekeeper go for help? Or would she see this as a chance to rid herself of Alicia once and for all?

In his brother's new bedchamber, Drake strode back and forth, his footsteps clicking on the marble floor. He still could not believe that Muira Wilder wasn't his true mother. Yet she had been a mother to him in all the ways that mattered. Even when they'd had nothing, she had scrimped to put food on the table. She'd given him a happy childhood, and he would always love her for that.

Claire had loved him, too. Her dying wish had been to secure his rights as Hailstock's heir.

Drake took a deep breath. He ought to be considering his windfall. Never in his gambling days, when he had amassed his fortune with single-minded ruthlessness, had he ever dreamed of taking so perfect a revenge on Hailstock.

He was Hailstock's heir. He would be welcomed by the finest families in England. He could walk among them, their equal.

Hailstock's equal.

But not even that triumph could distract him from the restlessness inside himself. He wanted Alicia with him. He wanted her to amuse him with her witty commentary, to seduce him with her smiles. But she had made her feelings for him all too clear.

I don't want you with me. I will do this alone.

His chest tightened. She had been referring to more than questioning her mother. Alicia didn't need him. Not ever.

His hands steepled beneath his chin, James sat near the fire and watched him pace. "She'll forgive you. Alicia isn't one to hold a grudge."

A grudge? Would to God it was only that. "How do you know what I'm thinking?" he said irritably. "I could be gloating about stripping you of your title."

"If you were gloating, you wouldn't be prowling like a caged panther."

Halting, Drake pivoted toward his younger brother. Now that the initial shock was over, James looked remarkably unperturbed. "And why aren't you cursing me?" Drake asked. "I'm about to rob you of your future."

James shrugged. "A future based on falsehoods doesn't appeal to me." Maneuvering his wheeled chair to a table, he set down his glass with a decisive thump. "First thing tomorrow, I shall consult my solicitor. He'll know how to handle such an unusual matter."

"It's too soon," Drake objected. "The proof may never be found. That letter alone won't hold up in court."

"The papers will turn up eventually. Alicia will find them."

"And I shall destroy them," Drake snapped. "I do *not* aspire to be the next Marquess of Hailstock." His own words stunned him. God help him, it was true. All of his life he'd craved having the power to bring down Hailstock. But vengeance wasn't what he wanted anymore. He had no desire to bear the name of the man he had hated for so long.

James rolled closer. "You haven't a choice," he said in a hard-edged voice. "You have a duty to the children you'll sire."

No one else knew that Alicia's body already sheltered a new life. And Drake couldn't admit aloud to the fierce tenderness that gripped him. "I can provide for my family," he said through clenched teeth. "I don't need Hailstock's money."

"Curse you, it's their heritage I'm talking about. Your son will be a peer. Your daughter will be called 'lady.' Don't let your stupid, selfish pride stand in the way of them claiming their noble lineage."

"I want my children to grow up believing all people are equal. The nobility is hardly the place to accomplish that."

"Then it's up to you to raise them to be thinkers and benefactors. And keep in mind, if you deny them their birthright, you'll be just like Father."

The truth of that pierced Drake. Hailstock had denied him. Thus had begun a series of deceits that had resulted in this intolerable dilemma.

Of course, he didn't wholly agree with James. There was a vast difference between him and his father. Drake would never abandon his child. But there was no point to arguing.

Wary of his brother's generosity, he crossed his arms and leaned against the mantelpiece. "And you? What about you?"

"I'll be happy with my duchess." The husky note in James's voice lightened. "And celebrating the fact that *I* shall never have to endure tedious sessions of Parliament."

Drake felt no humor. Thoughts of Alicia besieged him again. He hadn't known a man could hurt so much, that he could so bitterly regret the hatreds that had guided him for most of his life. He hadn't realized that a woman could have such a hold over his heart. The power of his feelings for Alicia unsettled him. If he didn't keep a grip on himself, she'd have him behaving like a lovesick tadpole. *More* like a lovesick tadpole.

The sound of hurrying footsteps came from the outer corridor. Eliza Yates burst through the doorway, her mob-cap hanging askew, her brown eyes wide, her breast heaving. "Sir! Ye're 'ere!"

Struck by alarm, Drake strode to her. "What is it?"

" 'Tis m'lady," she said, lapsing into cockney babble. "In the ballroom. Wid his lordship. 'E 'as a gun."

A chill gripped him. "Hailstock."

Her fingers scrabbling at his coat, she bobbed her head up and down. "Beggin' yer pardon, I let 'im in, I did. I didn't know 'e were a bad sort."

"The devil you say," James snapped. "This can't be true."

Drake paid no heed to either of them. Fear icing his veins, he leapt past the housekeeper and raced out the door.

Though she had arrayed herself as a queen, Mama looked small and defenseless in Lord Hailstock's grip. The dueling pistol glinted in the lamplight. Dear God, *he* was the demented one, to threaten her sweet mother.

Taking a deep breath, Alicia eased the stranglehold of panic. She couldn't depend on a rescue that might never come. She must use her wits to procure Mama's safety. And the letter might be her only bargaining chip.

"You're right, my lord," she said, forcing a sheepish laugh. "I did indeed put all the pieces together. Then I went looking for the proof." She rattled the paper to tantalize him. "Claire wrote this letter on her deathbed. In it, she confirms my suspicions."

"Bring it to me."

Despite her fear, a wave of anger swept over Alicia. He had abandoned an innocent baby. Thinking of her own child, hers and Drake's, she could understand Claire's desperation to protect her son from this man's cruelty.

"No," she said. "You'll burn it. Drake will need proof that he is your legitimate son."

"He is Claire's by-blow." The marquess took a menacing step toward her, dragging Mama with him. "By God, I won't allow a common bastard to lay claim to my title."

"The child *is* your heir," Queen Eleanor declared, not appearing to be frightened in the least. "I decree it to be so."

"Cease your raving. Alicia, open the letter. Show me what's inside."

She considered refusing. But he might shoot Mama. Her throat constricted, Alicia slowly unfolded the paper and displayed it for his inspection.

"Where are the documents?" he demanded. "Where have you put them?"

"I haven't seen them. I suppose at one time Mama knew, but she doesn't remember anymore. So you may as well let her go."

"I do indeed remember," Queen Eleanor said indignantly. "This man is a villain. He would overthrow the crown and seize the treasury."

"Madwoman," Lord Hailstock muttered, giving her a shake. "Tell me where you put the affidavit from the midwife."

She drew herself up, a diminutive but regal figure beside his sinister form. "Though you might draw and quarter me, I shall never breathe a word to one such as *you*." Then she pressed her lips shut.

Did Mama understand what she was saying? Alicia wondered wildly. If she came to her senses, she could guide them to the place where she'd hidden the documents. Lord Hailstock would let her go.

But in the next moment Alicia knew the futility of that. Claire had instructed Mama never to give the papers to Lord Hailstock. And Mama, bless her devotion, had kept that promise for thirty years.

"You belong in Bedlam," Lord Hailstock growled to the countess. "Where you can confine your ravings to the other lunatics."

Queen Eleanor lifted her chin. She kept her mouth tightly closed.

Alicia's stomach churned. "That's the real reason you wanted to marry me," she whispered. "You didn't care for me. You only wanted to lock Mama away. To keep her from revealing your secret."

A fiery determination burned in his eyes. "And to keep you or anyone else from stumbling upon the proof. Just as your father did."

"Papa?"

"He found the letter and realized its worth. Then he came to me, begging a loan to pay his gambling debts in exchange for his silence. Until then, I didn't know any proof still existed."

Bile rose in her throat. She felt dizzy with disbelief. "You *murdered* Papa?"

"No! I would only give him the money if he gave me the documents. The fool refused. Said he wouldn't force Eleanor to betray her promise to Claire. Then he went home and shot himself."

Mama made a small sound of distress. Her lips trembled. A tear rolled down her cheek, the droplet sparkling in the lamplight.

Anguish clutched at Alicia. Mama *did* understand.

Beset by the urge to claw Lord Hailstock's arrogant face, Alicia clenched her fingers around the paper. "My lord, I will exchange this letter for my mother."

"Bring it to me," he said. "I want to know exactly what Claire says."

"Release Mama first."

"No. Come closer and show me the letter."

Alicia took a cautious step toward the marquess and stopped just short of his reach. Without the aid of a lamp, he wouldn't be able to decipher the faded penmanship. She must convince him the letter was valuable, a worthy barter for Mama.

"Shall I read it to you?" she forced out. "In it, Claire avows that Drake *is* your son. She calls him by name. She describes your jealousy, your refusal to recognize your own child—"

"Her bastard," he spat. "She deceived me into thinking her a lady, but she had no morals in the bedchamber. She behaved like a bitch in heat. Her child could have been fathered by any riffraff."

From the doorway of the ballroom, a familiar voice rang out. "It doesn't matter who sired me. By law, any child born within the bounds of your marriage *is* yours."

With a gasp, Alicia spun around to see her husband enter

the darkened ballroom. Broad and strong and tall, Drake walked with the determined stride of a warrior heading into battle. His decisive footsteps echoed in the cavernous room.

Lord Hailstock snapped, "Stop right there. You can't prove you're my son."

Drake halted a few feet from the dais. His gaze went to Alicia, penetrating deeply into her, before returning to Lord Hailstock. "That letter will help verify my case to the authorities. If nothing else, it will cast a blot upon your sterling name. Let the countess go, and I'll let you burn it."

The rasp of Lord Hailstock's breathing filled the silence. Alicia felt her heart pounding against her rib cage. Then abruptly he gave her mother a shove, sending her lurching toward Drake. "Go to Claire's whelp."

In the same motion, he grabbed Alicia. His fingers dug into her arm as he yanked her hard against him. The paper slipped from her fingers and fluttered to the floor. She pushed frantically, trying to escape his iron grip. Then something made her go perfectly still.

The gun barrel nudged her neck.

Lady Eleanor tumbled off the dais and into Drake's arms. Though she was a small woman, the impact caused him to stagger backward. Her veil draped his head, blinding him. He gripped her for a second, then let her slide to her feet while he clawed away the gauzy stuff.

Too late.

Hailstock held Alicia. He pressed a dueling pistol to her neck at the vulnerable place just below her ear.

Uttering a savage growl, Drake released the countess and sprang forward, his muscles tensed to leap.

Hailstock cocked the pistol. "Stay back," he snarled. "I won't hesitate to use this weapon."

The click of the gun froze Drake. His nerves thrummed with a wild rage, a rage he dared not indulge. His gaze bolted to Alicia's wide blue eyes. He couldn't risk her life. Or the life of their unborn child.

In a rustle of heavy skirts, Lady Eleanor glided to his side. "You certainly took your time in answering my summons," she chided, as if this were a game. Gentleness entered her voice. "But now I know why you look so familiar. You're Claire's son. You've her coloring, the black hair and blue eyes. So very striking."

Drake kept his eyes on Alicia. Softly he said, "I must ask you to move away, my lady. There is danger here."

"I am not afraid. I am Queen Eleanor of Aquitaine."

"Even queens must protect themselves, Your Majesty. Go now."

Fumbling with the clasp of her moleskin cape, she vanished into the shadows. Relief touched him, but only for a moment.

He focused on Hailstock, who held Alicia on the raised dais. "Let her go. I don't want your damned title. Nor your wealth or anything else you own. All I want is my wife."

"You expect me to believe that?" the marquess sneered. "You don't know the meaning of honor."

Drake refrained from retorting that Hailstock was the most heinous sort of criminal, to threaten a woman. He could see fire in the marquess's eyes; a wrong move might push him over the edge. Forcing his voice to remain steady, he repeated, "Let her go. This is between you and me. She has nothing to do with our quarrel."

"You may have the letter, my lord," Alicia said, her voice remarkably strong. "I dropped it right there." She moved her foot slightly, pointing with a pink-slippered toe.

Pulling her along with him, Hailstock edged toward the paper. Drake gripped his fists. He hated his own helplessness. He hated seeing his wife threatened by this nobleman. He hated himself for instigating the revenge that had brought them all to this crisis.

Wheels clattered from the doorway. "Father!" James

called out, his voice echoing in the immense ballroom. "What the deuce are you doing?"

Hailstock had started to reach down for the letter. His face stark with alarm, he straightened. "Leave here at once. You shouldn't be here."

"Indeed I should. I want to know why you're holding a gun to Alicia."

"I'm protecting your inheritance from this vulgar upstart."

"I told you, James can keep his inheritance," Drake said in a tight voice. "Harming Alicia will gain you nothing but a hangman's noose."

James rolled to the dais, staring up at his father. "Have you gone completely mad? Put down the gun. Release her and we'll forget this nonsense."

"It isn't nonsense. If I don't stop him, he'll take everything when I die." Hailstock's voice quavered with strong emotion. "You'll be left destitute. A helpless cripple."

"I'm not helpless, and I never was," James said forcefully. "I was sulking, and you encouraged me so I'd be dependent on you. As for the title, I shan't take what isn't mine. *You* raised me to be a better man than that."

His forehead furrowed, Hailstock stared down at his younger son. "You don't understand. You have blue blood—your mother was a Quincy. The title *must* go to you."

"No, Father. I shan't accept it. So you see, there is no purpose to holding Alicia hostage."

The pistol wavered. Drake tensed his fists, concentrating, willing the marquess to drop the gun. He feared to say anything that might antagonize him.

Lady Eleanor chose that moment to reappear out of the gloom. She tugged on Drake's sleeve. "Hsst."

"Stay back, Your Majesty," he whispered.

She jerked harder on his arm. Standing on tiptoe, she

murmured in his ear, "But I have something for you, my lord."

My lord.

Clenching his teeth in denial, Drake glanced over to see her standing beside him, the moleskin cape draped over her arm. A piece of the blue satin lining gaped open, the threads dangling. She probed inside and drew forth an oiled paper, folded over several times, brown and bedraggled in the dim light from the lamps.

Her games didn't interest him now. Only Alicia, still in Hailstock's power. But Alicia was frowning, watching her mother. Then Lady Eleanor pushed the unfolded paper into his hand.

He looked down, and his gaze riveted to the page. Spidery handwriting on an official-looking document. Beneath it, a second paper, a statement signed and notarized.

Ghostly prickles ran over his skin. He gripped the papers tightly. Lady Eleanor had had these documents with her all the time. A marriage certificate. And proof of his birth. If he'd had any doubts before, he didn't now. He *was* legitimate, born of Claire, Lady Hailstock.

"Are those the papers?" Hailstock asked hoarsely. "Give them here."

"I'll do better than that," Drake said. "I'll save you the trouble of burning them."

Striding to the edge of the dais, he pulled the lamp closer and lifted the glass chimney. Alicia uttered a choked gasp as he touched the documents to the flame. He looked straight at her, willing her to believe in him again. The oiled paper took a moment to catch.

Then he jerked his gaze to Hailstock. "Let her go now."

His face stark with surprise, Hailstock said in a raw, incredulous voice, "You really do mean it. You don't want the title."

"I never did."

Moving as slowly as an old man, the marquess lowered

the pistol and loosed his hold on Alicia. She darted away, descending from the dais and drawing her mother back into the shadows. Drake felt a boundless relief at her safety, greater even than his satisfaction at burning these documents. He wanted to go to her, to hold her in his arms, to reassure himself that she belonged to him.

The racket of wheels sounded from behind him. He kept his gaze on the smoldering documents, watching the edges blacken. "You'll want to witness this, James. Now you can keep your bloody damned title—"

The chair careened into him. Drake staggered sideways; his shoulder struck the lamp. He heard the shattering of glass as momentum threw him to the floor.

Without the documents.

James had snatched the papers away. He'd lunged for them with such force, he'd thrown himself out of his chair and landed onto the parquet floor. With his bare hands, he beat out the flame. But larger flames raced toward him, the spilled oil pouring down from the dais in a stream of fire.

Even as Drake leapt to his feet, Hailstock scrambled off the dais, slipping on the spilled oil as he shoved James to safety. Drake sprang forward to drag James well away from danger.

Then gut instinct sent him surging toward the doorway to shout, "Fire!"

Mrs. Yates must have been waiting outside in case a scuffle arose. Carrying rugs to beat out the flames, she and several footmen ran into the ballroom.

Drake tore off his coat and raced back toward the blaze. An agonized cry echoed through the ballroom.

The sound made his stomach curdle. He spied a figure by the dais, encased in flame, a living pillar of fire.

Hailstock.

The marquess staggered away from the dais. Alicia frantically tried to put out the flames with the moleskin cape. In a flash of movement, Drake reached his father, thrusting him to the floor, smothering the flames with his coat. But it was too late. The marquess lay badly burned, breathing in ragged gasps, his face a mass of charred flesh.

Drake crouched beside him. He called to one of the footmen, "Fetch a doctor!" The man dashed toward the doorway.

Caught in his own private hell, Drake had a numb awareness of the other servants extinguishing the last flames, and the choking smoke in the air. Alicia had shielded her mother from Hailstock. They knelt by Mrs. Philpot, who sat up, coughing. Mrs. Yates helped her to her feet.

James hitched himself forward by his elbows. His voice rough with pain, he whispered, "*Father.*"

The marquess groaned. His breath rattled in his throat and then ceased. James uttered a low cry, reaching out to touch his father's unmoving chest. Then he bent his head and wept.

Drake pressed his fingers against his burning eyes. A welter of emotion choked him, the longing he'd felt for a father's love, the regrets that he couldn't change the past. Hailstock had given his own life to save his younger son. And Drake had to admire him for that.

He didn't know how long he and James remained there. But when he lifted his head, Alicia and her mother were gone. An overwhelming panic struck him. He told himself she would be putting her mother to bed, seeing to Mrs. Philpot. There would be time enough to speak with his wife. Time enough to hold her, to coax her, to work himself back into her good graces.

The footmen bore away the marquess's body on a makeshift stretcher. Another servant righted the wheeled chair and brought it to them. Drake helped to lift his brother, while James caught the arms of the chair and levered himself into it.

Soot streaked his face and shirt. A lock of hair drooped

onto his brow. He looked weary and saddened, his eyes shadowed. Clearing his throat, James muttered, "He said I didn't understand. But he was the one who didn't."

Drake could say nothing to that. He knew no adequate words of comfort. The loss was far greater for his brother.

The ballroom was dim, lit only by the remaining lamp. Two footmen would stand guard here tonight, to ensure that no smoldering places caught flame again. They had opened the windows to air out the room, though Drake knew the reek of smoke and charred wood would linger until the damage was repaired.

James wheeled himself to the unscathed end of the dais. "Fetch me that letter," he said to the footman. "And the dueling pistol."

The servant brought both to him.

Drake strode to his brother's side as he examined the long-nosed gun, turning it in his hands. Hailstock must have dropped the pistol when he'd run to push James out of the way. "We're lucky it didn't discharge," Drake said, his throat dry. A wild shot could have struck Alicia.

"Lucky?" James asked. Without warning, he pointed the gun at the shadowed ceiling and pulled the trigger. An empty click sounded. "Just as I'd thought," he whispered. "Damned thing wasn't loaded."

The realization stunned Drake. How much he truly hadn't understood about his father. That was all the more reason not to want the title.

He put out his hand. "I'll take those documents now."

James tucked the letter inside his coat along with the marriage certificate and the affidavit of birth. "No, I'll keep them until your claim is established."

"Don't be a damned noble fool!" Drake flared. "Hailstock wanted them destroyed. You should comply with his last wish."

"On the contrary, I shall protect these papers with *my* life." James afforded him a keen stare. "Resign yourself to it, brother. *You* are now Lord Hailstock."

Chapter Twenty-eight

Three weeks later, Alicia opened the door at Pemberton House to another floral delivery.

These were wildflowers, purple hyacinth and white hawthorn and yellow buttercups arranged in a Chinese porcelain vase, the bouquet so enormous it hid the deliveryman's face. He walked jauntily past her, flashing her a familiar grin, his honey-brown hair tousled from the spring breeze.

"Gerald!" she exclaimed. "I thought you'd gone to the club."

"I did," he said, carrying the vase through the foyer. "And your husband sent me on this errand."

Drake.

As she followed her brother into the drawing room, Alicia felt the rise of an involuntary thrill, a sensation she promptly squelched. She mustn't let Drake charm his way back into her heart. And he had certainly tried during the weeks since she and Mama had returned to their old home.

An extravagance of blooms decorated the drawing room—and every other chamber in the house. Roses in red and white and pink. Delicate hothouse orchids. Pink camellias and yellow marsh marigolds and purple violets. A profusion of lovely scents filled the air.

And there were other gifts, too. Tins of bonbons and

other fine confections scattered the tables. Perfumes and jewelry crowded her dressing table upstairs. In the library, there were books in fine leather bindings, poetry and philosophy, histories and novels. Drake seemed to have an unerring instinct for her taste in reading.

But he did not understand her heart.

Beneath a spray of apple blossoms, Mama sat at a pie-crust table on which stood a crystal ball. She wore the garb of a gypsy: a saffron-yellow turban, shiny gold earrings, and a cape of midnight-blue satin sprinkled with crescent moons. The costume was another gift from Drake, of course. Alicia thought it especially diabolical of him to make Mama his ally.

Lady Eleanor clapped her hands, her bracelets jingling. "Ah, more flowers! Didn't I predict their arrival not ten minutes ago?"

Mrs. Philpot cleared a place on the pianoforte for Gerald to set the new offering. "You certainly did, my lady," she said, clucking her tongue in amused dismay. "I must say, it is kind of his lordship to send along a vase. We seem to have run out of containers." She left the room to fetch an ewer of water.

Gerald brushed the golden pollen off his leaf-green coat. "You should know, Ali, your husband went to the country and picked these himself."

"Now, there's a Banbury tale," Alicia scoffed.

" 'Tis true," her brother insisted. "He returned only a short while ago. Indeed, I've never seen a man so—" Before he could finish, he whipped out his handkerchief and sneezed.

A man so . . . *what*?

Alicia wouldn't ask. She didn't care to know.

To distract herself, she patted her brother on the back. "You aren't catching cold, are you?"

"Blasted bouquet tickled my nose, that's all." Then he reached into an inner pocket of his coat and produced a square of ivory vellum, folded and sealed with a wafer. Flashing a grin, he handed it to her. "This goes along with the posy."

She took the note, surreptitiously gliding her fingertips over the fine paper. Drake hadn't attempted any communication since that first week, when he had endeavored to convince her to return to his house, alternately cajoling and demanding, subjecting her to the full force of his scoundrel's allure. He had avowed his regrets over the lies he'd told and claimed that he had resigned himself to being a peer only for the sake of their children.

Their children.

A wistful warmth enveloped Alicia, the ever-present knowledge that their baby nestled safely within her womb. She knew Drake would be a good father. He liked children and children liked him. But he was determined to win her back only because he had too much stubborn pride to admit defeat. She resented him for thinking he could buy her affections with his bounty. She would not allow herself to be swayed by lavish gifts and persuasive letters. That wasn't what she wanted from him.

She would never forget that night when she had stood outside James's room, trying to work up the courage to tell Drake that he was legitimate, and overhearing him say, *I'll never kneel before any woman.*

That one remark summed up his inability to love. It wasn't that she wanted him to prostrate himself. But she had always dreamed of a man who would be willing to walk over hot coals for her, a man who regarded her as the center of his existence.

"Open the note," Gerald urged.

Mama waved her hands, then peered into the crystal ball. "I do believe . . . yes . . . it is from one who yearns for you."

Alicia's fingers itched to open the missive. Perversely, she resisted the temptation. "Then he shall go on yearning."

"Ah, have pity on the poor fellow," Gerald said. "I vow, he's at his wit's end."

Was he? Feeling a moment's softening, she walked swiftly back and forth, reminding herself of all her grievances. "I cannot pity the man who stole the title from James."

" 'Tis Drake's by right," her brother said, with typical male obtuseness. "The courts should confirm that soon."

Mama looked up from her crystal ball, her eyes clear and blue, her brow puckered. "My dear girl," she said in faint horror, "are you suggesting that Claire's son should *not* be the Marquess of Hailstock?"

More and more these days, Mama seemed to grasp what was going on around her, though she still dressed up in costumes and played out her daydreams. Not wanting to upset her, Alicia demurred, "I simply don't think it's fair to deprive James, that's all."

"Neither is it fair to deny Claire's son," Mama said, a trifle anxiously. "The dear boy was lost all these years. And Claire's dying wish was to protect him. That is why I hid the documents for so long."

Repentant, Alica slipped her arm around her mother's slight form. "I know, Mama. You are to be admired for keeping your vow so faithfully."

Realizing the truth in that, she took a deep, shaky breath. Perhaps she herself was the obtuse one, afraid to risk her heart again. Afraid to accept the fact that her husband hadn't wanted this final revenge. He despised the notion of being the Marquess of Hailstock.

In her mind she saw Drake touching the documents to the flame of the lamp. He had intended to destroy the evidence that would prove his legitimacy. All the while, he had gazed straight at her. As if willing her to believe him an honorable man.

She fingered the folded notepaper, wondering what message it contained. Could Drake have overcome his vengeful nature? If he conquered the hatred inside himself, might he then learn to love? She wanted to believe it. Too much.

Gerald's green eyes bored into her. "You should also know that Drake gave away the old marquess's fortune to James—except for the entailment, of course."

Alicia straightened, scarcely noticing the shower of petals when her shoulder brushed a spray of drooping roses. "James didn't tell me that."

"Drake wanted it kept quiet. Doesn't like to brag, especially about his brother. They've become fast friends, you know."

She had surmised as much. James, too, had nothing but praise for Drake. He'd come here every day to teach at their school, often accompanied by Sarah. The two of them had privately announced their betrothal, though out of respect for his mourning, they would wait until the following spring to marry. Their love stirred a yearning in Alicia, the awareness that a part of herself was missing.

It seemed forever since she'd felt Drake's embrace, his arms strong and warm, holding her close. Over the past weeks, she had thought about him often, in anger and pain . . . but also with love. She had reflected on his befriending of James and his generosity to the misfits who had experienced the hardships of life on the streets.

And she had imagined Drake as a little boy, eager to meet his father for the first time and profoundly hurt to be accused of thievery instead. Such cruelty might have defeated many a child. Instead, Drake had fought back, using his wits and his genius to amass a fortune at the gaming tables. In the only way he knew how, he had striven for recognition from his father. Who was she to blame him for that?

Besides, if he hadn't been bent on revenge, they might never have met and married. She wouldn't have his child inside her now, the miracle of their lovemaking.

"Open the letter, Ali," Gerald urged again. Working his

boyish features into the severe countenance of an earl, he placed his hand on her shoulder and added, "The fellow's besotted with you. It's only fair that you give him a chance to redeem himself."

Mama tapped the folded letter. Her gaze full of mysterious wisdom, she whispered, "Go ahead, my dear. Do not be afraid. The crystal ball says 'tis time to seek your future."

Basking in their love, Alicia allowed herself to let go of her doubts. The hurt and confusion of the past weeks floated away like petals on a warm wind. She felt light and free, secure in her decision. She was Drake's wife, and she wanted to be with him. Even if he kept his emotions locked away, even if he could share only his body and not his heart, she would love him anyway.

And so, with trembling fingers, she broke the seal on his letter.

Chapter Twenty-nine

At precisely three o'clock that same afternoon, Alicia followed Fergus MacAllister up the grand staircase at Wilder's Club.

Their brisk footsteps echoed in the vastness of the entrance hall, with its elegant white columns rising against the dark green walls. Few members occupied the premises at this early hour: only a pair of gentlemen engrossed in a card game in the salon, and another man by the bow window, his nose stuck in a newspaper.

Alicia remembered the first time she'd come here, desperate and determined, intending to offer herself as mistress to the most notorious gambler in London. Now she would come to him willingly as his wife.

A shiver of yearning prickled her skin. She had bathed and primped and changed her gown at least ten times, finally settling on this soft copper silk that clung to her curves. A gold-braided spencer covered a bodice cut low for a man's pleasure.

For Drake's pleasure.

" 'Tis time ye put the auld fusspot out of his misery," Fergus said as they reached the top of the stairs and started down the corridor. "The master's been moping 'round here like a whipped dog."

In spite of herself, Alicia appreciated knowing that Drake, too, had suffered. "Has he, now? I should rather enjoy seeing such a sight."

Fergus peered down at her, his unpatched eye showing a secretive amusement. "There's an even better sight awaiting ye, m'lady. He's gone daft fer ye, that's fer certain."

Without further ado, he swung open the gilt-trimmed door and motioned her inside. Then he bowed out, leaving her alone.

An even better sight? What did Fergus mean by that?

She would find out in a moment.

Awash in giddy expectation, she hurried through a dim antechamber and into Drake's office, the carpet muffling her footsteps. Her gaze swept the marine-blue walls, the wine-dark leather chairs, the shelves of books that she now knew to be well-read. The draperies were drawn against the afternoon light, and a branch of candles cast a glow onto the polished surface of the big mahogany desk.

Her smile faltered. Where was Drake?

I have something that is yours.

His note had been brief, just that one sentence, along with a request that she come here at this appointed time. She had assumed he'd be waiting for her. He would be contrite yet seductive, ready to ply his charm and entice her with his touch. And this time she would let him. He would pull her into his arms, and she would succumb to his scoundrel's seduction. . . .

Her gaze alighted on the mantelpiece with its statue of naked lovers locked in an eternal embrace. Walking to it, she let her fingers drift over the smooth alabaster. How shocked she had once been to think of behaving so wantonly with a man. But now she knew intimacy to be a fine expression of love. Before Drake had finagled his way into her life, she had been well on her way to becoming a puritanical spinster. Because of him, she had flourished and grown into the fullness of womanhood. Because of him, she would be a mother. How had she ever thought she could live without him?

Behind her, a door opened.

Whirling around, she saw her husband standing in the shadows across the room, where dark blue draperies half concealed a doorway. His brawny form riveted her attention. Her throat went dry and her pulse quickened. He wore an ancient Roman-style garment, a plain linen tunic that ended at his knees. Beneath it, his legs were bare.

No wonder Fergus had been so amused. She couldn't help smiling, either, though more with interest than humor.

Drake bowed deeply. "I am here to serve you, my exalted mistress."

A wild excitement coursed through her as she remembered her fantasy. He would play her slave and do her bidding? Drake, who was too arrogant to obey anyone?

"Come closer," he said in a voice that was deep and stirring. "I live to satisfy your every whim." Then he gestured at the doorway.

More than willing, she walked past him and into a cozy blue bedchamber with a fire burning on the hearth and candles glowing on the bedside table. Her gaze riveted to the big, canopied bed. The linens were strewn with rose petals, and their scent perfumed the air. Her heart racing, she turned to find Drake standing directly behind her, his eyes dark and compelling, holding the promise of delights to come.

"I am pleased you would come to me," he said. "I have missed serving you."

She couldn't stop staring at his firm, sensual mouth. And thinking how much she craved his kiss. "As I have missed you."

She would have moved into his arms then, but he caught her hand and led her to a chair by the fire. Mystified but eager to play along, she sat down while he took something from the mantelpiece.

His manner deferential, he bent low, his tunic gaping open to a view of his muscled chest. He extended his hands, a small jeweler's box cupped within his palms. "For you, my lady."

I have something that is yours.

Was this what he'd meant?

Reaching out, she tentatively touched the leather case. "Oh, Drake, you needn't purchase gifts to win me back. It truly isn't necessary."

"I wish only to give you the courtship you never had."

Her throat went taut with tenderness, and she understood how she'd misjudged him. He hadn't been trying to buy her affections these past weeks. He had been *wooing* her. To make up for their forced marriage.

He opened the case. Against a backdrop of white velvet lay a diamond-studded band of gold. As if in a dream, she looked at him questioningly, afraid to ask what it meant.

Then he did something astonishing. He lowered himself to his knees, and his gaze beseeched her. "Your wedding ring, my lady. Will it please you to wear it?"

He wasn't telling her. He was *asking*.

Tears misted her eyes. She couldn't contain her eagerness. "Yes. Oh, yes!"

Taking her hand, he slid the ring onto her finger, and the gemstones sparkled in the firelight. As he brought her hand to his lips, his eyes glowed with mysterious depths. "I have something that is yours," he said.

So it wasn't the ring.

"You," she murmured, leaning forward to twine her arms around his neck, no longer able to contain her unruly desire. "*You* are mine. Oh, do make love to me."

Closing his fingers about her shoulders, he held her back. "Not yet."

Confused by his suddenly domineering manner, she wanted to play their fantasy. "But you're my slave. You're supposed to do as I say."

He smiled, a brief quirk of his lips that showed his dimples. "Patience, my lady. All will be as you wish." Then an unguarded longing shone in his eyes. Drawing a harsh breath, he went on, "It's been hell living without you these past weeks. I want you with me for always, you and our child."

"I know," she whispered. "I want that, too. I shouldn't have been so stubborn and unforgiving—"

He gently pressed his finger to her lips. "Let me finish. What I have for you, Alicia . . . is my heart. I love you."

I have something that is yours.

Joy poured through her in an extravagant rush of emotion. She wanted to weep and exult all at the same time. Burrowing into his arms, she relished the steady beating of his heart against hers. "Oh, darling, I love you, too. *Now* will you seduce me?"

This time, his smile took on that erotic tilt. "I am yours to command, O mistress mine."

Rising, he drew her to her feet and unbuttoned her spencer. He kept his gaze lowered in deference, though there was nothing servile in the way he stared at her bosom. Her breasts had grown heavier, preparing for the time when she would nurse his child. As if by accident, his fingers brushed the ripe swells. She might have been the mistress of a Roman villa, dallying with a handsome slave. "Touch me," she decreed.

"Your will is my pleasure."

His hands moved in lazy strokes, tracing the curves of her body. Stepping behind her, he slowly undressed her. He slid the copper silk gown off her shoulders, letting it slither to the floor, leaving her clad in only a lace-trimmed shift and a single petticoat. With a tug on the ties, he sent the petticoat drifting downward. He leaned closer, his breath warm against her ear, sending shivers over her skin. "No corset today," he said in a rough murmur. "Mistress, you make my duties so . . . enjoyable."

Oh, she did like this game! She lifted her arms. "Finish, my slave."

He complied, disposing of her last garment. Then he cupped her bare breasts in his hands. With a sigh, she leaned into him, relishing the abrasion of his coarse tunic on her soft skin, the radiant heat of his body, the urgency of his iron-hard arousal. "Kiss me," she whispered. "Oh, Drake, do kiss me or I'll go mad."

He brought his mouth down on hers with gentle pressure as if he controlled his passion. But she didn't want discipline; she wanted wild, uninhibited seduction. Winding her arms around his neck, she parted her lips and enticed him with her tongue. He responded with a hoarse groan, tasting her, caressing her, his hands sliding downward from her breasts to her hips, stopping just short of the place she wanted to be touched.

"To bed, slave," she said. "Take me to bed *now*."

He obeyed, half carrying her across the chamber and pressing her down onto the sea of red petals. The scent of roses wafted around her and mingled with his exciting essence. Stripping off his tunic, he loomed over her, broad and strong, his muscles bronzed by the candlelight. He was all man, *her* man.

Crouching over her on the bed, he took one nipple into his mouth and suckled her, then did the same to the other. Alicia uttered a breathless cry, her fingers sinking into his thick black hair. All the while, he caressed her in a leisurely fashion, teasing her between her legs until she could no longer bear the torment, and she reached for his heavy shaft, guiding him to her.

Then he joined their bodies, no longer the slave but her master. Seizing control, he moved inside her, and she moaned with the pleasure of it. Each thrust heightened the exquisite agony. When she would have closed her eyes, he caught her cheeks in his hands and his gaze locked with hers. "Look at me," he ordered. "See the man who loves you."

She did look. His blue eyes held no secrets now; they burned with the beauty of love. He penetrated deeply, filling her, pressing harder and faster. She strained to meet him, matching his passion with a wildness of her own. Gazing into his eyes, she saw his face darken with the approach of climax and felt a surge of emotion so powerful that she convulsed with ecstasy.

For long moments afterward, she lay in his arms, utterly content and sated. The aroma of roses enveloped them along with the musk of their lovemaking. Her wedding ring glinted in the firelight. She stretched and sighed, cuddling against his warm, hard form. How she had missed this—not just the closeness of their bodies, but the sense of completion, the feeling that she belonged with Drake, now and forever.

His hand traveled in lazy strokes over her hip. "I see my lady is pleased with her slave."

The arrogance was back in his voice, and she thrilled to it. Smiling, she plucked a petal from his shoulder. "I believe I'll keep you after all."

"So long as you don't expect me to dress like a damned fool anymore."

"What, and deprive Fergus of his amusement?" she teased. "I can see you clad as an Indian in a loincloth, an Arabic prince in gauzy trousers, a—"

"Enough." His eyes twinkling, he kissed her. Then, with a look of concentration, he tipped up her chin, touching her as if she were beloved to him. His voice gruff, he said, "In all honesty, Alicia, I'd have come crawling on my knees to get you back. I even considered selling the club, since you so despise gambling."

She quickly shook her head. "Oh, but you mustn't put Mr. Cheever and Mr. MacAllister and all the others out of work. Where would they go?"

He nodded. "That's exactly what I thought—and what I'd hoped you would say."

"But surely you won't be spending as much time here. You'll have other duties now."

"Quite so." All charming rogue, he let his fingers circle her breast, causing the rise of arousal in her. "I shall be keeping my wife contented."

"I meant your duties as the Marquess of Hailstock," she said gently.

Grimacing, he flopped onto his back, sending rose petals fluttering off the bed. "Don't call me that. I never wanted the damned title."

Seeing his discomfort, she perversely reveled in it. "Such are the wages of vengeance, my lord."

"Jade. Don't forget that vengeance brought me into your life."

"Jackanapes," she said tartly, wriggling against him. "Don't *you* forget that I made you a better man."

He focused his scoundrel's smile on her, the smile that always made her heart beat faster. "You'll have a lifetime to remind me of my sins. But for now, dear wife . . ."—his hands drifted possessively over her—"for now, I intend to seduce you again."